14⁹⁵

5⁰⁰

D1708467

DON'T STOP THE CARNIVAL

Island of
Amerigo

LITTLE DOG   BIG D

PITT B.

SIGNAL MT.

Hasting's Estate

old sugar mill

Waterfront Road

HOG POINT

Sub Base

SHARK BAY

Crab Cove

White Beach

blue
yellow
green
white
pink

cottages

CLUB

DOCK

TERRACE

Gull Reef Club

Broadstairs

Government House

MOSQUITO HILL

Sir Francis
Drake Inn

GULL
REEF

Prince of Wales Street

Hogan's
Fancy

FORT

Charlotte's Fancy

Works by Herman Wouk

HERMAN WOUK

DON'T STOP THE CARNIVAL

A NOVEL

LITTLE, BROWN AND COMPANY

Boston   New York   Toronto   London

ISBN 0-316-95512-4

Library of Congress Cataloging-in-Publication
information is available.

Author's Note

There is no island of Amerigo, or "Kinja," in the Caribbean Sea. In this tale of imaginary
people on an imaginary island, fictional freedoms are taken with calendar dates, political
and theatrical events, astronomic occurrences, and the like. The book contains no
intended portraits of, or references to, actual individuals living or dead; any such
resemblance that may be discerned is a coincidence, and without intent on the author's
part. Where celebrated public personages are mentioned or seen, no historic accuracy
concerning them is intended. Finally, regarding the native dialects in this story: Calypso
accents vary from island to island, and even from one part of an island to another. The
intent here is only a general indication of the West Indian patois.

Grateful acknowledgment is made to the following for copyrighted material:

Norma Millay Ellis
Lines of "Wine from These Grapes" from *Collected Poems* by Edna St. Vincent
Millay, Harper & Row, Publishers. Copyright 1921, 1928, 1948, 1955 by Edna St.
Vincent Millay and Norma Millay Ellis. Reprinted by permission.

Hollis Music, Inc.
Lines of "Zombie Jamboree" ("Back to Back"). Words and Music by Conrad
Eugene Mauge, Jr. © Copyright 1955 and 1957 Hollis Music, Inc. Reprinted by
permission.

Leeds Music Corporation
Lines of "Joe Hill." Words by Alfred Hayes. Music by Earl Robinson. © Copyright
MCMXXXVIII by Leeds Music Corporation. Reprinted by permission.

Shari Music Publishing Corporation
Lines of "Jamaica Farewell." Copyright © 1955, Shari Music Publishing Corp.
Reprinted by permission.

10 9 8 7 6 5 4 3

MV-NY

*Published simultaneously in Canada
by Little, Brown & Company (Canada) Limited*

Printed in the United States of America

Part One

THE
SMARTEST
MAN
IN
NEW YORK

chapter one

Lester Atlas

I

Kinja was the name of the island when it was British. Now the name on
the maps and in the Caribbean guidebooks is Amerigo, but everybody
who lives there still calls it Kinja.

The Union Jack flew over this enchanting green hump in the blue
ocean for almost two hundred years. Before that the island was Danish;
before that, French; before that, cannibal. Smoky gun battles between
sailing ships and the old stone fort went with these flag changes; whizzing cannon balls, raiding parties, skirmishes, and an occasional death.
But the fort guns have been silent for more than a century. The United
States acquired the island peaceably in 1940, as part of the shuffling of

old destroyers and Caribbean real estate that went on between Mr. Roosevelt and Mr. Churchill. The Americans ended up in this instance not only with the submarine base in Shark Bay—now gone back to tall guinea grass and catch-and-keep, the piers sagging and rotting, the rusty Quonset huts all askew—but with the whole island. The details of the transaction were and are vague to the inhabitants. They were not much interested.

Keen-ja was the short, musical native version of the actual British name, King George the Third Island. Obviously this was a bit awkward for an American possession, so somebody in the Department of the Interior thought of Amerigo. The new name is used mainly on official stationery and in the school classrooms. There the pupils docilely scrawl themes and recite facts about Amerigo, but in the streets and playgrounds they call the place Kinja, and themselves Kinjans. All through the Caribbean they still say of a native of this island, "He fum Kinja."

The West Indian is not exactly hostile to change, but he is not much inclined to believe in it. This comes from a piece of wisdom that his climate of eternal summer teaches him. It is that, under all the parade of human effort and noise, today is like yesterday, and tomorrow will be like today; that existence is a wheel of recurring patterns from which no one escapes; that all anybody does in this life is live for a while and then die for good, without finding out much; and that therefore the idea is to take things easy and enjoy the passing time under the sun. The white people charging hopefully around the islands these days in the noon glare, making deals, bulldozing airstrips, hammering up hotels, laying out marinas, opening new banks, night clubs, and gift shops, are to him merely a passing plague. They have come before and gone before.

Long ago they came in their white-winged ships, swarmed over the islands, slaughtered the innocent cannibals, chopped down magnificent groves of mahogany that had stood since the Flood, and planted sugar cane. Sugar was money then, and it grew only in warm places. They used the felled mahogany to boil molasses. Those were the days of the great stone plantation houses and sugar mills; of seasick slaves hauled in from Africa, the ancestors of the Kinjans; of wealthy landowners with pink cool wives back in England, and warm black concubines on the premises. Then the sugar beet, which can grow in the north, came in, and black slavery went out. Bankruptcy and insurrection exploded along the island chain. The boom collapsed. The planters left. The plantation houses fell in. Today the natives put tin roofs over one nook or another in the massive broken walls and live there.

The West Indians do not know what will cause the frantic whites to leave next time. Perhaps a bad earthquake: the entire chain of drowned mountains rests on a shaky spot in the earth's crust. Or a tidal wave; or a very bad hurricane; or an outbreak of some dormant tropical disease; or the final accidental blow-up of the white man's grumbling cauldron in the north, which will send the Caribbean white remnant scurrying to—where next? Tasmania? Tierra del Fuego? Unlike the natives they cannot subsist, if the ships and planes stop coming, on crayfish, mangoes, coconuts, and iguanas.

Meantime, in a fashion, Amerigo is getting Americanized. The natives like the new holidays—Thanksgiving, Fourth of July, Presidents' birthdays, and the rest—added to the old British holidays and the numerous religious days, none of which they have abandoned. The work calendar has become a very light and unburdensome thing. The inflow of cash is making everyone more prosperous. Most Kinjans go along cheerily with this explosion of American energy in the Caribbean. To them it seems a new, harmless, and apparently endless carnival.

2

Two men came out of Prince of Wales Street into the white sunshine of the waterfront, on a November morning in 1959. One was a big oyster-pale fellow in a rumpled black silk suit, with a thick bald head like half a bread loaf rising out of fat shoulders. He was bawling, "Trade winds, hey? All right, here's the waterfront and where's your goddamn trade winds? That's what I want to know, Norman. This whole island is one god damned furnace. This island is hell with palm trees. How the Christ can a white man breathe in this hole?" He was holding a can of beer in one hand and a cigar in the other, and he gestured with both, scattering ashes and splashing beer.

The other man, who kept making pleading, soothing noises, was smaller, slighter, and tanned. He had a well-brushed head of silvering hair, and a lean face of young middle age; he looked perhaps forty-five.

He wore a navy linen blazer, gray slacks, an open turquoise shirt, and a gray-and-yellow silk scarf tied inside the shirt. The costume was faultless for a color advertisement in *Holiday*. After a while one learns that in the Caribbean only tourists or homosexuals wear such clothes. The little man was a fastidious dresser, but new to the West Indies.

The big man yelled, "Okay, okay, I know I'm in a strange place. Strangest goddamn place I've ever been in. Now where the hell is this Gull Reef Club?"

"They said we could see it from the waterfront—ah, Lester, just *look* at all this, why don't you? Just look at where you are! It's like landing in another century. Look at that church! It must be two hundred years old. I bet those walls are seven feet thick. That must be for hurricanes."

"I wish one would start blowing," bellowed Lester. "Cool the place off. This beer! It's piss!" He hurled the can spraying and clattering across the cobbled plaza. "Don't they even have refrigerators here? I bet they don't, you know something? I bet they cool the beer with the goddamn trade winds."

The smaller man was looking around, with the air of a child just come to a birthday party—at the clumsy old island schooners tied up at the water's edge, with red sails furled; at the native women in bright dresses and the black ragged crewmen, bargaining loudly over bananas, coconuts, strange huge brown roots, bags of charcoal, and strings of rainbow-colored fish; at the great square red fort, and at the antique cannons atop its slanted seaward wall, pointing impotently to sea; at the fenced statue of Amerigo Vespucci, almost hidden in purple, orange, and pink bougainvillea; at the houses of Queen's Row, their ancient arching plaster façades painted in vivid colors sun-bleached to pastels; at the old gray stone church, and the white-washed Georgian brick pile of the Sir Francis Drake Inn.

"It's beautiful," he said with sudden loud firmness. "It's the most beautiful place I've ever seen in my life. If you don't think so, you ought to get your head examined."

The patio of the Sir Francis Drake Inn, an old brick yard shaded by two gigantic mahogany trees, stretched to the edge of the water along one side of the square. The only people in the patio at the moment were the Tilsons. They had the neat, flushed, freckled, corded, dried-out look of long-time white dwellers in the tropics. The Tilsons usually sat immobile and silent as lizards over their first three white rum-and-tonics, scarcely blinking. But when Tom heard the little man talk, he turned his white-and-pink head heavily toward his wife. "New York," he said. "Both of them."

She nodded. "And in November. This island has had it."

The Tilsons did not speak another word, but they watched the two invaders with vague hostile interest. A tall colored boy in old slacks and a ragged shirt approached the men, taking off a flat broad straw hat with dangling red and yellow ribbons.

"Mistuh Papuh?"

The little man smiled in relief. "Paperman. I'm Norman Paperman."

"I de Gull Reef boatman." He led them to an odd little vessel with a curving, comb-like prow, and the long rounded shallow black hull of a gondola, abruptly trailing off into a plain shabby rowboat, with a square stern and uncushioned thwarts.

The big man stared skeptically. "Is this thing safe?"

"It safe." The boatman took the two suitcases from the boy who sauntered up.

"Where are we going?" said Paperman, stepping into the boat. "Where's the Club?"

The boatman flicked a thumb toward the harbor. "Dah."

Out in the harbor, beyond the red slanting mass of the fort and separated from it by a couple of hundred yards of green shallows, Paperman saw a small island feathered with palm trees; and through the trees, a rambling white terraced building. The man called Lester stepped into the sawed-off gondola. The boat sank a foot, rocking; Lester cursed and waved his arms, the boatman sprang to him and grabbed his elbow, and down on the seat beside Paperman he dropped with a splintering thud.

"Christ, this thing's worse than a canoe. Is that it, that white building?" The boatman nodded, and pushed off with an oar. "Well, if this isn't ridiculous. Why don't they build a bridge?"

"It's kind of charming," said Paperman. "The little boat ride."

"Charm, my ass." Lester mopped his fat face and his naked conical head. "It's a way to scare off customers."

The boatman rowed powerfully toward the cement pier of the little island. A woman emerged from among the palms and hibiscus of the island, a tall, broad-shouldered woman dressed in a yellow shirt and white shorts, with orange hair piled on her head. She came striding like a man across an emerald lawn and down a curved flowery path to the pier, where she stopped and waved. "Hello there! I'm Amy Ball," she called. "Welcome to the Reef."

"Hi. Can we land without passports?" Paperman shouted back.

Mrs. Ball's laugh was pleasant, if somewhat baritone. Paperman leaped from the boat to the pier, grasping the strong freckled hand the woman held out to him. The two of them, with the aid of the gondolier, got the fat man safely out of the boat.

"This is Lester Atlas. I wrote you about him," Paperman said.

"Ah, yes. How do you do?" She offered Atlas her hand.

Paperman was afraid that Lester would instantly compromise both of them with a horrible burst of coarseness. Mrs. Ball intimidated him by her negligent assured air, and her strangled British diction. Her lips scarcely writhed when she spoke. It suddenly struck Paperman that the Gull Reef Club was a place where a Jew had perhaps never before set foot.

Atlas took Mrs. Ball's hand and collected himself, feet together and back straightening. "Are we really welcome?"

"Of course. Why not?" Mrs. Ball said through her teeth.

"Well, I just don't know how anybody could actually want to sell such a beautiful place."

She opened her mouth to laugh, then shut it firmly. "I'm probably crazy. But that's an old story. What'll it be? A nap after the plane ride? Breakfast? A drink? A swim?"

"A swim sounds perfect," said Paperman. "To begin with."

"I want to get out of these clothes," said Atlas, "and then I'd like to talk. If," he added with a surprisingly pleasant smile at the woman, "you don't mind getting right down to business."

"Not at all. American style," she said.

The white stucco cottage to which she led them was on the other side of the lawn, clear across the narrow island. It was much cooler here; a light flower-scented breeze blew. Over the arching doorway of the cottage a faded scrollwork sign hung, with one word on it: *Desire*. "This is the White Cottage," Mrs. Ball said, producing a key and opening the door. "The boys who ran the Reef before me were a little mad, I'm afraid. Larry Thompson and Tony Withers, sweet lads but queer as coots. I'm always meaning to take those idiotic signs down." The gondolier arrived just as she was saying goodbye and closing the door. Setting the two suitcases inside, he left before they could tip him.

"So. This is the Gull Reef Club." Atlas's heavy bloodshot eyes swept the cottage interior, which smelled of mildew and insecticide. There were four large beds covered in red nubbly cotton. The rough white walls were splashed here and there with framed water colors of palms, flowers, and fish. "Sizable cottages. They get two families in here easy, in season." He rattled the red plastic divider collapsed against a wall, then flung his jacket on a bed and took his suitcase into a bathroom. "Got to have a quick shower. I unquestionably stink."

Dazed by fatigue and excitement, Paperman opened his valise and swigged scotch from a bottle. He did not enjoy doing this, it was not his way of drinking. But nothing eased off palpitations like a little alcohol.

He was in a shaky state after a bumpy all-night plane trip with Atlas, who had never stopped guzzling bourbon out of paper cups all the way to Amerigo, to calm his nerves; first on the big plane to San Juan, and then on the little island-hopper. From the start Paperman had endured acute spasms of embarrassment. Atlas had bullied the ticket clerks at Idlewild, yelled at the skycap porter to get the lead out of his ass (and calmed the man's rage with a five-dollar tip), and annoyed the stewardess with ribald remarks each time she walked past. He had also made persisting indecent gestures at the poor girl's swaying rear, winking the while at a horrified white-headed lady across the aisle, and shouting, "Con permisso! Haw haw!" Atlas had roamed up and down the aisle when the seat-belt sign was off, talking to the other passengers, offering them whiskey, and every so often roaring out "Con permisso! Con permisso!" with hoarse howls of laughter. The aircraft, which was continuing on to Venezuela, carried many Latin Americans; and this repeated bawling of a Spanish phrase, with an added harsh "s" in *permiso*, was Atlas's idea of wit.

Paperman was a sensitive individual, who prided himself on dressing and acting with taste. He was self-made. He had run away at fifteen from middle-class parents who kept a furniture store in Hartford, Connecticut. He was a Broadway press agent, with some industrial clients; and the assorted vulgarians, tinhorns, and loudmouths of the show business were types he was at great pains not to resemble. Just as abhorrent to him were crude businessmen of the Atlas variety. *Square* was the deepest term of anathema in his circle. It was an excruciating discomfort for Norman Paperman to have to travel in public with such a boorish, booming, atrocious square as Lester Atlas.

Paperman's friends were writers, actors, newspapermen, television people, and the like. Many were real celebrities. In a company of these he spent most of his nights at one Broadway restaurant or another, drinking coffee, smoking cigarettes, and talking. Paperman's circle worked hard at dressing correctly and at reading the right books. Paperman and his friends, indeed, made a second career, beyond their professional work, of being up to the moment, and of never wearing, saying, or doing the wrong thing. This was not easy. In New York the right thing to wear or to read, to think or to say, to praise or to blame, can change fast. It can be damaging to miss a single issue of one or another clever magazine. Doctors complain of the flood of periodicals they must read to stay abreast of their profession; but their burden is almost light compared to that of being a New Yorker like Norman Paperman.

That was one reason Paperman was in the West Indies. He had broken down in the task.

3

About half an hour after he arrived Paperman almost drowned.

He was wearing rubber fins and a face mask for the first time in his life, and he was charmed by the underwater beauty of the reef: by the parrot fish browsing on dusty pink coral, the gently waving purple sea fans, the squid staring with tragic human eyes set in little jelly bodies, and jetting off backwards as he drew near; and by the glowing clean pink color of his own magnified hands and legs. He was pursuing a cloud of little violet fish past a towering brain coral, and having a wonderful time, when he turned his head under water, and the breathing pipe pulled out of its socket. The mask filled. Before he managed to yank it off he had inhaled and swallowed a lot of warm, very salty water. Coughing, gasping, he retrieved the sinking pipe, and tried to put it back in the mask, noting that he had wandered out too far from the beach. He was a good swimmer. The trouble was that since his coronary attack he got out of breath easily, and it was bad for him to exert himself in thrashing, flailing motions. He fixed the mask, clumsily pulled it on, and again was breathing warm water. Again he tore it off, snorting and choking, and now he was scared, because he seemed unable to catch enough breath, and his frantic treading was failing to keep his head above the surface. He went under; he clawed himself up, uttering a feeble "Help!" With his eyes fastened on the beach, which now seemed five miles away, he kicked and splashed and groped in one spot. He thought, "This would be one hell of a stupid way to die," and he thought of his wife and daughter, and wondered what idiocy had brought him to this island three thousand miles from New York to sink and be lost in the sea like a punctured beer can. His heart thundered.

A strong hand grasped his elbow. "Okay, easy."

He saw a big red fish impaled bleeding on a spear, inches from his face. The person holding the spear gun had thick black hair, twisted in curls and streaming water. The face was a blank skin-diver face, all yellow mask and tube. "Lie on your back and float." The voice was boyish, quiet, good-humored. Some of the knots went out of Paperman's muscles; he obeyed. The hand released his elbow and took a cupping hold on his chin. "Okay?" Paperman managed a nod against the hard hand.

The skin diver towed him to the beach. He let go while they were still in deep water, so that Paperman could turn over and swim the last dozen strokes. Anxiously glancing toward the hotel veranda, Paperman saw Atlas talking with Mrs. Ball and two Negroes. Nobody had noticed the panic or the rescue. The skin diver stood in the shallow water, pushing his mask up on his forehead. He had a narrow sunburned face, a big hooked nose, shrewd smiling brown eyes, and a masculine grin. He flourished his staring red fish at Paperman. "Think that'll serve two? It's my dinner."

"I'd say four."

"Nah. Take the head and tail off these brutes and there's not much left. But it's fresh. I guess it'll feed two."

The soft hot beach sand felt inexpressibly hospitable and good underfoot to Paperman. "You and who else?" he said, making talk to cover his embarrassment.

The man's grin became ribald. "Oh, you know. This babe." The intonations placed his origins unmistakably in New York or New Jersey.

"Well, look, thanks for pulling me out of there."

The skin diver slapped his ribs. He was a skinny sort, no taller than Paperman, and his bones showed in knobs under stringy muscles and coppery skin. "I got chilly out there. I'm going to have a dose of medicinal whiskey. You too?" He signalled toward the veranda.

"Sure." Paperman was trembling in the aftermath of the scare.

They fell into wooden lounge chairs on the sand. The coarse red canvas cushions, burning hot in the sun, soothed Paperman like a heating pad. "I'm getting old and stupid," he said. "I was up all night in an airplane. I just got here. I've never snorkelled before. I'm in lousy shape. And there I was roaring out to sea, the boy frogman."

His rescuer hung the mask on the back of his chair. Black wet ringlets fell on his forehead. "That's me. I'm a frogman."

Paperman glanced at him uncertainly. He had the New Yorker's usual horror of having his leg pulled. "Is that so? What are you, in the Navy or something?"

"UDT. Underwater Demolition Team, that is. We train here."

"Are you a naval officer?"

"Just a lowly enlisted man."

The swimmer lit a cigarette from a green shirt hanging on his chair, and told an odd tale of having volunteered in the Israeli navy in 1948 at the age of seventeen, to the dismay of his American parents, who had then been in Palestine for business reasons. He had forfeited his American citizenship. Then he had studied aeronautical engineering in England, with an idea of working for El Al. Now he was in the navy to get his citizenship back. "Israel's a great place. But I was just a kid," he said. "I'm an American. I want that green passport I lost. Luckily the navy needs lots of UDT nowadays."

The bartender came, a bronzed blond man, barefoot, with ice-blue eyes and huge shoulders. His right hand lacked two fingers. The frogman took the stubby glass full of dark whiskey and ice, and pointed at the dead fish. "How about that, Thor? Can Sheila clean it now?"

"You be figure eat here tonight? You better ask Amy. The governor having a party, I tink ve full up."

"Okay. Chuck it on the ice, anyway."

The bartender nodded, twisted the fish neatly off the spear, and left. Paperman sipped the whiskey, feeling better with each passing moment. The main beach of Gull Reef was a curve of clean white sand, bordered with palms and the round-leaved gnarled trees called sea grapes. The sand was warm and silky, trickling in his relaxed hand. Never had Paperman seen such an ocean, so tranquil that it reflected the puffy white clouds. Off to the right rose the hump of Amerigo, the serried green ridge stretching north and south, with red-roofed white buildings of the town climbing from the harbor along three rounded hillsides, and the bold carmine splash of the fort at the water's edge.

"This is not hard to take," he said, yawning and stretching.

"Amerigo? It's a dream. I've been in Italy, the south of France, Tangiers, and all that. I think this is maybe the most beautiful place in the world."

"But peculiar," said Paperman.

"How so?"

"Well, take that bartender. I never saw a bartender like that. He looks like the fourth or fifth Tarzan they had in the movies."

"Thor's not a bartender, really. He crossed the ocean by himself in a sailboat. He's one of those. A Swede."

"What's he doing tending bar?"

"Saving money for a new boat. He piled up his yawl on the reef out in Pitt Bay."

Paperman hesitated, then said, "I'm thinking of buying the Gull Reef Club."

The frogman cocked his head, crooked teeth flashing in his brown face. "Really? Is it for sale?"

"There was an ad in the *New Yorker* three weeks ago."

"Oh. The *New Yorker*."

"Don't you read it?"

"If I come across it. It takes six or seven weeks to get here."

This startled Paperman. He was in the habit of pouncing on the *New Yorker* each week within an hour after it was delivered to his favorite newsstand at the corner of Eighth Avenue and Fifty-seventh Street. In the same way he pounced on the New York *Times* each night as soon as it appeared on the streets, and he bought all the editions of all the evening and morning newspapers one after the other, though nothing changed but one headline, and though he knew well that these changes were made mainly to sell papers. He was an addict of ephemeral print. It had never occurred to him that the *New Yorker* was not instantly available all over the world—perhaps a day or so late at most, at the far end of the jet routes. He said, "You could have it sent airmail."

"At about a dollar a copy? Why?"

Paperman shrugged. Such a question merely betrayed the frogman's mentality: a square. "What do you think of the Club? I mean, as a business proposition?"

"I don't know anything about business. I'm sort of surprised she's selling it. She seems to go with the place." He sat up in a cross-legged slouch. "Is that what you do in the States? Hotel business?"

"No."

Paperman sketched his background, told about his heart attack, about his acute depression afterward and his disenchantment with Manhattan: the climbing prices, the increasing crowds and dirt, the gloomy weather, the slow bad transportation, the growing hoodlumism, the political corruption, the mushrooming of office buildings that were rectilinear atrocities of glass, the hideous jams in the few good restaurants, the collapse of decent service even in the luxury hotels, the extortionist prices of tickets to hit shows and the staleness of those hits, and the unutterably narrow weary repetitiousness of the New York life in general, and above all the life of a minor parasite like a press agent. He was quite as hard on himself as on the city. The long and the short of it was that his brush with death had taught him to make one last try to find a better way of life. Once he had seen the advertisement for the Gull Reef Club he had known no peace, he had been unable to sleep nights thinking of it, and now here he was. "And I'll tell you something," he said, "I didn't realize how disgusted with my life I actually was until I came here this morning. Coming to this island is like being born again. It's like getting a reprieve from a death sentence." He smiled with a tinge of embarrassment. "It's almost like finding out that there's a God."

The swimmer listened, with a twisted little grin, nodding now and then. "Well, I sure go along with you on New York. But this place is a real big change."

"That's the idea," Paperman said with vehemence. "A real big change. I guess you're like my wife. She thinks I've slipped my trolley."

Laughing, the frogman got off the chair. "Hell, no. To live here, to be the boss, to have *this*"—he swept his arm around at the beach and the hotel—"three hundred and sixty-five days a year? It's heaven, if you can swing it. Our unit goes back up north in March. Right now, I know three guys that aren't going to make the plane." He picked up his mask and spear gun.

"Thanks for the drink," Paperman said. "Let me buy one for you tonight. And for this babe."

"Sure thing. My name's Bob Cohn."

"I'm Norman Paperman."

"Right. See you in the bar around seven. Look, don't swim alone in deep water, Norm. Water safety rule number one."

"You were out there alone."

Cohn was putting on the green shirt, which had a gray parachute emblem over the breast pocket. "Do as I say, not as I do. Navy leadership rule number one." He grinned amiably, and went trotting up the beach with his spear gun.

4

Paperman could hear Atlas as he walked up the red concrete steps to the bar.

"Just an old truth teller," Atlas was saying. "All I do is tell people the truth about their own business."

Paperman's spirit sank. Yes, there it was, the same old issue of *Time* with Eisenhower on the cover. Two Negroes in dark blue city suits were sitting forward in low wooden armchairs, glancing at the story. Lester sat sunk in another such chair, a glass of beer in one fat paw, a torpedo-shaped cigar in the other, his hairy white legs spread apart, his paunch resting on his lap, pince-nez glasses perched on his heavy nose. His tropical costume was an orange shirt covered with scarlet-and-green watermelons, creamy linen shorts that were much too brief and looked like nothing but exposed underwear, brown city shoes, and drooping black cotton half socks.

"Hello there!" Mrs. Ball waved a beer glass from a square lounge chair for two, on which she was curled in a pose too kittenish for a big woman. "We're having our elevenses. Come join us."

"I'm all sand and salt. I'd better shower first."

"Nonsense. Give him a beer, Thor. How was your swim? Why didn't you tell us your partner's a celebrity?"

"Just an old truth teller," beamed Atlas.

Paperman suspected the woman was being sarcastic. The *Time* article was an acid attack on corporation raiders. Lester came out almost worst of all the nine men whose brutal shifty faces bordered the story. But all Lester cared about was that his picture had appeared in a national magazine. He had a leather-bound copy of the issue in his office, another in his home, and a reserve pile of them which he was using up one by one in ignorant boasting.

"Do meet Walter Llewellyn, Mr. Paperman, he's the president of our bank," Mrs. Ball articulated through immobile jaws. "And my accountant, Neville Wills."

The two Negroes stood, arms at their sides. When Paperman put out his hand they took it, and he experienced the limp hesitant handshake of the West Indian. The banker was a round-faced slight man with gray hair. The accountant was tubby and young, with a couple of gold teeth showing in a shy smile. Both men were quite black; indeed the banker, perhaps because of the gray hair, looked purple-black.

"Norm, I was telling Amy here, and these gentlemen, that my only stock in trade is truth. Now, to give you an idea, Amy, let's say there's this Corporation X—" Paperman sank into a chair, resigned. Lester was not a man to be diverted.

On he went with it, the old tiresome fable. Corporation X had been making money on rubber belting and tires, but losing its profits because of a subsidiary that manufactured buggy whips. Lester Atlas became a stockholder. He studied Corporation X, saw the truth, and told it to the board of directors. They could get rid of the buggy-whip plant for a big cash profit, because the building and land were valuable, and thereafter they could stick to making products that were in demand, and earn large dividends. But the directors, a decrepit old family group, ganged up against Atlas, because they were sentimentally attached to making buggy whips. They called him a wolf and a raider, and threw him out of their office. Then, and only then, did Atlas go to the other stockholders, and tell them the truth. The stockholders started a legal fight, threw out the directors, and elected a new board. The new board sold off the buggy-whip building, and turned the corporation into a big money-maker.

"Now sometimes it happens, Amy, that these people offer to elect me as a director, or even as chairman of the board. Just out of gratitude for telling them the truth. Well, if I can accept, I do. But I'm a busy man. Usually my only reward is the knowledge that once more I've told the truth and saved a sick corporation. That's what I do. That's *all* I do. If that makes me a raider, I'm proud of it."

The banker said, "Why, I feel you are perform*ing* a genu-*wine* public sar-*viss*, Mr. Atlas." He had a gentle, musical voice, and he hit the last syllable of every word, in the manner that had so amused Paperman for years in records of Calypso songs.

Paperman wondered how Lester had the gall to go on repeating this simple-minded story of his, when this very issue of *Time* that he kept flaunting described how he actually operated. Lester had recently bought into a Southern furniture company, which—it was true—had been badly run for years. He had gained control in a vicious stock fight, sold off all the buildings and timberlands, and pulled out with better than a million-dollar capital gain in cash. The family owners had also made money, but the corporation was now a gutted shell. Some four hundred people had lost their jobs. *Time* quoted Lester as saying, "All I did was wind up the affairs of a company that had to quit anyway. Instead of going bankrupt, those old fuds who were running it retired rich to Palm Beach. I did them a favor, didn't I?" To a question about the four hundred employees, Lester answered, "They were boondoggling. They were making bad furniture on bad machines at a bad price. When you get boondogglers off the government payroll you're a hero. When you do it in industry, you're a raider."

Time's story of Lester's stock fight depicted an operator who used any means short of crime to win votes: cash, cajolery, girls, threats, financial squeezes, and if necessary, his fists; an opposing lawyer at a rough meeting had called him a dirty name and Lester had knocked him unconscious. There was little trace of this violent brute in Lester now, as he sat beaming in his pince-nez glasses, watermelon shirt, and

cream-colored drawers, describing his own modest altruism in the mellif-
luous manner he could turn on when it suited him. This honeyed crafti-
ness, combined with his physique of a debauched gorilla, gave Lester
Atlas in these moments a peculiar crude charm.

Mrs. Ball said, "Well, it's all utterly fascinating. Perhaps you'll tell us
the truth about the Reef, too."

Paperman cleared his throat. "Isn't the place a money-maker?"

"Oh yes." Mrs. Ball pointed a long finger with a long orange nail at
ledgers and blue-bound balance sheets piled beside her. "But it should
make ever so much more. I haven't the foggiest idea why it doesn't."

Atlas said, "I've looked at those figures. I'd like to ask some questions."

"By all means. That's why Neville and Walter are here." The woman
signalled with her empty glass at the bartender. He brought her more
beer, and went back to doze on a bar stool. He wore ragged khaki shorts
and a blue frayed shirt laundered almost gray, and he had a gold ring
in one ear.

Paperman decided that if he bought the hotel he would keep this
eight-fingered bartender. He was changing his notion that the Gull
Reef Club needed smartening up. It was seedy, but—as in some of
the best hotels in England and Paris—the idea might be to keep it so.
Dowdiness was sometimes chic. This piratical bartender, snoozing on a
stool, added to the color. The bar décor was fish nets, great sea fans
painted white and gone a little gray, green glass-bubble net floats, dusty
conch shells, and bleached coral. One solid wall was painted with
amateurish pictures of fish. Nothing screened the corrugated iron roof
but a few withered palm branches. A frangipani tree thrust limbs
starred with pink flowers under the roof, and each gust of the breeze
stirred a wave of perfumed air. It was certainly primitive; yet, Norman
thought, authentic and right.

Atlas was questioning Mrs. Ball and the two Negroes about payrolls,
off-season and on-season prices, and taxes. "Amy, tell me one thing,"
he said abruptly, lighting a fresh cigar, "what are you selling here?"

The woman looked startled. "Why—we sell drinks, of course, and food
—we did try coral jewelry, but—"

Atlas shook his head. "You're selling sleep."

"Slee-eep?" Mrs. Ball's voice slithered up two octaves.

"Sleep. How can you make money when you don't know what

your merchandise is? People come here in the winter to be warm. At night they have to lie down. Your bar and your dining room are frills. Your merchandise is beds. Sleep. That's your profit item." He stabbed two fat cigar-clutching fingers at the ledgers. "Those books say you're not selling enough sleep. A dozen more beds, and you've probably got a business here. He set his glass down hard, and pushed himself out of the chair. "Let's go."

Lester had authority. Mrs. Ball and the Negroes stood, and so did Paperman. The bartender turned his head on his arms, and opened one cold blue eye.

Mrs. Ball said, "Oh, I've often talked about building more cottages. We have the space, but—"

"Build? Here?" Atlas squinted at the banker. "This kind of construction in the States now is nine bucks a square foot. What is it here? The contractors promise it to you for about fifteen, right? And they bring it in at twenty to twenty-five, depending on what kind of bums they are."

The Negroes exchanged an amazed glance. The accountant burst into a rich and wonderful laugh, throwing back his head, slapping his thighs, staggering here and there, and showing red gums and gold teeth. "Dat de troot. I do declare dat de troot. Dem de figures for true."

The banker held his dignity, but he too was laughing. "Mistuh Otloss, you have done business before in the Caribbe-*an?*"

Atlas thrust his cigar in his mouth and grunted. "I'm just an old truth teller. Let's see where we can put ten more beds."

As they crossed the lobby, Norman saw two girls batting a ping-pong ball back and forth in a gloomy room full of card tables. Tired as he was, Paperman felt a warm stir, for one girl wore a bikini that showed her whole naked back view, highlighted by a tiny shivering green triangle. It was a beautiful view. The Gull Reef Club was looking better and better! The ball flew into the lobby, and the girl turned to chase it. As she came wobbling nudely toward Paperman, the spell subsided. She had a big nose, a pear-shaped red face, freckles, and pink crinkly hair.

"Hey, Norm. Coming?"

Atlas and the others were mounting the stairway near the reception desk. Paperman followed, thinking that ten years ago the face might not have mattered. Possibly the gargoyle was Bob Cohn's "babe." She had the body for it. He wistfully recalled the raw appetite of youth that could enjoy such fare; and as he mounted the too steep and too long stairway at a slow pace—stairs bothered him a bit now—he thought that only waning energy, for which he deserved little credit, had made him harder to please.

Upstairs Mrs. Ball was unlocking doors and Atlas was glancing into the rooms.

"Where are your guests?"

"Most of them are out on a sail. November's our slow month, and the whole island's pretty dead."

"You've used up the space on this floor."

The banker said, "You could build out over the south side."

Atlas shook his head. "No, no. Nothing structural. Let's keep looking."

They went back down. Atlas was casting an appraising eye around the lobby, when a ping-pong ball rolled to his feet. Out galloped the naked pink-headed horror, quaking from neck to knees.

"So sorry," she giggled.

"My pleasure," said Atlas, handing her the ball with a leer. She marched back into the game room. Atlas watched her jellied dancing behind, then his interest faded as he took in the large room full of tables. "What's this? You must have fifteen hundred square feet here."

"I've never measured it," Mrs. Ball said. "It was the dining room, but now everyone eats outside, so we made a game room of it. But—"

Atlas crouched and rapped the wooden floor with his knuckles. "Partitions and plumbing," he said to the banker. "Not much to it. The rooms would be small, but all anybody wants here is a place to fall down at night. Throw in a toilet of their own and you got luxury."

"On the ground floor," the banker said, glancing around the room with a sudden shrewd cast to his gentle face. "So conveni-*ent.*"

Mrs. Ball said, "The room's never been used enough, that's true—possibly this idea should have occurred to me. As I say, I'm no business-woman."

"Norman is about to fall on his face," Atlas said. Paperman did have a drained look, and he was weaving a little. "We'll grab a nap and then talk some more."

5

In the cottage named Desire, Paperman collapsed on a bed. The bed cover irritated his sweaty, salty skin, but he felt that he could sleep on red coals.

Not Atlas, though. Atlas poured himself half a tumbler of bourbon and walked up and down the room.

"Norm, I look on you and Henny as a couple of kid cousins or something, you know that. How serious are you about this thing? Has it all been a pipe dream? Is it for real? Now that you've seen it, you'd better decide fast."

Paperman rolled on his side, with a small groan. He didn't want to talk business; his body was crying for sleep. But Atlas was doing this out of kindness to his wife and himself, and if the old thug felt like talking, Norman had to oblige.

Henrietta Paperman had been Atlas's secretary long ago. A sort of friendship had continued, based mainly on Atlas's greedy interest in meeting Broadway people. He was a lonely man, separated from his wife and detested by his two grown children, and he liked to take the Papermans to dinner now and then and tell them his troubles. What he enjoyed most was going to an opening night with them and then sitting at a table in Sardi's, staring at the celebrities, sometimes collaring one who happened to greet Norman or Henny, forcing him to join them, and pressing big dollar cigars and champagne on him.

Norman said in a small, tired voice, "Well, Lester, it's about what I expected. It's what I want to do. I don't know about the money part, but—"

"Oh, the money part could work, Norm. I'd see to that. I've said many times I'd like to put you into something better than that fly-by-night publicity racket. I mean it's a small situation, but this dame's pulling fifteen thousand a year out of the place. Six more rooms and you could clear twenty-five easy. Your overhead would stay the same, maybe one more cleaning girl. The cost of improvement is nothing, just partition walls. The only real cost is the plumbing. I'm a nut on giving everybody their own can. You ought to get Henny down here right away, if you're actually serious."

Paperman raised himself heavily on an elbow. "You'd go ahead with this, Lester?"

"You're the one who'll be going ahead with it."

"I have no money to invest. That's the whole problem."

"That's no problem." Atlas sighed and sat on the bed next to Paperman's. "It's as hot as hell in this cottage. This island is hot. I don't care what anybody says."

Indeed it was choking and damp in the large white plastered room, though the porch was open to the sea. Norman said, "November is the worst. The trade winds die down. Then in December—"

"Trade winds! For Christ's sake stop with the trade winds. It's hot. Hot! In the winter people want to be hot, so you're in business. You got merchandise." Atlas drank off his bourbon and poured more. "Now about the deal. You don't really think you can buy a piece of real estate like Gull Reef, with the hotel and these beaches and all, for fifty-five grand, do you? This thing has got to be worth two hundred fifty thousand dollars right now and at that it would be a steal."

"Lester, the ad said fifty-five thousand."

Atlas shook his head with tolerant patience. "It belongs to some native family. It's been handed down for generations. You'd have to round up about seventy-five people to even talk about a deal, and some of them can't hardly read and write, and some are in England, and some are God knows where. This banker says that back in 1928 some Englishman did round them up and he got a fifty-year lease and built this place for the American trade. Then 1929 came along and he went bust. The place went back to the goats and the rats and the lizards for twenty years and more. That's why it's got this crappy look. About eight years ago two fags came down from California and bought the lease, and fixed the joint up like it is now. That gondola and all the rest. Well, then, one of them fell in love with this Turk who opened a gift shop here, and the other California fruit got mad and stabbed the Turk— that banker told me all this—and the Turk survived and the two fags got reconciled, only they had to blow the island because this one was up for attempted murder, and that's when Mrs. Ball bought it. The upshot of it is, you're not buying anything but the last nineteen years of the lease. You got to get your dough out in that time."

Despite his fatigue, Paperman was laughing. "What happened to the Turk?"

"That's what I asked. He's still here, he's one of their leading citizens. He runs the Community Chest drive."

Paperman laughed harder.

"Norm, this thing has angles. Suppose you're sitting here on this reef with a nineteen-year lease, and a Sheraton or a Hilton comes along and wants in? This is the best site for a new tropical hotel I've ever seen. *Those* guys don't give a good god damn. They'll sink a hundred thousand in legal fees just to clear the title. They're apt to pay you anything you name for the lease, I mean a quarter of a million, three hundred thousand, who knows? Those bastards, they don't fool around.

"The other thing is, Norm, the Caribbean is a growth area. The smart money, I mean like the Rockefellers and some of the big Europeans, they're buying thousands and thousands of acres on some of these islands you never even heard of. They're looking fifty years ahead. That's how they operate, they think of the family two generations from now. In Puerto Rico and the Virgin Islands, the boom's hit already, prices are sky high. Amerigo's on the edge. You can still pick up the choice stuff reasonably, and when you get into the big wild patches over on the north side, from what old Llewellyn said there's some real bargains. But you got to be here. You got to be on hand when some old poop dies up in the hills and the stuff comes on the market. I like the idea of you and Henny being down here, keeping an eye out for things I might buy. Anything like that, I'd cut you both in, of course. A finder's fee."

Paperman was wide awake now, sitting up and hugging his naked knees. "Les, I don't know anything about real estate."

"Nothing to it. All you'd have to do is keep your ears open, and holler for me if something good turned up. No, this can be a good thing all around." Lester Atlas yawned and threw his cigar out over the porch. "You've got to face up to it now. Do you really want to give up New York and come to the Caribbean? It won't be easy, you know." He pulled the cover off the bed and settled down on the sheets, yawning and moaning with pleasure. "Jesus, I'm tired. Say, how about that green bikini?"

"She has a face," Paperman said.

"Isn't it hell?" said Atlas. "Those goddam bikinis always cover the wrong part. Norm, this is fun. Maybe we'll both end up beachcombers."

He was snoring in a minute, his naked gray-furred chest perspiring in running streams. Paperman sat hugging his knees, staring straight ahead.

6

The bar was jammed. The talk and laughter were loud; it was almost eight; a low brilliant evening star cast a narrow silver path on the still sea. Negroes and whites were roosting on the terrace rail or sitting on the steps. Paperman's immediate concern was whether he was properly dressed. He had longed to wear his new custom-tailored white dinner jacket, but overdressing was abhorrent to him. He had settled on black Bermuda shorts and knee socks, a madras jacket, and a maroon bow tie. He saw at once that it hardly mattered. There were men dressed like himself, and men in light shirts and slacks; girls in cocktail dresses, in toreador pants, and in shorts. A party in evening dress sat around the big low circular table in the center: Negroes, whites, a naval officer in a beribboned white uniform, and two ebony Africans in red-and-gold robes and crimson skullcaps. Mrs. Ball sat with them.

Lester was not in sight. He had disappeared while Norman slept.

"Hey, Norman!"

Bob Cohn, dressed in an olive gabardine suit, was waving at him from the bar. Muffled in a shirt and tie, the frogman looked insignificant, an ugly little young man with an outsize nose. Sitting beside him, her back to Paperman, was a tall blond woman in white.

"Hi, Bob. I'm paying for those drinks," Paperman said, approaching them. The woman turned her head. Before he saw her face, Paperman knew that it would not be disappointing. Ugly women did not carry their heads or turn them in this way.

"Sure thing. Mrs. Tramm, meet my new swim buddy, Norm Paperman from New York."

"Hello there," said the woman, with a slow blink of large alert hazel eyes.

Cohn started to slip off his stool. "Come on, join us. Sit here."

Paperman put a hand on his shoulder. "What's this? Respect for gray hairs? Get back on your chair. Martini, please," he said to the bartender. "Bombay gin. Boissière vermouth, two to one. Lemon peel. Chill the glass, please."

"Bless my soul," said the woman in white. "That's precisely how I like a martini. Cold, and tasting like a martini. This idiocy of waving the vermouth bottle at a glass of plain vodka!" She tinkled her glass at him. "But I gave up on the chilling long ago. I drink them with ice."

"Wrong, wrong," said Paperman. "Lumps in the oatmeal. The coward's compromise. You have to fight for the things you believe in. The martini before dinner is a sacrament. A chilled glass. To those who believe, no explanation is necessary. To those who do not believe, no explanation is possible."

Mrs. Tramm burst out laughing. "*The Song of Bernadette!* Ye gods. Somebody else remembers." She pushed her glass at the bartender. "Thor, please make me one exactly like Mr. Paperman's."

"Yes, ma'am."

"My name's Norman."

"Mine's Iris."

Paperman held out his hand, and Mrs. Tramm shook it, still laughing. She had a cool bony hand. There were no rings on her unusually long fingers. Earrings swayed and sparkled with each motion of her head; to Paperman's practiced eye, platinum and diamonds. It was obvious to Paperman that he had had a very wrong idea about "this babe." For some reason it had amused her to accept a dinner invitation from the young swimmer, but she was not the kind to bother with Cohn. She was a powerful woman on the loose.

Iris Tramm was—on a quick inventory of what was visible—a divorcee in her thirties; a woman with a lovely face of English or Scandinavian cast, with strong sloping bones, a small tilted nose, and fine teeth. There was a curl to one side of her lips, a flattening, a touch of unbalance to the mouth, and her eyes were strikingly brilliant. She was the kind of woman Norman found most appetizing, though he still admired, with wry regret, the pretty Broadway girls whom he had played with for so many years. Now he knew they preferred the dark-headed boys, and in truth he was embarrassed by their callow ways, which more and more reminded him of his own growing daughter. Norman was an almost habitual philanderer; but since his heart attack he had behaved himself, mainly for medical reasons.

Cohn said, "Listen, Norm, I took another look at that fish. It's a hefty beast. Have dinner with us."

Paperman shook his head. "Three's a crowd. Thanks."

The slight curl in Mrs. Tramm's mouth deepened. She said in a theatrically sexy voice, "Bob, don't you want to be alone with me?"

Cohn grinned. "It's a good fish. Why should the waitresses get most of it?"

"He's afraid of me," Mrs. Tramm said to Paperman. "Imagine. An undersea warrior like that."

The bartender put two frosty glasses before them, and poured. Paperman picked up his glass. "Let's toast the undersea warrior. I might be under the sea right now if he hadn't come along and pulled me out this morning."

"Oh hell, Norm, you were just having a little trouble with your mask."

Mrs. Tramm lifted her glass. "Fortunate encounters."

"Fortunate encounters," said Cohn and Paperman. The glance Mrs. Tramm gave Paperman over the rim of her glass shook him, though it only showed appraising curiosity.

She said, "So help me, a real martini. Lovely. Look, why don't you help us eat that fish? Since Bob seems to fear I might eat him."

Paperman looked at the frogman, and said, "Well, Mrs. Tramm, I don't know—the inducement, you both understand, would be the fish."

Mrs. Tramm did a startling thing. She popped her eyes, sucked in her cheeks, and gave a couple of goggling gasps, in a very fair imitation of a fish. It went by in a moment, her face resumed its peculiar curling smile, and both men were laughing hard.

"I believe this is one evening," said Mrs. Tramm, "when I will step off what passes with me for a wagon, and have two martinis. We won't count that lumpy oatmeal I was drinking when Norman arrived."

"We're having wine, too, Iris," Cohn said.

"Sweetie, we're having something wet, nasty, and furry in a bottle.

There isn't a wine in the world that can travel to this island." She turned to Paperman. "It's a scientific mystery. Guadeloupe's just over the horizon. You can see it from Government House. The wine there's excellent. The Caribbean's not to blame. What is it?"

"I know about that. It's like thunderstorms and milk," Paperman said. "It happens in all latitudes and climates, and there's no accounting for it. The American flag turns wine sour."

Mrs. Tramm choked over her martini, and laughed with sudden gusto. "My God, that's marvellous. I've even drunk wine in American consulates, Norman. It's absolutely true. Outside the gates glorious wines, inside vinegar. Before you buy the Reef talk to the governor, won't you? Make it a neutral enclave for wine drinkers."

"Who says I'm buying the Reef?"

"My friend, in Kinja everybody knows everything about everybody at once. You're a front for a billionaire who was on the cover of *Time,* and he's going to put up a thirty-five-story hotel. The Sheraton Kinja, or something." Paperman laughed and shrugged at these absurdities. Mrs. Tramm continued, "What's going on in the New York theatre right about now? I haven't been up there since April."

To this cue Norman rose like a trout taking a fly, and he held forth with inside Broadway gossip and the new Sardi's jokes until they went to dinner. Norman was a fine raconteur. It was a delight for him to talk smartly over martinis to a shining-eyed pretty woman who laughed in cascades at his jokes. The young frogman sat and listened with a good-natured smile, looking rather out of it.

The great red fish, which arrived baked whole on a board, had an exquisite flavor, and despite the jesting the white wine was pleasant enough. This dining terrace of the Gull Reef Club at night, Paperman thought, must be one of the most charming places on earth. On the table were white linen, an overflowing centerpiece of yellow and scarlet flowers in a white glazed bowl, and an oil lamp of mottled clay, burning with a salmon-colored flame that flickered in the cool salt breeze. This terrace faced the town. Underwater lights illumined the green shallows, and made sparkling showers of the swells breaking on the rocks. Beyond these lights the water was black between the reef and the floodlit red fort, the white-and-gilt clock tower, and the dark lamp-dotted hills. Street lights curving along the waterfront silhouetted the moored schooners, and lit up the houses of Queen's Row, and the old gray church.

"What I want to know is," Paperman said at one point, "why would anybody want to sell this place? Where's there to go from here?"

Mrs. Tramm's mouth wrinkled. "Ah well, I suppose Amy Ball has her sad little secret, like everybody on Amerigo, and it's compelling her to leave."

"I have a hell of a sad little secret," said Cohn. "I blew two months' pay this afternoon in a crap game."

At the long table next to theirs, where the governor's party sat, loud bursts of laughter were rising, amid excited conversation. Paperman said, "Which one is the governor? The white-headed fellow?"

"Why, no. That's Tom Tilson," said Iris. "It's the man at the head of the table. Governor Sanders."

"Is he colored? It's hard to tell."

"Yes, he's colored."

Paperman peered at the man at the far end of the table: sallow, scrawny, with a long hollowed face and a straight thin nose.

"That woman at this end of the table—his wife?" Paperman was talking about a black woman in a short red evening dress, whose black hair was pulled flat, and piled and banded high at the back.

"Yes. Don't you think she's pretty?" said Iris.

"Well, different. Looks like Nefertiti, a bit."

"She's a Washington bureaucrat. He used to be one, too. She works in housing and only flits down here now and then to visit friend husband."

"You know all the gossip, Iris."

"When I first came here I took a job at Government House for a while."

At this moment the governor's wife turned and beckoned to Paperman. He glanced about, puzzled. She nodded, and beckoned again. "Does she mean me?" he said to Mrs. Tramm.

"It appears so. Go talk to the first lady. Mind your manners."

As he walked to the other table the woman held out a jewelled dark hand. She had very large green eyes. "Hello, I'm Reena Sanders. You're Mr. Paperman, aren't you?" Mrs. Sanders had the speech of a Western college graduate, clear and easy. "I just wanted to ask you not to run away, and to join us after dinner in the bar. The governor wants to meet you."

"That's awfully kind of him. And of you."

"You speak French, I hope. Our guests are from Chad."

"In a Hartford high school fashion."

"Where's your friend? The man who was on the cover of *Time?*"

"I'm afraid I don't know. I'm with these other people—"

"Of course. Iris, and one of Lieutenant Woods's swimmers. Please ask them to join us too."

Iris Tramm said when he returned to the table with this invitation, "The governor wants to cross-examine you about that thirty-five-story hotel, no doubt."

"I can't hang around long," said Cohn. "We're supposed to swim from Shark Bay out to Little Dog tomorrow, starting at dawn."

"Isn't that six miles?" said Iris.

"Yes. That's the beginning of the exercise. Then we do warlike things for two days and nights among the thornbushes. Eventually the survivors swim back."

"Why, you're a hero. You make me feel all shivery," said Iris.

"It beats working," Cohn said.

Paperman was silenced. There was a trace of menace about the frogman, for all his light tone. Smart comment on the New York theatre did not seem, for the moment, quite the most brilliant form of male display.

Soon afterward the steel-band music began, and they went to the terrace that faced the beach. Part of this terrace was the bar, the rest an open red-tiled space where many couples were dancing. Barefoot lean black boys, in ruffled red-and-yellow shirts and old slacks, stood in one corner, shuffling and hopping as they beat out strange music with sticks on old fuel-oil drums, hacked short, brightly painted, and hung around their necks on straps. The shallowest drums, cut to pans, produced treble notes; the larger ones rang in lower octaves, and on three whole drums one boy was pounding bass rhythm. Paperman couldn't understand how these chopped-off oil containers produced melody, but the music was real enough: mournful, monotonous, a few minor-key phrases pounded over and over and over. This insistent syncopated monotony was disturbing and sweet: *Boum-di-boum boum, tim tim tim, boum-di-boum boum—* The dancing couples rocked their hips in a step that wasn't the

rumba, or the samba, or any dance he knew. Negroes were dancing together, so were whites, and there were black men with white girls, and
white men with black girls. Paperman had seen this kind of mixing in
gloomy dives in Paris and New York, but the striking thing about this
scene was the respectable look of the dancers, black and white alike.
The Negro men all wore suits and ties, and the girls bright dance frocks.
Only some whites were dressed in shorts and sandals. There were older
couples too; one enormous black woman in brown satin was twirling
and swaying with elephantine grace, and her partner was a gray-headed
white man who might have been a minister on vacation.

Iris Tramm at his elbow said, "Something different, isn't it?"

"God, yes."

"Well, you go and join His Excellency. Bob and I will have one dance,
and then we'll be along."

"Can you do that dance?" Paperman said to Cohn. "It looks so complicated."

"It's in the knee action. Watch."

Cohn took Iris easily in his arms and the two of them rocked away,
Mrs. Tramm's hips tracing a sinuous curve across the floor.

Reena Sanders welcomed Norman with a warm smile as he approached the round table in the bar, where the governor's party had
returned. "Hello, there. Sit next to me. Alton, this is Mr. Paperman."

The governor stood, and gave him the strong quick handshake of an
American. Sanders had a white man's face, long-jawed and lean, with a
small mustache, and two deep vertical creases on either side of his thin
mouth. But his skin was lemon yellow, and his grizzled hair was woolly.
"I hope you're enjoying our little island," he said with a dour grin.

"I'm falling in love with it."

"That's what we like to hear. I'm sorry your partner isn't with you
tonight." The governor lit a cigarette with skinny stained fingers.

"Well, I daresay Lester'll show up."

Mrs. Ball, sitting straight in a chair next to the governor's, said
through a toothy smile—she was heavily painted, but it was not unbecoming—"Mr. Atlas has boundless energy. I called a cab for him about
five. He was going to explore the island."

Paperman said, "I understand there's a rumor that Lester's going to
put up a huge hotel here. There's really nothing to it, Governor. I'm

interested in buying this club. Lester's a friend of mine, and he came along to advise me on the money end. That's all."

"We like financiers visiting us, for whatever reason," the governor said.

Paperman was soon drawn into the conversation with the Africans. He knew French better than he had admitted; he had whiled away a year in Paris, in his early twenties. He found it piquant that the black men in barbaric robes spoke this cultured tongue so well. One was a doctor, the other an engineer, and they were both United Nations delegates. At the moment they were talking about housing, but when Mrs. Ball said of Paperman *"monsieur s'occupe à Brodvay,"* they showed magisterial interest, offering him studious opinions of the serious American playwrights. Norman let them talk, and then sailed forth with an airy lecture to the effect that the real American theatre was now the musical stage, and that all playwriting after O'Neill was trivial. They listened with a sober air of making mental notes. Iris Tramm, joining the party with Cohn, was clearly amused by this persiflage tossed off in more than passable French.

The white-headed man, Tilson, who had struck Norman at first glance as a surly narrow-minded old Gentile, spoke up in surprisingly good French, with a salty comment on the obscenity and sex aberration in the theatre. Mrs. Sanders defended the playwrights. The talk grew lively. The steel band thumped and jangled, the brandy and coffee went around, the swaying hips and whirling skirts of the dancing women spiced the scene, and Paperman thought he had never chanced into a more exotic or pleasant evening.

He deftly switched the topic to African sculpture. It was the fad in his Broadway set, and he had bought a couple of pieces and read some books. The diplomats were amazed at his offhand evaluations of the statuary of the West Sudan and the Gold Coast; at his connoisseur's preference for the Kifwebe masks of the Congo, and the Tellem style in Dogon sculpture. They spoke up, smiling and eager. The governor, his wife, and Mrs. Ball regarded him with growing respect. Even Tilson and his red-faced wife unbent to ask questions. As always in such company, Paperman was sharply aware of being a New York Jew. But he had long ago mastered this self-consciousness. The thing to do was simply to be himself. It always worked. It was working now. He was in command of this little party, even talking in a foreign language. The play was between himself and the Africans; the others were a charmed audience. He was a witty, cultured, amusing man, and people couldn't help liking him. Cohn, sitting next to his straight-backed commanding officer, had taken on a thoughtful look. Paperman was on top of the world, and he hardly noticed when the music stopped, and the dancers began chattering. But then he heard a roar over the chatter, and he faltered.

"*Con permisso!* Haw haw haw! *Con permisso!*"

There was a discordant banging on metal, and Lester Atlas came in sight, a steel drum around his neck, whacking away with two sticks and waggling his enormous behind. He wore a crimson jacket, sagging white shorts, a yellow shirt, and a black string tie, and he was barefoot. Tilted on his head was a straw carnival hat ornamented with dangling red monkeys. Behind him, holding a drink in either hand, shuffled the pink-haired girl, also barefoot, dressed now in strapless green silk, chanting a Calypso song:

> "*Carnival is very sweet*
> *Please*
> *Don't stop de carnival—*"

"Haw haw! *There* he is! There's the old trade-winds boy! Hey, Norm! I'm staying right here in Kinja, you know? I'm getting me a job in a steel band. How about this? *Con permisso!*"

He headed straight for the governor's table, followed closely by the girl, whose face was not improved by what appeared to be several layers of paint put on one over the other at odd times. Norman Paperman thought he might now welcome another heart attack, if it would bring instant final blackness.

"Look, Norm, I can play this thing! I swear, it's easy. I just borrowed it off the kid five minutes ago—and listen! *My country 'tis of thee, sweet land of liberty*"—he bawled the words and clinked out the tune—"*of thee I . . . where the hell is 'sing'—sing.*" (The note he struck was very sour.) "No, no—*sing.* Sing! Oh, SHIT! *Sing.* Hey, that's it, *sing, sing, sing, of thee I sing.*"

Paperman was on his feet, tugging at Atlas's sleeve. "Lester—Lester!

Lester, this is Governor Sanders. This is the governor of Amerigo. Lester, meet the governor. The governor—"

"The governor? Heh? What? The governor? You're kidding. The governor?"

Sanders stood and held out his hand. "Welcome to Amerigo, Mr. Atlas."

"Holy Jesus! I wasn't exactly expecting to meet the governor."

"Glad to see you're enjoying our little island. Come join us."

Lester divested himself of the drum and the hat. "Flossie, give this thing back to the kid. Bring me my sandals. Governor, this is Flossie. Flossie Something. She loves your island."

Atlas's embarrassment lasted no longer than it took him to jam a chair next to the governor's. He lit a giant cigar, and took charge. First he informed the delegates from Chad that he had once almost gone into a large cotton-raising enterprise in their country, similar to one that he owned in Mexico. The scheme had broken down because of tax difficulties. Next Atlas explained to the governor how to improve the economy of Amerigo. He spoke of citrus possibilities; the chronic water shortage could be solved by a ring of earth dams around the mountains. There was no need for the people to live in huts. Five hundred prefabricated units could be put up at a crack, using nothing but federal loans, and he could guarantee to do it himself and make a profit. Mrs. Sanders showed interest in this, throwing questions at him which he answered with blurry ease. The music started. Paperman instantly asked Mrs. Tramm to dance. She came along, half-dragged by him, smiling in her lopsided way. "What's your hurry, Norman?"

"Lester doesn't fascinate me."

"He's sort of cute, in a subhuman way."

Off in a shadowy corner of the terrace, she slid her tight skirt prettily up to mid-thigh to show him the dance step. Paperman was an adept dancer; soon he was rocking like everybody else, if a bit uncertainly. "Very good, very good, you've got it," said Mrs. Tramm, tapping his shoulder. Her body moved in powerful undulations which he felt through his arms. "How long are you staying?"

"Right now I never want to leave. I guess I'll go home tomorrow or the next day. As soon as our business is done."

"Why don't I drive you around a bit tomorrow? You should see the island."

"I'd stay just for that."

The steel-drum music hammered on his nerves, a strong, harsh, blood-warming noise. It stopped. A moment's pause, and the musicians began a slow, out-of-key, ragged *Stardust*. The magic lapsed. They were boys banging on oil drums. "Oh, hell, wouldn't you know?" Iris said. "The only music they can play, they despise. All they want is to out-do Guy Lombardo, whacking tin cans with sticks. And that's the Caribbean for you."

"I don't want to go back to the table," Paperman said.

The dancers were shuffling primly to the makeshift music. Iris Tramm was heavy and slow in his arms. "Nuts to this." She pulled away, leading him by a hand back to the table. "Reena, I have a brute of a headache. I'm turning in," she said in a low tone, not breaking into the argument that Lester was having with Tom Tilson about African copper mining, which the men from Chad were intently trying to follow. Bob Cohn and the naval lieutenant were gone. The saturnine governor, slumped in his chair, glanced at Mrs. Tramm with one raised eyebrow. He said to Paperman, "Are you leaving us, too?"

Mrs. Tramm swung Norman's hand. "He's just seeing me home."

"Well, be sure to come back," said Sanders. "We'll be going up to Government House for a nightcap."

"Melancholy dog, your governor," Paperman observed, as Iris led him through the lobby.

"He's not my governor. I'm a California girl, and that's where I'm returning. Maybe sooner than anybody thinks. The Caribbean's fine, but after a while it's like a steady diet of cream puffs."

"You'd be against my buying this place, then."

"Not at all. It's entirely different if you've got something to do. And I assume you'll be bringing your wife."

"Don't you have anything to do, Iris?"

"Oh, some sculpting, and I really came here to work on a book—or so I tell myself. I've actually written some of it. But there's no urgency in that sort of thing, you know. Nobody cares whether you do a day's work or not. And it's awfully pleasant to do nothing here."

They were descending a short stone staircase to the jasmine-scented moonlit lawn. Paperman was silent. Iris glanced at him sidewise. "Your wife might adore the island. What's she like? We go this way. I live in the Pink Cottage." She cut across the lawn, walking fast. Paperman strode beside her, thinking that the conversation was taking an unfortunate turn. It was no time, and no place, to be discussing Henny. They were almost at the door of the cottage when Iris said with a mocking edge in her voice, "I said, what's your wife like, Norman?"

Under a yellow insect-repelling lamp, a wooden scroll-sign hung over the entrance: *Surrender*. Insects swarmed around the light. "Honest, if that dumb sign hasn't embarrassed me more than once," exclaimed Iris. She turned to him, arms folded, and leaned against the door, her twisted smile blackly marked by the light from above. "Well, this has been fun. I hope you liked the fish."

Paperman was wondering, as almost any man under seventy would in these circumstances, whether he would be invited into Iris Tramm's cottage, and if so, what would happen inside. He said unsteadily, "My wife's wonderful, Iris."

"Is she pretty?"

"I think she is."

"Tall?"

"No. Not like you. You see, I like them short. Henny informed me of this fact when we got married. Once or twice she has reminded me."

"She sounds all right."

"Henny's a terrific woman."

"Would you like to come in for a drink?"

"Yes indeed."

"Come along. It's a hell of a time to end an evening, quarter to eleven." She opened the unlocked door, and he followed her in. As she flipped on a wall switch, Paperman heard a growl. "All right, it's just me and a friend, so shut up," she called, whereupon somewhere out of sight a dog began to snarl and bark, clanking a chain and scrabbling strong claws on wood. "My protector. Just stand your ground. You're not afraid of dogs, are you? —Okay, okay, I'm coming, shut your yap, darling." She went out to the porch. There were leaps, thumps, clanks, barks, and into the room bounded a large black German shepherd dog. It charged straight for him, eyes as red as its tongue, teeth gleaming in rows like a shark's. Paperman stood still; to retreat one step before this animal, he was certain, meant the loss of all of his throat that mattered. The dog halted an inch or two from him, glowering and slavering. Iris came in and cuffed the beast on the nose. "I said he's a friend, stupid. Don't you want out on the beach? Beach? Beach?"

The big animal looked at her, then at Paperman, and with a bound it catapulted out the back door.

"He's very clever," said Iris, "and he's lots of company. His name is Meadows. When he comes back he'll be all right. Sit down. What'll it be, more brandy?"

"Scotch with—ugh, with ice, if you've got it." Paperman was annoyed at his involuntary swallow.

"Unnerving, isn't he?" she said, from the kitchenette. "That's the idea. I bought him two years ago, after my divorce from Mr. Tramm, when I was alone in a big house in the Santa Barbara hills."

Paperman now became aware of how different this cottage was from the one he and Lester occupied; no hotel furnishings, no room divider. There was a large peach-colored divan with black throw cushions; an enormous round rug of lacy yellow straw; chairs, couches, and a dinette in modern Swedish; gaudy oil abstractions on the walls. One far wall in shadow was all books and phonograph records, floor to ceiling, except for the space taken by a formidable hi-fi. On that dim side of the room stood a plank table on sawhorses with clay figures, stained cloths, and sculpturing tools; and beside it an open portable typewriter and a stack of yellow paper on a wheeled stand. The place seemed split into a working, studio side, and a living side; and the smell on this living side was a strange mixture of delicate boudoir and coarse dog.

"Here's your booze," Iris said.

"What's this? I'm drinking alone?"

"I don't drink much, Norman. Coffee for me."

Meadows trotted into the room, favored Paperman with an absent-minded snarl, and flopped at the feet of his mistress. "Hello, fool. Were you a good dog out on the beach?" He looked up into her face with bright adoration.

Iris was curious about Atlas, or said she was, so Paperman described Lester's business; a flat topic, but with Meadows at her feet, any latent romance in the evening seemed to have died. Iris got more coffee after a while, refilled Paperman's drink, and brought out of the kitchenette a meaty beef bone, saying, "Bedtime for little doggies." The beast capered after her out to the porch, and Paperman heard the clank of a chain and some cooed silly endearments.

He wandered around the dark side of the room, inspecting her books and records; also the sculptures—a clenched hand, the head of a Negro boy, a sleeping dog. He said as she came in, "Is this what you do?"

"I play at it."

"You go in for heavyweight books."

"I read."

He had noticed grouped on a high shelf, above dozens of austere highbrow paperbacks and a shelf of mysteries, some worn books from a buried time in his own life: Marxist treatises of the thirties, thick tomes which he had once plowed through with dogged energy and —he now realized—unwitting religiosity. How long ago *that* was! He had gotten rid of those books during the McCarthy panic. Now he was ashamed of having done so. Henny had given him hell, but at the time it had seemed simple prudence. He said, "I'm surprised you bother your pretty head with economics."

"A heritage from my first marriage. I have four times this many in storage back home. An old book brings back memories. When I read John Strachey, I'm seventeen and in love again, and the smell of jonquils in a window box on Perry Street rises from the pages." She took up a guitar leaning in a dark corner. "Do you play?"

"No."

"I think I'm going to have to give it up. I liked cowboy music and folk songs long before they got to be the thing."

Paperman said, "That happens to everything in the States these days, Iris. The avant-garde can't keep ahead of the squares."

"Isn't it the truth?" Iris swept her hand over the guitar in a rich chord. "Well, let's pretend every second college boy isn't doing this, okay? It used to be fun."

She played and sang a lively Caribbean song he had never heard, *The Zombie Jamboree:*

> "*Back to back, belly to belly,*
> *I don't give a damn 'cause I done dead a'ready—*"

All she did was strum chords, she was an inexpert player, but her singing was surprisingly good. Paperman was stung with a sudden notion that he knew this woman; whether she was really a performer, or the wife of an old friend, or—hardly conceivable—someone he had had a fling with in the dead past; but could you forget somebody like Iris Tramm? Perched on the edge of the divan, her charming legs tucked to one side, she struck strong low chords, and began to sing *TB Blues;* then *Streets of Laredo;* then *It Makes No Difference Now.* He sat in a low chair opposite her, sipping his drink, awash in nostalgia. She shot him a mischievous glance, and plucked out the first bars of a melody, very slowly, single note by single note:

> *tonk . . . tonk . . . atonk*
> *tonk . . . tonk . . . atonk—*

He sat up, shocked.
"Recognize it?"
"*Recognize* it!"
She sang:

> *"I dreamed I saw Joe Hill last night*
> *Alive as you or me;*
> *Says I, 'Why Joe, you're ten years dead—'*
> *'I never died,' says he.*
> *'I never died,' says he."*

"Iris, where do I know you from?" said Paperman.

> *" 'The copper bosses killed you, Joe,*
> *They shot you, Joe,' says I;*
> *'Takes more than guns to kill a man,'*
> *Says Joe, 'I didn't die.'*
> *Says Joe, 'I didn't die.' "*

Paperman had not heard *Joe Hill* for perhaps a dozen years. The prosperous ex-communists he knew didn't sing it, even if they got very drunk. But this song, especially in the throaty, sad way Iris was singing, brought back to Paperman the feeling of being young, strong, and throbbing with sexual drive; the wonderful comradeship of the left-wingers at the smoky boozy parties for Loyalist Spain, the exaltation of being on the inside of a movement that was going to save the world from Hitler and bring on the golden age; the excitement of conspiring against the evil bosses for the cause of the common people, the naïve workers, who were hoodwinked followers of the capitalist press; above all it was a song of youth. Of youth! Of spaghetti dinners and red wine, of the kisses and embraces of many girls and at last the different kisses of little Henrietta Leon, and their love affair that burned through Marxist discussion meetings and picket-line marches and all-night arguments in cafeterias; yes, and through protest rallies on Union Square and in Manhattan Center, and in left-wing night clubs and at the "social significance" cabarets and shows—those gay biting shows that he had helped to stage, and Henny had danced in, when he had still dreamed of being a producer—and after the shows, the late Chinese meals, and then the walk up spangled Broadway to his tiny shabby room in a fleabag hotel on West Forty-eighth Street, just Henny and himself, holding hands and singing with the once-in-a-lifetime joy of young lovers on their way to make familiar and perfect love:

> *"Says I, 'Why, Joe, you're ten years dead,'*
> *'I never died,' says he.*
> *'I never died,' says he."*

—singing so happily that even morose Broadway strollers smiled through the rain at them—

Paperman stood, scanning the woman's face. "I'll be damned," he said in a quiet wondering tone. "That's who you are. Iris, you're Janet West. Aren't you?"

chapter two

Janet West

I

The new white convertible was only a Chevrolet, but it seemed enormous on the narrow highway to the airport, whizzing past little European cars, and rust-rotted old American machines. Meadows sat erect and pompous on the front seat. Atlas, in his black silk suit, slouched in the back beside Paperman, who wore new water-buffalo sandals, a pink-and-white striped sport shirt, and white shorts.

"Sixty miles an hour, and it's boiling hot," said Atlas. "And it isn't even eleven in the morning. Tell me again about the trade winds, Norm."

Iris said without turning around, "It's the sun, Lester. Shall I put up the top?"

"No, I want the burn, prove at least that I've been down here." Atlas mopped his naked head. "What do I tell Henny, Norm? When will you be back?"

Paperman's eyes met Iris's for a moment in the driver's mirror. "Tomorrow, Lester, or Friday. I'll phone her tonight."

The airport, ten minutes from town, was a flat field full of waving guinea grass and assorted brambles. One tarred strip ran east and west through the greenery. The terminal was a spacious brown wooden shed, open to the field. Inside was the ticket counter of an obscure airline, and a tin refreshment booth offering dusty candy, last week's New York papers, and scuffed copies of *Time* going back to September. About a dozen brightly clad tourists sat on wooden benches, looking hot and hung-over. Several hundred yards away there was a sound like a riot. In the concrete shell of a half-finished building laborers swarmed, abusing each other with great good cheer.

"Governor said last night Pan Am's going to route its Venezuela run through here once that terminal's up," Atlas said. "Figure what that'll do to your land values. Three hours non-stop from New York."

They were standing at a window where there was a little breeze, and Paperman was watching Iris approach from the parking lot. He said absently, "Oh, the boom's got to come. One day this'll just be a hot Larchmont."

"You made out better than I did last night," said Atlas.

Paperman took his eyes off Iris and faced into Atlas's wise grimace. "I didn't make out. Look, Lester, if I decide to go ahead with the hotel, what do I do? What kind of deal will it be?"

"Norm, just make up your mind first."

"But there's a plain big question of money."

"I know. If you want to do it, tell Amy I'm the money man and she'll hear from me. We'll work something out that won't be too hard on anybody. Let me worry about the money end."

"Your plane's landing," Iris called to Atlas. "Get up to the gate so you can grab a front seat. The tail on these planes sort of whips around."

Atlas groaned. "Who ever heard of an airport without a bar? I want a drink. I hate flying. Anybody who ever said he didn't is a liar. That goes for the Wright brothers and Lindbergh."

At the gate he held out his hand to Iris and put on his courtly manner. The small blue plane was swooping in with a roar. "Well, so long, Iris. Thanks for driving me to the airport, that was very thoughtful. Take good care of Norm, now. So long, Norman. Have fun."

A sudden gust of wind whirled dust and papers all over the airport. Thick gray rain began hammering the tin roof, making starry splashes on the concrete apron. The sun continued to shine, and a low rainbow arched over the mountains. A loudspeaker squawked at the passengers to board the plane at once. Atlas exploded with foul talk, apologized to Iris, and then lumbered out of the terminal and into the downpour. He heaved himself up the plane steps, and once inside he turned, waved his fist at Paperman, and shouted something clearly uncomplimentary about the trade winds. The rain continued until the plane started to taxi down the ramp; then Paperman could see the shower drifting along the airstrip and out to sea, a blowing curtain of gray under a single billowing cloud in a serene blue sky.

"Odd weather you have here," he said.

"We have half a dozen different weathers, all at the same time."

"How's the weather going to be for our picnic?"

"Well, Pitt Bay is the place where it doesn't rain even in the rainy season. We should be okay."

With the departure of the plane, desolation shrouded the terminal. The porters, the mechanics, the girls at the counters and the booth all vanished. Nobody was in sight; not one living thing except the flies and a single dust-colored dog lying in the middle of the building, fighting off flies with sad, loud thumps of his tail. The distant noise of the laborers on the new terminal suggested that blood was being spilled in rivers, but walking out into the blaze of the sun Paperman could see about half of them moving slowly and peaceably, and the other half standing quite still, watching them.

The airport lay in the flattest part of Amerigo, amid unbroken square miles of sugar cane. An old stone mill humped its brown cone out of the green carpet, the one structure between the airport and the mountains. The only sounds close by were the cries of birds, and the footfalls of himself and Iris on the cinder path to the parking lot.

"I hope Meadows isn't roasted alive. I have to put up the top and keep the windows half shut or he gets out and terrorizes people."

Meadows was all right, as he demonstrated by howling and lunging in the closed car at Paperman.

"Shut your big face," she shouted, opening the door, and the dog quieted. "Well, now, Norman, where to? I'll take you up through town and around the long way to Pitt Bay, so you'll get a pretty good look at the island. Anything special you want to see?"

"How about that sugar mill? Can we visit it?"

"Not that one." She started the car, and drove out of the lot. Iris drove fast, nervously, but well. "It belongs to one of our rich homos. He has it fixed up as a guest cottage. Quite delightful—Victorian furniture, Corots, and what have you. Marvellous place for parties."

"Are there many of the gay boys here?"

"Whole prides of them, sweetie. They live on the income of uncounted shares of U. S. Steel, Allied Chemical, A. T. & T., and so forth, most of them, and their taxes go to meet a good part of the island's budget. Of course we have poor ones, too."

"Balanced economy," said Paperman.

They were driving down the highway between high straight walls of cane. They passed a withered black woman riding a donkey loaded with pineapples. Meadows growled. "There's more to Amerigo than meets the eye," Norman said.

"More than you'll find out if you spend the rest of your life here. Just this little island of twelve thousand people. Layers under layers under layers."

He said after a silence, "Do you think you'll act again?"

"I expect not."

"Why not? You were marvellous. Such a gift doesn't disappear."

"Well, you're very kind, Norman, but the sort of reputation I got myself seldom rubs off. And besides—" Iris glowered at the road, driving very fast. "Oh, hell, if I do ever act again, just make sure you're not around, that's all. The fallout poisons reservoirs five hundred miles away. Anyway, what am I talking about? The next time would be the death of me. It's absolutely out of the question."

Talking about her career, she now seemed more like the Janet West he remembered. Motions of her head, a trick of pushing out her lips, the powerful rise and fall of her voice brought back to his mind moments of her performances in movies. He could recall how awed he had been, seeing the skyrocketing young film star backstage at the rehearsals of the second Follies for Free Spain. Her hair had been light brown then, rippling to her shoulders. Hardly more than nineteen, she had moved like a squaw in the wake of her husband, Melvin Swann, a suspected communist, but such a success at playing brutal likable villains that Hollywood was then tolerating him. He was either dead now, or drifting around Europe. Paperman was reluctant to ask Iris about him. He knew that some time during her public crack-up, so pitifully early in her career, they had been divorced.

My God, what a beauty she had been! How touching her inexpert willing efforts to sing and dance in the radical skits! Iris Tramm, as a thirtyish blonde encountered on a tropical island, was attractive enough. As the red embers of the briefly incandescent Janet West she was pathetic, startling, and even more appealing.

They drove into the town. (Georgetown was its name; in native parlance it was "dung tung.") The Chevrolet began a tortuous climb along ill-paved streets, steeper, narrower, and more winding as they went up, lined with perilous open sewer trenches, unpainted little wooden houses, and shacks of tin cans hammered flat. None of these places had glass in their windows. The people lived in mazes of plasterboard partitions not reaching to the ceiling, but the interiors were neat, and some walls had bright-tinted religious pictures. All along the way flowering shrubs grew from patches of earth or big lard cans. Children below school age scampered about in little shirts, or less. The progress of the gigantic Chevrolet through the tiny streets was greeted with many a bashful grin and unconcealed penis.

"These people don't live well," he said.

"This is the Caribbean."

"Is there unrest here?"

With a crooked smile she maneuvered the car past a sharp and narrow corner. "Remember, Norman, these people haven't just arrived from Idlewild. They've never seen Park Avenue or Westport."

As they zigzagged uphill, head-on meetings with other vehicles stopped them twice. Once Iris backed around a corner to make way for a taxi. The next time it was she who halted, while the driver of a rickety truck full of live goats waved merrily, gave her a white-toothed grin, and backed out of sight up a steep curving hill, to the loud protests of the terrified goats. "There's a gentleman," said Paperman.

"Oh, mostly they love driving backwards. It's the direction of choice in the Caribbean."

The shacks became fewer as they reached a cooler altitude far above the main town. Soon they were in green countryside, driving along a high ridge on a new two-lane road, with splendid views of the town and the harbor. The houses up here were of a different class: some of white-plastered cement block, with red tile roofs, some of fieldstone, and some eccentric constructions of redwood and glass. These homes ranged from medium size, by American standards, to sprawling mansions, all with large gardens of bougainvillea, scarlet poinsettia, high thickly flowered hibiscus hedges, and lavish plantings of tall-fronded banana trees.

"Beverly Hills," said Paperman.

"Signal Mountain. Same thing. The people here are known as the hill crowd."

"Who are they?"

"Some shop owners. The old plantation families. Retired rich folks. Retired military. Homo couples. Assorted drunks living on trust funds. Mostly white, but there are some old leading colored families."

"Sounds interesting."

"I wouldn't know. The minimum time for acceptance by the hill crowd, so they say, is ten years."

"How about that governor? Is he accepted?"

"Sort of tolerated."

It was a spectacular ride. Paperman delighted in the ever-changing panoramas of the town, the azure sea, and the green hills. The road grew more winding and the scenery became wilder: forested hills and valleys plunging down to red-brown crags and the breaking sea. They rounded a sharp curve, and the town went quite out of sight. This was the other side of Amerigo, more precipitous and even greener, a jungle green. Norman said after a long silence, "Iris, what's eating the governor?"

She briefly turned her head full at him, her large eyes wide. "A number of things, I believe. He did a lot of work to bring out the colored vote on the West Coast for Eisenhower, they say. Expected the Virgin Islands as his lump of sugar, but got Kinja instead. Then I guess there's that wife of his, up in Washington with his two boys, and evidently not about to come down and make him a home, or to divorce him either." She paused. "I also expect His Excellency's never been too happy about finding himself inside a colored skin." Iris swerved the car into a dirt road. "Hang on now."

They went bumping down through tangled woods: some wild palms, papayas, and mangoes, but mostly tall trees like birches with swollen lumps on their trunks, big wooden tumors. She said these were termite nests. The road became steeper and stonier. They were going down and around a hill, entering another climate of dry hot wind, and the car was raising a cloud of red dust with an acrid smell. One cactus plant after another appeared: clumps of straight spiky tubes, barrel cactus, prickly pear. The ground became flinty rubble. More and more the trees gave way to cactus, thornbush, and the great spikes of century plants. The car stopped, for the dirt road ended. Beyond lay a narrow stone trail into the thorns. "I don't know," Iris said. "I've only done this in a jeep before. It's a hell of a walk down from here and we have all that picnic stuff—shoot, let's see what kind of *cojones* they put in a Chevy nowadays."

They jolted forward. He rolled up his window in a hurry, after a long thorn branch raked blood from his cheek. The car groaned, bounded, shuddered, clanked; it struck its axles and underside with jarring, screechy blows. Meadows whimpered. Iris fought the wheel coolly. "All right, you Detroit son of a bitch, what did you expect, turnpikes all your goddamn life?" This plunge probably lasted two minutes, then they were on level hard sand, purring through a grove of high coconut trees, where the only hazard was a scattering of rotted fallen nuts. Ahead was the sea.

"Whew! How do we get back up?" he said.

"Worry about that later."

The beach was a deserted wide sweep of snowy sand. Palm trees lined it all the way to its end, about half a mile away, in high rock. At the near end it trailed off in thickets of cactus. There were no waves in Pitt Bay. Clear water sloshed up and back on the sand, not breaking. Coral reefs made jagged dark patterns in the green shallows; farther out, the bay was blue. One large island, three or four miles off, hid much of the horizon. Beyond it to the right was the green knob of another island.

"Big Dog," Iris said, pointing, "Little Dog. Bob's out there by now, doing his warlike deeds. Like broiling fresh lobsters on a driftwood fire, and so forth."

The silence was extraordinary. The swooping and diving pelicans uttered no cries. So still was it that when one of the birds hit the blue water, far out, Paperman heard the splash. Meadows alone broke the peace, racing down the beach and barking at the pelicans.

"Housekeeping chores first, then swimming and stuff," Iris said, unzipping her flared orange frock, and stepping out in a snug black jersey swimsuit that sent a tingle of pleasure through Norman. He peeled down to red trunks, glad that at forty-nine he had no paunch. Iris, unpacking a hamper, gave him a lively look. "Well! Where'd you get that tan?"

"Fake. Sun lamp. Athletic club."

Soon she had the picnic set out on the sand in the shade of a low-slanting palm tree. Food, far too much of it, was arrayed on a card table. Beer was piled in a cooler, and charcoal smoldered in a portable grill. "Okay." She brushed hair off her damp forehead. "Hot as hell even in the shade. Forty-five minutes for a swim and a drink."

The underwater scenery here was stunning. The coral arched and twisted in baroque pillars and caverns, dusty green and pink, and dotted with bright plants. The fish were larger than at Gull Reef; the first parrot fish that went by must have been three feet long. Iris swam ahead, her scissoring pink thighs a fair sight; now and then she swished around to point out a fantastic growth of elkhorn, an octopus writhing along a coral ledge, a big grouper lurking under a rock. She led him to a sunken wreck, where yellow and purple fish were gliding through the ribs in schools. Paperman was hovering over the wreck, watching the play of living color with delight, when he felt Iris's finger poke his shoulder. He turned, and saw, not ten feet away in the water, a gray diamond-shaped flat thing as wide as a tent, with white spots, and a barbed black tail. It flapped by him, swirling water against his chest, and slowly passed from sight. This incident clouded his pleasure, and he was glad when Iris headed for the shore. On the beach she told him that he had seen a leopard ray. "They can't hurt you. Bob shoots rays all the time. Says there's nothing to it. How about a martini to quiet your nerves? Two to one, Bombay gin, Boissière vermouth, lemon twist, chilled glass?"

"Don't torment me. Beer's fine."

"But it's right here." She drew glasses from the cooler, which frosted on striking warm air; produced a rattling shaker, and poured pale martinis.

"You're an amazing woman."

It was a spicy, beery picnic: frankfurters and hamburgers sizzling off the coals, beans and sauerkraut; Norman even broke down and wolfed potato salad, thinking, oh hell! They sat on straw back-rests on a broad Indian blanket, all zigzags of red, yellow, and blue. This bay was the loveliest, most peaceful place he had ever seen. They were utterly alone.

Iris tossed aside a beer can and yawned. "Take the blanket over in the sun, Norm. I'll clean up and we'll have a snooze, yes? And another swim."

A little while later she came, stretched on her back on the blanket in the sunlight, cradled her head on her arms, bent a knee so that one thigh curved over the other, and smiled sleepily up at him. Paperman recognized, or thought he did, open invitation. He lay beside her, propped on an elbow. Meadows, having gorged on the scraps, was dozing in the shade, about twenty feet away, his head on his front paws.

"You not only spread a great picnic, Iris," Norman said softly, "and you're not only exceptionally kind to the lonely wayfarer—you're beautiful."

She murmured, "What? Full, fat, and drowsy, at the moment."

"Beautiful, I say. Beautiful and sweet." He leaned over and took her lightly by the shoulders.

Meadows leaped in the air as though stung by a bee. He closed the distance in four bounds, snarling and yelping. Paperman snatched his hands off the woman. The dog stopped short on the other side of Iris, bristling, red-mouthed, making homicidal sounds.

Iris said with a lazy half-turn of her head, "Oh, Meadows, shut up. What a bore. Yes, Norman? Pay no attention to that boob. You were saying—"

"Iris, I understand devotion, I admire it," Norman said, annoyed and quite intimidated, "but isn't this kind of unhealthy? I mean this joker is your dog, he isn't your husband."

"Isn't it ridiculous? I can't even dance with a man when he's around. He thinks it's a kind of attack."

The dog was glaring at Norman across Iris's midriff, rumbling evilly in his throat.

"Well, I mean, is all this a lot of noise, or does he bite?"

"Norm darling, I actually don't know. Nobody's ever pushed him that far. He once tore up a burglar frightfully in California, but that was different, of course—"

"Don't you think he'd be happier in the car?"

"Probably, dear. I'm sure he would be. Put him in."

"Me? *Me* put him in? Are you kidding? This dog looks on me as a sort of sex-mad hamburger. I wouldn't make it halfway to the car. He'd arrive there spitting out my sandals."

Iris sat up, laughing, and put her hand to his face. "Have I told you I think you're funny? I do. Come on, little bow-wow."

The dog ran with her to the car and bounded in, evidently thinking that he and Iris were going to drive off and leave Paperman behind. He whined long and dismally when she shut the door and went back to the blanket.

"Well, now, where were we?" she said, settling herself on a back rest and igniting a cigarette.

"You were about to have a nap."

"Yes, and you were about to get fresh. Meadows knows your kind. All you are is a gay deceiver." She giggled. "That was a good joke, the sex-mad hamburger. Did you ever write jokes? I guess all press agents do, those quips in the columns." Paperman, gloomily sifting sand through his fingers, didn't answer. "Oh, come on, Norman. You don't really want to smooch, do you? *I* don't. When you bring your Henny here, I want to be friends with her."

Paperman lay down, his head on his arms. She ran her fingers through his thick gray hair. "Norman's mad, and I am glad, and I know what'll please him. A bottle of wine to make him shine, and a bottle of ink to make him stink, and Iris Tramm to squeeze him."

He couldn't help turning his head and grinning at her. "I haven't heard that since I was ten."

"Sh!" She put her finger on his lips, and cocked her head. "Car coming. Now who on earth? On a plain old Thursday? There's nobody here even on Sunday, half the time."

A white-painted jeep came weaving through the coconut grove. It drew up near the beach, and out jumped the governor and the two diplomats from Chad, in swimming trunks. A driver wearing shirt, tie, and a black chauffeur's cap remained at the wheel. Sanders waved. "Hello there. Pardon the intrusion. You have the right idea, Iris, showing visitors the nicest beach we've got."

"No intrusion, Governor, it's your island," called Iris.

Both Africans were magnificent men: broad-shouldered, narrow-waisted, with muscles heavy and marked under their gleaming black skins. The governor by contrast was a meager whey-colored object. The Africans shyly waved and called greetings in French; followed the governor splashing into the water and swam and laughed.

Paperman said, "Shall we offer them beer, when they come out? There's plenty left."

"Nothing doing. This is our party. God, a black man should be black, shouldn't he? Look at those two, and look at him. A yellow stork. What's more, they're smarter than he is. Here he sits on a silly rock in the sea. They're in the United Nations. Which at this point is practically the number-one black social club."

Though Paperman was hardly a radical any more, he was a good New York liberal. This remark offended him. He said, "You know, I'm surprised that you stay on an island like this, with your prejudice against Negroes."

She turned her head slowly and stared at him. "Me? Are you insane? *Prejudiced?* I don't like anybody much, but I like blacks a lot more than I do white people."

"Maybe I'm mistaken. Just from things you've said—"

"You're mistaken."

"Okay."

It was a snappish, tense little exchange. Paperman thought it best to let it drop. He put his head down on his arms. The sun, the beer, the silence soon lulled him into a sweet doze. He jerked when he heard her say, "Oh damn."

"Huh— Wha—?"

"Out of cigarettes."

"Are there more in the car?"

"Packs. Glove compartment. Stay put, I'll get them."

"Nonsense." He stood, yawning. The three Negroes were just coming out of the water, fairly close by. At the car Paperman peered through the closed door at Meadows. The dog was fast asleep on the back seat. Cautiously Paperman turned the front door handle, making a noise. Meadows did not flick an ear. He slowly opened the door, and pressed the catch on the glove compartment. It fell open with a thud. Meadows sat up. The next instant Paperman was knocked sprawling, and the dog was racing toward the three Negroes, ears back, uttering fearsome snarls.

"Iris, Iris!" Paperman's yell was useless, the dog was upon the men. He leaped like a cougar, straight at the governor's throat, and bore him to the ground, where the man and the animal rolled in sprays of sand.

Iris was sitting up, impassively watching the struggle. Paperman ran toward Meadows and the governor, shouting, "Iris! For Christ's sake, call the dog—" He broke off, and stopped in his tracks.

"Hey, Meadows! Hey, you're going to eat me, are you? Hey, pup, how goes it? Long time no see." Sanders, flat on his back, was holding off the dog by the jaws, and Meadows was snarling and shaking his head, but his tail was wagging. The Africans laughed and chattered in baritone French.

After a moment of stupefaction Paperman came to Iris. She said with a wry smile, "Something, isn't it? He made friends with Meadows the first day they met. His Excellency could burgle my place with ease. Meadows would just tiptoe around and open the drawers for him."

Sanders was sitting up, brushing off sand, and Meadows was frolicking in circles around him. Paperman said, "It's incredible. Has he seen the dog often?"

"Meadows came to Government House with me every day when I worked there. It got so he would go and flake out in His Excellency's office. All right, Meadows." Iris raised her voice. "All *right*. Enough."

The dog was frisking and lunging at the lean yellow governor, who was getting to his feet. "I don't mind, Iris," he called.

"I do. Meadows!" The dog hesitated, then came trotting to his mistress, tail wagging, full of good humor. He even made a friendly little lunge at Paperman. "Lie down, you. Norm, let me have another beer." There wasn't much difference in the command tones, and Iris caught herself and laughed. "See what comes of living alone with this monster. I'm getting the manners of a lion tamer."

The governor plunged in the water to wash off the sand, and then approached them. "Did you enjoy your picnic?"

"We're still enjoying it, thank you." Iris sipped her beer, leaning with her back against Paperman's shoulder.

"I'm afraid you'll be rained out." He pointed to thunderheads that had boiled up on the horizon near Big Dog, and that now appeared to be drifting toward Amerigo. Norman had already felt a few cold drops.

"Not a chance. Those things always pass over Pitt Bay and hit Signal Mountain."

"How did you manage to get down here with that Chevrolet?" The governor was obviously trying to be pleasant, and Iris—for all her talk of liking Negroes—was obviously not making it easy for him. Paperman thought it very awkward that she refrained from offering him beer. He saw Sanders glance at the cooler.

She said, "Just did it."

"I wonder if you'll be able to get out?"

"We'll manage."

He gestured toward his chauffeur. "Would you like Ronald to take it up to the road for you? I'll be glad to drive you two up in the jeep."

Iris gave him an extremely twisted smile. "No, thank you."

The governor raised thick grizzled brows, and reached down to pull the dog's ears. "Don't mention it. Enjoy the rest of your picnic." He stalked away.

When the jeep started to drive off through the palm trees, Iris flung her beer can after it.

"What's the matter with you?" Paperman said.

"All I ask," Iris said, "is that they don't act *superior* to us. Is that asking such a lot?"

With a cat's quick turn she knocked Paperman backward, and pinned his shoulders to the blanket. Her blond hair was in a tumble, her eyes shining. Paperman was delighted, flustered, and a bit embarrassed. He could still hear the squeaking and bumping of the jeep. Moreover many big drops were splattering him. It was certainly starting to rain.

"What's all this?"

"Just shut up." She kissed him long and hard, seemingly unaware of the rain, but it was falling hard, all at once, falling like a thick bath shower. She looked up at the clouds and laughed, rain running from her hair, her face, her shoulders. Nearby the charcoal embers were hissing and pouring white smoke. "No, no, this is Pitt Bay," she yelled at the sky. "Pitt Bay, stupid! It *never* rains in Pitt Bay!" She twined her arms and legs around Paperman and rolled over and over with him on the hot sand in the beating rain like a tomboy, almost the way Sanders had been rolling with the dog. Half a rainbow appeared, arching low in the east. "Come on, Norm, let's get on home. Picnic's over, and a damn good thing. Go back to New York, and don't return without your wife!"

chapter three

The Sending

I

Henny leaned her head against the icy window glass, wondering whether Norman's plane could land in this weather. Clouds of big snow-flakes were tumbling by outside. A cold draft rattled through the paint-crusted window, a pleasant little puff of relief from the blasting steam heat. Nothing in this building fitted any more or was decently kept up. The heating system was shot. From October to May you froze or you roasted. But at rent-controlled prices, in mid-town Manhattan, the apart-ment was a luxury, the envy of their friends. On their income, with Norman's habits of casual spending—he lived, as he liked to say, "the cashmere existence"—they couldn't move without going to the low-ceil-inged cubicles of the new apartment houses, where you could hear every toilet flush, every wife nag her husband, four floors above and below you; or else out to the suburbs, and that was less thinkable for Norman than the Caribbean.

Here was Norman's room, almost twenty feet square, ten feet high, facing south, bright enough when the sun shone, a little gloomy maybe in its old brown paint, but with all the space in the world for his big steel desk, his electric typewriter, his large library, the new red leather couch for his prescribed naps; all the wall area he needed for signed pictures of celebrity clients and framed bright posters of plays he had publicized; all the office furniture he had accumulated through two decades, including the old brown armchair and ottoman set which came from his one-room bachelor apartment, and which she had reuphol-stered three times. He wouldn't part with it, because she herself had bought it for him during that long depression time when they had been lovers instead of husband and wife; lovers, the rationale had been, be-cause Henny could live more cheaply with her parents; lovers also, to be truthful, because Norman had liked it that way and she had had some slight difficulty getting him to propose.

("You're going to marry me, you son of a bitch, do you hear!" with hot tears all over her face. "I'm tired of this, five years of screwing around is *plenty*. We're going to get married in two weeks or you're never going to see me again, I swear to God!") Twenty years! With all the agony, those had been the days! Henny settled into the old armchair, and put her feet up on the ottoman to sentimentalize; whereupon the telephone rang and she jumped for it.

"Henny? Lester. We just landed blind. I've never been so scared in my goddamn life."

"Hello, Lester. Where's Norman?"

"He stayed over. Henny, my mouth's full of blood. Why the hell do those broads give out gum when you come down? I damn near chewed off my own tongue. I think I swallowed a piece of it, Henny. This wasn't gum. It was meat."

"Why didn't Norman come home? I was expecting him. I have a big dinner—"

"He's phoning you tonight. A proposition like this takes a little looking into."

"Jesus, I was hoping this trip would cure him, Lester."

"Baby, look out of your window. Who needs this? I think Norman may be smarter than all of us. That island is paradise, and that hotel's a find. With what I told him to do with it, you're good for twenty-five, thirty thousand a year there, living easy in a goddamn garden of Eden. Hey, there come my bags. So long. I got a closing at four o'clock in the Chrysler building, and I'm boiled as an owl."

"You sound it."

"They give away booze free in first class, Henny. You got to drink up that difference in the fare, or Pan Am's buggered you. Bye—"

"Lester, Lester! Didn't he say *anything* about coming home?"

"He said tomorrow, maybe. Bye, small fry."

Henny sat dismayed, her hand still on the telephone, staring out at the whirling snow. This was Norman, all over. Yesterday, their twentieth anniversary day, he had spent on this dizzy excursion to the Caribbean. She had a turkey ready for the oven, champagne in the icebox; a belated celebration was better than none. Evidently, it was going to be even more belated.

2

The blast of sleety air shocked Paperman when he arrived next evening. The plane was three hours late. It was dark in the vast flat plain of Idlewild crisscrossed with miles of runway lights; dark, freezing, and windy. He encountered thick slush underfoot until he entered the terminal; then a long long trudge amid hurrying crowds, through lamplit corridors leprous with advertising, to the baggage claim counter; then a long wait in stifling steam heat through which frigid drafts lanced, chilling his neck and ankles, in a continuous clamor of loudspeakers; then a long shoving contest over the bags as they arrived, then a long search for a porter, as he wasn't supposed to carry luggage; then a long stand in wind and needling sleet amid a horde of angry combative people all jousting for the rare taxicabs that appeared; then a scary ride on an icy parkway, in a crawling river of skidding, headlight-blazing cars, with a cab driver who smelled unclean, smoked a foul cigar, and roared obscenities randomly all the way to Manhattan.

Norman Paperman was home.

She murmured, "The tropics agree with you, obviously."

"Fountain of youth," he said. "Get those elbows out of the way."

"Oh, break it up, Norm." Henny pulled free, laughing. "I've got to get back to that turkey. What a marvellous color you've got! How come you're not exhausted?"

"I slept on the plane, and—I don't know, Henny, I feel as though I've just been born, that's all. Where's Hazel?"

"I guess with the Sending. She's bringing him to dinner."

"Oh no. No." He went back to his bags, bent and tottering. "Not the Sending. Not tonight. I feel old again."

"It was her idea. No Sheldon, no Hazel. What could I do?"

"Nothing, I guess," Norman groaned. "That's bad, though, isn't it? She never brought him to dinner before."

"It's not good," Henny said.

"Well, to hell with it," said Norman, opening his Mark Cross calfskin suitcase. "To hell with it. Let us be gay, at all costs. Here's a trivial souvenir of the tropics for you. Happy anniversary."

She unwrapped the gold paper in a flutter. "What is it? I should have bought you something, I guess, but—*Norman.*" Henny was looking at an antique bracelet of Florentine silver and small diamonds nestled on purple velvet. Her voice became shaky and low. "You take this right back to the man who sold it to you."

"It's all right, isn't it?" He was removing his tie at a mirror. "It'll go with some of your things."

"It'll go with *anything.*" She was screwing up her face in a characteristic way. Henny had a round pretty face with a small nose and a fairly full chin, and when she did this to her face she rather resembled a pug dog. "Norman, where ever did you find this? We can't afford it."

"Sure we can. There it is."

On the whole Norman thought it as well not to mention that Iris Tramm had guided him to the shop of the homosexual Turk on Prince of Wales Street; had vetoed several gewgaws which the mincing dealer had brought out; had compelled him at last to produce this bracelet, and had then proceeded to cut down the Turk's price to half. The bracelet had cost Paperman nine hundred and fifty dollars. He did not have much more free cash in the world. The plunge had come partly out of guilt over his flirtation with Iris, and there was the tropical sense of release and what-the-hell in it, too, but mostly it expressed the real way he felt about the wife of his youth. Norman Paperman loved his wife. Henny put up with him, despite his philandering, mainly because she knew he did; also because he amused her. Still, there had been times when she had been close to throwing him out.

Henny came close to him, holding the box. "Thanks," she said with some difficulty.

"Why? That's just for services rendered. And may I say I'm looking forward to twenty more years of the same? Don't change a thing."

"But what next, you nut? The Caribbean, honestly? A hotel?"

"Only if you want to, Henny. You see what's doing on Fifty-seventh Street? The sun was shining in Amerigo when I left. The hills were green. The sea was blue. The temperature was eighty degrees. And the breeze smelled like Arpège."

This was a misstatement. It was Iris Tramm, kissing him goodbye at the plane gate, who had smelled like Arpège.

"Keep talking," Henny said, "I'll probably weaken." She glanced at her watch. "Where in the lousy hell is our daughter? My dinner will be ruined. I'm going to telephone the Sending's apartment. I'll bet she's there."

3

It was a good thing Henny called. The girl with a giggle said that she and Shel had been painting his kitchen and had forgotten all about the anniversary dinner, but that they would come in fifteen minutes. Henny wisely took the turkey out of the oven, and they arrived an hour later.

Sheldon Klug was the sorrow in the parents' lives. They both covered their pain by trying to laugh at it. He was Hazel's present love, the latest in a rather long string—Hazel was nineteen—an English instructor at her college, broad-shouldered and handsome, if a bit too fat and a bit too bearded. The Papermans had very little doubt left that this young man had deflowered Hazel some months ago, and had been sleeping with her ever since at random opportunities. Hazel wasn't pregnant, and she wasn't talking. That was all they knew. Henny, still a crusading freethinker, swore often to Norman that she didn't care if Hazel had found sexual fulfillment; she was all *for* sexual fulfillment, before marriage or during marriage; but how could the girl find sexual fulfillment with such a horse's behind?

Since the boiling up of the Sheldon affair, Hazel was seldom in a hurry to get home. When she did get home, she often gave her mother the strong impression of being fresh out of a warm bed. But on this occasion she did appear to have been painting a kitchen. Her tangled hair, tied up with a red ribbon, had a frost of white paint over one ear. Paint stained her gray sweatshirt and also her patched, faded blue jeans, washed threadbare so as to strain explosively over her ripening hips.

The Sending, on the other hand, looked quite presentable: dark suit, white shirt with French cuffs and heavy silver cuff links, polished grainy black shoes. The pointy reddish beard outlining his somewhat pudgy oval face was well trimmed; his heavy dark red hair was carefully groomed. He did not always look like this. A few times, especially during the summer, he had showed up at the Paperman apartment in tight Western pants, dirty sneakers, and torn T-shirt. He then tended to have a fuzzy growth of beard, and to smell like a subway at rush hour.

Sheldon Klug had been dubbed The Sending by Norman's mother, who had met him only once for a few minutes. She had actually used a Yiddish word, *onshikkeness,* to describe him. The closest English version of this term, instantly adopted by Norman and Henny, was "The Sending," with its overtones of a curse, a haunt, a burden, a blight. Klug had not charmed the grandmother. To her immediate question as to whether he was a Jew, he had responded with some talk about ethnic origins, heretical faith, alienation, live options and dead options; both his parents were Jews, in short, but he considered himself an existential pagan whose religion was art. That part, the grandmother had shrugged off; he was Jewish, at least. Her objection to the young man arose from his beard, and from his failure to discuss marriage after almost a year of hanging around Hazel. Old Mrs. Paperman thought that young

American men with beards tended to be either phonies or immoral adventurers, and she feared for Hazel.

Hazel was a tempting girl. Her great blue eyes, set far apart and very slanted, were her best feature. They gave her without effort the startled-doe look that other girls needed paint to simulate. Hazel was aware of this advantage, and she tended to keep switching her head here and there, her eyes wide and startled, even when nothing startling was going on. Hazel had an unusually long upper lip, and a full lower one, so that when she smiled her mouth assumed a V-shape. Nothing was more characteristic of Hazel than a startled look and a coy V-smile. She had a lithe figure, and a marshmallowy bosom, concealed at the moment under the paint-smeared sweatshirt. This girl had mowed down many sophomores and juniors at New York University. Perhaps this very glut of triumph had bored her, and sent her questing among the instructors.

To Hazel's view, Klug was not only good-looking, mature, and clever, but a source of prestige. This was not just her own notion; the girls and boys at the college concurred. Hazel's status had soared in the past year. For Klug not only taught, he wrote; and what he wrote was printed; usually in bickering small journals, but a few of his pieces had appeared in literary supplements, and in the new popular magazines that featured dense prose and bare girls.

In crowded New York nothing confers more gleam than any public recognition, any thrust however tiny, above the gray human sea. At New York University, where Hazel went, it was not forgotten that Thomas Wolfe had once taught English, an unrecognized genius, walking those very halls. Who could say that Sheldon Klug, at twenty-five, wasn't another Wolfe on his way up? Klug was not from the South, he came from Newark; but he bore himself, and he lectured, with persuasive ironic superiority. He was surely one of the more glamorous faculty members. When he drove up outside a cafeteria near the school late in the afternoon, in T-shirt and blue jeans, and Hazel Paperman got into the bucket seat of his decrepit red Jaguar and roared off under the eyes of her girl friends, she knew a brilliant exaltation far beyond her parents' middle-aged imaginings. And they called him the Sending! Hazel thought she treated them with remarkable forbearance. They were blind.

She treated them kindly this evening, too, ignoring their dour irritation at her sloppy appearance, her lateness, her bringing of Klug. She blew in with a bubbling air, and much kissing, laughing, jokes about the Caribbean, and excitement over Henny's new bracelet. Her parents' glumness soon evaporated. They doted on her. Norman halfheartedly tried, over the champagne cocktails, to make her clean up before dinner, but she overruled him; it would take her hours, everybody was starved, it was pointless. They all gulped two cocktails—except the Sending, who managed three—and Hazel sat down to the twentieth anniversary dinner of her parents looking like a hod carrier; with exquisite eyes, however, and a V-shaped sweet smile.

The dinner got off to a bad start. Klug revealed a surprising appetite, and a cheery willingness to ask for more and yet more. He ate most of the butter rolls in the basket that went around; he filled his salad bowl twice; he drank a lot of wine fast, and he requested a second portion of Henny's barley soup. If this was an attempt to win Henny's heart, it was not a success. She cooked well, she did nearly everything well, but she did not fancy herself as a cook. Henny and Norman kept glancing at each other as Klug attacked the food. Hazel noticed these glances, of course. There is no *a priori* reason why a great lover and a man of genius should not also be a very big eater; it is a fact, though a little-known one, that Byron had a bad weight problem. Nevertheless Hazel was embarrassed, and she began to chatter.

First she said that she had never been so starved in her life. Painting a room was hard work; my, it certainly gave you a colossal appetite! Maybe it was something in the turpentine fumes. Then she declared that she had great news. This was really a double celebration, because Shel's book had just been accepted by a publisher! Klug stopped eating soup long enough to caution her genially that nothing was certain until the contract was signed, and many wrinkles still had to be ironed out.

"What book is this?" Norman said to him. "I didn't know that you were writing a book. What's the title?"

"I'm afraid that's classified information," Klug said with a smile.

"Oh, I know," Henny said. "It's *The Homosexuality of Balzac.*"

Norman, pouring wine, was so startled that he splashed some on the table. "Balzac?" he said, peering at Klug in disbelief. "Surely not Balzac?"

Klug turned an annoyed look at Hazel, who was blushing. "That wasn't for broadcast, dear. It's a half-finished thesis."

"Oh, mother," said Hazel angrily.

Norman said, "I mean, my dear fellow, Balzac did absolutely nothing but boff women all his life. Surely you know that. I think that was what he died of. That, and eating like a hog."

"It was the women who killed him," Henny said. "Too much shtoop. However, that's Sheldon's theory."

Klug shrugged and smiled, his good humor restored. "The satyriasis was a familiar pattern. Overcompensation, plus a flight from self-knowledge."

"It's an interesting idea, anyhow," Norman said. "Balzac must be about the only one left."

Klug's smile faded into a tolerant, pitying look. He said to Norman, smoothing his hair, "There's always resistance to these discoveries. Read *A Passion in the Desert* again. And *Louis Lambert*."

"Thanks. I'll wait for your book. I did Balzac in my twenties. You say this is going to be published?"

"I'm hoping to finish it on a Guggenheim fellowship next year. And I have a publisher interested, yes."

Norman briefly cast his eyes at the ceiling.

Henny carried in the turkey, browned and fragrant. Norman carved it and Henny, dishing out the meat, the stuffing, and the vegetables, piled Klug's plate with an enormous, insulting mass of food. It was not a dinner for a person at all; it was garbage heaped up for a Great Dane. Klug took no offense, and serenely proceeded to eat.

But if the Sending wasn't offended, Hazel was. She kept switching her head this way and that, glaring at her parents with huge hurt eyes. Paperman found himself feeling sorry for her. With her shiny shell of self-confidence, created by her power over boys and by the egotism of an only child, she had been patronizing her parents for years. All at once she was vulnerable, because she really cared about a man. She could not help seeing him this evening, Norman thought, through her parents' eyes; and from that viewpoint, Sheldon did have the clear imperfection of being an eager free-loader.

Hazel's defiant-doe look melted his resentment. She was lovely. She was his daughter. She was all they had. It caused him sharp pain to think that this pudgy, supercilious young man was almost certainly violating her crystalline young body at will and that—manners today being what they were—there wasn't a thing in the world he could do about it. Not a thing. Shotguns were too obsolete even to be funny. No, he had to accept this ravisher at his own table, at his own anniversary dinner —and even smile at him!

"Hazel, turn on the radio." He wanted to shut out these stabbing thoughts.

Henny said, "Oh, please, no, Norman. It's too depressing."

Hazel leaped for the portable radio on the buffet, glad of the distraction. It was just past the hour. The announcer was speaking with resonant relish, the voice of oncoming doom:

". . . offshore islands, the United States Seventh Fleet off Formosa will be ready for all eventualities, the President gravely declared. Meantime Soviet Premier Nikita S. Khrushchev warned that the Soviet Union now has rockets with thermonuclear warheads capable of reaching any target on the planet, including slow-moving fleets at sea, and he added quote any unprovoked aggression against the brave Chinese people will bring down on the aggressors swift reprisals of INCALCULABLE . . . MAGNITUDE. . . . Unquote."

There was a short silence. The announcer chirruped gaily:

"In other developments, the nationwide teamsters' strike, now scheduled for Thursday, will totally paralyze the economy of the nation, according to . . ."

"Oh, that's nothing, turn it off," said Henny.

Norman said, "Hell. What I wanted to know was whether the Chinese bombed the Seventh Fleet. They said they would."

"He didn't sound that excited," Hazel said. "I guess they didn't."

"How could they? What bombs have they got?" Henny said. "Chowmein bombs?"

"Russian bombs," said Hazel.

"Do you know the best thing about Amerigo?" Norman said to

63

Henny. "Down there they don't know there's a Chinese crisis. They have no television. You can't buy a paper that isn't five days old. The radio just plays records and commercials. In the three days I was there I heard one news broadcast. The announcer did start to say something once about the Chinese islands, but he couldn't pronounce their names. Do you know what he did? He giggled. I swear, he just giggled and dropped the whole thing, and went on to something else, something about a PTA picnic! And the strange part was, I didn't care. I laughed like hell myself."

"Jesus, let's all move there," said Henny.

Klug had finished his gigantic plateful. He said, "The calculations are that the fallout from the first thermonuclear exchange will poison everybody in the Northern Hemisphere down to latitude nineteen. What's the latitude of Amerigo?"

"Who knows?" said Norman. "It's near the equator somewhere. It's an improvement over Fifty-seventh Street and Seventh Avenue."

"Indubitably. We're probably sitting on Ground Zero, right here at this table, for H-bomb number one," said the Sending. "Cocked and ready at this moment, somewhere on a Siberian tundra, to shoot over the North Pole and land here in about twenty-six minutes. A full hundred megatons."

"Coffee, anybody?" Henny said, her face extremely pugdog-like.

Norman said uneasily, "I'm not really worried. There's not going to be any atom war. Who would be so crazy as to start it?"

Klug smiled at him, as at a student giving a bright answer. "You put the exact question. Who would be so crazy? But, alas, all of history is the case report of a deepening mass neurosis, and at this stage—if one cares to face the truth—the record points straight to an imminent and cataclysmic nervous breakdown of the entire human race."

Norman shrugged. "I suppose the Russians are goofy enough, with their bizarre Dostoevsky make-up, to do almost anything, but even they—"

"Oh, there isn't the slightest danger from the Soviet Union, clearly," Klug said with calm assurance. "It's a naïve optimistic society, full of the simple cheery myths of Marx, and quite pacific. It's only the United States that's threatening to destroy the world." Klug smiled blandly at everybody, and drank off a glass of wine. "The United States, you see, has reached the psychoneurotic dead end of the industrial culture. We've actually created the abundant society. We've found that it's a mirage, a dead end, a paralysis of tense frustration. No country in history has ever become so totally polarized to the thanatos instinct, or—"

"The what?" said Henny.

"The thanatos instinct, dear. The death urge," Norman said wearily. "Eros instinct, life urge. Thanatos instinct, death urge. Late Freud."

Klug arched a surprised eyebrow at Norman. "Exactly. Late Freud. And sheer prophecy. Look at us. We build giant highways and murderously fast cars for killing each other and committing suicide. Instead of bomb shelters we construct gigantic frail glass buildings all over Manhattan at Ground Zero, a thousand feet high, open to the sky, like a woman undressing before an intruder and provoking him to rape her. We ring Russia's borders with missile-launching pads, and then scream that she's threatening us. In all history there's never been a more lurid mass example of the sadist-masochist expression of the thanatos instinct than the present conduct of the United States. The Nazis by comparison were Eagle Scouts." The Sending arched an eyebrow again at Norman. "If I were you I'd buy that hotel in the West Indies tomorrow."

"Tell me this," Henny said. "With those ideas, how do you feel about getting married and bringing more vicious, dangerous Americans into the world?"

With a roguish lift of his brow, Klug replied, "Well, there's always some hope in a new generation, and anyway, the life process is its own categorical imperative. I've never been sorry about Russell, for example, and I'm sure he isn't."

"Russell?"

"My son."

"You have a son?" Henny peered at Hazel, wrinkling her brows.

"Of course." Klug also glanced at Hazel, whose eyes had gone oddly blank. "He's three. Russell lives with his mother in Chicago. I seldom see him, but I'm very fond of him."

This statement brought a pause.

"You're divorced," Norman said.

"No."

"You're still married?"

"My wife teaches. So do I. A divorce is complicated and expensive. I can't just pick up and go to Reno for six weeks. Besides, there are many unresolved things—Anne is still in analysis, and we're both hoping that maybe—"

Hazel said loudly, "It's nobody's business but yours, Shel. Why discuss it?"

"There's a mince pie," Henny said to Klug in brutal tones, "if you have any room left, that is."

Klug hesitated, and grinned. "Well, I can certainly try to do it justice—"

Hazel switched her head wildly at her mother. "I can't eat another bite. Neither can he, so don't go forcing pie on him. We want to see this French movie at the Fifty-fifth. It's late. Let's go, Shel." She started to rise.

Klug laid a hand on her arm. "Your folks seem surprised, Hazel. Surely you've told them about Anne."

"Who cares? What's it got to do with them? Come on."

"Now, now. Calm down." He turned benignly to the glowering parents. "I trust you're not actually upset. I don't have to justify my way of life to you, any more than you have to explain yours to me, but I do have a code. I live by it. It's an honorable code, though it may not be yours. I live by my autonomous choices. I married a bit too young. Well, that's part of my identity now, which I accept and affirm. This doesn't mean I have to forego other feminine company such as Hazel, not in the least. My chief task is to discover and affirm myself, to say *yes!* to myself. It's a process in which I'm still engaged."

"Will you say yes to the pie?" growled Henny, standing. "I'll just trot out and get it—"

Hazel shrilled, "You bring that pie, and I'll throw it at you. Sheldon, let's GO."

"Perhaps we had better run along," Klug said to the parents, with an affable smile.

The outside door closed hard, with a metallic *chonk!*—a familiar Hazel farewell.

4

They were in a taxicab on the way to Sardi's, and they were caught in the after-theatre jam on Forty-fourth Street. Henny was still trying to calm Norman. "But I *ask* you—America's thanatos urge!" he shouted, flinging out both hands and sawing the air. "The homosexuality of Pershing's horse! The mythos and the ethos of Athos and Porthos! Jesus Christ, Henny! My daughter taken in by one of *those!* And the son of a bitch has a wife and child, and she knew it all along! The girl is schizoid!"

"She is not. She's in love, the poor jerk. Stop working yourself up. We're almost there now. Anyway, there's not a thing we can do about it."

"Why? Why can't we try? She was going out with some nice kids, wasn't she? Wet behind the ears, but—"

"Listen, Norm, the one thing that made me stick to you through five lousy years was the way Mama kept fighting against you. All my self-respect got tied up in it, and—" Norman was making an extremely sour face. She said hastily, "Not that I'm comparing the two of you, but—all I'm trying to tell you—"

"I was lean," said Norman. "I was wiry. I was gay. I made jokes. I never took myself seriously, like this fat pontificating slob. I was no angel, but I never slept with another man's wife, and I never deflowered a virgin, even though—"

Henny said tartly, "Okay, dear."

"Look, I mean no offense. I was *glad* you'd had some experience, and I—"

"Shut *up*." The pugdog jaw jutted at him, and Norman subsided. Henny stared through the steamy window at the fluttering snow. When she turned to him, after a minute or so, he was surprised and sobered to see tears running down her face. "We brought her into the world, didn't we? She's our daughter. If she's screwing around, who's to blame? He's a drip and let's pray she gets over him, that's all."

"Look, suppose we did go to the Caribbean? Maybe she'd come along.

She's learning nothing at N.Y.U., and as for the ballet lessons, she's never been serious—"

"Forget it, Norman. She wouldn't come. She's trying to marry the bastard, that's why she brought him to dinner, and so far he's not having any. He's got the oldest and best out." Henny struck a little fist on the armrest of the cab. "Letting her be is our best chance. He's pretty rich. I think she's going to get fed up and puke. I just hope he doesn't hurt her too much."

The cab stopped. Henny put a hand on the back of Norman's neck and rubbed, an old intimate gesture. "Here we are. Listen, kid, I want some fun tonight, do you hear? Not another word about the Sending. Not tonight. Henceforth, joy and wassail."

"It's a deal," Norman moaned, passing a dollar bill to the cab driver. "Joy and wassail."

There was an opening-night mob in the restaurant, all buzz, jewels, white bosoms, black ties, and alert clever faces, but the headwaiter bowed the Papermans to one of the better tables in the middle of the room. Norman expected this. He entertained clients and columnists here; here too he exchanged jokes and gossip with Broadway friends; his monthly bill came to a couple of hundred dollars. The purpose of all this activity was to get the names of his clients printed in the papers.

"I wonder how the Olivier opening went?" Henny said as they walked to the table.

Norman's cronies at various tables were making small cabalistic signs to him: a faint hitch of a shoulder, a roll of the eyes, a flat hand rocked back and forth on the table. "I think they're in trouble," he said. "But you know something? I don't care. I don't care, Henny, if this show is a hit or a flop. I really don't. I don't give one good god damn. Any more than I do about some show that opened last night in Copenhagen."

"Something's happening to you," she said.

After ordering drinks he took up tomorrow's *News*, which he had bought from a street vendor, opened it to the theatre columns, and with glum pleasure saw the names of four of his clients in print. He had always been a good workman, even if his work was contemptible. He turned to the front page. The headline was about a brunette beaten to death in her apartment. In the story on page three, the "brunette" as usual was fifty-four, just another aging lady done in by bungling thieves. He sat erect, startled. "Hey, Henny! Did you know about this?"

He showed her the story. She exclaimed, "Gosh yes, I remember! There was a crowd across the street this afternoon. Ambulance, and cops, and all that. I thought somebody had had an accident. Ye gods, *murder!*"

"Across the street from us, Henny. A hundred yards away."

"I know. I wonder what part of New York is safe any more."

"The cemeteries are safe," said Norman, "for the customers."

At the front of the restaurant there was a commotion, for Sir Laurence Olivier was entering with a large party. Sometimes on a first night the diners applauded the star of the new show but tonight, perhaps because Olivier awed them, there was no handclapping. Olivier's party filed to the large vacant table at the front.

"Wait a minute!" said Paperman hoarsely. "Henny! Henny, do you see what I see?"

Henny was staring, her face all wrinkled up tight. "Ye gods. I think I do."

"But—how come? Is it possible? What's happening to this town? To this world?"

The unlikely sight that the Papermans were beholding was a huge apelike figure in a bulging dinner jacket and a frilled dress shirt, with a bald cone-shaped head, taking a chair beside Sir Laurence Olivier, throwing an arm over his shoulder, saying something in his ear, and guffawing loud enough to be heard all over the restaurant. "Haw haw haw!"

Lester Atlas was in the Olivier party, without a doubt in the world.

"I'll be goddamned," murmured Norman. "I really will be goddamned! I think my life is over."

Her face still wrinkled, Henny said, "Who produced the Olivier thing? Dan Freed? That's Freed at the table."

"Sure, Freed."

"Well, that's it, then. You introduced Lester to Freed, Norm, back in March. Don't you remember? The night of the Boyer opening. Lester cross-examined him about play financing for an hour. Lester's got money in this show. That's all."

"But why has he never mentioned it? Never even hinted it! How could he resist? Olivier! Lester always runs off at the mouth about himself like a five-year-old."

"That's how much you know about Lester," said Henny. "When he wants to, he talks. When he doesn't want to, he can keep mighty quiet. If it's a flop, he won't mention it. Lester Atlas never loses."

Paperman watched Atlas and Olivier laughing together, with stricken gloom. He had spent his days in the service of glamour. Nothing had ever been more real or more important to him than the radiance of a stage star. All his work, all his life long, had been an effort to generate tiny sparks of that radiance for his clients. Here was Olivier, the most effulgent of living actors, in the embrace of the squarest of squares, Lester Atlas. It was a total collapse of values. Brightness had fallen from the air.

He knew the reason for it. This was a foul triumph of the dollar. Broadway, with its strangling costs and shrinking audience, needed so much money to survive that it had no recourse left but to fall on its knees to the Lester Atlases. And Atlas would give money. The price was his public embrace, and his vulgar hee-hawing in your ear, at the number-one table in Sardi's.

In a flash like a waking vision, Paperman found himself picturing what the Gull Reef Club must be like at this instant: the glittering moon path across black water, the dancers, Negro and white, on the terrace, the hibiscus flowers scarlet in the flare of kerosene flames, the lights jewelling Queen's Row and the dark hills, the pure ocean breeze scented with frangipani . . .

Henny had not lived twenty years in wedlock with Paperman, and five years out of it, without becoming expert at reading his face. She said, "Norm, tell me, how serious are you about that hotel?"

He said with a sharp, almost guilty turn of his head, "I think I'm just waiting to die here in New York, Henny. There has to be something better to do with the time I've got left."

She played with her bracelet. "It's really Eden, and all that jazz? It really is?"

"Look, the natives live in shacks. It gets too hot. It's a pleasant place. Sweetheart, the point is I know sixty people in here tonight, and every one of them goes south in winter. Every one. Dan Freed would come to

Gull Reef. Half of them would. It's something different. It's making money now, and we'd make more. But that isn't the main thing. What I picture, for both of us, is a chance to—"

"HAW! HAW! HAW!" The violent bellow made them both jump. "NORMAN HILTON, I PRESUME? Haw haw! How's the old trade-winds king?"

They had been too absorbed in their conversation to see him bearing down on them. He loomed over them in evening dress, his pince-nez glasses perched on his sunburned nose, his bald head peeling in odd patches. He carried a fat cigar as usual and a dark brown highball. His frilled shirt was a light blue. This was the color for people going on television, and Paperman thought that Lester Atlas was likely to appear on television, if ever, only in a brief interview at the gates of Sing Sing. But it was like him to affect the blue shirt.

"Hi, Lester."

"How about our wandering boy, Henny? Two days in the tropics and he sheds ten years. Gone with the trade winds. Haw haw! Listen, I've been telling Larry about the hotel. You know, Sir Laurence Olivier. He's dying to meet you. He says you sound like the smartest man in New York."

Henny felt Norman's hand in a restraining grip on her knee. She said, "Thanks, Les, but we have to get home."

Atlas, however, was already hauling Norman out of his chair and telling the waiter to bring him the check at Olivier's table. Paperman's skin crawled at the thought of being introduced to the star by Lester Atlas, but the only alternative was a physical scuffle, which he would lose anyway. He came along.

The star was gracious; he did appear curious about Gull Reef, and mildly amused at Atlas. There were three columnists at the table, besides Dan Freed and his wife. All these people were old friends of the Papermans, and they made room quickly, while Mrs. Freed exclaimed over Henny's bracelet. The columnists at once asked Paperman probing questions about the Gull Reef Club. Norman began to perk up. He was an old columnist-charmer, and for once now he had something fresh to talk about. He warmed to a word picture of the island, well aware that he was giving everyone a welcome diversion from the grim wait for the notices. Little details came back to him—the plash of the pelicans in Pitt Bay, the "hill crowd," the Turkish homosexual, the free mingling of blacks and whites on the dance floor, the underwater lights on the rocks, the Chad diplomats, the eight-fingered bartender with a gold ring in his ear. All these he used with his old raconteur's flair. Even Henny was drawn in. She knew his tricks and half imitated them: the ingratiating hoarse little chuckles, the play of the eyebrows, the eyes humorously crinkled almost shut, the outward flinging of both curved palms, the spice of an occasional Yiddish word: but she was still his best audience. Her face was alight, her laugh quick and loud.

Part of Paperman's charm was his care never to weary his listeners. He knew that the notices would soon arrive. With the questions still lively, the laughter still high, he stood, taking his wife's hand, and said he had to go home. Olivier drew a laugh by saying that he wanted to reserve the cottage named Desire right now. One of the columnists said, "Norman, how does the thing actually stand? Have you and Mr. Atlas bought the hotel yet? Or are you going to buy it, or what?"

Norman was not at all ready for the final wrench; nor was his wife, judging by the amused uncertainty on her face. He said, "Well, Henny and I are going down there, anyway, probably next week."

"To look at it again? Or buy it?"

"To buy it," Atlas interposed, "to buy it, of course. It's all set."

Paperman took a deep breath, and pressed his wife's hand. "To buy it."

chapter four

The Deal

I

Henny loved Amerigo, from the moment she first saw its green hills in the morning sun through the windows of the bouncing inter-islands airplane. And Paperman's fear that, on second look, the enchanted island would prove a tawdry, hot, stupid little backwoods; that his infatuation with it had been a dream of a night and a day, woven of rainbows, moonbeams, wine, frangipani, and the bright glances of Iris Tramm—this, too, proved groundless.

They drove with Mrs. Ball in her Land Rover on a narrow broken back road along the sea, with magnificent vistas of hills and water, and glimpses of the gray ruins of old plantation houses set back in wild valleys. The ruins were what conquered Henny, and beat her quite to the ground. She had a passion for ruins. In European countries she could wander for hours amid crumbling walls open to the sky, even in heavy rain. She inquired hopefully whether the Gull Reef Club was a ruin, and showed her first sign of disappointment when Mrs. Ball told her that the building was twenty-nine years old.

Norman said, "Look, Henny, dynamite doesn't cost much. We can blow the place up and you can restore it."

Mrs. Ball laughed through her teeth and said that was a lovely thought; then, her long face sobering, she added that she had some rather glum news for Norman. Another buyer for the Gull Reef Club had appeared; three partners, actually, from Chicago. The men had visited the place a week ago and had decided straight off to buy it. She had not notified Paperman because the deal hadn't yet been concluded. "I don't know why not, exactly," she said, her voice shaken by the bumping of the car. "I'm a complete nitwit about these things, but there seems to be some involved haggling over the financing. For all I know you can still buy the Reef. I rather hope it'll be you, because these were rather coarse fellows, but you'd better talk to my solicitor today."

Norman's glance at his wife showed his shock. If the deal fell through now, after the story had appeared in half a dozen columns in New York and Hollywood, what a fool he would seem!

"Will you drop me at your lawyer's office, then?" he said. "Henny can go on to the Reef with you."

"Nothing easier." Mrs. Ball drove into Georgetown and parked on Prince of Wales Street by an arcade of shops. "His office is on the second floor," she said. "Let me just dash up and see if he's free."

Prince of Wales Street lay parallel to the ocean front. No breeze penetrated its rows of two-story stone buildings. The morning sun beat down white and fierce. Paperman felt the sweat rolling under his worsted suit, and he expected Henny to start complaining. But she was taking in the pink plaster arcades, the quiet street almost empty of automobiles, the black natives strolling by, with lively pleasure. "My God, the *peace*," she said. "I'd either be the happiest woman on earth, or I'd go absolutely nuts. Say, there's Little Constantinople!" Henny climbed out of the car. "Got to see Little Constantinople. Got to tell the Turk how I love my bracelet."

The proprietor, whose name was Hassim, greeted them with great ogles, bounces, and smiles. He was a rotund bald man in a striped sport shirt and orange slacks, with a scraggy mustache, a complexion of shiny khaki, and a bottom swaying like a woman's. He produced strange baritone twitters about Paperman's fine taste and ruthless bargaining, making no mention of Mrs. Tramm, but rolling his large humid brown eyes slyly at Norman, and licking his lips. Henny said when he flounced away into the back of his shop, "Gawd, I do believe he has designs on you." Hassim returned and pressed a little gray-and-white porcelain cat on her. She was ashamed of herself, and reluctant to take it—it was a fine Danish piece—but Hassim was importunate and charming.

"It is pure selfishness. We want people like you and Norman on the island. I will cheat you of ten times the value of it in due course."

Henny said as they left the shop, "He's nice, after all. Like so many of them." Behind her back, Hassim bestowed on her husband an obscene grimace, wallow, and wink.

Mrs. Ball was at the wheel of the Land Rover. "Hi. He's waiting for you," she called. "Through the alley, straight up the stairs. The firm is Collins and Turnbull. You want Collins."

Paperman entered a sunny courtyard brilliant with flowers, and climbed old steps of cracking red cement. In a roasting-hot anteroom lined with brown lawbooks, a man stood holding out a meaty hand. "Hello. I'm Collins." He had a big cheerful face, remarkable for a baby nose and a heroically large chin. He wore a short-sleeved white shirt, a ribbon tie, and dark trousers. "Come on inside. Sorry I don't have an air-conditioner. Never saw a November this hot. My inside office is cooler, we get the sea breeze."

Norman did not notice any sea breeze in the small whitewashed stone room, but a clanking fan disturbed the air a bit. Feet on desk, head cradled on interlocked fingers, the lawyer disclosed that he was from Philadelphia, that he had played left tackle for Penn State, that a back injury developing into arthritis had compelled him to seek a warm climate, and that this had been the luckiest thing in his life. He had been living in Amerigo for twelve years now, and loved it more every year.

"About the Reef, now. Here's the story." He tossed Paperman a four-page letter from the attorney of the Chicago men. Glancing at the pages, Norman couldn't understand all the verbiage, but it was obvious that the negotiation was real, and far along. An arrangement of bank loans was the only remaining problem.

"Suppose, for argument's sake, I offered you a check this minute?" Paperman said, handing the letter back, and concealing his dismay with, he hoped, a nonchalant air.

Collins, sucking on a cold pipe, narrowed his eyes at Paperman. "My dear sir, these people have done a lot of talking, cabling, and writing, but we haven't seen their money yet. My client can't let a sure sale go for a possible one."

"How large would the check have to be?"

"About ten per cent is the usual binder. If you give me a check for five thousand dollars before they do, Gull Reef will be yours."

"May I call New York? I'll reverse the charge." Paperman gestured at the old heavy telephone on the desk.

"Please."

Placing an overseas call in Amerigo was not simple. The local operator did not answer for several minutes, and the overseas operator didn't answer at all. Collins sent his secretary, a pretty Negro girl in a yellow cotton frock, to hunt for her. The girl flushed the operator out of a nearby ice-cream parlor, and she came on the line rather out of breath and surly. She took the call and reported back in a little while that the New York office of Mr. "Ot-loss" said he had gone to Butte, Montana. He would be at the Capitol Hotel about five in the afternoon, Amerigo time.

Collins said cheerfully, "Well, that's probably time enough. I don't see these Chicago fellows coming through with a binder by then. Why don't you just go along to the Reef, and have a swim and enjoy yourself?"

Norman placed the call to Montana, and told the operator he would be at the Gull Reef Club. Collins walked with him through the anteroom, and shook hands with Paperman in the sunshine at the top of the staircase, in a doorway festooned with a vine of yellow flowers. "You know, this island isn't for everybody. I don't know about those Chicago fellows, but you strike me as a real Kinjan."

"Oh? Why?"

"It's a question of human quality." Collins squinted at him through the blue smoke of the pipe clenched in his oversize jaw. "Of course, if those Chicago fellows do come through today, there are other properties here. Hogan's Fancy just came on the market. Tell you what. Why don't you and your bride have a drink tonight with me at Hogan's Fancy? Say sixish? The sunset is out of this world up at Hogan's Fancy."

2

Henny waved a tall red drink at him; not her first, to judge by her furtively gay grin. She sat at a table in the bar with Mrs. Ball and a lean, tanned man who badly needed a shave. Architects' sketches lay scattered on the table. Everything about Gull Reef and the bar was the same—the peace, the dusty sea fans, the dazzling beach, the azure water, the frangipani—and more charming, with Lester Atlas out of the picture. "Hi, dear," Henny said. "We're having our elevenses. Old tropical custom. I think I'm going to like the tropics. Meet Tex Akers. He's a builder. Tex, this is Norman."

The man arose, with ramshackle unfolding motions, until he stood six and a half feet high. He had unkempt fringes of graying hair, an engaging smile, and hollow tapering jaws like a nutcracker. He held out a long brown arm streaked with yellow paint; there was also a dab of the paint on his cheek. Akers looked even taller than he was, because of his costume: a khaki shirt, paint-stained khaki shorts stopping well above the knee, and bare brown legs all the way down to little white sweat socks and mud-caked work shoes. "Hi, there, Mr. Paperman. Your little lady here sure does know construction."

Henny laughed. "Amateur stuff."

They plunged back into their talk, and Norman saw that she was showing off. Henny helped all her friends in decorating or remodelling their apartments. During a couple of Norman's leanest years—a period now seldom referred to—she had brought into the house what money there was by working for a decorator, while Norman lay around the house sunk in gloom, or tried to write short stories for the *New Yorker,* or went out and made a quick conquest of some Village slut to keep up his self-esteem.

"Do have a beer, Norman." Mrs. Ball waved at the bartender, who sat at the bar with the fat little Negro accountant, working over ledgers. The ragged Viking gave Norman a friendly smile, and brought the beer at once. "Velcome back, Mr. Paperman."

Mrs. Ball had told Tex Akers about Lester's ideas for adding rooms to the Club, it turned out, and Tex had worked up the sketches. Henny was volubly delighted with the Club, with Akers, with the sketches, with the island. Norman was not sure this rum-flavored approval would survive a solid lunch, but meantime she was rapping out ideas for colors, materials, and space-saving tricks, and revelling in the admiration of Mrs. Ball and the builder.

"By the way, how did you get on with Collins?" said Mrs. Ball.

"Very well. I've got a call in to Atlas."

"Oh, have you? Fine. Decent chap, Chunky. Best lawyer on the island. He didn't try to unload Hogan's Fancy on you, did he?"

"Well—he did invite us up there for a drink this evening."

Mrs. Ball laughed. "Poor Chunky. He bought Hogan's Fancy when he came here. He's never been able to get rid of it. But do go for the drink, the sunset is divine. Don't wear wooden clogs or anything, the termites will chew them right off your feet."

Paperman said to the builder, "How much would this job cost?"

"Hard to say. Your missus here is knocking off dollars by the minute."

"Well—ten thousand dollars?"

"Why, Mr. Paperman, I had it roughed out for five. I think your girl friend's got it down to three and a half, easy."

Henny beamed.

"See here," said Mrs. Ball, "if you're going to dig into these grubby details, why don't you join Thor and Neville over there? They're totting up last month's accounts. You can get a fair idea of how we run this silly place."

"Good idea."

The accountant and the bartender cordially took him into their conversation. Between the Scandinavian and Calypso accents, Paperman couldn't follow the arithmetic, but he soon perceived that Thor was the real manager of the Club. All money was collected right here at the bar, where Thor had his small business desk set up beside the cash register. Departing guests came here to pay their bills; outsiders who wanted to dine at the club bought dinner chits from the bartender. It was a simple system, and obviously easy to control. Thor knew to a dollar the receipts week by week from the hotel guests, the bar, and the outside diners. He kept account books, bought the liquor, and supervised the cook's food purchases. Mrs. Ball's work, Norman gathered, was answering the letters and wires for reservations, keeping track of the reservation board, and spreading charm and sympathy. Norman was sure he could fill that role well, if in a different style.

"Tell me, Thor," he said, "how long have you been working here?"

"Year and a half, joost about."

"Supposing the Club changed hands? Would you stay on?"

With a savage smile, the bartender said, "If I stay in Kinja, I guess I stay on. Vy not?"

"Well, will you stay in Kinja?"

"I dunno. I come here in a boad. I don't leave till I sail avay in a boad."

"Sailing boats leave here all the time, don't they?"

"I don't sail in a boad unless I'm captain. Dad's vy I sailed across the ocean alone. No competition for captain." Thor uttered a grim laugh.

"Would you do this same job for me? I mean, accounts and all?"

The bartender hesitated, a crafty look clouding the intense blue eyes. "Amy don't pay good money. I come here dead broke off a wreck. I make a bum deal."

"We could talk about a better salary."

"I be tam glad talk about dad, dad's for sure," said Thor, and he and the accountant laughed.

Norman went back to the table, where Henny was holding a nearly empty glass high in one hand, and running the other across a sketch. "Why break down the whole wall, Tex?" she was saying. "Suppose you just cut a doorway here for access?"

"Say, that could work real good, Mrs. Paperman." Akers made a pencil scrawl on the sketch.

"Henny, how's for a swim?" Norman said. He still wore his dark New York suit, and he was damply uncomfortable.

Amy Ball stood at once. "Now you're talking. Business before lunch gives me a headache. And after the swim, how about drinks and hamburgers for everybody, on the beach?"

Akers laughed. "That's for the leisure class. I've got to tool out to Crab Cove." He rolled up his sketches and handed them to Norman, saying that there would be no charge. He was glad to accommodate Amy Ball, but he couldn't do the actual construction himself. He was too busy with his development at Crab Cove, where he was finishing up twenty-five large houses. This remodelling of the game room was a routine little job; any of a dozen island contractors could handle it. He wished the Papermans luck and ambled off, covering ground like a giraffe.

Mrs. Ball said, "If you go ahead with this, you keep after Tex. He'll do it. He's a sweetie pie, and he's the best on the island. Go look at his Crab Cove homes, they're magnificent. Your bags are in the White Cottage. See you on the beach in a few minutes, okay?"

Henny said as they walked across the lawn, "Well, Norm, I'm beginning to see your point. That gondola ride! That incredible beach! The smell of the air! That cute bartender! And baby, those planter's punches!"

"You really like the place, Henny?"

"What's not to like? Wow! Elevenses. I must remember that. Where do all these handsome men come from? That fellow Tex! Yum yum. Are they all like that on this island? Me for the Caribbean, kid."

Paperman said a little stiffly, "You call that long drink of water handsome?"

Henny looked at him aslant. "Why dear, I thought you liked them tall. How about these cottages? Right on the water! Terrific. Who's in this pink cottage?" They were walking past it, and Meadows was barking.

In his many descriptions of Amerigo, Paperman had as yet never mentioned Iris Tramm, following his old rule, in all matters regarding women, of golden silence. He said, "I don't know, but I think it's on a long lease. Here's our place, honey."

"The cottage named Desire!" Henny squinted up at the sign, linking her fingers in his, and swinging their hands. "It really exists! Razz ma tazz! Shtoo-oop! Hit me on the head and call me Shorty!"

3

Hogan's Fancy was a ramshackle wooden colonial house on the western slope of Government Hill. The mossy flagstone terrace jutted out on a knoll, and the lower town, the waterfront, the fort, and the Gull Reef Club were all part of the view. The terrace itself was an overgrown choke of flowering shrubs, palms, great-leaved green plants, and glass-and-iron tables, bathed in the rose light of a waning sun.

Chunky Collins rose from a table when he saw Paperman. "Hurry, hurry! Just in time for the green flash!"

At that moment Norman noticed Iris sitting at a gloomy table set back among the palms, with Governor Sanders. They did not see him. Iris, a mean twisted smile on her face, was tapping her foot as she talked, while the slouched governor regarded her with frigid remote amusement. So much Paperman observed before the lawyer collared him and hustled him and Henny to the railing.

"I'm just a city girl," Henny said. "What's the green flash?"

Greatly excited, Collins said it was a marvellous astronomic freak. Just before the sun sank into the sea, on certain clear days, the bit of red rim above the horizon would turn bright green. Hogan's Fancy, he said, was the best place in the Caribbean to see the green flash. It was famous for that. A row of tourists, drinks in hand, were making lively chatter at the rail, watching the sun. Paperman was less interested in the green flash, whatever it was, than in the pair he had seen among the shadowed palms. But of course he could not turn and stare, so he watched the sun too. It sank and sank, and was gone.

"The green flash!" bellowed Collins. "See it? See it? A perfect green flash!"

Paperman had observed nothing. Henny said yes, she thought she had noticed something green. The people at the rail were in a clamor; some had seen the flash, some hadn't. Collins shepherded the Papermans to "the best table on the terrace," and insisted that Norman sit in the chair with the best view; which put him squarely with his back to Iris.

The evening darkened fast, and by the time their drinks came lights were blinking on everywhere. The Gull Reef Club, with its strings of lamps and flares reflected in long wavering streaks on the indigo harbor waters, was the jewel of the panorama. Henny said it looked like Shangri-la.

"It does indeed, and that's just what it is," Collins said. "Gull Reef is the prize property of Amerigo, no dispute on that. What's the good word from Montana, by the way, Mr. Paperman?"

Norman told him that the call had not yet come through. He had left word with the operator that he would be at Hogan's Fancy, and he expected to hear soon—perhaps at any moment—from Atlas.

Collins looked somber. "I hope so. The Chicago people wired me this afternoon. They're flying down tomorrow to close the deal. It's a real hairbreadth finish, isn't it?" His gravity dissolved into genial merriment, and he waved an arm in a broad sweep around. "But if they do win out, this island's full of opportunities. How about Hogan's Fancy, for instance? Small operation, very easy terms, and you just can't beat the view."

"Don't touch it." Old Tom Tilson came up scowling at this moment, in black shorts and a Hawaiian shirt, leaning on a knotty stick. He sat at the table without being asked. "You back already, Paperman? You've got the island fever bad. Let me warn you, the island joke is that if the termites stop holding hands, Hogan's Fancy will fall down."

"There isn't a termite here, Tom. Just some aphids," said Collins, quite unruffled. "Aphids from the gardenias."

Norman said, "This is my wife, Henrietta—Mr. Tilson."

The old man stood, made a creaky bow, and dropped in his chair. "Have you ever done business in the tropics before, Paperman? Ever managed a hotel?"

"No."

"This isn't New York, you know."

"I realize that. But that fellow Thor really runs the Reef. I found that out. I've talked to him and he's willing to stay."

"Then you've got it made," said Collins. "There's nobody like Thor on the island."

"He's a boat man," said Tilson, shaking his stick at Norman. "Those boat people are a race apart, I warn you. Every one of them's crazy." He leaned toward Henny, dropping his voice, and his withered, freckled old red face lit in a lecherous gleam. "Mrs. Paperman, ever hear of a film star named Janet West?"

"Why, sure. Ages ago. She ended up in the d.t.'s ward."

"Well, she's at that table under the palm tree, right behind you."

Paperman could not resist any longer. He turned and looked, and so did Henny. Iris sat alone now in the shadows. She made no sign of recognition, though she was looking straight at them.

Henny said, turning away, "Why, she's blond. Wasn't Janet West a brunette?"

"There's been some changes made," said Tilson, showing his tongue at the corner of his mouth and eyeing Paperman.

Norman said, "Is *that* who that woman is? Why, I danced with her."

"I know you did," sang Tilson with a schoolboy's teasing note.

"She said her name was Traum, or something."

"Tramm. Iris Tramm. Well, mister, you were dancing with nobody but Janet West. She doesn't talk about it, but that's who she is."

"I'll be damned," said Paperman.

"I can't see at this distance," said Henny, "but she doesn't look too bad, for an old drunk."

"She looks pretty good," said Tilson. "Doesn't she, Paperman?"

"Very good, considering."

"She's a pleasant woman," Collins said. "She rents the Pink Cottage at the Reef."

"That's it, Henny," said Paperman. "I told you that place was leased."

Though Norman had done nothing but kiss Iris Tramm a few times, he was getting more and more uneasy, and he wished himself and Henny well off this terrace. Tilson seemed to be having some senile fun at his expense.

"Let's invite Iris over," said Tilson.

"Oh, leave her be," said Collins, with an odd look at Paperman.

Tilson turned and waved his stick. "Iris! Come join us."

"May I?" called the rough sweet voice.

She wore her hair this evening in a tousled style falling around her ears. The light of the sky was fading; a kerosene lamp in the center of the table illuminated her, and she looked young and lovely. She wore a sleeveless dress of Indian material shot through with random blues and browns.

"Hi there," Iris said to Norman with cool distant good humor, as Collins made introductions. She sat beside Henny, and smiled at her. "Well? Has the island magic got you, too? Or do you have good sense?"

"I'm not sure. I'm not feeling very sensible right now."

"Good. Amy Ball says you intend to redecorate the Reef when your husband buys it. Will you do the cottages over, too?"

Henny shrugged, peering curiously at Iris. "So far it's all just talk."

"What do you plan for the lobby?"

"Well—I just have some vague notions."

"Tell me."

With a couple of planter's punches under her belt, Henny was quite ready to display her decorating knowledge again—especially to a movie star, however faded. The two women began to talk color schemes and furnishings, and in a few minutes they were chattering away amiably. Iris seemed as knowledgeable as Henny.

"Mistuh Papuh? Dey somebody here name Papuh?" A tall black boy in a waiter's white-piped red shirt was passing among the tables.

"Here, boy. I'm Paperman."

"Ovahseas, mistuh."

"Oh my gosh," Henny said. "Lester."

"That's right, Henny. What do you say?"

She wavered, looking around at Tilson, Collins, and Mrs. Tramm. "Good lord, Norman. All of a sudden this is *it*, isn't it?"

Iris was watching them with a melancholy little smile.

"Just about." Norman put his hand on hers. "Well? Think you can stand the Caribbean?"

Henny made a mock-gallant gesture with her glass. "Oh, you know me, Norm. Anything for a few laughs."

"All right, then. Here goes."

The telephone rested on top of a small upright piano near the bar. Atlas was bellowing at the other end of the line, his voice fading in and out, recognizably coarse and recognizably drunk, "Hello, hello—Walter? Is that you, Walter?"

"Lester? Hi! This is Norman."

"Norman? Norman who? I don't know any Norman. Get off the line, mister. God damn it, operator, I'm expecting a call from Walter Sandelson in St. Louis. Let's get on the ball here."

"Lester, it's me. Norman. Norman Paperman! I'm calling from Amerigo." The line went dead, then came on with a burst of Lester's unintelligible roars and three shrill operators talking at once. Next he heard Atlas, calmer and clearer, "What? Isn't this St. Louis?"

Paperman shouted, "Lester, for God's sake it's me! Norman! Norman Paperman! What's the matter with you?"

"Oh. *Norman*. Why the hell didn't you say so?"

"Lester, I'm calling from Amerigo. Henny likes it here. She's willing to string along. But we have to move fast. There are these other people from Chicago—"

"Say, Norm, this is one hell of a lousy connection. You keep fading."

"We've got to act FAST, in fact tonight, if we want to buy that hotel." Paperman was talking very loud. The idlers at the bar, the colored bartender, the tourists at the nearest tables, made up an interested grinning audience.

"Listen, Norman, I'm expecting a call from St. Louis—Phil, there's another bottle of bourbon in that black suitcase—Norman, let me call you back."

"No, no! It's hell getting a connection, Lester. This is a very simple thing. If I can give them a five-thousand-dollar binder tonight, we can still buy the place." In mentioning the money Paperman dropped his voice far down.

Atlas yelled in his ear, "I can't hear a goddamn thing you're saying. I've got the lieutenant-governor of Montana in the next room and—Phil, why are you messing with my pajamas and shirts? That bourbon is right there under the hot-water bag—Norman, please get off the line, I've got to talk to St. Louis."

Paperman shouted, "All I want to know is, can I give them a five-thousand-dollar check?"

"Five thousand! Five thousand for what? Phil, give me some of that bourbon first—Norman, I've got to hang up now."

Paperman bawled, "Atlas, I want to know one thing. Can I give them a binder, a BINDER, for five thousand?"

"Oh, a binder. —Hey, Phil! Are you blind? You opened a bottle of Southern Comfort! That's for the dames! The lieutenant-governor will vomit. Get that drink back from him. —Go ahead, Norm, you give her that binder, I'm with you. Is that all?"

Paperman hesitated, under the double embarrassment of Atlas's impatience, and the public noise he was making. He didn't have five thousand dollars or anything near it, in his bank account. What he wanted from Atlas—what he had telephoned him to get—was an assurance that Atlas would cover a check for that amount. But he could not bawl all over Hogan's Fancy his own lack of funds.

"Well, if you're completely with me, Lester, I'm giving them the binder."

"Sure, you do that. Good luck, Norm, we'll have a ball on that island one of these days. Give Henny a goose for me. Bye."

A small parrot, walking upside down in a cage on the amber-lit bar, said clearly, "Goodbye now," and the tourists laughed.

Paperman drew out his checkbook as he walked back to the table. "Cable those Chicago people and call them off," he said to Collins. "We've got a deal."

The lawyer jumped up and shook his head. "Bully!"

"So everybody gathered," Henny said. "Everybody clear to Puerto Rico, I think." She looked gay, vexed, excited all at once.

"So I've got myself a new landlord and landlady," said Iris, with a waggish little tilt of her head that Norman remembered from her films. "I couldn't be more pleased."

"And Paperman's got himself a new life," Tilson said. "Let's all have another round and wish him luck. Waiter!"

Norman wrote out a check for five thousand dollars and handed it to Collins. "How long does it take for a check to clear to New York?" he said. "I'll have to make a deposit, of course."

"Oh, ten days to two weeks," Collins said. "No strain whatever."

4

All the way home on the plane next day, they discussed the surge of new problems. What was to be done with Hazel? How about the apartment they had lived in for seventeen years? What would become of Norman's publicity business? It was only a client list, but it gave a steady income, and it was the fruit of twenty years' work. The jet fled the tropics at ten miles a minute, and with each mile Henny grew more sober and dubious. "That goddamn island," she said. "I'd like to have one more look at it, plain. I kept seeing it through a fog of planter's punches."

"It looks even better the second time, Henny. I found that out. Anyway, we're in it."

"We sure are. Writing a bum check is fraud, tootsie."

"Lester will cover the check."

"Did he *say* he would? Did he say so in those very words—*I'll cover the check?*"

"Henny, don't worry about the money. That part's all right."

They rode from Idlewild to Manhattan in an unheated cab with their arms around each other. It was an evening of solid iron-gray low sky, bitter cold. "My God, how cold New York is," Henny said at one point through teeth that kept clicking like loose dentures. "How cold, how huge, how dirty, how crowded, how gloomy, how *cold* this town is!"

"You lack poetry," Norman said. "This is the city of gold, and here all around you are the faery lights of the billion-footed manswarm."

Henny said a dirty word.

They found Hazel humming about the apartment; Sheldon was taking her to dinner and then to an off-Broadway show. "Who's Bob Cohn?" she said. "He called twice and wants you to phone him. I wrote his number down."

Norman had to think for a moment. "Oh. That frogman. Is he up here?" He went to the telephone.

"The frogman? The man who pulled you out of the water, that Israeli?" said Hazel. "He sounds like Brooklyn, and real fresh."

First, Paperman telephoned Atlas's office, but Lester was still in Montana. Then he called Cohn. Cohn said he had come to New York on his citizenship problem. He was returning to Amerigo in the morning, and he had just called to say hello.

Henny said, "Ask him to dinner. I'd like to meet him."

Norman nodded. "God, he jumped at it," he said, hanging up. "I think that's why he called. I'll bet he's broke and hungry. He gambles."

"How old is he?" the daughter said.

"Well, he was in the Israeli war in 1948. He must be at least thirty."

"Oh." Hazel went into her room. Half an hour later she emerged panoplied for a midweek date, and poignantly pretty, despite a ridiculous explosion of hair straight up from her head. Her neckline exposed more unsteady white bosom than Norman thought seemly, but he was tired of losing that fight. She was putting on her fur-collared coat when the doorbell rang, and she answered it. Cohn stood in the doorway, hatless, in an old tan raincoat, tightly belted. He was not much taller than Hazel in her high heels. He had gotten a close navy haircut which did not fit with his big nose and sharp brown face.

"Hello. You must be the girl with the funny voice. Hi, Norm."

Norman introduced the frogman to his wife and daughter. Hazel said, buttoning her coat, "I don't mean to be rude, but I have an appointment. I'm glad to meet the man who saved my father."

Cohn shrugged, flicked off his raincoat, and dropped it on a bench. He wore an out-of-date gray city suit, the jacket too long and the lapels too wide and flaring. "Your dad wasn't in any trouble. Not like I was, the next day." He turned a white-toothed grin at Norman. "I almost drowned, out at Little Dog. They had to work me over."

"What do you mean, I have a funny voice? What's wrong with my voice?" Hazel's eyes were getting wider.

"You sounded like you'd just run up eight flights of stairs, and also had a sore throat. You sound better now."

Norman and Henny both laughed out loud. Hazel's breathless, hoarse, presumably torrid telephone voice was a household joke.

Norman said, "What happened to you at Little Dog?"

"What's Little Dog?" said Hazel pettishly. She leaned in the doorway of the living room.

"It's this small island about six miles off Amerigo," Cohn said to her. "It has a coral shelf all around it about sixty-five, seventy feet down. That's good for submarine exercises, see, because periscope depth is sixty feet, more or less, and that's the depth at which we do all lock ins and lock outs." Hazel was listening with the eyes of a gazelle about to have its throat cut, staring at the knife. Cohn went on, talking now to Norman, "Locking out and in when the sub rests on the bottom is routine. But in combat the sub will have way on, of course—it can't keep stability otherwise, subs don't hover—and that's what our exercise was this time, escaping from a moving sub at sixty feet, and then later climbing down a line and locking back in while under way. That's where I fouled up. What happened—"

"You came here for a drink," said Henny. "What'll it be?"

The Deal

"Scotch and water is great."

"Can I have the same?" said Hazel, glancing at her watch. "What do you mean by locking in and locking out?" She perched on the arm of the chair nearest the door of the living room, unbuttoning her coat, and crossing her beautiful legs.

Cohn described the air lock, the small chamber that opened into the submarine and also to the sea, and the valving and pumping scheme by which men went into the lock, stood and waited while water filled the tiny room, and then swam out. He could hardly make them believe that in the new escape method they left the submarine without air apparatus, and just blew their breaths out continually till they got to the surface.

"But don't you run out of breath?" Hazel said. "You *can't* exhale for more than a few seconds." She puffed her cheeks and blew.

Cohn laughed. "The only problem is exhaling fast and hard enough. That air in your lungs is under pressure, Hazel. It keeps expanding as you rise. You'd explode if you didn't get rid of it on the way up. Your mouth is your safety valve. You open wide and blow and blow for your life. It's hairy, the first few times you do it in the practice tower, but you get used to it."

"It sounds frightful," Hazel said.

"The really bad part is getting back into a submarine that's making three or four knots, sixty feet down," Cohn said. "That's work. I don't care what anybody says. A man doesn't swim that fast, you see. The buoy drifts by going like a train. You have to grab or you've missed it. Then down you go hand over hand on this moving line. All this is at night. You can't see anything, it's all by feel. So you grope your way back into that lock, still on that last breath you took at the surface, and—"

Norman said, "Henny, to hell with the Gull Reef Club. I've just discovered my line of work."

Henny and Cohn laughed, but Hazel remained solemn-faced, staring at the frogman. Cohn said, "Well, that was the point at which I goofed, the first time. I don't know yet what went wrong, but I had to be pulled inside the lock by the safety man and sort of emptied out. It was okay the second time, and now I can do it like the others. It was one of those things."

Hazel said to her father, "Where are you going to dinner?"

"I don't know. I guess Sardi's."

"Would you mind if Sheldon and I joined you?" She added to Cohn, "My friend is a writer. I'm sure he'd like to meet a frogman. It's so interesting."

Cohn looked to Paperman, shrugging. "If he's a writer, he'll feel short-changed. He'll expect a pale-eyed killer with no lips."

Henny said, "By all means, call Shel. Have him meet us, dear."

Hazel went to the telephone. Norman followed his wife into the kitchen, where she replenished the ice bucket. "For Christ's sake," he said, closing the door, "why do we need that depressing creep at dinner? He'll ruin my appetite and he'll eat twenty dollars' worth of food."

"This frogman is a contrast to the Sending. I thought maybe we ought to lean on it."

"Henny, he's nothing but a different kind of cuckoo." His wife shot him a look of contemptuous irony. He added, "I mean it's all very admirable, very admirable indeed, what he does, but normal guys, you know, don't go in for swimming in and out of submarines a hundred feet down, or whatever."

"No, you're quite right. Normal guys spend their lives sucking up to columnists to get little jokes printed." She thrust the ice bucket in his hands. "Give the cuckoo another drink while I dress."

Hazel had her coat off and was sitting on the couch beside Cohn, hands clasped on crossed knees, head atilt, and eyes huge. Cohn was talking about Israel. This was a subject which bored Paperman acutely. His parents had always been Zionists; his mother was still president of her Hadassah chapter. In escaping from home at fifteen, Norman had left all that behind, as well as his father's strict religious observances, with great relief. He had felt some pride in the unexpected victories of the Israelis, and had even made contributions to Zionist drives when the battles were at red glow. The wars had also served for wonderful joking at his Broadway tables about jet pilot communications in Yiddish, and the like. Beyond that, Israel meant not much more to him than Afghanistan.

It surprised him that Hazel seemed interested, but this he ascribed to the glamour of the frogman. Hazel had not met a man of action before. There were not many of them in middle-class New York circles.

Some of the lads who pursued her were getting reserve officer training, and they were pretty fellows in their new uniforms, but they did not lock in and out of moving submarines. Hazel wanted to know what Jerusalem was like, and how the Israeli girls dressed. She was astonished when Cohn told her that most Israelis weren't religious; her idea had been that they were all as fussy as old Mr. Paperman. What surprised Norman more was Cohn's praise of the scenery, for he had pictured Israel as more or less like Miami, flat and sandy and hot, and too cluttered with old Jews. Cohn, calmly sipping at his scotch and water, spoke of the stony mountains of the north, the red gorges around Sodom, and the dusty plains of the Negev, turned to dark green wherever the water came. In his dry way, he became rather eloquent.

"You should have worked in their tourist bureau," Paperman said.

"Well, you could do worse than go there sometime, Norm."

Paperman made a deprecating face. "We thought of squeezing it in between France and Italy two years ago. Time got short."

5

The Sending was waiting at Sardi's, and Paperman wondered at his wife's folly in allowing Hazel to invite him. He was almost a head taller than Cohn, and broader in the shoulder. The frogman's wiry muscles were hidden by his floppy old suit. Klug's attire was straight out of *Esquire,* all skimpy and narrow, and errorless to the arrow-thin dark blue tie. Cohn's heavy broad red tie, badly knotted, had a frayed edge. Klug was handsome, and had rich long chestnut hair; Cohn was ugly and had almost a prison clip. The confrontation was pointless anyway, for Hazel greeted Klug with blatantly undimmed love light in her eyes.

Quite as Norman had feared, the Sending ordered oysters and a filet mignon, and several side dishes, none of them of the cheapest, such as fresh asparagus hollandaise and eggplant parmigiana. Dropping the menu with a contented sigh, he said to Cohn, "Hazel tells me you're a navy frogman. I think that's fascinating." Cohn nodded, and said nothing. "Can you tell me, I wonder, what the motivation of the men in your outfit is? That's what's truly interesting. The motivation. Why do they do it?"

"Motivation? It depends on the guy, I guess."

"Of course. But speaking generally."

"Speaking generally, there are two motives. Poverty and fright."

"Fright?" Klug arched one brow in skeptical amusement.

"And poverty. It's double hazardous-duty pay, you see, and that extra dough looks big. Most of the fellows are married."

"But fright, you say?"

"Why, sure. I guess most of us are cowards who have to keep proving to ourselves how brave we are."

Klug laughed. "You're being ironic. But there may be something in that."

Henny said, "I think you're heroes."

Cohn said earnestly, "No, ma'am. Heroes don't go for this duty. They like the parachuting, locking in and out of subs, and the rest. But there's too much drilling. It never stops, even after you qualify. You go on running three miles every morning and swimming ten miles a week, and that's most of what you do, and heroes get disgusted and quit. No, the ideal frogman is an unimaginative coward with a lot of unpaid bills."

Hazel said, "Parachute jumping? You do that too?"

"We have to qualify. Demolition is our job but it shades over into reconnaissance. You can't always swim to an objective."

"Gosh, they do *everything*," Hazel said to Klug. She turned back to Cohn, bright-eyed. "And do you learn karate, and all that? Can you kill a man by hitting him once on the neck?" Cohn chuckled. "Well, can you? What's so funny?"

"See, I can't tell you whether I can do it, Hazel, because they don't give us live men to practice on."

Norman said, "It's that stupid old Congress again, and their peacetime economizing. Damned shortsighted."

Cohn's eyes gleamed at him. "Right. It's Congress's fault for sure."

"But you're thirty years old," Hazel said. "Isn't that too old for such strenuous stuff?"

Cohn coughed over his drink. "It sure is, Hazel. I've told my C.O. that, many times, and offered to quit. He just orders me to run three extra miles, to prove I'm wrong."

The arrival of the food put an instant stop to the talk, at least for

Klug; he fell to madly on the oysters. Hazel, picking at a melon, began to press Cohn for stories of his war experiences in Israel. He tried to dodge her questions, saying that the Israeli armed forces were the most fouled-up on earth, and nothing ever happened but a lot of low comedy. To prove this he told a story of a frogman group swimming from a fishing boat into the port of Alexandria to attach limpet mines to Egyptian warships. As he narrated it, the expedition was a series of silly mishaps, culminating in the fact that of the six old Italian limpet mines which they did manage to affix to the Egyptian ships—in one case with the aid of an Egyptian sailor, who readily obeyed orders barked at him in Arabic—five had failed to go off. However, the one that did go off had sunk the largest destroyer in the Egyptian navy.

"Was that one you set?" Henny asked.

"God, no. The man who set that one is the commodore of the Israeli navy now. I couldn't get mine to stick to the ship. The magnets had rusted out or something. I thought of staying there and holding it against the side till it went off. But as I told you, this duty attracts cowards. So I missed my chance to have a street in Tel Aviv named after me. Rehov Robert Cohn."

"Let's go to Israel one day, dear," Hazel said to Klug. "I'd love to see it."

"Sociologically it's an interesting place," Klug said. He had polished off his steak and the side dishes, while Cohn talked and merely nibbled at a slice of cold salmon. Klug lit a cigarette and leaned back in his chair. "Of course, there's a lot of nonsense written about it. There's been development capital of about a thousand dollars per head put into Israel by the Jews. You put that much money into any other country and you'd see results just as remarkable. In India development capital figures out at about twenty-one cents a head."

"Well, you'd be right except for one thing," Cohn said. "The way Israelis do things, a thousand dollars goes about as far there as twenty-one cents does in India."

Klug smiled tolerantly. "Then how do you explain the amazing progress?"

Cohn shrugged. "I hate to say this, but I think it's a Jewish plot."

Hazel stared at him, then broke into peals of laughter. "You know, he's just plain crazy," she said to Klug. "This man is crazy."

93

Klug looked at his watch. "Much to my regret I think we're going to have to skip dessert, dear. It won't be easy to get down to Sheridan Square."

When Hazel and Klug had gone, Cohn exchanged a quizzical glance with each of the girl's parents. "I like him," he said.

Henny said, "He's a horror."

"A mess," said Norman.

"A nothing," said Henny.

Cohn said, "What does he do? Is he really a writer?"

"He teaches English," said Henny. "He's writing a thesis about how Balzac was a fairy."

"Balzac, eh?" said Cohn. "I have a brother who teaches comparative lit at Brandeis. He wrote a dissertation about how Homer was a fairy. Is Hazel going to marry this fellow?"

Henny said, "Well, the only thing is, he has a wife."

"And a kid," Norman added.

"I see. You're in great shape with your daughter."

"Peachy," Henny said. She went off to the ladies' room.

Norman said, "How about coming home and having a brandy with us?"

"No thanks. Say, Norm, if this isn't an imposition, can you lend me a hundred dollars?"

The abrupt demand startled Paperman into making an unpleasant face. Cohn laughed. "All right, forget it. You don't know me from Joe Zilch. It's nice of you to give me a feed."

"Why, no, I'll lend you the hundred. It's just that—well, I don't have a hundred on me. I guess the restaurant will cash my check—"

"You'd be a real pal. I'll send you the dough from Kinja tomorrow. One of the guys owes me two hundred."

Norman's opinion of Cohn was taking a sharp drop, but he signalled for a waiter and wrote out a check. Cohn rattled on cheerily, "I ran into these officers off the *Jerusalem,* you see. I knew them in the Israeli navy. Working an ocean liner sure puts an edge on your card game."

Henny returned as Norman was taking the hundred dollars from the waiter and handing it to Cohn.

"What on earth?"

Cohn said, thrusting the loose bills into a pocket, "Norm's staking me to the fare back to Amerigo. The fact is, I have to sort of step on it to make the plane." He grinned. "Do you mind if I barrel off?"

"Why, of course not. But—"

"Well, then, see you in Kinja." Cohn stood. "Bring Hazel along. The youngsters in the team will give her a big rush. Thanks for everything, Norm. You too, Henny."

He made off, and they watched him get the old raincoat from the checkroom girl and go out.

"I'll be goddamned," said Henny.

"That's the only reason he called me," Norman said incredulously. "He needed the hundred."

"How is it I still have my bracelet?" said Henny.

The next night, about half-past eight, a special delivery letter came from Cohn, swarming with stamps. It contained a hundred-dollar bill and a note scribbled in pencil:

Henny and Norm—Iris sends her love, and says tell Henny Hassim has those six Hong Kong chairs. This sounds like a spy code and we may all end up in the brig. I've thought it over. I bet Balzac really was a fairy. Sheldon's going to be famous, and you're very lucky people. Back to Little Dog in the morning.

> *Glub glub—*
> *Bob.*

6

A week passed. Each day Lester's secretary told Paperman that Mr. Atlas was due back in New York the following day. Norman kept trying to telephone him at the Capitol Hotel in Butte, but he was never in, and Paperman's urgent requests that he return the calls went unanswered. In desperation, at the end of the week, Norman talked to the hotel operator. "Oh, Mr. Paperman. Oh dear. Yes, Mr. Atlas is still here. He most *certainly* is," said the girl in a flirting Western lilt. "But he *is* the hardest man to reach, isn't he?" She uttered a deep, lewd giggle, which made Norman visualize naked orgies that Lester was probably having with her in odd hours. He pleaded with her to have Atlas call him back, and she promised to do her "bay-est." Lester didn't call.

A pleasant distraction that same night was a party for Sir Laurence Olivier at Dan Freed's penthouse. Freed, the most successful producer on Broadway, a little sharp dark man with a creased face, a crew haircut, and doggedly collegiate clothes, had been a rival of Norman's in the publicity business long ago. They were still friendly, but Freed now tended to invite the Papermans only to his second-class parties. This bid was a clear sign of Norman's new status as a temporary celebrity. In dressing for the occasion he forgot his worry over the oncoming check from Amerigo. He owned an elegant Italian dinner jacket, and wearing good clothes always cheered Norman up.

He and Henny usually went late to such affairs, for a star like Olivier wouldn't arrive until an hour after the last curtain. When the Papermans walked into the long cavernous living room looking out on the park, the noise, the eye-stinging smoke, the crush showed that they were right on time. The smoke was worse than usual because a sleety gale was blowing outside. Here on the twentieth floor, the wind shrieked at the casements, and the opening of a single window would have torn dresses off women. Dan Freed darted at Norman out of the fog and the din, and Mrs. Freed flung herself at Henny, kissing the air as she came.

"Here they are!" Freed bawled over the talk, the piano-playing, and the wind. Everybody in the room turned, looked, and began to applaud. The Freeds led them to the buffet table near the rattling windows, laden with meats and salads. A big white cake, iced with a picture of a man under a palm tree cuddling a brown girl, was the centerpiece; and arched in pink sugar over the picture was

Norm the Beachcomber.

The "Olivier party" was a hoax; it was a surprise farewell party for the Papermans. The guests were mainly his Broadway friends, but the stars of Freed's three current shows were also there. Norman instantly grasped that Dan Freed was exploiting his passing notoriety for a fresh little promotion of the plays. He fell in with this graciously, making a brief speech with suitable jokes, to great laughter. Champagne foamed all around; Olivier did come by for a few moments; the whole stunt was a merry success. Three different publicity men came to Norman as the party bubbled along, and offered to buy his client list and his good will whenever he was ready to sell it.

Besides the Papermans, the one person who attracted unusual attention at the party was—of all people—Freed's production manager, a man named Lionel. Lionel had a long green-gray face, forgettable little features, pale hair, an unknown last name, and a patient beast-of-burden demeanor. Usually people acted as though Lionel were not present (whether he was or not) until something needed doing, from fetching a sandwich to retyping a contract; whereupon the cry was "Lionel!" and then "Oh, there you are," if he happened to be standing there. He had a gift for choosing clothes that made him almost invisible, but these were not necessarily drab. Tonight, for instance, Lionel wore a bright green suit; but it was almost the exact color of Mrs. Freed's wallpaper, so he more or less blended into the background. Nevertheless he was a center of attraction. Lionel had once visited Amerigo. Everybody was pumping him, but they could not draw out of him an unkind word about the island. It was, according to Lionel, nothing but Paradise on earth, the happy isle, the place where he himself would retire one day. The climate was fabulous, the natives were fantastic, the scenery was smashing, the beaches were the end, Gull Reef was cloud nine, and so forth. Because he was so very nondescript, no one could suspect him of trying to upstage the Papermans; it wasn't in his blood, if he had blood. They believed Lionel, and by the time the party ended Norman had received assurances from uncounted people—surely thirty or forty—that they were going to take their winter vacations at the Gull Reef Club.

Next morning, Norman once again telegraphed Atlas, with a note of panicky urgency. A reply came from Western Union, an unexpected one: Atlas had left the hotel. Norman called Atlas's New York secretary. She said it was absurd, Lester was in Butte, she had talked to him at the Capitol Hotel that very morning. So once more he telephoned the switchboard girl at the hotel in Butte. "Oh, Mr. *Paperman*. Oh dear, oh yes," she said. "Mr. Atlas said if you called again to give you a message. He had to dash to St. Louis. He'll call you from there."

"St. Louis? *Where* in St. Louis?"

"He didn't say. Honestly, isn't he a sketch?" and she laughed throatily and reminiscently. Paperman slammed down the telephone in a rage.

There was another farewell gathering that night: old friends, mostly with radical pasts, all now sober, respectable, and middle-aged. One had written some farce hits, another directed films, a third composed popular songs. The rest were businessmen, doctors, and lawyers, or they filled interstices of the amusement world as Norman did. Assembled with their wives in the composer's Fifth Avenue apartment, they passed an evening of joking and alcohol, of wallowing in old music sung around the piano; and—as the hour grew late—there were even some tears, assuaged by the serving of a large Virginia ham and a massive Dutch cheese, with rolls, coffee, and cakes. Afterward, when they clustered at the piano again, and the couples with smaller children had left, the composer at the keyboard looked up slyly; and then with whispering touches on the keys, he played *Joe Hill.* Probably nobody else felt quite the warm thrill that coursed through Norman Paperman.

During this evening, nearly every person there told Norman or Henny, usually in a private moment, that they were doing a marvellous, enviable thing. The Russians at the time were firing off new awesome bombs in Siberia, and the mood in New York was jittery, but there was more than that behind the wistfulness of their friends. All these people were at an age when their lives were defined, their hopes circumscribed. Nothing was in prospect but plodding the old tracks until heart disease, cancer, or one of the less predictable trap-doors opened under their feet. To them, the Papermans had broken out of Death Row into green April fields, and in one way or another they all said so.

It was a very late and very boozy party, and the telephone jangled him awake much too early next morning. The manager of his bank was calling. Norman had told him to telephone the moment the check came in from Amerigo. The check had arrived; five thousand dollars, payable to Mrs. Amelia Ball. The balance in the Paperman account was four hundred and seven dollars. What, the manager inquired, was Mr. Paperman's pleasure? Norman promised to talk to him again before noon. He spent two hours in bleary frantic attempts to locate Atlas, but Lester had vanished into St. Louis as other men get swallowed by the Arctic.

Then he tried to argue again with Henny about selling the apartment. The building had become a cooperative several years earlier, and Norman had paid in seven thousand dollars to buy his flat. He had friends who, he knew, would pay ten thousand for it now, if he picked up the telephone and offered it to them. But on this point Henny was obstinate.

Their original plan had been to sublease it for at least a year, until they were sure that the Caribbean move was a success; and she would not budge from this. When he pressed her, she turned ugly, and snarled that they were not selling the apartment now, that was all—"and if you don't like it, mine host," she concluded, "screw you." Norman might have won this argument; Henny's worst noises were often made just before she yielded; but deep down, he realized that she was being prudent. Supposing something went wrong? Supposing, for instance, Atlas backed out? At this point it was beginning to seem all too likely.

But the check had to be covered. Norman was in a vise. Bitter and beaten, he at last began telephoning the competitors who, at Freed's party, had offered to buy his client list.

At half-past five that evening, as Norman sat alone in his office behind a closed door, downing his third martini to ease the raw ache at his heart, Atlas called. He had meant to phone from St. Louis, he said, but then he had decided to rush back to New York. Here he was, at Norman's disposal. What was on his mind? Why all the calls and wires? He had been tied up on the largest deal of his life, the Montana thing, so Norman would have to forgive him if he had been a little remiss. "Tell you what," he rasped, "why don't I take you and Henny to dinner at Sardi's and we'll talk? I want to look in on Larry anyway."

Norman declined frostily, and told Atlas of his embarrassment with the check, and the way he had solved it. He had disposed of his list and his good will, the product of a life's toil, at a distress price of seventy-five hundred dollars, to an odious little newcomer in publicity named Spencer Warwick.

"Say, you did all right," Atlas said. "Good will isn't worth a fart in your racket. That Warwick must be a cluck."

"I think my client list was worth something."

"What's the matter, Norm? You sound peeved. Listen, I can still give you the five thousand. I can give it to you in bills tonight; what's five thousand? Hell, you could have asked my secretary and she'd have written you a check for five thousand. I guess this means we go ahead."

"Does it? It'll take another fifty thousand dollars to close this deal, Lester."

"I know the figures, Norm. When do we go down there and close?

How about Tuesday? No, Tuesday I've got a meeting in St. Louis. Wednesday. Let's go Wednesday."

Norman said, catching his breath, and with much more cordiality, "You mean next week? Six days from now?"

"What's to wait for? There's no title search or anything, it's just a lease. Give me the name of that lawyer down there."

"Lester, I have to know this—are you prepared to put up the entire fifty thousand dollars? I have nothing to invest. The little money I've got left, Henny will need until—"

"I *said* I'd handle the money end, didn't I? I'm going to take care of the fifty, and you're also going to get back the five you paid. I operate on my word, Norm. What's the lawyer's name?" Norman told him. "Fine. My office'll set up the whole thing, and get the plane tickets for you, me, and Henny. We're going down to Amerigo on Wednesday, and Thursday you start in the hotel business. Norm, I've got to make four million if this Montana thing works out. It's fabulous. That's why I've been a little tied up. All capital gain. This is doing it the girl's way, with no risks or anything. I'll tell you all about it Tuesday. No, Wednesday. Wednesday. Tuesday I've got to be in St. Louis. Bye."

It was surprising how many and how tenacious Norman's Manhattan roots were. Parting from his barber—to take an absurdly small thing—was quite hard. The little Italian, in a dingy Lexington Avenue shop patronized by famous actors, had been cutting his hair for seventeen years. Every ten days he went at it with anxious artistry. Whenever Norman returned from abroad with his hair mangled by strange hands, Frank would shed real tears of anger. The news that Norman was moving to the Caribbean shocked him. He turned pale, and his eyes filled. He was inconsolable until Norman swore that business trips would bring him back at least once every month or so. Then Frank with red eyes and unsteady hands pulled himself together and gave Norman his last haircut.

This kind of scene recurred with Norman's haberdasher, with his family doctor, with his heart specialist, with his dentist, with his allergy specialist (he had a tendency to asthma and hay fever), with his bookseller, with the blind man at the newsstand, with his shoemaker (Norman wore custom-made shoes), with his tailor, and with the headwaiters of restaurants. Each thread twanged sadly as he broke it. There were more farewell parties too; evenings of adieus, drinking, old songs, tears, jokes, and congratulations. The Papermans were as thoroughly and spectacularly said goodbye to, in these last whirling days, as though they were being shot off to the moon.

On Sunday night, coming home from a party, Henny complained of a stomach pain. They blamed it on a midnight snack of shrimp curry. Next morning she was better; by afternoon the pain came back, worse. She went to the family doctor, who examined her skeptically and said that in her circumstances he, too, would be having a bellyache. She had told him of their plan; which was that she would fly to Amerigo with Norman, see to the construction and decorating of the new rooms, return to New York to dispose of the apartment and settle Hazel somehow, and then go back to the Caribbean for good. He gave her pills for her nerves. These put her in an amiable grinning stupor, and banished the pain. But on Wednesday evening, a few hours before they had to leave, Henny's pain came back. She quite agreed that it must be psychosomatic. She took an extra dosage of pills, and fell into a fit of sleepy giggles. It was a night of rain and lashing winds, and Norman called the airline, half-hoping for a postponement until the morning. Oh, no, came the report, the flight was going; and the plane in which Lester was returning from St. Louis was also on time. So to Idlewild they went.

They heard Atlas roaring somewhere around a far turn of a corridor in the terminal, quite a while before they saw him. He came steamrolling through the wet ill-humored crowd in a tweedy cape and a plaid hat, evidently modelled on the costume of Henry Higgins in the opening scene of *My Fair Lady*, ridiculous beyond words on his whale shape. He was drunk, merry, and unwearied, though his eyes were completely bloodshot and the flesh under his eyes hung in frightening blue bags. "Got to make five, Norm," he said, in a voice scraping like an overplayed record. "Five and a half, if I don't break two legs and an arm. What a fantastic deal." He herded the Papermans straight to a bar. But Henny wouldn't drink. She sat withdrawn and pale while Atlas, downing a double bourbon, grated on about his wonderful deal, the taking over of a copper-mining company with gigantic assets in land. His battle for stock control, he said, was already about won.

All at once, when Lester paused for breath, Henny said, "Norm, you go on down to that island. I'm going home."

"What!" both men said at once.

Arguments glanced off her. She was going home, she said, gathering up her things, and she was going home now. She would come to Amerigo in a few days, probably. Right now she was going home. Her opaque look of pain changed only once. Paperman said, after trying jokes, logic, and cajolery on her, "Well, okay, let's all turn in our tickets, then. I'm not going without you."

Henny said, smiling most peculiarly, "Norm, you have to go. Don't you understand? You've got to make a living, mine host."

7

It was fiercely hot in Collins' small inner office. Sunlight beat through slits of the green blinds in blazing white bars. The noisy fan rustled documents on the desk as it swept back and forth, its puffs briefly cooling Norman's perspiring brow. They had arrived late, and still wore their New York clothing. Norman had had nothing for breakfast but a very old doughnut bolted at the Amerigo airport without coffee. He felt awful, and he could not understand Lester's cool, chipper bearing. Lester sat erect in the leather chair in a double-breasted blue serge suit, glancing at documents, his eyes bright and fairly clear behind his glasses, no sweat visible on his face.

Soon he turned on the little gray-headed Negro banker. "That service charge is ridiculous."

"It is our standard charge, Mistair Ot-loss."

"Well, we'll change the standard for this transaction." Lester flipped a page of the document, reading intently, his pince-nez glasses glittering, his mouth contracted. One fat hand slowly, evenly tapped the desk as he read. "Let me see the promissory notes." Collins at once passed a sheaf of slim blue papers to him.

The lawyer was in a hard little chair on his right hand, the banker on his left. Lester sat in Collins' own leather chair, at the desk. Norman and Mrs. Ball were in armchairs in front of the desk, side by side. The

Englishwoman wore a sleeveless blue silk dress, a rather high paint job, and a continuous, helpless little smile.

Norman didn't know what a service charge was. He was still reading the contract, trying to puzzle out the terms of this deal. At last it was in his hands, a smudged, blurry carbon copy of solid legal jargon on six long onion-skin legal sheets. He was going to get a check for five thousand dollars, as Atlas had said; a sentence on the fourth page specified this. Mrs. Ball was going to get fifteen thousand dollars, and there were long paragraphs about some promissory notes. But he could not penetrate the lawyers' prose to the facts. He had to count on Lester to spell these out for him—now, or later.

Atlas threw all the papers on the desk. "Except for that service charge, this thing looks all right."

The banker spread his hands. "Mr. Ot-*loss*, we would like to accommo-*date* you."

Collins said, "I can assure you, sir, that on this island that's the charge for prime credit risks."

Atlas scowled at the banker, and said in a sudden coarse hard tone, "You pulled a bank credit report on me last week. By cable."

Llewellyn looked at him askance. "Why, I—we have our rules, it is standard practice in large transac-*tions* involving newcomers—"

"Well? Didn't New York tell you that I can borrow a million and a half dollars on my unsecured name?"

"Ah—" Mr. Llewellyn looked around in embarrassment, and nodded.

"Then where do you get off hanging a service charge of four per cent on a twenty-thousand-dollar loan that I'm endorsing?"

Collins interjected, "The loan is actually to Mr. Paperman."

"Fine. Then we'll take my name off the loan."

"Mr. Ot-*loss*, if it were possible—the bank does not make special rates—of course we require your endorse-*ment*—"

Atlas looked at his watch, and stood. "Norm, this is too absurd. You can fly back with me if you want to, on the charter plane. There's no deal. Let's go."

The lawyer and the banker stood, each laying a hand on Atlas's arm. Norman was too amazed to move, and Mrs. Ball looked at Atlas with comic bafflement. A suspicion shot through Norman that Atlas was picking on a small point to back out. How like the old bastard that would be!

"Mr. Atlas, you're talking about a total service charge of eight hundred dollars," Collins pleaded. "It's an insignificant sum, when you—"

"Is it? You pay it, then. Come on, Norm." Atlas again moved to leave. Collins blocked him with all his football-player weight. "I mean," the lawyer said, "in a deal of fifty-five thousand, what does that amount to?"

Mrs. Ball spoke up with swift clarity. "Collins, this all seems terribly confused, but if eight hundred dollars from our side will take care of it, let's not muck everything up for that."

Collins said at once, "Well, Mr. Atlas, will that satisfy you, if we assume the service charge?"

Atlas dropped into the chair, with a total change to genial good humor. "So long as Norm doesn't pay it, I don't care who does. Okay, Norm, let's get on with the signing. I'm kind of late. I just don't like exorbitant charges."

The ceremony began. Norman signed whatever was handed him, glancing each time at Atlas, and writing his name if he nodded. There were many copies of many documents. Mrs. Ball signed some papers and not others, and so did Atlas and the banker. Paperman seemed to be signing everything. At one point the banker handed him a check for five thousand dollars, with warm chuckles, and shook his hand. "Well, now, I can truly say, wel-*come* to Amerigo, Mr. Paper-*mon*."

"There's one small thing that we didn't make quite clear in our telephone talk," Collins said with a smile to Atlas. "The matter of the notes. I assume you and Mr. Paperman are both signing them."

"Notes? *I'm* not signing any notes," said Atlas.

Collins' huge jaw sagged in astonishment. "But—surely you two gentlemen are acting together?"

"Paperman's the buyer. I'm on the bank loan as an act of friendship. There's nothing in this deal for me."

Atlas's tone was getting brutal again. Norman, afraid of a new last-minute difficulty that could wreck everything, struck in. "What are the notes, exactly, Lester?"

Atlas looked at him in real surprise, and took off his glasses. "Norm, didn't you read the contract?"

Paperman laughed nervously. "I'm not a lawyer or a tycoon. I didn't exactly follow it."

"It couldn't be simpler," Atlas said, rubbing his eyes. "There's a balance due here of fifty thousand, right? Amy's getting fifteen thousand from the bank, and she's accepting promissory notes for the other thirty-five thousand. That's all."

"But I also got five thousand," Norman said, waving his check. He felt foolish, exposing his confusion, but at this point he had to know the facts. It was getting to be life or death.

"Why sure, Norm. That's why the bank loan is for twenty," Atlas said with gentle patience. "That's the binder you paid, see? You're getting it back like I promised. You'll need that five for your new construction. You've got two years to pay off the bank. Amy's notes don't begin to come due until after that, and they stretch out over four more years. With interest and all, you've got about six years to pay off."

Paperman was becoming more and more alarmed; alarmed, and a little sick, as this deal of Atlas's began finally to come into focus. "Lester, I'm not the world's smartest businessman, I know that—"

"Neither am I, Norm. Just an old truth teller, trying to get along."

"Let me see if I understand this," Paperman pressed on, finding himself oddly hoarse. "I'm going to have to pay the bank twenty thousand dollars. Then after that, I've got to pay Mrs. Ball thirty-five thousand dollars. Is that it?"

"Sure. Plus interest. You agreed to that price, Norm."

"But this means I'm committing myself to pay out—what? Almost a thousand dollars a month, isn't it? Every month *for the next six years.*"

"Right. The club's throwing off a good fourteen, fifteen hundred a month, so there's no strain."

Norman was doing some frantic pencil work on the back of one of the documents. "Lester, that's what I thought I'd be living on. Maybe my arithmetic's cockeyed, but that leaves me maybe five thousand a year for me and my family, at best. I've been living on twenty thousand a year, and more."

"Well, baby, that's why you're going to install the new rooms, see? They're going to put you over the top."

Paperman subsided, picking up the contract and peering at it; not to read it, but merely to avoid the eyes of the banker, the lawyer, and

Mrs. Ball, who were all looking at him with unbelieving amusement, as his ignorance of the transaction became naked.

Collins said, "Actually, it's a fine deal. With those new rooms you'll have a comfortable fifteen thousand a year, and after the debt retires, you'll be rolling in money. Mr. Atlas, we conducted our telephone negotiation on a gentlemanly basis." He put the sheaf of blue promissory notes in front of the fat man, who was regarding him coldly. "I assured my client that you were a gentleman, and would endorse the whole deal. I know you will."

Atlas glanced at his watch. Then he put a thick hairy finger within an inch of Collins' nose. "Listen, you, I'm getting a little tired." He spoke in a tone of growling power that made Norman quake, a sound like an earth-moving machine working in low gear. "Amy paid those two fags six thousand dollars for the Club. Don't you think I know that? I found it out before I'd been on this island four hours. She's walking out of here today with fourteen thousand dollars cash profit. The notes are just gravy on top of that. You expected *me* to endorse the notes? Me? You think I got to where I can borrow a million and a half on my name by getting into such deals? How much can you borrow on your name?"

The lawyer ran his tongue over his lips and swallowed, staring at the finger. "My dear sir, all property in the Caribbean has increased in value—"

"I know that. Otherwise I wouldn't have let Norman make this deal. I'm going on the bank loan so he can get into the business he wants. If he drops dead I'm stuck for twenty thousand dollars. That's my lookout. I'm not taking any more of this sucker deal. You knew I wasn't, so let's cut out the nonsense! Sign the notes, Norm, and I'll go back north. I'm busy."

Collins made a defeated gesture at Mrs. Ball with both hands.

The woman sat up straight and turned her smile at Norman. "I have perfect confidence in your signature, Mr. Paperman. I'm sure it'll be quite enough. So—" She gestured invitingly at the blue notes lying on the desk.

Collins took a pen out of a desk holder, and extended it toward Paperman.

Paperman looked at the pile of blue slips, and then at Atlas. He cleared his throat, and made no move. "Do I sign these, Lester?"

"If you want the Gull Reef Club, Norm, sure."

Norman Paperman was in a panic. The deal was not in the least what he had pictured. He knew now that he had been pitiably vague about it. Vaguely he had thought that Atlas would advance him fifty-five thousand dollars, and vaguely that he would pay it back some day. But Lester Atlas was different, Lester was not a vague man. He acted, it was obvious, on a clear hard rule: never part unnecessarily with a dollar. In arranging this deal he had put Norman into the hotel business. He had done it without parting with a dollar. He had even managed to make Norman pay for the new rooms by selling his client list. The five thousand Norman was getting back now was only his own desperately obtained money that had covered the check; he was just borrowing it again from the bank. All this was true, yet who could say that Atlas had not kept his word?

The four people in the hideously hot room were staring at Paperman. The fan hummed and clanked in the silence. He had the strongest possible impulse to bolt out, while he still had the chance. His heart was hammering, sweat trickled from his armpits, his mouth was dry, he could still taste the abominable grease of the airport doughnut. But what could he do if he did back out? Return to New York, try to find other clients, face the friends who had cheered his departure to a glorious new life? Face Henny with this grotesque fiasco?

"Lester," he said after a long time, in a strained voice. "This isn't what I expected."

Atlas was looking straight at him. "What did you expect, Norman? Charity?"

Paperman stood, taking a pen from his sweat-soaked inner pocket. He walked to the desk, and there, on all the blue slips, he signed his name.

Part Two

MINE
HOST

chapter five

The First Day

I

Atlas went off in great spirits. The last thing he said to Paperman, out of the window of the taxicab, was, "Keep an eye peeled for any good land that comes on the market, hear? That's how we'll make our real dough on this island." He displayed not the slightest sense of having misled or injured Norman. From his point of view he had been Santa Claus throughout, complete to jingling bells and ho-ho-ho. He was nothing but a human rhinoceros, Norman decided, and there was no sense in wasting another ounce of nervous energy being angry at him.

He took his luggage to the Reef, and moved into the White Cottage, since Mrs. Ball was not quitting her suite in the main house until the morning. After a long, delicious shower, he dressed as befitted the host of a tropical hotel: a pink shirt, black shorts, black knee socks, black loafers, all casual, immaculate, smart. Crossing the lawn, Norman found his shattered spirit pulling itself together. Come what might, this was his lawn now. For the first time in his life, his feet were on ground of which he was the master. Authority and dignity flowed up out of this grassy coral island into his veins. He was in a tough spot, of course, the toughest of his life, and Atlas had behaved with slippery villainy. But why should he have expected anything else? And after all, what difference did it make whether he owed fifty-five thousand dollars to a bank and an Englishwoman, or to Atlas? Perhaps he was better off this way. In action, Lester had been a horror.

The dining terrace was crowded. It was getting on to December first, and the northern weather was already driving the fish down into his newly purchased net. It was a valuable net! The Club was charming, the climate was a golden enduring asset. He sat alone at a little table by the rail, and ordered a martini and an Iceland brook trout. Thor came out of the bar in his picturesque rags to serve the martini, with small European airs of welcoming his new lord.

"*Lycka till,* sor. Dat's Svedish for good luck."

"*Lycka till* to you, Thor. We seem to be doing well today."

"Not too bad. Maybe dis afternoon you vant to look at de books? I explain everyting, is not much to it."

"Very good. Let's say four o'clock in the office."

"I be dere four o'clock."

"This is a splendid martini, Thor. One of the things we'll talk about this afternoon is your raise in salary."

The bartender's blue eyes flashed brilliantly. "Sure ting."

"By the bye, ah, you haven't seen Mrs. Tramm today, have you?"

"No sor, I tink she not here."

The trout was excellent, the coffee was hot, there was a crisp salad with Roquefort dressing, and the service was very fast. Two pretty black waitresses in beige uniforms hovered over him, all coy smiles and quick attentions. Paperman began to perceive the advantages of being a boss; he had never been served with such deference in his life. Two o'clock. Just time, he thought, yawning, to get an hour's sun on the beach below the White Cottage, and a swim, and a nap; then would come the glance through the books. So far, so good! A few hours ago he had felt that the world was coming to an end. Perhaps, for him, it was beginning.

2

Thor had ledgers open on both desks when Norman arrived at the office, and he was taking rubber bands off thick bundles of receipts and checks. The office, behind the registration desk and the switchboard, was actually the space under the staircase to the second floor. The ceiling sloped sharply, with indentations of the underside of stairs. There was no window. A squeaky rattling wall fan did little to relieve the stagnant heat. Ceilings, walls, and floor were painted a smeary morbid green. The dusty furnishings were two old desks, two old chairs, a small safe, a large rusty adding machine worked with a handle, and an antique typewriter. There was also an inky-smelling mimeograph on a little stand beside a pile of blank menus. Fighting the boredom that filmed his brain at the sight of this room, these devices, and these records, still sleepy after his nap, Paperman sat down to his first lesson in hotel-keeping.

He asked the bartender, first of all, why the office wasn't air-conditioned. Thor said that Amy had priced the job; it would cost over three hundred dollars. This gave Paperman pause. But he foresaw many hours for himself and Henny in this slanting, choking green hole. "Well, it'll be a good investment. Let's do it."

Thor nodded and grinned. "Fine. Be more comfortable."

The bartender went over the payroll, and sketched the workings of the hotel. Sheila, the cook, managed the scullery maids and the six waitresses, he said. There were also six chambermaids; their leader was "de vun dat's so tam pregnant," the unmarried girl named Esmé. Paperman expressed wonder at the size of the staff. The hotel with all its cottages held only forty-four people; and seventy on the dining terrace was more than capacity. Thor agreed that it was ridiculous. After Mr. Paperman had been on the island for a while, he said, he would understand. Kinjan help wasn't paid much, and didn't do much, and that was how things were. He showed Norman a large cork bulletin board hung on the wall, marked out for the months and the days, with colored cardboard strips tacked up for the room reservations. Each strip had the name of a future guest, and the length of the strip showed the duration of the stay. Norman noticed that January and February were already stripped in solidly.

"That's good," he said. "Your whole season at a glance."

"Oh, yes, I figure dat out," said Thor. "Dat work good. December and March, dey fill up last, but dey good monts too."

Next he launched his tale of the bookkeeping, handing ledgers and sheaves of vouchers to the new proprietor, indicating this column and that, and talking at great speed. After a quarter of an hour Norman gave up any effort to understand him. Occasionally a recognizable term would swim up out of the Scandinavian murk—*inventory* or *current balance* or *cash journal*—and at such times he would nod brightly and perhaps say, "I see, yes, inventory." It was a mystifying but reassuring session. Obviously Thor had the books under tight control. The Negro accountant, Thor said, came in every Monday to double-check and balance the books. Norman could see that so far as financial records went, he had nothing to worry about. But he sat and smiled and nodded patiently for another hour in the slanting sweatbox. He wanted Thor to feel appreciated.

"Well, you've got a first-rate system there," he said when, to his relief, the bartender closed the ledgers and began banding up the vouchers. "Let's keep it just as it is. I'm extremely pleased, Thor. Now then, is there anything else?"

"Vell, vun more ting. Ve pretty near out of vater."

"Water? Here?"

Thor laughed. "Sea vater don't do us no good." He explained—slowing down and talking more clearly—that rainfall in Amerigo, as in most of the small Caribbean islands, was spotty, varying at odd times from flood to drought. Georgetown had a public water system fed by wells, and boosted once a week in the dry seasons by a water barge from the French island of Guadeloupe. Homes outside the town caught rain on their roofs and stored it in cisterns, and that was what the Gull Reef Club did, too. It had a vast roof area, the cistern held more than 150,000 gallons, and each cottage had its own cistern and pump, all interconnected with the main house. The total capacity was very large

—nobody really knew the exact figure—and usually there was no trouble, but due to a bad dry spell, the whole system was down to a two-day supply. Grinning at the consternation that crossed Norman's face, Thor assured him that it was no real problem. The French barge was due tomorrow, and it always supplied the Club when water was low. Somebody just had to stand on the pier at eleven o'clock and wave as it entered the channel. The captain was often too drunk to notice any other signal.

"Do we pay him for this water?" Paperman said.

"Oh, no. Dis government vater."

"Then we pay the government?"

"No. Notting to pay." Thor ran fingers through his thick blond hair. "I tink maybe I go out to de bar. It get busy now—"

"One moment, Thor. How is it we get free barged water from Guadeloupe? That's damned strange."

"Vell you see, Mr. Paperman—" Thor dropped his voice. "Lorna, she Senator Pullman's gorl friend."

"What? Who's Senator Pullman? What's he senator of? Who's Lorna?"

Senator Evan Pullman, Thor said, was one of the seven members of the legislature; a party leader, and chairman of the public utilities subcommittee. When not serving as a lawmaker, he kept a bar. Lorna was the girl who tended the registration desk and the switchboard of the Gull Reef Club. (Norman had noticed this ravishing black girl at the desk, of course, and had wondered about her.) Thor explained, with a faint leer, that the hotel paid her a lot more than the going rate for female help, but very much less than some half a million gallons of barged water per year would cost. This was an arrangement dating back several years. Everybody was happy about it, and there was no chance of any trouble.

"Dey joost vun ting you got to be sure, Mr. Paperman," said Thor. "You got to catch dat barge coming in. Going out she's empty, and you stuck till next time."

"Well, then you'll see to that tomorrow, won't you, Thor?" Norman was both dizzied and amused by these revelations.

"Oh sure, sure. I joost vant you to know about it."

The door of the office opened, and Senator Pullman's loved one looked in with a lascivious little smile, evidently the cast of her face in repose. Lorna always dressed in crisp lacy white. She had perfect features, a skin like black velvet, and large wide gray eyes. "Mister Paper-mon, you want your New York call? It's ready now."

"Good. Thor, don't go. I still want to talk to you about your raise."

"Ho! Plenty time for dat." The bartender went out.

After some ear-splitting clicks, Henny came on the line, sounding dispirited. The pain was gone at the moment, she said, but the doctors now suspected that she might have—of all things—a gallstone. They wanted to keep her under observation for two or three weeks.

"Why three weeks? What's to observe?" said Paperman. "If you've got one, an X ray will show it."

"Well, the X ray is clear, but they say there's a kind of stone that's transparent to X rays. Doesn't that sound ridiculous? It seems I may be secreting square-cut diamonds."

"That would solve our problems," Norman said. "You're a woman of great resource."

"Don't let's talk about it. I'm fit to be tied, and if I'm all right for a couple of days I'll come down and to hell with them and their transparent stones. Tell me about the hotel. Is everything set?"

Norman recounted the deal, not without indignation. She objected when he called Lester a lying old son of a bitch. "How did he lie? He said he'd take care of the money end. He did, didn't he? You've got the hotel, and you didn't put up five cents in cash."

"What? I put up five thousand dollars."

"But you got that back."

"Sure, to spend on the new rooms."

"Well, don't you need the new rooms?"

"Look, my point is that *Lester* didn't put up five cents in cash."

"Naturally. He's the world's master at that. What's the difference, so long as he got you the place?"

"He also got me a fifty-five-thousand-dollar debt to pay off in six years. That's the difference."

"Honey, that was the price. Did you expect Lester to give you the Gull Reef Club for Hanukka?"

"I thought we'd be partners or something. I thought he'd put up the money at first and I'd put up—well, I'd put up—" Norman paused.

"Your hotel experience," Henny suggested.

"All right, all right," Norman said.

"Have you seen that Cohn fellow? Hazel keeps mentioning the crazy frogman," Henny said. "And she's starting to talk about spending Christmas in Amerigo."

"Really? Maybe I'd better find out if *he's* got a wife."

"Well, I don't know. She's going to Asbury Park for the weekend with the Sending. Folk musical festival, she says."

"Asbury Park? Ye gods, why are you allowing *that?*"

"Well, they went and made the reservations. At the Pine Grove Hotel, funnily enough. You remember, the one we used to sneak off to. Imagine, it still exists."

"Tell Hazel I forbid her to go," Norman stormed.

"I will," Henny said. "She's sort of blue, like me, and it'll give her a laugh. I'll call you if there's anything urgent, otherwise let's just write. This is no way to start paying off fifty-five thousand dollars."

As he came out of the office Lorna gave him a feline glance. "Seventeen minutes," she said. "Fifty-nine dollars plus tax."

The flower-scented cool air in the lobby was a relief after the stifling, stale, dusty atmosphere of the office under the stairs. Paperman wondered whether to include a large modern office in the reconstruction, and at once decided against it. New money-making space would be the one aim of that job.

Strolling into the bar in the hope of encountering Iris, whom he hadn't yet seen, he noticed Collins and Tex Akers at a small table with the banker Llewellyn. All three men wore ties and dark business suits. Akers looked entirely different out of his work clothes, washed, and shaved. He had a distinguished air. No time like the present, Paperman thought, and he took his martini to their table. They were in a solemn discussion over untasted beers.

"May I intrude for just a little while?"

"Please!" The banker motioned to a chair.

"Mr. Akers, how about changing your mind and building those new rooms for me?" Paperman said. "It may be some time before my wife can come down here. I'd like to have these rooms ready by Christmas. She approved of your sketches, so why not get going right away? It's not a big job, and I'm sure you can work it in."

Akers glanced at the banker and the lawyer, and scratched his scanty hair, smiling. "It's funny you should come along like this. I've got a short holdup on the Crab Cove job," he said in his warm, relaxed voice. "That's what we've just been talking about. Actually I guess I could bring my Cove crew around tomorrow and just get rolling. In a way, it would fit in real good."

Collins said to Paperman, "That would be a break. His crew could do your new rooms in a week, probably."

"Easy," Akers said.

"You estimated about thirty-five hundred dollars," Paperman said.

"Well, to protect myself I'd call it four thousand on paper. I'd just charge you for labor and materials. If it comes to less, that suits me. Just so the crew keeps going." He laughed and shrugged. "This is too small a job to figure profit. If it works out under thirty-five hundred, maybe you can give me a case of scotch."

"Well, that's cordial of you, but I think you ought to have a profit. And I'd want a written estimate for the record."

"No problem."

"Will you want a construction loan?" the banker said to Paperman. "We'll be glad to extend one to you—and to Mr. Ot-loss, of course."

"It's a minor job," said Paperman with a touch of grandeur. "I'll handle it with cash."

Akers held out his hand. "I'll be here at noon with my crew."

Norman went to bed early, exhausted but encouraged. The night's dinner business had been capacity. The bar cash register was jingling as couples filled the moonlit dance terrace; and Thor had already given him one small canvas bag of money to be locked away in the old office safe, for deposit in the bank in the morning. This most eventful day in his life, which had begun so badly, was ending well enough. He didn't like sleeping alone in the White Cottage, and his last drowsy thoughts were of poor Henny and her transparent stone. He also wondered where Iris could be. Just as he was dozing off he heard the door of the Pink Cottage open and close, and Meadows yipping joyously. He was too tired to move.

3

Pounding at the door: bang, bang, *crash*. "Inside! Mistuh Paper-mon! Inside! You in dah?" BANG!!

Paperman forced his eyes open, sat up, and blinked at the sun glare off the water. Seconds passed before he understood where he was, and what he was doing there. He had been in a deep sleep, dreaming of New York. "Yes? Who is it?"

"Sheila. I sorry to hoross you, suh."

"Oh. One minute, Sheila."

Sheila was the cook of the Club. Norman had met her in his first tour of the premises, weeks ago: a mountainous irascible black woman with dark eyes and thick satanic eyebrows, rolling sweat in a tiny malodorous kitchen, and snapping peevish orders at two sulky, terrorized, darting girls. Paperman did not understand how such excellent meals issued in quantity from that fiery, squalid hole of a kitchen, but he knew they did, and he proposed never to venture near Sheila's domain. Now here she was.

"Sheila, what time is it?" he called, as he tumbled out of bed and reached for a dressing gown.

"Quarter past."

"Quarter past what?"

"Ten."

As he opened the door she held out a scrawled, bloodstained paper. Sheila wore a large apron and a chef's hat, and she was perspiring heavily.

"What's that?"

"Mario's Market. Mario don' give no credit. He up de main house wid de meat but we got to pay."

"Well, tell Thor to pay."

"Thor ain't dah. Got to have meat fo' lunch, suh."

"How much is it?"

"Hunna fifteen dolla'."

Paperman wearily took the bill, and wrote a check. Sheila departed fanning the check, and shouting angrily at herself.

He dressed and plodded across the lawn toward the main house; but halfway a startling sight arrested him. A large red sailing yacht, aswarm with white people having a party, was tied to the pier. A merry roar, and snatches of bawled song, rose from the deck. Norman approached this boat, puzzled. It was a beautiful new vessel; the scarlet of its hull looked like Japanese lacquer, its towering masts were yellow-varnished, its brasswork glistened in the sun.

"Norman Paperman! Dah-ling! Here he comes! My hero, my love! Come aboard, sweetheart, and have a glass of champagne! Hurry!" He heard Mrs. Ball's voice, and saw a muscular brown arm waving above the clustered heads.

He crossed the little rubber-matted gangway, and the Englishwoman thrust out of the mob, stately in a white pleated dress, painted like a doll, and holding a champagne glass. She threw a brawny arm around him. "Welcome aboard *Moonglow*, you dah-ling! You're *just* in time, love, we cast off in fifteen minutes. Come along and have a drink. Isn't this boat a *love*? It was Tom Tilson's and now it's mine. There isn't a schooner to touch it in all the West Indies, and I've been aboard them all."

Paperman observed that she was towing him through the "hill crowd." There was no mistaking it: self-assured, sunburned people, middle-aged or older, dressed with informal clean elegance, Gentile to the last man and woman, serenely superior in their bearing, in their smiles, in their intimate laughing ease with each other; most of them with the glittery eyes of steady drinkers, some with the poached eyes of excess; here and there a chic pair of homosexuals, brilliantly dressed and with close-cropped gray heads. "Champagne, love? —Oh, dear, are we out of champagne? Well, more's coming. Do have some caviar." Open cans of gray caviar labelled in Russian stood on the small wheeled bar, with trays of crackers and a hacked-up blue cheese.

"I don't know, Amy, it's kind of early in the morning—"

"Ah, here we are! Quick, Captain, champagne for my dear friend."

Out of a hatchway climbed a very big red-faced man in a yachting cap, a tailored white long-sleeved shirt, white duck trousers, and canvas shoes. "Hey, Mr. Paperman!" The man threw his arms wide and brandished two frosty bottles of champagne like Indian clubs. "I got it! Vat you tink? I got my boad!"

His costume was such a change that Norman did not recognize Thor until he spoke.

"*My* boat, lambie, *my* boat," cried Mrs. Ball, snuggling up to the bartender, putting an arm around him, and looking dewily into his face.

"I'm de captain, py God!" roared Thor, pulling the cork out of a bottle with a gunshot sound and a spill of foam, "Captain of *Moonglow,* finest tam boad in de islands! And today ve sail for Panama! Panama, py God! Dat vas my port before I got wrecked, and dat's my port now! Mr. Paperman, I owe it to you! Here, champagne!"

Stunned, Paperman took the glass, raised it, and managed a smile. "*Lycka till,* Thor," he said. "Is that right?"

"Hey, Amy, you hear dat! *Lycka till,* you betcha, dat's right, Mr. Paperman. Py God, I drink vit you, you're a man."

The three of them drank. Mrs. Ball then glued a kiss on Thor's lips, cleaving to him like a bride, an impatient amorous bride, unsteady after a long wet wedding breakfast. Thor submitted to the kiss, glancing slantwise at Paperman. "Amy, I tink I see de governor come aboard," he said, as soon as he could disengage his mouth.

"The governor! Come, bring a bottle and a glass, lamb." Mrs. Ball made off through the crowd like a quarterback. Thor followed in her wake, giving Norman a sardonic man-to-man grin.

"Paperman, you look kind of put out." Tom Tilson was at his elbow, scooping up caviar with a cracker. His red freckled face, all cords and bones, was wrinkled at Norman in crafty appraisal.

"I'm surprised."

"You had no warning?"

"Not a word."

Tilson gulped the caviar, and shook his knobby stick at Paperman. "I tried to tip you off, you know, about Thor. At Hogan's Fancy. I couldn't say much more than I did, with Collins sitting right there. I knew about it. *Moonglow*'s my boat. Amy's been blowing hot and cold about buying it for a year. I thought it was just talk to keep Thor happy, but by Jesus yesterday afternoon she did it. Damn fool, if you ask me. As long as she didn't buy it, she *had* him. Now he's got *her.*"

"I gather they're very good friends—as one might say."

Tilson uttered a lecherous hoarse giggle. "Them? Mister, since the day he piled up on Cockroach Rock a year and a half ago. If you ask

121

me, all he's been doing since then is working up to this moment. Amy doesn't know boat people. I do. She'll find out."

"Well," said Norman with a heavy sigh, "it seems that I don't have a manager."

"You sure do," said Tilson. "Name of Paperman."

The deck rocked and vibrated. "What the devil!" Norman exclaimed. "We're moving." The boat was, in fact, powering away from the pier. "How crazy is he? Are we all off to Panama?"

Tilson laughed. "Just to the waterfront. That gondola is a hell of a bore. As you'll soon discover." The old man squinted at him. "I'm afraid you're in for a rough time."

He swallowed another immense gob of caviar and stumped away.

Thor came shouldering along the deck, bawling orders at a black boy in the cockpit. Seeing Paperman he stopped, looked abashed, threw his head back in a savage laugh, and wrapped an arm around his shoulders. "I tell you, Mr. Paperman, I feel kind of bad, you know?"

"Why? You said you'd stay till you got a boat. You've got a boat."

"De books are hunnert per cent, right up to last night, joost like I showed you. It's a easy system, you catch on fast. Don't hoross yourself, like dey say. Gilbert can run de bar. I been breaking him in. He mixes good drinks. I showed Gilbert de main water valves, and de fuse boxes, and all dose tings. You be okay."

"Who's Gilbert?"

"De boat boy. He honest and he not so tam stupid, only you better watch him till he get used to de job, you know? All you got to do is keep de books and handle de reservations. Dere be no problem. Sheila run de kitchen fine, she de best tam cook in Kinja."

"Thor, I don't know much about keeping books."

"Ha! I know less dan you ven I come. You pick it up fast. You call Neville Wills, tell him come in every day for a veek or so, check tings over. He de only good accountant on dis island. —Hey, Artur! Slow down, you vant to run dis tam boad up on de beach?" Thor held out his hand. "No hard feelings? I like you, Mr. Paperman, honest. De only ting is, I'm a sailing man."

Paperman accepted the powerful handshake. Thor hustled forward. "Stand by! Clear de starboard rail!"

The hill crowd disembarked on the waterfront, Norman among them, and stood in a huddle, shouting farewells, many still holding highballs in paper cups. A strong breeze was blowing across the harbor, and Thor at once hoisted sail, disdaining to clear the channel under power. *Moonglow* looked brave and lovely, falling away from the bulkhead, slowly gathering way and dipping her scarlet hull as one and then another white sail ran up flapping and caught the wind. The hill crowd began to sing *Auld Lang Syne*. Amy Ball stood in the stern with her arm around a shroud, swaying and waving, and laughing through streams of tears. *Moonglow* had to maneuver to avoid an ugly vessel that was bearing down on her, an enormous flat chugging thing, solid rust from its square bow to the small iron deckhouse at the stern. Thor cleared this ungainly scow by a foot or two, and the onlookers cheered.

Paperman observed that the big rustpot was flying a French tricolor. It occurred to him that this could only be the water barge from Guadeloupe. It was already passing the Gull Reef pier, and nobody was there to wave! He started running up and down the waterfront, sawing both arms in the air and screaming at the oncoming barge, "No, no. *Non, non.* Stop! Stop! *Arrêtez-vous!*" He made a megaphone of his hands and howled, capering here and there, *"Arrêtez-vous!! A-RRRRETEZ-VOUS!"* The barge moved steadily on. There was nobody on deck. The enormous old contraption was coming in with snorts and clanks; the Frenchman in the wheelhouse, directly over the engines, could not possibly hear him.

Paperman suddenly ceased his dancing and screeching, aware that the entire hill crowd was staring at him in silent amazement. The waterfront strolling and bargaining had also stopped dead, and perhaps forty Kinjans were goggling at the berserk white man, not very surprised, but willing to be entertained.

Paperman put his hands in his pockets and sauntered along the waterfront, whistling, trying to look sane. The barge came alongside, and stopped. A fat mustached old man in white trousers, a peaked cap, and an incredibly shabby brass-buttoned blue jacket limped out of the deckhouse, threw two thick manila lines on the waterfront pavement, and went back inside. Two burly Negroes, stripped to the waist, tied the lines to bollards and climbed aboard the barge, dragging a thick black hose.

Norman jumped up on the low deck, the iron plating of which felt fiery through his rubber soles. At the open door of the deckhouse, he knocked. The barge captain sat inside at a little table, pouring himself pink wine from a half-gallon jug. He had a drooping big belly, and his thick mustache was streaked pink from the wine, and yellow from an old pipe lying on the table in a spill of ash. Ignoring the knock, he drank half the glass of wine and stared straight ahead out of far-off, filmy eyes.

Paperman thought that the man might be deafened by his own engines. *"Monsieur le capitaine!"* he bellowed.

The Frenchman pulled open a drawer, took out a greasy green record book, laid it open before Paperman, and lapsed back into his melancholy trance. The open pages showed columns and columns of numbers entered in brown ink. Paperman explained at the top of his voice, in a tumble of agitated French, that he did not want to see the book, that he was not an official, that he was *le nouveau propriétaire* of the Gull Reef Club, and that he needed water. The captain only stared straight ahead, once or twice groaning in a heartbroken way, as though seeing phantom German columns marching down the Champs-Elysées. When Paperman paused he looked up and spoke several hoarse hostile sentences in strange French, waving his arms stiffly with palms upward. Then he poured more wine and sighed, and stared, and drank. Nothing Paperman said after that had the slightest effect on him.

Norman went forward to the two Negroes, who squatted beside the thumping, pulsing hose. "Can you tell me where Senator Pullman's bar is?" he said.

The men shifted their eyes at each other.

"You know who Senator Pullman is, don't you?"

There was a full minute of silence. "Senat-uh Pull-mon?" said one, with an air of repeating a phrase in Chinese.

Beside himself, Paperman jumped off the barge. In all his life he had never been confronted with a shortage of water. To his New York mind, water was something that flowed from taps. The supply was instant, limitless, and as certain as air to breathe. There were thirty-eight people registered at the hotel and in the cottages, only six under capacity. All those taps running dry at once; all those toilets ceasing to flush—!

In the arcade of shops opposite the fort, leading off Queen's Row, he saw a small hanging sign in red, white, and blue, *Peace and Prosperity Bar*. Surely on this little island, he thought, the barkeepers knew each other. He ran across the cobbled square. There were several Negro and white drinkers in the Peace and Prosperity Bar, but he saw no bartender. Leaning in the doorway was a moon-faced, short young Negro in a light blue drip-dry suit and a black knitted tie, smoking a cigar with a sensuous rounding of his mouth. Paperman said to him, "I beg your pardon. Do you happen to know where I can find Senator Pullman's bar?"

"I'm Senator Pullman. This is my establishment. Can I be of any assistance to you?" said the Negro, in clear mainland accents.

Paperman threw his arms around him. "Senator Pullman! Thank God!"

The senator, surprised and amused, endured the hug and asked what the trouble was. Paperman poured out his tale.

"Well, well, so you're Mr. Paperman. Lorna was telling me about you. You're just as handsome as she said, too. Welcome to Kinja."

"Thank you. Do you know French? Can you talk to the barge man?"

"About what?"

"About the water! Tell him to save some for the Club."

Senator Pullman wrinkled his nose and his brows, and looked much older and shrewder. "Well, you see, he's commenced pumping into the municipal system now, and he's got to discharge his entire capacity." When the senator used long words, a slight beat on the last syllables disclosed his island origins.

"But we're down to one day's supply. One day! All those people, Senator."

"Yes, it would be a definite health hazard." Pullman looked up at the cloudless sky, screwing one eye shut. "I do think we're going to get some rain. The Club has a very expansive roof, and you can catch a week's supply from one generous precipitation."

"Supposing it doesn't rain?"

"That's a prudent question, but you needn't worry. In that case talk to Lorna. She'll tell you how to get emergency water. Incidentally, if you encounter any electrical problems, I have a degree in electrical engineering. In our community a liquor license is more remunerative, so—" He winked at Paperman and went behind the bar.

Paperman hurried off down the square to the landing. The gondola was tied to a cleat, the boat boy was gone, and a knot of white people stood there muttering and arguing. Several of them were tourists in heavy dark clothes, with luggage heaped around them. A guest who recognized Norman told him that there had been no boat service for an hour. The gondola had been tied empty at the pier across the water until a few minutes ago, when some guests had rowed over and left it.

Paperman had no choice. "New arrivals first, please, get in and I'll take you across," he said. This occasioned a jostling rush into the craft, very nearly overturning it. Then he had to swing a number of heavy suitcases onto a rack at the bow. This exertion in the vertical noon sun, followed by the effort of rowing the laden, unsteady boat three hundred yards, plus the job of tying up the boat and helping out the passengers, put Paperman in a drenching sweat. He ran up the lawn to the main house, and through the lobby to the bar.

There, sure enough, was the boat boy, in ragged blue shorts and shirt, new and obviously slashed up by a knife. Still wearing his gondolier's hat, he was rattling a shaker with a look of exalted pride all different from his usual veiled sullen glare. Paperman paused. There were about thirty people drinking in the bar, and on the beach. This was revenue.

"Gilbert, please give me that hat."

"Dis my hat, suh," said Gilbert, looking hurt. "Mistress Ball she did give me dis hat."

"A bartender doesn't wear a hat. Only a boat boy wears a hat."

"Oh! Dat right?" Gilbert at once removed the hat, grimaced at it, and passed it to Norman.

"I see you're doing a fine job. Keep it up."

"I doin' everything just like Thor," said Gilbert. "I can work de cash register."

"Splendid." Paperman raced out on the lawn again, straight to a man whom he had observed clipping a hedge near the pier. When the people across the water saw Paperman they began shouting.

"Hello," Paperman said to the gardener, a stout Negro in khaki work clothes, all buttoned up against the sun. "I'm the new owner of this club, you know."

"Yes please." The man touched his hand to his headgear, a brown paper bag folded like an overseas cap; smiled in a mournful, kindly way, and went on clipping.

"What's your name?"

"Millard."

"Millard, I'd like you to row that boat for a while. Just take the people back and forth, you know?"

"Mistress Ball she said clip de hedges Torsdays."

"Yes, well, this is just for now. It's an emergency. You can let the hedge go."

Millard looked at him in perplexity. "I de gardener, please."

"Of course. But I'm making you the gondolier. Just for now. Here's your gondolier's hat."

He offered Millard the shallow yellow- and red-ribboned straw. The gardener hesitantly took it, removed his paper hat, and set the straw on his head. A look of bashful delight crept over his face.

"I row de boat good, suh."

Millard went to the boat and cast off, smiling proudly all the while at Paperman. He rowed with clumsy strength, and closed the other shore fast. Paperman was watching him help passengers into the gondola, when the arrival of another vessel at the pier cut off his view. This was a battered old power boat gasping up from the waterfront, with Tex Akers in the bow, at the head of a phalanx of perhaps twenty-five tool-carrying workmen.

"Hi, there," Akers called. "Ready or not, here we come."

He jumped from the moving boat across eight feet of water, his long bare legs taking him easily to Paperman's side.

"Quite a work force you've got there," Paperman said. The boat bumped to a stop and the men streamed off.

"Sure do, but that's my lookout," said Akers, grinning down at Norman in the friendliest way. He was about a head and a half the taller of the two. "I've got a payroll to keep going. This is the whole Cove outfit. You'll just get your job done three times as fast. Actually with this all-out kind of operation I'm hoping to wrap it up in less than a week. I figure to work Sunday, but the overtime will cost me, not you.

All right, fellows, this way." He led the battalion of workers—there were about two Negroes to each white man—across the lawn toward the main house.

The old power boat snorted away, and Millard came rowing alongside, with the gondola so crowded that its gunwales were level with the water. He helped everyone out without mishap, still wreathed in dignified smiles under the ribboned hat. Paperman told him to carry up to the main house the bags accumulating on the pier, and to take fewer people in the boat next time.

Millard said, "I can row de boat all full."

"Yes, but we don't want you drowning them."

"No please," said Millard, roaring with laughter. He loaded himself with an astonishing number of bags and strode up the lawn.

For the first time since Sheila had awakened him with her pounding, Paperman now drew a couple of quiet long breaths, standing in the sunshine on the pier. The upsetting withdrawal of Thor seemed to be contained. Norman had to get the accountant in to keep the books, until he could take them over; he had to start to work on the reservations, answer the letters and telegrams, and so forth. Perhaps he would even have to double as a bartender for a while. But he would survive. Tom Tilson had put the matter fairly; the new manager's name was Paperman.

He had sweated right through all his clothes. His new yellow shirt hung in black wet blotches, and he could feel trickles running down his nose and his neck, and under his arms. He returned to the White Cottage, and put on trunks. As he walked down the path to the water, he saw a blond masked head break the surface, far out. Iris came streaking in toward him, swimming with loose neat arm strokes. "Hi! Welcome, Norm! Or should I say, mine host? What's the good word?"

"The good word is, I'm doubling your rent."

"Oh, you Americans. What know-how!" She took off her mask, shaking back her heavy streaming hair. "Gad, things must be well in hand, if you're swimming at noon. I hear Henny didn't come with you."

"She'll be along in a few days." He dived into the sweetly cool water and floated beside her. "I've had a hell of a morning."

Iris was astonished by the news of Thor's defection. She said she had slept until noon, and hadn't seen the yacht arrive or leave. "Of course I heard Amy talk off and on about buying *Moonglow,* but I never thought she would. Amy's a close girl with a shilling, but she was mad for Thor, all right. She's bought herself a package, believe me."

They came out of the water. Lying beside Iris on her Indian blanket, in the shade of high oleanders heavy with pink blossoms, Norman told her about Henny's ailment.

"Oh, Lord, what a time for that to happen. Everything's hit you at once." Iris shook her head. "This place needs a man and a woman, Norm. Or two faggots, like before, same difference. The man looks after the upkeep, the driving, the money, and all that. The woman's in the office, and watches the service, and makes pretty noises at the people. Amy and Thor were very good."

Norman said, "There's nothing really wrong with Henny. She often shows up with odd aches and pains when she's tense. She'll be down in a week or two. I just have to get through until then."

Iris sat up. "Look here, let me help."

"Nonsense. I'll manage."

She said, getting to her feet, "I'll just get the salt out of my hair and spiff up. Honestly, it'll be fun. I'm bored to death anyway."

"Iris, the worst is over. I'm all right."

"You don't know that. Somebody should check the books and receipts, for instance. Gilbert's just a boy. I'll see you up in the office in an hour." She bounded up the embankment, waving off his protests.

As she did so, Norman heard a distant crash, and then continuing loud noises of demolition—hammerings, smashings, the fall of stones, the yelling of men, the shattering of glass. He was planning a short nap, but this sound could only be the Akers crew getting to work. He wanted to see that. He dressed quickly and hurried toward the main house, where at the rear, clouds of plaster dust were rising above the roof into the sunshine.

In the lobby, a gigantic greasy brown tarpaulin billowed in the breeze, masking the doorway of the old game room. The sounds of breakage and collapse were coming from behind this tarpaulin, and wisps of plaster dust floated through holes in the heavy cloth, like smoke from a fire. Fortunately it was the lunch hour. The lobby was deserted.

Paperman lifted an end of the tarpaulin and slipped behind it, into a scene of sad ruin. Half of the back wall of the room lay in rubble on the floor. A ragged egg-shaped hole was open to the sea and to the sun, which blazed into the room through tumbling eddies of dust. Even as Paperman arrived, a ringing smash of many sledge hammers at once sent another great chunk of the thick cement wall crumbling inward, unveiling more blue sky, grass, and sea.

"Hold everything!" bawled Paperman, half blinded by the dust boiling up at him.

"Easy, fellows," he heard Akers say. "Here's the boss."

His arms before his eyes, Paperman groped and stumbled to the hole in the wall, and climbed through into the sunshine.

"What's all this?" he said. "The job's just inside construction. Why are you knocking down the wall?"

The contractor said he had two reasons. There was the problem of getting men and materials in and out of the room. This way, the entire job would be done behind the tarpaulin. The heavy noise would be over today, and then the guests would have undisturbed use of the lobby. Otherwise workmen would be passing through the hotel with construction materials and rubbish for a week. Moreover the wide dining-room window, which they had already demolished, would have been unusable for the new small rooms. It was cheaper to knock the wall down and put up a new one than to break it partially and then rebuild it.

"This thing's looking real good," he said. "We came on a couple of one-inch pipes under the floor, from the days when they had a kitchen back here. We just hook in our hot and cold water, flush out the rust, and I reckon that'll cut the plumbing cost maybe in half."

He drew Paperman a little away from the men. The six who had been smashing the wall were leaning on their sledge hammers. The rest of the workers, a very large group, were lying around on the grass, drinking fruit nectar out of cans, listening to Calypso songs on portable radios, and making loud incomprehensible jokes, with bursts of jolly laughter.

"If it's convenient," Akers said, "can you let me have an advance on the job now?"

"I suppose so. How much?"

"Well, the usual thing is a week's costs, but that's the whole price in this case. How's about half?"

"Two thousand dollars?" Norman said dubiously.

Akers' lantern-jawed face, with dust caked on the reddish bristles of his chin, broke into a gentle, engaging smile.

"I'd much rather bill you at the end, but these local suppliers don't give credit, you see, they've had too much trouble with a few fly-by-night characters who've come and gone since I've been here. The responsible contractors are left holding the bag. I've ordered all the materials for the job from Amerigo Supply, and the stuff'll be here in the morning, provided I get a check over there before bank closing time today. That's how things work here. Call Chunky Collins, and ask him."

Paperman was embarrassed at the suggestion. "It's quite all right," he said. "You're entitled to an advance, of course. Would you like the check now?"

"I'd sure appreciate it."

"Well, fine. Let's go to the office."

Lorna said as Paperman went by the desk with Akers, "De afternoon plane just came in wit five guests. Ain't nobody to meet dem."

"Well? Those people this morning got in all right."

"Dey come very mad. It says in our brochure we meet dem. Thor he always met dem." She held out some keys on a chain. "Dese are for de Rover. Thor said for me give dem to you."

Norman took the keys with a shrug, went into the office, and wrote the check for Akers. The contractor said, blowing on the check, "Thanks. If you're going to the beach now, I'll come along."

"Don't you have to stay with the men?"

"All they have to do is finish off that wall. I told them to stop there and quit, so I don't reckon they'll knock down the rest of your hotel." Akers giggled, tucking the check in a dusty khaki pocket.

The new gondolier, exerting himself to put on a show for his employer, drove the boat to the shore with a dozen strokes, his ribbons a-flutter in the wind. "Millard, I think maybe you've got yourself a new job," Paperman said. The man's ebony face glistened with elation.

Akers showed Paperman how to start the Land Rover, an oversized British machine like an enclosed jeep. "They're great machines. I've got one," he said. "The only thing is, if you need a spare part it comes by slow boat from England. See you in the morning. Those rooms are going to start sprouting up tomorrow like mushrooms after a rain."

4

Seven angry tourists with a high heap of luggage awaited Norman at the airport. Their anger was directed equally at the Gull Reef Club and at a cab driver asleep at the wheel of a taxi parked close by: a Buick of about 1938 vintage, newly painted bright yellow, with patches of rust eating through the paint, and half of one door rotted away. When they had asked the driver to take them to the Gull Reef Club, he had said that he was busy, though there was no other visible business for him at the dead terminal. He had then slumped in a doze.

Paperman saw that without this taxi he would have to make two trips. The Land Rover couldn't hold seven people and the great pile of luggage. He went and rapped at the cab window. The driver opened one eye, then both, and sat up with a spry grin. "Yes, suh, whah to?" He reached for the rear door handle.

"Gull Reef Club."

"Sorry," said the driver. "I busy." He slouched back and closed his eyes.

There was no time to probe this puzzling outrage. Drawing on his vast experience with New York cab drivers, he rapped again, this time with a hand holding a ten-dollar bill. "Are you very busy?" he said.

The driver contemplated the ten and swallowed. "I got to leave dem off by de post office. Den dey got to walk."

"All right. Take the people, and I'll take the luggage."

Nobody offered to help him load the Rover, and of course there was no porter. So Paperman, who was not supposed to carry heavy weights or otherwise overexert himself, piled seventeen large suitcases into the car, with the western sun frying his back. He was not expert at this kind of thing, and when he started to drive off, the first stiff lurch of the Land Rover sent nine of the bags slithering out on the sticky tar road. He got out, repacked the bags, and tied them with a rope he found on the floor, mopping his streaming face with a sleeve, and easing his spirit by roaring at the waving sugar cane all the obscenities he could think of. He climbed into the Rover, jammed the accelerator to the board, and held it there. He was distinctly lightheaded by now. Rocking and swooping like a roller coaster, the machine tore along the highway, whistling past the decayed Buick about halfway to town.

The wharf once again was crowded with irritated whites. The gondola was moored alongside, and at the oars Millard slumped, his face tragic. His hat was gone. Nearby on a bollard sat Senator Pullman, and the senator was holding the hat.

"Hello Mr. Paperman! I'm glad you're here. I think I've saved you some very serious inconvenience, not to mention legal difficulties of humiliating proportions."

"Why? What's the matter now?"

The senator waved the hat. "Did you knowingly allow that person now sitting in your boat to operate it?"

Paperman explained why he had drafted Millard as a gondolier. The senator looked increasingly serious, lighting a cigar and puffing at it with nursing lips. "Mr. Paperman, that person is not a citizen. He is an alien, a bonded worker from the British island of Nevis. His bond only allows him to work as a gardener, since there is a shortage of Kinjan gardeners. There is no local shortage of unskilled labor, such as rowing a boat and wearing this hat would entail. You have to employ a Kinjan citizen for this position."

"I'll be glad to. It's an emergency, Senator." He reached for the hat.

The senator pulled it away. "I'm endeavoring for the friendliest motives to spare you considerable hardship. If an Immigration inspector were to find this person performing unauthorized employment—and they snoop around constantly—you might have all your alien workers' bonds cancelled forthwith. All your chambermaids and kitchen maids are bonded from Nevis. You'd have to close your hotel."

"Senator, tell me what to do and I'll do it," Paperman said. "Where can I get a Kinjan to row this boat?"

"There's only one place. The Amerigo Employment Division keeps a current list of Kinjans seeking job opportunities."

"Fine. Where is their office?"

"Across the street from the church. Unfortunately on Thursdays they close at one o'clock. I doubt that you can get a man anyway, to be frank. The season is on, and the list is usually empty by Thanksgiving."

Paperman stared at the senator's placid, sober round face. "But Senator—if I can't use bonded help, and I can't get a Kinjan, who is going to row this boat?"

The senator nodded with approval. "Well, you understand the situation, then. I feel you have a knotty problem."

"Jesus H. Christ," said Paperman.

"Perhaps you should put back the former boat boy. You can see that we cannot allow aliens to fill temporary shortages," said the senator. "Otherwise there would never be any shortages, and this island would have an unemployment problem. As it is, there is no unemployment in Kinja."

"I can well believe it. I'll take the hat." The senator passed it to him, and Paperman added, "Can you tell me while we're at it, why a cab driver wouldn't pick up my guests at the airport, and then wouldn't deliver them to this landing?"

Senator Pullman rolled his cigar inside a tolerant smile. "That is the fault of your policy."

"*My* policy? I got here yesterday."

"The Gull Reef Club sends a car to meet its guests. The taxi drivers' association feels this takes the bread out of the mouths of Kinjan citizens." He wrinkled his face, and seemed to age twenty years. "Now that the Gull Reef Club has a new proprietor, it's a golden opportunity to revitalize your policy on meeting guests."

Paperman walked to the gondola. "Millard!" The gardener looked up dolefully. "Give me a hand with the bags."

"Yes please." Millard scrambled eagerly out of the boat.

Paperman felt a tap on his shoulder. Senator Pullman said, "Handling luggage also is not a job certified by the Amerigo Employment Division for alien labor." But something in the suffering, cornered-rat look on Paperman's face caused him to add, "I don't see any Immigration inspectors on the waterfront right at this moment. I'm speaking of policy."

"This is completely against the policy of the Gull Reef Club," said Paperman. "Pile as many as you can on the rack, Millard."

"I feel that you will soon adjust to Kinja," said Senator Pullman.

Once again Norman Paperman rowed a boat full of luggage and people, including the big sad gardener, across the harbor, leaving behind a squalling, complaining huddle. Having no place else to set the hat, he put it on his head. It was nearly three o'clock now, and he was glad of the shade. The western sun on his head was making him very giddy.

Putting at defiance any Immigration inspectors lurking in the shrubbery, he ordered Millard to bring the bags to the main house. He hastened to the bar and told Gilbert to man the boat. Gilbert was shocked and balky. "Suh, I make good drinks. I got a order now for six planter's punches."

"Gilbert, I'll make the punches. Or they can wait. Those people have to get over here."

"I work de cash register, just like Thor. I handlin' de money good."

"I'm sure of that. This is just until we figure something out. Please go to the boat. *Now*, Gilbert." A cloud descended on Gilbert's face; his African lips pouted; his eyes became slitted and opaque. "Yazuh."

Paperman followed him through the lobby, not at all sure that he meant to obey. But he saw Gilbert saunter to the gondola and cast off.

Lorna at the desk was staring at Paperman, and giggling behind her palm most peculiarly. "Suh, Mistress Tramm she in de office."

"Oh, yes, of course." In the rush of events—this was easily getting to be the longest day of his life—he had forgotten Iris's offer to help.

She had several ledgers open on the two desks, and she was sorting out dining and bar checks of different sizes and colors. Big black glasses gave her a cool executive look. She was not alone. A bearded white youth, perhaps twenty-one or so, with a heavy shock of straight brown hair, stood slouching against the wall, his elbows clasped shyly behind him. He wore red bathing trunks and a faded blue sweatshirt with a flung-back cowl.

"Hi, we're doing big business today," Iris said. "I've got Thor's system figured out. It's good." She took off her glasses, looked somewhat startled at him, and then burst into silvery giggles. "My, my, well—anyway, this is Church Wagner. Church is an artist. There are some of his pictures. He wants to know if he can display them in the lobby. They're rather nice."

With a sheepish smile, Church showed oils and water colors: palms and the sea, tumble-down houses, dancing natives: mere bright vapid posters. Church himself, however, was a wonderfully handsome lad, with a lean rugged face softened by sensitive, almost girlish brown eyes.

"Is that what you do for a living?"

"Well, sir, I've been teaching painting at the high school. It sort of didn't work out, and so—I apologize for the way I look, sir, I just sailed over in my cat."

"Your what?"

"Catamaran, sir. That blue one, the two-hulled boat by your pier, with the blue-and-gold sails."

"Oh, *Lovebird.*" Paperman had had to maneuver the gondola to avoid the odd craft.

"Yes, sir," said Church.

Paperman, reduced to clutching at straws, said, "Can you by any chance mix drinks?"

Church's poetic face broke into a beguiling grin. "Well, I worked my last year through college tending bar at parties."

"Want a job?"

"Gosh, yes."

"Right now?"

"Sir, I'll jump at it."

"Come with me."

He installed Church Wagner in the bar, showed him the bar and dining checks and the cash register, and stayed long enough to watch the lad start the planter's punches. "This is a well-equipped bar," Church said, happily pouring and stirring and rattling. "I'm not dressed very appropriately—"

"You look fine. Picturesque."

"Well, this is sure my lucky day. I was a little short of eating money, sir, to tell the truth."

"I'll talk to you about salary later. Meantime you can eat here."

"Sir, thank you. That's a real help."

"He's a boat fellow like Thor," Paperman said to Iris, returning to the office. "So he has a screw loose. We'll just have to wait and find out which screw. I can keep a close watch on how he handles money.

Meantime he's a lifesaver—what in the hell are you laughing at? What's
Lorna been giggling at?"

"Look in the mirror," said Iris, compressing her mouth.

Paperman turned and regarded himself in the dirty little round mirror
on the wall. He saw his face dust-streaked, sweat-beaded, sunburned,
haggard, his gray hair hanging down, dishevelled and dark with sweat,
and crowning all the gondolier's hat with the red and gold ribbons.

He turned to Iris and flung his arms wide.

"*O sole mio,*" he bawled, "*O sole mio*—"

Collapsing with laughter, Iris came and put her arms around him,
and they harmonized.

Lorna looked into the open doorway, startled. With an understanding
and salacious giggle, she backed away and closed the door.

5

Norman staggered off to the White Cottage for a bath and a nap, too
"horossed" for lunch, or a swim, or even a beer. He had done far more
running around and more heavy labor in one morning, all under high
nervous tension, than he had believed he could do and survive. Yet his
heart was behaving; or, if he had had palpitations and pains, he had
been too busy to notice them. He thought he would pass out for hours,
but a soak in a tub restored him. He drew the bath hot and full, with a
defiant snort at the sign on the wall: *Please don't waste water. Take
brief showers.* Afterward he felt so good that he couldn't sleep. He was
anxious but buoyant, and very wide awake. He tossed, and tossed, and
finally got up and dressed. It was useless. Something terrible might be
going wrong up at the main house. That was where he belonged.

But everything was fine at the main house. Nothing had changed in
forty minutes. Guests were frolicking or sunning on the beach. The bar
was full of idle gossiping drinkers, and in the lobby elderly people were
reading magazines or making talk. The tarpaulin swayed and bellied;
behind it, silence. He slipped into the old dining room. The wall was
gone, the rubbish swept away. A rectangular space like a huge picture
window opened on the calm sea, the bright sky, and some promising
thunderclouds.

If only it would rain! It was the terror of running out of water, he decided, that was eating his nerves. The thing was to learn the hard facts about the water system right now. He fetched Gilbert out of the gondola.

"Gilbert, Thor showed you all about the water, didn't he?" Gilbert regarded him with heavy, unhappy eyes. "I mean the valves, the cisterns, the pumps—you know. The water."

From below his diaphragm Gilbert brought up a growling "Yazuh."

"Well, show me."

"Yazuh."

Gilbert trotted ahead of him to the main house, and through the lobby to the kitchen passageway. Norman heard Sheila trumpet, "*What?* Gilbert, you git on out of my kitchen. You just trouble, mon. Go on, git out."

Gilbert mumbled, "Mistuh Papuh he say show him."

"Yes I did, Sheila," Norman said, as bravely as he could. "We won't be long."

Driving the girls before her, talking disconnectedly at the top of her voice, the cook left.

The heat in the tiny kitchen was unbelievable; Paperman thought it must be a hundred and twenty degrees. A heavy fish odor jetted from a grumbling vat on the stove. Gilbert slipped an iron hook into a ring sunk in the wooden floor, and heaved; most of the floor came up; he took a flashlight from a shelf and shone it into the square black hole. "Dah," he said.

Paperman edged up to the hole, bent over, and peered in.

"Why, I can see water, quite a bit of it," he said in tones magnified by the resonance of the cistern. "How much is there? Do you have a gauge?"

Gilbert dropped a plumb line, and brought it up dripping. The line was dry except for the last foot and a half, which was soaked black.

"Well, with all that area," Norman said, "even that much must be thousands of gallons."

Gilbert pointed near the top of the wet part. "De pipe suck dah."

"You mean all the water below that goes to waste?" Gilbert nodded. "That's an idiotic way to build a cistern. I'll get Akers to move the pipe down."

Gilbert ran his finger down the cord. "Below is wha' de stuff settle."

"Stuff? What stuff?"

"Stuff offen de roof. Like leaves an' bird droppin's, an' mud, an' dead caterpillars, an' dead centipedes, an' dead tree toads an' spiders, an' a few field mice, an' like dat."

Since his arrival at Gull Reef, what with all his perspiring, Norman had already drunk a large amount of this interesting water. He felt a strong wave of nausea, and backed hastily from the hole. It would hardly do to add vomit to the strange contents of the hotel's drinking water. He walked unsteadily out of the kitchen and leaned against a wall. Gilbert put the floor back over the cistern, and came out.

"Are you serious, Gilbert? How is it everybody who comes here doesn't die of typhoid or cholera?"

"De water does filter troo charcoal."

"Isn't the cistern ever cleaned of that—that stuff?"

"Yazuh."

"When was the last time?"

"When de earthquake done crack it and all de water gone out."

"When was that?"

"Dunno. Hippolyte clean it."

"Who is Hippolyte?"

"He de fella don' work here no mo'."

Gilbert led his queasy employer through a back door into sweet fresh air, down a sandy slope, and through a vine-covered trellis masking the iron support beams beneath the bar. Underfoot was beach sand, and one could look out through the trellis at the sparkling sea and the guests at play. Gilbert crouched and vanished through a crawl hole in the foundation, and Norman followed him.

"Don' stan up straight," said Gilbert, as Norman did so, fetching his head a crack against metal in the gloom. The flashlight beam showed that he had struck the handle of a valve, painted red, projecting downward from a maze of interlocking and crisscrossing pipes. Close to it was a valve painted green. This low airless crawl-space smelled of decay, mildew, drains, and machine grease. It was full of the detritus of hotel-keeping: broken chairs, odd lumber, cans of dry paint, rusty screens, stacks of basins, bales of roped paper. Dominating all was a large machine clanking, wheezing, and chugging on a concrete platform. Pipes radiated from it like the tentacles of an octopus, and it was lumpy with odd knobs, gauges, and chambers. Paperman had a slight fear of all machinery. This thing looked very diseased, and evil.

"De pump," said Gilbert.

"How does it work? Gasoline?"

"'Lectric." He pointed to the two painted valve handles, and a dozen others, gray or rusty, projecting everywhere. "Don' mind dem other valves. Dey goes to de cottages. De red one de main. De green one de 'mergency. Well, I guess I go back to de boat." Gilbert started out.

"One minute." Uncomfortable though he was, Norman felt that it was now or never for learning the mysteries of the water system. Hunched like a miner, there in that foul-smelling damp dark place, he asked question after question, hammered away at the boy's taciturnity, turned the pump on and off himself, and worked the two colored valves. The emergency tank, he found out, held about a day's supply, so that if the main cistern water did run out, he had an extra day for procuring more. Paperman thought this nugget of fact was enough reward for all the dreary and uncomfortable investigation. The nightmare of forty unflushed toilets dissolved. There was a margin for error.

"All right, Gilbert. You can go back to the boat. Thank you."

"Yazuh."

Paperman now returned to the lobby. Lorna was busy at the switchboard, deftly plugging and ringing and answering. He waited for a lull.

"Lorna, Senator Pullman tells me that you know how we can get emergency water, if we happen to run dry."

"Senator Pull-mon?" Lorna's eyes rounded in blank innocence; her mouth curved and her tongue flickered in a smile that might have shocked a Parisian whore. "Senator Pull-mon say dat?"

With some coaxing, he got the story out of her. Lorna had a brother named Anatone, who owned a tank truck, and he made his living hauling water up to the homes of the wasteful hill crowd. Anatone procured his water from the municipal reservoir. He could bring water to the Club, but it would be expensive. No hose in Amerigo was long enough to stretch from the waterfront to the Reef. There was an old World War II landing craft in the harbor, used for hauling municipal garbage out to sea and dumping it. Anatone could hire this craft; he could drive his truck aboard, and so get the water to the Club. Paperman would have to pay for the water, the landing-craft hire, and Anatone's extra time. "I tell you what, Mr. Paperman," she said. "You better hope it rains."

"Your brother's name is what—Anatole?"

"Anatone," she giggled. "Everybody make dat mistake. Anatone."

Anatone sounded like a desperate remedy to Norman, but decidedly better than none at all. This had been an hour well spent, he thought. On the water problem, he now knew what there was to know.

Iris was still in the office, putting away ledgers and checks. "Hi," she said, "did you get any rest? You still look rocky."

"Do I?"

Paperman, feeling pleased with himself, embraced her and gave her a kiss, which she apparently enjoyed. "Ye gods, does a nap do that for you? Lucky Henny. These books are simple, Norm. Posting once a day is all that's necessary. We'll do it together tomorrow."

Norman said, "Splendid. I now propose a long swim, and a few martinis, say six or seven, served to us by Church Wagner in the privacy of the White Cottage veranda, and then dinner."

Iris's eyes sparkled at him. "It's all lovely, except dinner, Norm. I can't have dinner with you. Let's go."

6

The thunderclouds were drawing near from the east, dumping gray streams of rain in the sea, when she joined him on the veranda after their swim.

"Look," he said jovially, pointing. "Bye-bye water shortage."

"Isn't it wonderful?" Iris said. "You bear a charm. Sheila said it wouldn't break until Christmas. Where are the martinis?" She sat on the wicker couch, swinging up her bare legs, and perched them on the black cushions, tucking her pink linen skirt close under her thighs.

"Church is on his way down with them."

She was smoking and looking thoughtfully out at the rain, now less than a mile off shore. "About Church," she said.

"Yes?"

"Norm, your bartender's your key person here. All your money comes in through that register at the bar. Even check-outs. It makes the record-keeping a cinch, and it worked fine with Thor. But—"

"I think this lad's as bright as Thor. Anyway, I'll be watching him," Paperman said airily. He wanted a less business-like tone to this cocktail hour, with gold rays of the low sun shafting around the rain clouds, and Iris looking so provokingly pretty, curled up pink and white on the black cushions.

She said, "Well, dear. I thought I'd better check. I called the high school—"

There came a knock and Church, still in bathing suit and sweatshirt, brought in a jug of martinis in an ice bucket with two glasses thrust among the ice shavings. He gave Iris a shy little smile. "Evening, Mrs. Tramm. Sir, we're real busy at the bar. They're all over the beach too, and it's starting to sprinkle. The girls are pulling the rain awnings on the terraces. They asked me and I said sure."

"Church, is it throwing you? The handling of the money?"

"Oh, no, sir. There's a cash journal at the bar, you know. I'm sort of keeping track as I go. We sold sixteen outsiders' chits for dinner. We'll be crowded." Church left with quick light barefoot step.

"Why, he's the salt of the earth," Paperman said, pouring the drinks, and tasting one. "He's a find and a jewel, and how's that for a martini?"

"He left the employ of the Amerigo Central High School," said Iris, "because he got the principal pregnant."

Paperman's eyes lit with amused surprise. "The principal! That lad?"

"Miss Lydia Pullman, a cousin of the senator, a spinster of forty-three, with nineteen years of seniority."

"Ye gods," Norman said.

"I talked to some teachers up there, Norm. There was hell to pay. Any unmarried teacher who shows up pregnant loses her job and her seniority. It happens all the time, but it's never happened to a principal before. They kicked Church out like *that*."

"What's become of her?"

"She's already left for the States. She was awarded a year's in-service fellowship in school administration. A rather hastily voted fellowship."

"I see it all," said Norman, "the Board of Education meeting in the dead of night, behind locked doors. The academic merits of the applicant presented by the local gynecologist. I'm falling in love with Kinja all over again. How's about a refill?"

She shook her head, laughing. "The question is, do we want this ravisher of respectable educators handling the Club's money?"

"Why not? If older women are his vice, he won't need money to stay happy. That stuff is plentiful and free."

"I wonder. Tastes differ and all that. But I could no more mess around with a fuzzy, peaches-and-cream tidbit like Church—"

A wisp of wind-driven rain struck Norman's face. The waving rain-curtain pouring into the sea from the oncoming thunderhead sounded like a distant waterfall. The sting of the cold drops elated him. He said, "How would you feel about messing around with a dehydrated tidbit like me?"

"Ah, Norm. Norm Paperman. What a name. Paperman." She regarded him with a sadly comic shake of her head. "You know, you did something damned stupid or damned smart, I'm not sure which. But anyway, you did it. You brought Henny down here. And she'll be down again."

Norman ran a thumb nervously along his lower lip. "She's far away now."

"I'm not what I was," said Iris, "but I'm not reduced to owing my pleasure to another woman's gallstones."

"It's got nothing to do with Henny's gallstones," Norman said irritably, "and she doesn't have any, anyhow. It's just that you're beautiful and I like you."

"Really, Henny is so nice," Iris said. "Why, she's got me looking for chairs and fabrics for the lobby. We hit it off like long-lost cousins. And anyway—" Iris breathed a heavy sigh and drank off her martini with a single motion of a crooked elbow. "You know all about me. I'm nobody to mess with, obviously. You're just talking. Mustn't drink another drop, and I must leave." She stood, shaking her skirt straight. "Why, what's the matter, Norm? What in God's name are you staring at? Aren't you well?"

"It isn't happening," Norman said. "Such a thing can't happen. Can it?"

He made an uncertain gesture at the sea. The squall was moving past Gull Reef. The White Cottage stood on the point that thrust farthest out into the sea, and it had scarcely been wetted. Behind the retreating black cloud and its gray fall of rain, a red-and-gold sunset was opening across a clear blue sky.

"Ah, too bad. That one seems to have missed us," said Iris. "Well, another one will come along."

"But Iris, look at all that *water*, falling into the sea. Thousands of gallons a minute into the sea! Why? The sea doesn't need water. *I* need it."

"Go ahead, Norman. Finish the martinis."

"If I had longer arms," said Paperman, "I could have held out a bucket and caught God knows how many gallons. It was that close. Now it's going away. To Cuba or somewhere."

"For all we know it's raining at the main house," Iris said. "That's what the weather's like in this silly place."

"Let's look!" Norman exclaimed. They went through the cottage and out on the lawn. The main house was glowing rosily and drily in the sunset. Beyond it, the island of Amerigo was almost invisible in a heavy downpour.

"Iris," said Norman, "it's raining to the west of us, and it's raining to the east of us. I don't think there's more than a mile between these two cloudbursts. We're sitting here beneath a blue sky, as dry as though we were under a tent. This is just not possible. I'm having a nightmare."

"Look, Norman, darling, come inside and sit down."

She took his arm, firmly walked him inside, pushed him down in a chair, and handed him another martini. "I may as well tell you that this happens here all the time."

"It does?" Paperman cocked his head at her like a sad inquisitive dog. "It really does?"

"It's a freak of the wind patterns. The mountains cause it. Amy Ball used to go out of her mind. The thunderheads either get sucked up against the ridge, or they bounce loose and drift out to sea. I've sat here and watched them go by on either side of this hotel like soldiers marching around a dead body."

"I'll be damned," said Paperman. "That's very interesting, and it might even be amusing, except I think it's going to give me a fatal heart attack."

"Oh, don't go on like that. The thing is, sweetie, sooner or later one of these three-day rainstorms comes along and the whole island gets blanketed and drenched. You've got such a huge roof area here that the cistern can overflow before the end of such a storm. I've seen it happen."

"Meantime," Paperman said, "I'll have to hunt up Anatone tomorrow and buy water. That's obvious."

"Anatone? Who on earth is that?"

Paperman repeated to her the story that Lorna had given him.

"Gosh, the names on this island," said Iris. "Anatone. Sounds like a headache remedy."

"I thought of an off-brand Japanese radio," said Paperman.

She said, chuckling, "I must go. If you write Henny, tell her Hassim's bringing in the black-and-gold grass cloth from Hong Kong that she wanted for the lobby. It ought to be here next week." Iris leaned over and gave him a brief kiss. "If you ever talk sweet to me again I'll set Meadows on you. All that is *out*, do you understand? I'm going to be a sister to you."

He groaned and cringed. "Iris, you embarrass me."

He followed her out to the lawn and watched her walk off, a swaying lovely pink figure, toward the dock. All the rain clouds had passed on, north, south, east, and west. A sapphire sky, with two planets shining in the west, bent its dry dome over the Gull Reef Club.

7

He came awake with a bodily jerk. The knocking went on, and still the voice cried, "Inside! Mistuh Papuh! You dah?" It was a woman's voice, and not Sheila's: thin, high. The seaward window was black dark; no moonlight, no stars. His phosphorescent watch dial showed quarter-past eleven.

"Inside! Inside! —Well, I guess he ain' dah."

Another girlish voice: "He dah."

Hammering of several fists, and yells of two women: "Inside! Mistuh Papuh!"

"All right, all right, one moment."

The girls—they were the waitresses in the bar—told him that the hotel water had just run out. Church had noticed it, while washing glasses, and had immediately sent them to him.

"Okay," said Paperman, with some elation. For once he was on top of a Gull Reef crisis. "Tell Church he'll have water in two minutes."

The two girls ran back to the main house and he followed in robe and flapping straw slippers. In the lobby half a dozen guests in night clothes clamored at him. He raised both hands. "Folks, it's a question of shifting from one cistern to another. I regret the inconvenience, but by the time you get back to your rooms you'll have water."

Many people were drinking and laughing in the bar, all oblivious to the water crisis, and more were on the terrace, dancing to the steel band.

"Church, get the big flashlight in the kitchen and come with me. You might as well learn how to do this."

"Yes, sir."

He led Church to the malodorous hole under the hotel. The pump was running with a queer dry rattle. Paperman flashed the light beam along an electric cable, coiling in the darkness to a wall socket. He pulled out the plug. A fat blue spark leaped after the prongs; the pump choked, rattled, shuddered all over, gave a screech and one loud clank, and fell silent.

Paperman did not remember, at this point, whether the red valve or the green valve led to the emergency tank. It didn't matter, he thought. All he had to do was close the open one and open the closed one.

He did this.

"Now," he said, and he plunged the plug back into the socket.

The pump reacted like a living thing, like a bull stabbed with a sword, like a woman grasped in the dark by a strange hand. It screamed, and writhed, and seemed to rise bodily off its concrete block, and shook at every point, its gauge needles dancing. Then it settled down to running noisily again.

"There we are," said Paperman, trying to appear unconcerned, though dry-mouthed at the pump's convulsion. "Run up and make sure we've got water. Just yell down to me, I'll be out on the beach."

"Yes, sir."

"No water," Church called down from the rail of the bar, about half a minute later. "No water, Mr. Paperman. And the lobby's full of people complaining."

"Get back down here," roared Paperman.

"Coming, sir."

"Now what the hell, Church?" Paperman said, playing the flashlight on the thumping machine. "It's running, it's drawing on a full emergency tank. I checked that tank today."

Church put his hand on the pipes. "There's no water going through, sir. There'd be a vibration and the pipes would feel cool. Do you suppose the pump has to be primed? Most pumps do, once they've run dry."

"You seem very knowledgeable. Go ahead and prime it, Church."

Church scratched his beard, and looked at his employer with a weak one-sided smile. "Sir, that's one thing I'm no good for. Machinery gives me the creeps. I have a long bad history of wrecking boat engines, sir. I really would rather not touch this pump."

Both men stared at the gasping machine.

"Well," said Paperman, "I sure as hell don't know how to prime it. That was one little detail I neglected to ask about. It wasn't volunteered. I guess I'll have to find Gilbert."

The somnolent night boatman, Virgil, was sprawled in the stern of the gondola, with the hat over his eyes. He was a small very scrawny man; Paperman had been unable to guess his age because he had no front teeth and he was cross-eyed. He was constantly munching, though he never seemed to put anything in his mouth. Thor had told Norman that Virgil was nicer than Gilbert, but he had made him the night man because "he look so tam fonny."

Norman, who had thrown on shirt, shorts, and sandals, came trotting to the dark pier and stirred him up. "Virgil, you don't happen to know anything about the pump, do you?"

"Pump? No, fah. I fink Gilbert, he know." Virgil sat up, looking several feet to Paperman's left.

"Can you tell me where Gilbert lives?"

"Oh, yeff. Dat fery fimple, fah." He munched out some incomprehensible directions, in which the words "Mofquito Hill" kept repeating.

"Mosquito Hill, eh? All right. I'll find him. Let's go."

Paperman leaped out of the gondola as it drew near to the shore. A couple who looked like honeymooners were waiting hand in hand, peering toward the lights of the Club with shiny eyes. The girl said to Paperman in a babyish voice, "Is that place as heavenly as it looks?"

"It's utterly fantastic," said Paperman, "and unbelievably reasonable."

"Oooh," said the girl, stepping into the gondola with a giggle.

Paperman ran up Prince of Wales Street and found a cab. "I want to go to Mosquito Hill," he said, jumping in. "And fast."

"Yassuh. Wha' on Mosquito Hill?"

"Well, I don't know. Where Gilbert lives. The boatman from the Gull Reef Club."

The taxi driver nodded. A scary ride ensued, around corners, through alleys, up and down hills, with at one point a screeching grind backwards in blackness between narrow stone walls. The driver explained that this short cut saved ten minutes; it was all right to back along the one-way alley but not to drive through it.

At last the taxi stopped. "We dah," said the driver. "Mosquito Hill. Dat be two dolla'."

Paperman got out of the car and found himself looking at the longest, steepest flight of stairs he had ever seen outside of pictures of Inca ruins in the Andes. The staircase went straight up and up into the night, gloomily lit by street lamps clouded with moths.

"What's this? Where's Gilbert's house?"

"He live up dah. De Tousand Steps."

"The *Thousand* Steps?"

The driver laughed. "It just a name. Dey ain't but two hunnert seven. Gilbert he live up near de top. Goat Row. You ask anybody up dah."

"Can't you take me up to the top so I can walk down?"

"Yes suh. Dat does take twenty minutes longer, you does have to go way round Gov'ment Hill and den de ole Jewish cemetery in between."

"I'm glad to know about the Jewish cemetery," Paperman said. "It may come in handy. Wait here for me, please."

"Sho."

Norman contemplated the steps. On the list of overexertions which his doctor had ordered him to avoid, climbing stairs had stood first, underlined in red ink, ahead even of "excessive sexual activity." It crossed his mind that if death had to come, he was not committing the misdeed of choice. Nevertheless the pump of the Gull Reef Club had to be primed. He began to mount the Thousand Steps.

The steps were lined with shacks of tin or wood; here and there were stucco structures that might be called houses; all presented blank walls or narrow high windows to the stairs. Where the street lamps stood, alleys ran off into the darkness. The signs on corner dwellings gave the names: Jensen Alley, Old Church Mews, Spanish Row, Simon Row. Garbage filled deep cement gutters bounding the stairway. Garbage removal on this hill, Norman saw, was done by the rain and by scavengers. The short storm at sunset had washed much of the refuse down to the large heaps where the taxi stood, and the rest lay tumbled along the cement trenches. Cats and dogs and a few small black goats were busy at the smorgasbord, all the way up the hill. The gutters were choked with broken bottles and punctured beer cans, stuck in a permanent black mulch, which diffused a smell of fetid decay on the hot night. Paperman tried to subdue his gasping as he mounted. He was less likely to die from the climb, he felt, than from inhaling this miasma. He paused to catch his breath at a broader alley than the rest, discouragingly named Lower Street. Here on one corner was a tiny tavern with glassless windows and unpainted little tables, where yelling, laughing, muscular black men in undershirts were drinking beer out of cans. A bit scared, Norman searched their faces. The men became quieter, and gave him truculent looks.

"I'm looking for Gilbert," he panted. "He works for me, and he lives in Goat Row."

After a pause of vacant staring, a man in the doorway shouted inside, "Hey, wha' Gilbert?" There were many noisy answers. He pointed up the stairs. "He up dah. He gone to sleep."

Paperman climbed; climbed till his head swam and his ears sang; climbed until the sign *Goat Row* loomed at last before his misting eyes. He halted, clutching at the stitch in his side, and gulping the air, which here, near the top, was sweet. Glancing behind him, he grabbed at the lamppost to keep from plunging dizzily head first down the gulf of steps to the shrunken taxi. There was a charming vista from this spot—the close lamplit town hills, the far curving waterfront, and the tiny gem of the Gull Reef Club—but Paperman was incapable of admiring it.

Goat Row was dark. His watch showed a few minutes before midnight. Far down the alley to the left he saw one light. He made for that, gasping like a stranded fish, stepping in squashy muck, kicking unseen tin cans, and once treading on a thing that writhed and made no sound. A stout woman sat in the lighted window, reading a worn little Bible. "Gil-*bert*?" she said. "Gilbert de next side de stairs, de red house."

Nothing looked red in the dim lamplight on the other side of the stairs. Paperman went striking matches from house to house, examining the paint on the walls. It occurred to him during this peculiar activity that he was quite a long way from his home, his wife, his daughter, and Sardi's Restaurant. The muck was especially thick here, and he felt it oozing warmly over his sandals.

"Wah you want, mon?" A flashlight from a window dazzled him. Before he could reply the voice altered its tone. "Mistuh Papuh?"

"Is that you, Gilbert?"

"Yazuh. Mistuh Papuh, I kin work dat cash register just like Thor said."

"I'm sure of that," Norman panted, "but it isn't what I came to see you about." His hand pressed to his galloping heart, he described the trouble with the cisterns. The light beam shone full on him as though he were doing a vaudeville act.

"You does have to prime de pump," said the boatman's voice through a yawn.

"So I gathered, and how do I do that?"

"You does pull de plug, den open de petcock, den take de spanner by de sump, den you does unscrew de vent nut, den you does pour in some water from de bottle by de sump in de pump, den—"

"Gilbert, listen, you'd better come and do it."

"It don' take but two seconds, Mistuh Papuh, dey ain't nothin' to it."

"May be, but my guests are rioting by now. I can't take a chance. I'm not climbing these steps again tonight."

"Yazuh." The flashlight snapped off, leaving Paperman half-blinded, still gasping, and up to his ankles in warm slime. The shadowy form of Gilbert came out of the house, and headed toward the staircase. Norman observed that the boatman hugged the wall, walking on a narrow stone curb, to avoid the mud.

There were great advantages he thought, as he staggered back to the Thousand Steps—advantages he had never before quite appreciated—in knowing one's surroundings.

About a quarter of an hour later he stood with Gilbert in the crawl space, flashing lights on the dead pump. Church was above, checking out two irate guests and trying to calm a mob in the lobby.

"Okay, Gilbert. Let's see how you do it."

Gilbert took perhaps a minute to bring a happy far-off shout from Church, "Water! There's water, sir!" All he did was unscrew a nut, pour a little water from a dirty bottle into the opening, tighten the nut, and plug in the pump. The machine came to life with its usual hysteria, but when it calmed down its thump was full and throaty.

He rehearsed the pump-priming motions with Gilbert half a dozen times.

"Gilbert, you're entitled to overtime for this," he said as they came out on the starlit beach. "You'll get it. Thank you very much."

"Mistuh Papuh, dat be all right. Thor he done show me de books and how to work de register. I does mix good drinks. I make brandy Alexander, de folks from up de hill does like dem, and sloe gin fizz and like dat."

The boatman's usually glum face was alert and smiling. He had enjoyed bringing deliverance. Here was a young man who really wanted to work, Paperman thought, and who did know something about the unforeseeable pitfalls of operating the Club.

But there were things against Gilbert. He was an inscrutable, morose, black lad. He parted with spoken words as though each were a ten-dollar bill. He lived at the top of the Thousand Steps, on Mosquito Hill, behind Government Hill and the Jewish cemetery. The bartender was the key man in this hotel. Church was white, understandable, and tractable. Moreover, replacing a boatman, under the strange labor laws of Amerigo, was apparently impossible.

"We'll see, Gilbert, we'll see. Let's leave things as they are, just for now."

The Negro's thick lips tightened until they disappeared. A murky spark came and went in his eyes, leaving his expression veiled and dull. He walked off down the beach.

Paperman left a note for Lorna at the desk: *Please call Anatone first thing. Tell him to fill the emergency tank and put three days' supply in the main cistern.*

He tottered off to bed. So ended his first full day as the owner of the Gull Reef Club.

chapter six

The Second Day

I

None of the new proprietor's awakenings so far had been pleasant. The following morning was a change, in that hammering fists on his door were not what roused him. He awoke gagging and choking. The cottage was filled with a smell so strong and so foul that his mind sprang to a wild surmise: a dead rotten whale had stranded on the beach. He groped to the seaward window, but there was no dead whale. He went and looked out at the lawn, noticing that he was still wearing last night's shirt and shorts and mud-caked sandals. He had no recollection of what he had done after leaving the message for Lorna; he had been so played out that it would not have surprised him to awaken on the lobby floor.

Beyond the rise of the lawn which hid the dock from sight, he could see the round bridge of a landing craft painted in fading camouflage patterns. This had to be the garbage carrier, he realized, bearing Anatone's water truck. But could it possibly stink with this strength at this range? He went out to investigate. A black hose from the tank truck on the vessel twisted across the lawn to the main house. Guests, gathered on the terrace with handkerchiefs to their noses, were watching two Negroes working at the truck. Norman clamped his nose between thumb and forefinger and ran to the pier. "Which of you is Anatone?" he said in something like a New England twang.

"Dat me, suh." The thinner and younger of the two, wearing a battered brown hard hat, flashed gold teeth in an easy grin. "De wind sure de wrong way today. Sorry."

"How many more loads do you have to bring?"

"Ten."

"Ye gods, you'll be at it till sundown. There won't be a guest registered in this hotel by then."

Anatone said the wind was bound to change; it never blew from this direction for long, except in the summer. He had already topped off the emergency tank, and there was almost one day's supply in the main cistern. "Goin' for de next load now," he said. The boat captain roared up the engine, and Anatone cast off.

"How much is this costing me?" Paperman yelled.

"Fifty dolla' a load, suh. Fifteen load."

"Seven hundred and fifty dollars? For water?"

"De boat does cost de money," Anatone shouted back amiably from the stern, as the landing craft pulled away. The breeze brought instant relief. Just an ordinary light sea wind, it smelled like a zephyr from a lilac garden after the fumes of the garbage boat.

Millard, in his paper-bag hat, now tramped onto the pier carrying half a dozen suitcases covered with travel labels. Behind him came a big man in a seersucker suit, with a fat red face, sunken eyes, and curly gray hair. A slight, elderly woman in a yellow sun dress leaned on his arm.

"Good morning, please," Millard said to Norman with a sweet smile.

"There he is, Harriet," rasped the man. "Say, you, aren't you this new owner, this Piper, or whatever?"

"Paperman. I'm the new owner of the hotel, yes."

"Well, mister, my wife and I have been coming here for seven years, but by God this club is seeing the last of us. My wife's just thrown up her breakfast. Jesus Christ! Where's that gondola?"

"Sir, we've been having a little water problem, but after today—"

"You're telling me? The things that went on with our toilet last night! You've stunk us out of your hotel, Paperman, that's all I know, and you'll stink out everybody else before nightfall, you mark my word. How do you feel, honey?"

"Better now," murmured the woman. "Now that that horrible boat's gone."

The man blinked and stared at Norman. "Wait, you say your name's Paperman? That's an odd name. Where are you from? Not Hartford, Connecticut, by any chance?"

"Hartford, exactly."

"Jesus, you're not poor old Ike Paperman's son, are you?"

"That's right. I'm Norman."

"Well!" The man looked up and down at Norman's unshaven face, tousled hair, creased clothes, and mud-caked feet. "What a small world. I thought you were a Broadway producer or something. I did a lot of business with your father. He was a fine man. I'm George Harmer. Hartford Electric Supply."

Paperman held out his hand. The man shook it awkwardly. "Look, I mean, Norman, can't you do something about that boat? It's going to kill Harriet. She's a high-strung woman and she's just getting over an operation—"

"I'll call off the boat, Mr. Harmer," Norman said. "Immediately, I promise. You're dead right. I just woke up, or I'd have stopped them sooner. They can come another day when the wind's normal."

"How about that, Harriet? Ike Paperman's boy," Harmer said. "Isn't it a small world?"

Lorna looked amazed at seeing the Harmers come to the desk again, and somewhat scared. The man said jocosely, "Okay, girl friend, I'll take the key to twenty-seven again. I call Lorna my girl friend," he explained to Paperman.

Lorna smiled uncertainly at the man. "Mr. Akers in de ole dining room," she said to Paperman. "He does be waiting to talk to you."

"All right. You take good care of the Harmers now. Is Church here?"

"Yes, suh. He come in nine o'clock."

Slipping behind the bellying tarpaulin, Norman saw great stacks of building materials—window frames, door frames, lumber, panelling, pipes, kegs, boxes, toilets, washbasins, and the like—and beyond these, on the lawn, Akers' battalion of laborers sitting or lying in the bright sun. Akers was lounging full length on one elbow on the grass, pouring himself coffee from a vacuum jug. "Ah, the boss!" He rose in a clumsy way to his unbelievable height. "How about this? Everything the job needs, down to the last nail and tile, right here before your eyes." He picked up and flourished a manila folder. "Got the whole inventory here, too, if you want to look at it, with that estimate you wanted. This job's going to be mighty cheap for the A-1 materials you've got here."

"That's fine. Why aren't the men working?"

"Couple of things I have to check out with you. You see, it's this way, Mr. Paperman—"

A woman's scream stopped him; a high, frightening scream, from somewhere on the second floor. "Good Lord," Akers said. There was another weaker scream, and then the deep noises of an angry man, and trampling sounds. Paperman went diving under the tarpaulin into the lobby. George Harmer was coming heavily down the stairs, supporting his wife, whose eyes glanced wildly here and there. "Easy, Harriet, easy. It's perfectly all right now."

"Oh my God," said the woman. "Oh my God."

"PAPERMAN!" bellowed Harmer, assisting his wife to a couch. "You get me a doctor, and fast. If anything's happened to Harriet you're going to have a lawsuit on your hands, brother, for half a million dollars."

"It was so awful, so awful," quavered Mrs. Harmer, lying down on the couch, and putting the back of her hand over her eyes.

"What happened, for God's sake?" said Paperman.

"Never mind what happened. I can't tell you what happened. Get a doctor!"

The commotion was attracting guests into the lobby. A baldish young man in black swim trunks stepped forward. "I'm a doctor. Can I help? What's her trouble?"

"She's been shocked within an inch of her life, that's all."

Harmer stepped away from his wife's side. The young man, his face grave, sat on the couch beside her and gently took her wrist. "What frightened her?"

"I just can't tell you. Not now." Harmer glared at the ring of guests and especially at Paperman.

"It was so awful," moaned the woman.

The doctor lifted her hand away from her eyes, and pushed back her lids.

Paperman said in anguish to the husband, "What was it? Did she see a scorpion?"

"A *scorpion*? Listen, mister—"

The doctor said, "Your wife's all right. Give her a little brandy and let her catch her breath. And everybody should go away and leave her be," he added to the clustering guests.

"I never drink brandy," said Mrs. Harmer, with her hand over her eyes. "A drop of Cherry Heering, maybe. Just a tiny taste."

Paperman darted to the bar. To his annoyance, Church was not in sight. He rattled the bottles around until he found the Cherry Heering, and brought a small glassful back to the lobby. Harmer sat beside his wife, patting her hand. The doctor was dispersing the guests with good-humored hand waves. "Come, ma'am, sit up. Just take a sip or two," the doctor said.

"How soon can I take her away from this place, Doctor?" growled Harmer.

Mrs. Harmer was drinking like a baby from the glass in the doctor's hand. He smiled. "Any time, really. She's all right."

The husband grabbed Paperman's elbow. "Look after her for just a second, Doctor, will you? Just one second." He dragged Norman across the lobby, behind the desk, and into the tiny office, banging the door shut. "All right, brother, now here it is. My wife and I went back up to our room, see? I opened the door for her. She went in first. She let out a scream and all but fell dead on my hands. You know that bartender of yours? That skinny kid with a beard?"

"Yes?" said Norman, with an awful presentiment.

"Well, brother, right there on the bed, this bartender of yours was *slipping it* to our chambermaid! Right there in broad daylight, on our bed. And my Harriet had to see a thing like that! The chambermaid!"

Too upset to think clearly, Paperman babbled, "Really? Are you sure?"

"Am I SURE?" The man exploded, his face going purple. "What the hell? Do you think I'm too goddamned old to even remember what it looks like? I'm telling you what we both saw! Harriet damn near died. I had to carry her back down the stairs. Am I sure!"

Paperman groaned, and buried his face in his hands.

This mollified Harmer and he said in more normal tones, "I tell you, that isn't the worst of it. He *never even stopped*. He looked at us over his shoulder and sort of smiled in a sickly way, and said, 'Oh, hi. I thought you checked out,' and went right on with it. That's when Harriet screamed again. Paperman, you've got a sex maniac there."

Paperman moaned through his hands. "I hired him only yesterday. It was an emergency—"

"Yes? Well, this is a bigger emergency. That boy's crazy. For one thing, the girl's pregnant as a hippo."

"Oh no, no. Not the pregnant one," Paperman mumbled, rocking his head from side to side. "Not Esmé."

"That's her name. Esmé."

Paperman's hands uncovered a bristling, haggard, drawn, deeply sad face. "Mr. Harmer, I can't blame you for leaving. I won't argue with you. I'll get rid of him."

Harmer said uncomfortably, "I mean, I feel sorry for you. But I've just got to take Harriet somewhere else."

"I completely understand," Paperman said with a gasping sob.

"Holy Christ, man, are you crying? Don't cry. That's no way."

"I'm not crying," said Paperman. "I'm allergic. When I'm under pressure these attacks hit me. I'll be all right."

It was true enough. The swelling in his nasal ducts, the stinging in his eyes, the involuntary tears, were coming on severe and fast. It was his first allergic attack since the coronary; he had thought that pattern was broken up for good, and here it was appearing again.

"Well, okay. Good luck. You've really got yourself into something here, Paperman, that's all I can say." Harmer left, closing the door gently behind him.

Paperman began feeling in his pockets for Kleenex. What a misery this was, now! He had not even brought the medicines for his allergy;

he would have to cable Henny to airmail them— Rap, rap, rap at the door; bony knuckles striking hard. "Yes, come in," he wheezed.

Akers came stooping through the doorway. "I hate like hell to disturb you, but we ought to get those men started working."

"What? Are they still lying around? That regiment? It's past eleven o'clock." Paperman went into a sneezing fit. "Wha-wha-what's the holdup?" Searching in the desk he found a dusty box of yellowed tissue, and blew his nose and wiped his eyes.

"Well, you see," said the contractor, "that's what I was explaining when all this trouble started. Mind if I sit down?" He put the manila folder of the estimate on the desk. "Gosh, the types that get attracted to this island. Isn't that bartender of yours something?"

"What? How do you know about it?"

Akers gave him a lean grin. "It's all over the hotel, naturally. The whole island will know about it in an hour. Jungle drums. The way I heard it, he had these two chambermaids of yours stark naked on the bed, and—" He described a bizarre sexual arrangement, a flight of fancy out of Hindu erotic literature.

"Why, that's ridiculous," Paperman said. "I don't even think it's possible. There was only one girl, anyhow. I wish I knew how I could stop that story."

"Why? It's free advertising. They'll be coming down out of the hills to see this bartender of yours. They'll be coming over from Guadeloupe."

Paperman said, "In special excursion steamers, no doubt. Well, they'll be disappointed. As soon as you and I finish our business, I'm going to kick that pervert the hell off my grounds, beard first."

Akers shook his head. "I hope you've got another bartender lined up. One thing that's hard to find on this island is a white bartender. One that isn't a booze hound, I mean. They're like rubies. Look, about the job, now."

"Yes. What's the trouble?"

"Oh, no trouble. We're in fine shape." Akers told him some construction ideas, savers of time and money, which Paperman couldn't understand. The contractor then chatted about his big Crab Cove development. His partner was in Fort Lauderdale, arranging a bank loan of a hundred thousand dollars to complete the job, because they had run a bit over the budget. Despite the momentary snag, they expected to clear two hundred thousand dollars profit apiece, in the end. During this meandering talk, Paperman discerned, or thought he did, that Akers was somehow asking him for another thousand dollars today. Since the contractor kept talking for a long while after that about Crab Cove and its huge profits, Paperman thought he might not have heard him right. Akers paused at an inconclusive point, and his long-jawed face creased in a carefree jocund smile. "Okay? Will that be all right with you?"

"Will what be all right?"

"Why, the thousand dollars," said Akers.

"What thousand? What about it? I'm afraid I got lost a little bit, there."

"Well, I thought I just explained to you, Mr. Paperman, that before the boys will go to work today, I need another thousand dollars."

Akers told most of his story again, calmly and pleasantly, but fitting in some new important facts. Due to running over the budget at Crab Cove, he had not met his payroll in three weeks. The leader of the workmen—"Emile, one hell of a nice guy and the best foreman on the island" —had told him that they had to be paid some money on account, before they would work again. "It's a reasonable request, and we certainly should grant it," Akers said.

Paperman was not a very acute businessman, and he knew it. But even he could sense that this was getting to be a peculiar conversation; that the contractor's cheerful plausible statements were a trifle off-key; that, in short, the situation contained either a dead rat, or one in rapidly failing health. But he lacked the instinct to handle this new mess. He used his snuffling, wheezing, and nose-blowing as a handy excuse to say nothing. There was a prolonged pause.

Akers spoke up with tolerant, kindly patience. "Well, look, why don't you give Chunky Collins a ring and ask him about this? He'll confirm all of it. Chunky's the best lawyer on this island. I'll leave you alone. You can ask him the most embarrassing questions, anything you want. I'll put those rooms up for you in three days if you'll let me have the thousand, and what's more I'll make that my total price. How's that? I'll give it to you in writing. Three thousand, no matter what it costs me, for the whole job. What could be fairer?"

"All right," Paperman said. "Let me call Collins."

"Want me to leave?"

"That was your suggestion."

Akers laughed, rubbed his bony chin, and after a moment got up and walked out.

Norman quickly leafed through the Amerigo phone book—a dusty green-brown pamphlet, seventeen small pages in all, a most ridiculous contrast to the vast Manhattan tome—and telephoned Tom Tilson. A maid answered. "I tink dey does be down by de pool. Wait, please."

Tilson's rheumy voice came on after a while. "Yes? Who is it? Talk fast, I'm dripping all over my rug."

Paperman hemmed, hawed, apologized, and then blurted out his problem. A considerable silence followed. He could hear the old man's labored breath. "Paperman, why the devil are you bothering me with this?" Tilson shouted at last. "Who told you to call me? I'm not in business here."

"I know that. I'm alone and new on this island. I thought you might talk straight to me. I don't know who else will."

"You're a fool to try to run a tropical hotel."

"That may be, but I'm in it now."

"You sure are. Don't give Tex Akers the thousand. Goodbye."

"Wait. Wait! Just a moment. I've got to get those rooms built, Mr. Tilson."

"Paperman, you asked me a question and I answered you."

"Yes, and I'm grateful. Can't you tell me why?"

"Sure I can. It's better to be out two thousand than three thousand. We never had this conversation, Paperman. If you say you talked to me I'll call you a liar."

Tilson hung up. Paperman opened the office door and saw Akers draped angularly over the desk, holding Lorna's palm. "And then you're going to have six children by this rich husband—"

"Dah de boss." She snatched her hand away, flashing her sexy ogle at Norman.

"Oh, hi." Akers straightened up smiling. "All set? Time's sure awasting."

Paperman beckoned him into the office, closed the door, and told Akers that he couldn't give him the money. The contractor looked utterly dumbstruck. "What did Chunky say that threw you off? Let's call him back."

"I didn't call Collins. I've been looking at my books. I don't have more money to give. Not till the job's done."

A relieved grin spread over Akers' face. "Oh, come on, why, your partner can get millions just by signing his name. He's been on the cover of *Time*."

"He's not my partner. He went on a note so that I could buy this place. I'm on my own here, and I'm a poor man. *You* call Collins and ask him."

The contractor's beaming look gave way to a cloudy, unfocused stare, and he went peculiarly red around the eyes. "You don't mean you want to call this job off? You can't mean that."

"Call it off? What are you talking about? I've already paid you half the price. Two thousand dollars! These were your terms. You say it'll take you three days to finish it. Put your men to work. Three days from now I'll pay you the rest."

The cloud passed from the contractor's face. "Well, okay," he said gaily. "Let me try to talk the boys into it." He went out, humming *Valencia* and snapping his fingers.

Norman shook his head, wheezed, and blew his nose, trying to collect his thoughts. Urgently, he had to drive that depraved Wagner youth off the grounds before he committed some new hotel-emptying outrage. A lad whose appetite spanned Kinjan spinsters in their forties and pregnant chambermaids was hardly to be trusted alone with anything that moved. He went out to the bar, rehearsing in his mind hard short sentences of dismissal.

Church sat on the high stool at the bar, Thor's favorite spot for napping, posting figures from dining-room and bar checks into a large black ledger. Still barefoot, he now wore a red-and-white barred sailor's shirt and white clam diggers. His dark beard was neatly trimmed, his full hair well brushed. Bronzed, lean, tall, his face at once sensitive and strong, he was a picture of the young virile American seafarer, the charmer out of Melville and London, the idol of the yachting magazines. He was a Billy Budd unhanged. Island people and guests were having their "elevenses" all through the bar and on the beach. Here was a scene of tranquil, efficient prosperity, and presiding over it a lewd monster. But who would make drinks, Norman thought, if he fired the monster?

"Church," he said.

The bartender looked up with a bashful grin. "Oh, hello, sir. Mrs. Tramm showed me how this system works. I really think I can get the posting done every morning, sir, before the big lunch business starts."

"Church," Paperman said again, and paused. Guests in the bar were watching him, and leaning their heads together to whisper.

"Yes, sir?" Church said.

"Ah—Church, you and I must have a serious talk today. Not a pleasant talk."

Church blushed like a girl, hung his head, and gave Paperman a faint wistful smile. "I know, sir." His voice was soft and melancholy. "I couldn't be more sorry."

"I'll be back. I'll be back very soon," Paperman said as fiercely as possible, and he hurried out of the hotel and down to the pier, to talk to Gilbert about taking over the bar.

The wind had already shifted sharply, for the garbage boat was alongside again, Anatone was coupling up the hose, and there was no smell at all. Nevertheless Paperman yearned to call off Anatone, who seemed to be delivering tankloads of water at the approximate price of a medium Chablis. But the sky was a cloudless hard blue; the sun burned high and roasting; faucets and showers and toilets were draining the cistern fast. It was a trap. He had to endure. If it cost him three thousand dollars for water before the Guadeloupe barge returned, he had to pay, and pay, and smile.

The gondola approached with several passengers. The man at the oars had his back to Paperman. When he jumped on the pier with the rope, Norman was astounded to see, under the ribbons and the straw, a toothless smile and crossed eyes. "Good morning, fuh. Dat fun real hot today. —Thiff way, folkf."

"Virgil!"

"Yeffuh?"

"What are you doing? Where's Gilbert?"

"Gilbert he did tell me to fay he quit, fuh. Forry, fuh."

"Quit? Why?"

Virgil munched, smiling in Paperman's direction but looking out to sea. "Fuh, I can work day and night."

"No, no. I can't let you work two shifts. I have to talk to Gilbert. Take me ashore. Where is he?"

"Fuh, I favin' money to buy teef. I'll work both fiffs. I be glad to."

Virgil's talk—like Old English printing, all *f*'s for *s*'s—made Paperman's head ache. The news about Gilbert was a reeling blow. He now heard the thudding of many feet, and turned to see Akers and his gang of workers marching toward the pier.

Akers looked less cheerful than usual, but he spoke buoyantly enough. "Hi, Mr. Paperman. The fellows won't play. I kind of thought they wouldn't."

"What? I don't understand. What about the job?"

"I sure wish you could give me that thousand. We can still get a good long afternoon out of them."

Virgil rowed away toward the landing, where more passengers waited; and at the same moment, the old boat for Akers' workmen came wallowing around the stern of the garbage hauler.

This apparition, which proved that the construction gang was actually leaving, sent Paperman into a sudden nervous frenzy.

"What the HELL!" he bawled at Akers. "What's going on here? What kind of contractor are you? You took my money. You knocked out my wall! My hotel is open to the winds, and it's piled to the roof with building materials. You *can't* walk off now. People don't do such things."

"Look, I want to get to work, sir. I told you that. Just give me that thousand, and those rooms will spring up like mushrooms after a rain."

The men were clambering aboard the boat in a drove, exchanging gay jokes. "Mushrooms! Ha! Sure! I've heard about those mushrooms before. You're just the old mushroom man, aren't you, Akers?" Paperman capered in a full circle, chanting, "Oh, do you know the mushroom man, the mushroom man, the mushroom man!"

Akers watched this performance with mild surprise. "Well, I realize you've had a rough morning. Be seeing you." He followed his men aboard, still smiling.

"Wait, for God's sake! When are you coming back? What about the job? *What about that wall?*"

"Gosh, I just hope you'll think it over. It's up to you. I can still bring 'em back after lunch." The motor roared up, and he shouted as the boat pulled away, "You can reach me any time. Just call Chunky Collins."

A dreadful suspicion struck Paperman. He scurried back to the office, telephoned the Amerigo Supply Company, and asked them whether Akers had paid for the materials delivered to the Gull Reef Club. The answer was, he had not. Akers had been five thousand dollars in arrears at the supply yard, and now his balance due was three thousand. "But we are not worried, Mr. Paper-mon," said the owner, Moses Llewellyn, a brother of the banker. "We know de gentleman what was on de cover of *Time* good for de money. We bill you de end of de mont'."

Paperman dropped his head on his arms, in the hot inky-smelling office, and allowed himself one minute of teeth-grinding, enraged despair. Then he called up the lawyer Collins, but the secretary advised him that Collins was at Hogan's Fancy. Norman next tried to telephone him there; but now something had happened to the operator. He jiggled and jiggled the hook, to no avail. Iris had warned him about this. The vanishing operator was a continuing hazard of communications in Amerigo. There was no telling what was wrong, or how long it might be before the operator came on the line. She might be chatting with her boy friend; she might have blown a fuse in her switchboard; she might be handling many calls; she might be dozing; she might be out having a beer. Many a time, Iris had gone across in the gondola and driven her car to see the person she wanted to talk to, sometimes far back in the mountains, instead of waiting for the operator to answer. This was standard practice, Iris said, and on the whole it saved time and nerve tissue.

So Norman, after a few more angry jiggles, trudged to the pier and went over in the gondola. Let Virgil work the day shift for the time being, he thought. He had more urgent things to straighten out before he could even attend to such matters as brushing his teeth, shaving, changing out of last night's clothes, and eating something.

2

Collins was on the terrace of his guest house, with a young couple sufficiently characterized by cameras, cloth airline bags, brightly horrible shirts and shorts, scorching new sunburn streaks on pallid faces and thighs, and expressions of fatigued dogged gaiety. "Well, speak of the devil!" exclaimed the lawyer. "Norman Paperman, meet the Jensens from Milwaukee. I've been telling them about the Broadway producer who just bought the Gull Reef Club, and here you come strolling along."

The girl said in an eager contralto rush of words, "You see, we're thinking of buying Hogan's Fancy. Barry paints, and I'm a dancer. We're wild to come here to live. Why, it's Paradise. We thought we could run this sweet little guest house, and I could organize dance classes, and Barry could have a chance to devote himself to his painting. We adore the island. We're both very fond of Negroes."

Jensen said, "In Milwaukee I manage the used-car lot of my father's Dodge agency. It's not too inspiring."

"Yes, well, I'd love to talk to you about it," Paperman said. "I happen to have this very urgent business with Mr. Collins. Maybe you could drop over for a cocktail later."

The Jensens soon left, juggling their impedimenta and exclaiming at the beauty of the Hogan's Fancy foliage. Paperman assailed Collins with a bitter account of Akers' misdeeds. Collins heard him out, his big jaw jutting in a faint, rather silly smile.

"You know, none of this is new to me," he said. "Tex phoned me six times this morning. He was very concerned. Tex is a real sweetheart, he's one of these fellows you can't help liking and he always seems cheerful, but things eat at him *in here*." Collins tapped his chest. "You'd think he hadn't a care in the world, but Tex has an ulcer, and very high blood pressure."

"You mean it isn't news to you," Paperman said, "that he used my two thousand dollars to pay off some of his old debts? Don't you know he can go to jail for that?"

Collins chuckled. "Oh, that's just Moses Llewellyn for you. He's a pill. Tex *said* the two thousand was for your materials. Moses claimed he was applying it on Tex's balance. Once Tex's partner gets the bank loan, it'll all straighten out."

"Why is he getting a loan in Fort Lauderdale, anyway? Why doesn't he borrow money here, the way I did?"

Collins blinked, and after a moment said, "Well, the bank here does hold the mortgage on Crab Cove. This is second-mortgage money. You see if you gave Tex that thousand, Norman—if I may call you that —he could keep his crew together for a week. It would tide him over this little cash bind he's in. Honestly, it would be so nice if you would. He likes you so much, he says you're a true gentleman. He told me that himself. What's the matter?"

Paperman had sunk his head in his hands again, overwhelmed by hopelessness. Now it appeared that unless he gave Akers the thousand dollars he was no gentleman. Business conversations on this island, he thought, were straight out of *Alice in Wonderland*; and his bank balance was shrinking with Wonderland speed; but that was really happening, that was no story.

"Collins," he said hoarsely, "can I have a beer? I'm a bit shaky."

"Right." Collins snapped his fingers and called, "How about two more beers, here, chop chop?"

"Yazzuh," called a voice that Paperman recognized. He straightened up and peered through the tangle of plants at the bar, where a white-coated figure moved. "Sebastian H. Christ," he said in a low, shaky voice, "this is the end. Collins, you've stolen my boatman."

"Gilbert? Why, how you talk," Collins laughed. "I've known Gilbert for years. He came to me today and said he'd quit the Club and wanted to try bartending. He's a real godsend. My bartender just left me, he was appointed assistant commissioner of public works. His uncle's the new commissioner."

"You stole him from me," said Paperman, "and I'm taking him back. I'm going to promote him to bartender myself."

"Why, I understand you have a real rip-snorter of a bartender." The lawyer's face assumed a roguish cast—droopy eyes and rosebud mouth— which was most unbecoming. "As a matter of fact I heard all about him and the three chambermaids. Heh heh. What a sketch! Somebody should have taken movies."

"Yazzuh." Gilbert set down the beers before them. He wore an ill-fitting white mess jacket, and black trousers. He gave Paperman a brief smile, his heavy lids almost closing. "Yazzuh, Mistuh Papuh. De pump okay?"

"Gilbert, I looked for you this morning to tell you I'm giving you the bartender job."

"I did tell Virgil I quit, Mistuh Papuh. Sorry, suh."

"That's how they are," Collins said in a low tone as Gilbert walked off. "A Kinjan is loyal. He hates to make a change. But once he makes it, that's it. You can't get him back with money or bayonets. Somehow you offended Gilbert. He loved the Club. Too bad." Collins heaved a deep sigh. "Well!" he went on, in a jolly change-of-subject tone. "How about it? Shall I ring Tex and tell him you're giving him the thousand? It would be an awfully decent gesture. It would solve a lot of problems for everybody."

Paperman set down his beer with an alarming clank on the glass-top table. "You can tell Tex Akers—" He arrested himself, took a long breath, paused, and said, "I'm new on this island. I'm sure there are other lawyers."

"Oh, yes, several."

"Well, you can tell Tex Akers that if he isn't on my grounds by eight tomorrow, with his whole crew, and hard at work, I'm starting a lawsuit against him. At nine!"

"As a matter of fact," Collins said, "Turnbull might be your man for that. He's handling several of the lawsuits against Tex now. He's sort of got the whole picture."

"Turnbull? Isn't Turnbull your partner?"

"That's him. He's the best lawyer on the island. At least that's what I always say," Collins simpered.

Paperman passed a hand over his moist brow. "You mean—Collins, you mean the same firm will take *both* sides of a lawsuit on this god-damned preposterous insane son-of-a-bitching island?"

"Well, it may seem odd," Collins said with an unoffended little laugh, "but you see the custom here is for a continental lawyer—that's what we call whites from the States, continentals—to have a local lawyer share his office. That's what we call the natives, locals. We use the same girl, and that's about all. I do think Turnbull's your man for suing Tex."

"Look, what I *want* is to get the rooms built."

"Tex appreciates that. But the boys have already worked three whole weeks without pay. How's that for loyalty? These Kinjans are marvellous people."

"Well, why did their loyalty break down now? This morning?"

"Ah, you see, they know that your partner is a rich man who was on the cover of *Time*. Jungle drums."

"But you know better than that! You know what my deal is with Atlas. Why don't you tell them?"

Collins' eyes popped, and he smiled and winked with profound cunning. "Oh, everybody understands that a man like Mr. Atlas has his little ways of doing things."

Paperman stared at the lawyer, on whose oversized face the grin of cunning was fixed as though a movie projector had stopped. A new gulf of dismay was opening here. If the Kinjans believed that he was just a front for Atlas, then as long as he operated Gull Reef he would be charged for everything like a New York millionaire. Contemplating the wise petrified grin on the lawyer's face, Paperman realized that he could only dispel this false idea—at least in the mind of Collins—by going bankrupt. Even this would probably be dismissed as a shrewd New York maneuver. He could shoot himself; Collins would figure that his suicide was a deep Atlas tax gimmick.

Paperman got to his feet wearily. "Just as a matter of curiosity, how many lawsuits are there against Akers right now?"

"Only four plaintiffs have really filed. Tex will clean all those up in one afternoon, once he gets his loan. Tex is the best builder on the island. He just got a little overextended. Shall I tell him you're giving him the thousand?"

"No. No, I'm not. No, tell him no. And tell him that if I do sue, I'll bring down a New York lawyer who'll mangle him."

"Okay, I'll tell him. How about another beer?"

Paperman shook his head, and walked to the bar, where Gilbert was dropping cherries in three planter's punches. "Gilbert, come back to Gull Reef. I need you."

The Negro kept his eyes down. "Nozzuh."

"Why not? You know the Club is your place. You belong there, not here."

The brief, smoky spark that Paperman had seen once or twice before appeared in Gilbert's eyes. "Mistuh Papuh, you did want de white boy wit de beard."

3

Paperman returned to his hotel office and sent for Church. The air in the office was like escaped steam from a boiler. Dimly he recalled his talk with Thor, aeons ago—two days, in calendar time—about air-conditioning this space.

"Sir?" Church stood in the doorway—tanned, handsome, smiling, modest, young.

"Church, close the door. Turn on the fan."

Church obeyed and leaned against the wall, hands clasped behind him, eyes downcast.

Unluckily for the harsh tone that Paperman wanted to use, the bartender's humble stance before him brought to his mind another scene. In much this way he had stood before the desk of Jay Frankel, a press agent now long dead, his first Broadway employer. Jay had given him hell for seducing an office girl. She had been a notorious roundheels, and Jay himself had had a turn with her. It wasn't at all the same thing as a pregnant Negro chambermaid. Still, Norman felt that half his moral indignation at Church Wagner might in fact be envy of his young energy. He could remember well how, nearly three decades ago, he had listened to the fat old press agent's reproaches with the mock repentance and inner amusement of a hot lad of twenty. The sins of youth looked marvellously different, he thought, depending on whether you were before or behind the desk. "Church," he barked, or tried to bark, "if I had talked to you half an hour ago I'd have fired you. I'm still considering it. I hope you realize that at the moment you'd find it hard to get another job anywhere in Amerigo, except maybe cleaning cesspools."

"Sir, please don't fire me. I really need this job. There won't be any more incidents." Church looked at him with wide pleading eyes.

"Won't there? How can I be sure?"

"Sir, I wish you'd let me explain. You see, Mr. Harmer only turned in one key. I went up to the room to look for the other one. Then, as it happened, Esmé was there, so—I mean, all I'm trying to stress is that I didn't plan anything, sir. It was actually an accident."

"An accident! What the hell do you mean? Did you trip over Esmé, knock her down, and land on her, copulating, by sheer bad luck? Don't you know yet that what you did was WRONG? Don't you know that much, Church?"

"Well, sir, I said it wouldn't happen again."

"It had better not. I'm not going to preach to you, your morals are no concern of mine, but by God when you're on my grounds your conduct is. When you step off that boat in the morning from now on, you're a gelding, do you understand, Church? A eunuch! A capon! A steer! A castrato!"

"Yes, sir," said Church, his white teeth flashing most charmingly in his black beard.

"I'm not fooling. One more incident and you're *out!*"

"Sir, I promise."

"All right. Now I'm going to my cottage." Paperman sneezed and blew his nose, and picked up a letter from Henny lying on the desk. "Tell Sheila to send over some bacon, scrambled eggs, toast, and coffee."

"Right away, sir."

"And two boxes of Kleenex."

"Kleenex. Yes, sir."

A shave and a bath, as always, improved Paperman's spirits. When dirty or unsightly, he was miserable as a tarred cat. He ate his breakfast propped on cushions on his bed, in a gold-crusted red kimono bought in Hassim's shop. He could hear the snorting of the garbage craft as it came and went. Each trip was costing him fifty dollars, but he was past caring, so long as the odor did not reach his hotel or his nose; though in truth he might not have been able to smell it by now. His respiratory system was totally clogged. Before he finished his breakfast a sizable pile of waste wet Kleenex lay on the floor beside the bed, and he was adding a used tissue every minute or two.

He read Henny's letter over the coffee. It sounded exactly like her: quick, acid, affectionate to him and also derisory, and above all angry at doctors and disgusted with New York and with her bad luck. She still had the pain off and on. She had now consulted three specialists. Shingles, allergy, "transparent gallstones," and pure nervous im-

agination were the chief current guesses, and she was undergoing a
series of uncomfortable tests.

*Honestly [she wrote], if you did some of the things to me that
these perfectly strange men have been doing, I'd punch you right
in the nose. Just because they wear white coats and rubber gloves
and smell like pickled frogs, these nasty gropers think they can do
anything to a woman. I'm getting damned tired of it. Beyond a
certain point I'd rather be dead than undignified. They've got until December 17th. That's when Hazel's vacation begins. I've made
plane reservations and Hazel and I are coming down, no matter
what I've got.*

*Hazel is all hot for coming. Do you know that that Cohn charac-
ter came up here again? He took Hazel out a couple of nights ago.
We haven't heard from him since. I hope you realize that this is
the first time in God knows how long that she's made a date with
anybody except the Sending.*

*Our little girl was at great pains, before the date and after it,
to explain to me that she's merely curious about Cohn, that he
seems to her as old as you do, and that she likes his sense of humor
because it's like yours. In fact if I recall her words she said at one
point, "He's really a sort of father substitute to me, except that
what he does is important and interesting." I thought you might
like that. Anyway it's strange the way he keeps zipping in and out
of the Caribbean and in your leisure time you might try to find out
something about him. With our luck he's got to be at least a card-
sharp, a smuggler, or a Soviet saboteur.*

*How about writing me a letter, mine host, describing what you
do with your leisure time? I have vivid visions, and they make me
furious. I see you lounging at your ease on that white sand beach
in the sun, charming the lady guests, especially any young and
pretty ones, with that sparkling line of yours. I see you dancing
with them on the terrace in the moonlight, and so forth—lots of
and so forth—just doing your duty as mine host, of course. Well,
mine host is going to get his hospitable ass broken when I come
down there, if there's been the slightest hint of an offside play. You*

*may as well know that I've got a spy in Janet West—Mrs. Tramm,
as she calls herself. She wrote me a nice letter about the lobby materials, and one thing and another, and I'm answering her when
I finish this. If that cutie pie Tex Akers has gotten started, perhaps you can have him do a few things before I get down there.*

Henny listed some decorating details, the irony of which made Norman wince. She ended with a rather sweet paragraph about how she
missed him, and added,

*—So, mine host, have fun in Paradise. But not too much fun,
damn your eyes, until I get there. I'm feeling lonesome, abused,
and mean. In fact very much my old self.*

Love,
Henny

P. S. *How far are you into* Ulysses?

Norman wrinkled his face at the sly postscript. Like many of his
Broadway friends he was a resolute reader of prestigious literature.
His boast to his friends had been that in the Caribbean, with all his
leisure as "mine host," he would at last be able to read Joyce's difficult
masterwork. But not only did the book lie untouched in a suitcase;
since his arrival, Norman had not yet looked at a magazine or a news-
paper.

He called the office with his bedside telephone. "Lorna, I'm going to
have a nap. Don't disturb me now unless it's absolutely urgent."

"No, suh. I do believe you does be too horossed. You needs a good
rest."

He set aside the breakfast tray, snuggled down among the pillows,
put all his worries out of his mind—Akers, money, wall, water, bartender, and the rest—and fell asleep. For once nobody and nothing
woke him. He slept deeply, peacefully, and long. He opened his eyes,
calmed and refreshed, and saw the sun slanting low through the bougainvillea. With a loose, lazy motion he glanced at his watch. Quarter
to five. Time to be "mine host" at the bar, and he felt very much in
the mood for that. He rolled over, yawning and stretching luxuriously,
and saw on the floor by the bed what appeared to be a black sweater. He
didn't remember dropping a black sweater there, but all his recollec-

173

tions were confused these days. He absently reached down to pick it up, but it wasn't a sweater. Something black came up in his hands, leaving most of the pile on the floor.

In his sleepy, stupid state it took him a second or two to understand that he was holding several sheets of wet Kleenex swarming with ants. By the time he realized this, and threw the tissues away with a strangled shriek, it was too late. His right hand and arm were acrawl with ants to his shoulder.

This would have disgusted anybody. But fastidiousness was Norman's chief trait. To find himself covered with creeping stinging black things like this gave him perhaps the single most horrible moment of his forty-nine years. He rushed to the bathroom, tearing off the kimono, making animal screams of revulsion; plunged into the shower and turned on both faucets full force. Water gushed on him, washing ants in streams down his twitching frame. He got them all off. Naked, dripping, he snatched up the aerosol insect spray bomb in the bathroom and forced himself to go back to that pullulating black pile.

There it was, loathsomely alive, loathsomely moving; and feeding it, he now perceived, was a black trail that crossed the floor, mounted a wall, and disappeared behind a water color of a laughing, dancing West Indian in carnival costume, beating a drum. He held his breath, tightened his lips in disgust, and blasted the insect spray at the heart of the vile heap.

What occurred next was not to be believed, but he saw it happen. It was as though he had dropped a stone in a pool, except that the stone was the spray, and the pool was the ants. Instead of wilting and dying, the ants came boiling away from the heap in black concentric widening rings. The sight was so blood-freezing, and it happened so fast, that the two outermost rings washed over Norman's bare feet before he knew what was happening. The crawling and stinging mounted speedily toward his knees.

Norman Paperman went sincerely insane. Shrieking, howling, buck-naked, he galloped out of the cottage and scrambled down the path to the sea, unaware of anything except the ants climbing and biting now up his thighs to his very crotch. He fell headlong into the water, bellowing "Aagh! Aagh!" not in the least conscious that he was making the sounds of a man being butchered. Hysterically he rubbed and washed himself, splashing and howling, keeping on the move to leave the drowning ants behind.

What brought him to himself was Meadows, standing at the water's edge and barking almost as wildly as he was yelling. Iris came running down the path from her cottage, in a green silk bathrobe that fluttered open on naked legs and pink underclothes. "My God, Norman," she called. "What is it? Are you all right? Do you want me to pull you out?"

"What? No, no, don't be silly, I'm fine," Paperman sobbed. "Just great. Just having a nice little dip. Go away, Iris."

"Norman, there's something wrong. I'm coming in after you." She began to undo the robe.

"No, Iris, *no.* For Christ's sake, will you go away? I don't have a stitch on. I'm bare as a baboon."

Iris paused, her hands on her belt, staring out at him. He was in shallow water. He sank down in embarrassment to his chin. "Really? Why, Norman, what on earth? Birthday suit in broad daylight? Have you dropped your marbles, dear? And what was all that hideous screaming?"

Norman felt his heart beating much too hard and fast. "Iris, honey," he said faintly, "will you bring me a towel and a big slug of scotch, or any other booze you've got?"

"Baby, why don't I just bring you some trunks from your cottage?"

"No, no, whatever you do, don't go in my cottage. And don't ask questions, Iris. Just do as I say."

"Come on, Meadows."

She returned without the dog, carrying a hotel towel, a pink terry-cloth robe, and a square crystal glass of whiskey. "We're almost the same size," she said. "Here." She dropped the robe and towel on the pebbles and turned her back.

"Okay," he said in a few moments, having hastily dried himself and put on her scented robe. "Ye gods, I smell like Hassim, or something."

She faced him, holding out the glass. "You smell like me, and no cracks. It costs plenty to smell that way. You look real darling, I must say. Pink becomes you."

"Oh, shut up." He drank half the whiskey and sank to the beach. "Iris, Iris, I've had one bitch of an experience."

She sat beside him. "So I gather. Tell me."

He cradled his head on her soft lap, and recounted the misadventure of the ants. Then, he told her about Akers, Church, Gilbert, Collins, and the liquid gold that Anatone was delivering, tankload by tankload.

"I'd heard about Church," Iris said, absently stroking his hair. "But what I heard sounded very unlikely, I must say. The way I heard it—"

He leaped to his feet, dancing, and slapping at his legs. "Ants! Ants! Iris, get up! The beach is crawling with them! They're all over me! I feel them biting!"

He splashed into the water, holding the robe up almost to his middle, shouting, "Ugh! Ugh!"

Iris looked at her legs, and at the pebbles. She remained seated, slapping at her ankles. "Sweetie, your nerves are really shot. It's just the sand flies. They come out this time of day, when the wind's from the south."

"Sand flies? What are sand flies?"

"You poor innocent," Iris laughed, "don't you really know? They're the great guilty secret of the Caribbean. Sand flies, mi-mis, don't-see-ems, they've got many names. Tiny biting horrors. It's no problem, you just spray your legs with repellent. Gosh, I do it the way I wash my face. Morning, noon, and night."

"Ye gods. Are they that bad? I haven't noticed them before."

"Norman, sand-fly bites can build up to an allergic collapse. Some people are immune to them, and maybe you're one, but I've seen tourists carried aboard a plane in a stretcher from sand-fly bites."

"Sand flies, eh?" said Norman in a dolorous, hollow, defeated tone. "Sand flies."

"Oh, so what? In New York they have rats and roaches, dear, don't they? Not but what we have our own roaches. There's a Caribbean roach that can fight a cat to an easy draw."

"Iris," said Paperman, standing ankle deep in water, his shoulders sagging in the pink robe, "I believe I've made the biggest mistake in my life in buying this hotel. I may have made the biggest mistake any human being has ever made. I mean, on the scale on which I function. I'm not talking about, say, Hitler invading Russia. I haven't got that scope for my bad judgment. But within my modest limits I believe I can claim to have been perhaps the goddamnedest jerk in recorded history."

"Nonsense. One day soon you'll laugh at all these petty things. Go dress yourself real handsome, the way you do. You're taking me to a cocktail party at Government House."

"I'm what?"

"See?" she said, holding out a pretty leg in the rosy waning light. "That's a sand fly. There on my ankle."

"That tiny speck? Is it alive?"

"Ha!" She smeared a thumb on it. "Not any more. His Excellency is having a reception for some congressman or other, Norm. Congress always gets very concerned about American interests in the Caribbean, right after the first bad snowfall in Washington. I need an escort, and you're elected."

Paperman interposed objections, the chief of them being that he had to watch over the Club; but Iris said that on the contrary, he badly needed to get away from Gull Reef for an evening of fun. They might have dinner together and perhaps go to the movie. She started to climb the path to her cottage.

"Iris."

"Yes?"

"Come with me while I—while I look at those ants."

She smiled, approached him, and put a cool hand to his cheek. "Gad, you're squeamish. A month in the Caribbean will sure cure that."

They mounted his path together, a colorful pair, the woman in smooth green, the man in fuzzy pink. The sodden pile of Kleenex was no longer alive, no longer black, but rather speckled gray with uncountable dead ants. The rest were gone. The black trail up the wall was gone. Paperman pushed aside the picture which covered their point of entry, a crack in the plaster two inches long. "God, is this where those billions and billions of horrors came and went? Is it possible?"

"Certainly. They won't be back for a while," Iris said. "That's the main thing." She contemplated the pile with a wrinkled nose. "They like wet Kleenex. I'll have to remember that. Hey! Where are you?"

From behind the bathroom door Paperman's bare arm appeared, extending the pink bathrobe. "Here. Thanks for the help. Brother will pick you up in half an hour."

Iris's face twisted in a smile. "Well, well," she said, taking the robe. "That's good. Apparently the experience didn't have the usual effect on you."

"What experience?"

"Ants in your pants."

"I'm coming out," said Paperman.

"The hell you are," said Iris, slamming the bathroom door shut on him. "Half an hour."

4

When Norman came up with Iris in the long reception line on the Government House lawn, Governor Sanders blinked in glum surprise, then offered his lank yellow hand. "Hello, there. Glad you could get away. I understand you're having your troubles."

"That's why I dragged him off the Reef, Governor," said Iris.

"Mrs. Tramm, Mr. Paperman—Senator Finchley of Nebraska. Mr. Paperman owns the Gull Reef Club, Senator." Sanders pointed at the Club, visible over the low stone retaining wall. Norman and Iris had come late, and the Club lights were already on, reflecting white and yellow serpentines across the violet harbor.

"Ah yes," said the senator, a dapper little ruddy man, with a full head of white hair. "I've been wondering what that was. It looks like fairyland. Mrs. Tramm, I'm delighted." He sized up Iris with appetite. She wore black and a pearl choker, and her eyes had a wild sparkle. "Do you live in Amerigo?"

"Right now, yes."

"I have a feeling I've met you. You're not from Nebraska, are you?"

"As it happens, Senator, I was born in Omaha. My folks took me to San Diego when I was three."

"Now I know what's been missing in the state of Nebraska," said the senator, waggling his heavy eyebrows.

"Gosh, a whole live senator," Iris said as Paperman led her to the bar. "I had it wrong. We don't usually get senators till February. It must be damned cold in Washington. I'll have bourbon and water, please, Norm."

A chilly damp breeze was blowing up the white cloth of the long table arranged as a bar, showing the sawhorses underneath. The crowd at the table was two deep; it took Norman a while to get the drinks.

"Ah, thank you," Iris said. "The main job of my escort, dear, besides giving me some face as an honest woman, is to knock all drinks out of my hand after the second one. Cheers." She took a deep swallow.

"Are you kidding?"

"No, I'm not. I'm apt to get very ugly about it, too. Just slap me down, and if necessary, walk out on me. I'll come trotting along, using some dirty words you may not have heard." Paperman looked her in the eyes, still not certain she was serious. She said, "I mean it, Norm. Usually I'm all right. I know my limits. It's just that Government House sort of gives me the hoo-ha's."

"Well, it's an odd crowd," said Paperman, glancing around. There must have been two hundred people on the lawn, making a deafening volume of talk in the dim light of swaying paper lanterns. Most of them were Negroes, dressed in good current fashion, and the taste of the women for color enlivened the scene with many bright splashes. The clothes of some older Negroes were dated and dowdy. One bent grayhead wore a yellow pith helmet and a double-breasted blue suit. Iris told Norman that this man's family owned three thousand acres of the best land in Amerigo, including four white sand beaches, and that he lived in an unpainted two-room cinder-block house with a privy out in back. There were strange-looking whites, too, remnants of British colonial families; and here and there hill-crowd people, men in loud jackets and women in last year's New York styles.

A handsome, tall young Negro, in a silk Italian suit not much different from Norman's, went by holding drinks. "Hello dah, Mistuh Papuh."

"Hello," Norman said vaguely.

"You don' rekonize me?" The young man disclosed many gold teeth in a grin. "I'm Anatone. De fifteen loads all delivered. I did give Lorna de bill. She say you asleep."

"I'll take care of it."

Anatone glanced at the sky, and laughed. "Funny ting, de customers dey does get mad at me when dis happen. One fellow up on de hill las' year he ask me pump de water back out of his cistern." Anatone laughed very happily. "I do believe we fixin' to get a big rain tonight. De party finish inside."

Paperman looked upward in exasperation as Anatone walked off. Iris said, "I didn't want to spoil your evening, dear, but feel that wind? And there isn't a star in sight."

Paperman said, "You know what? I'll sue God."

Iris burst out laughing, and took his arm. "Let's get me another drink. Why aren't you drinking yours?"

"I am," said Paperman, a little nervous at the speed with which Iris had downed a large rich bourbon and water.

"I'll tell you," Iris said when Paperman brought her the drink, "let's go inside. Or does the sociology of a Government House lawn party interest you? If it does rain, the panic will be a nuisance. I react badly to being shoved and jostled by Kinjans."

"Okay."

"They mean no harm, they do it to each other and think nothing of it, but—" Iris led him through the crowd to the wide stairway into Government House. "I know a nook where we can drink in peace."

The first floor of the old stone building was thoroughly Americanized —white fluorescent lighting, soundproof partitions, rows of shiny steel cabinets, and even at this hour ringing telephones and one banging mimeograph—in strong contrast to the state rooms on the floor above. Here were grand salons full of gleaming old English furniture, their walls a-clutter with obsolete weapons, and faded prints of sea battles or West Indian scenery. The museum elegance of these antique rooms was crowned by a sweeping view, through tall French windows, of the Georgetown hills and the lamplit harbor. Iris showed Paperman the semicircular council chamber built in 1740, all dark mahogany and green leather, where the legislature still met. They passed down a long high mirrored hall.

"Here we are," Iris said, opening a tall door covered by a mirror.

"Speak of the devil!" said Chunky Collins, when Paperman came in. "Norman, do you always show up on cue like this?"

He and Tom Tilson sat with their drinks in a startling replica of the drawing room of an old London house. The arched creamy wood molding, the green damask on the walls, the spindly furniture, the Adam fireplace with a red light glowing behind glass coals, the china and silver pieces, the leather-bound books in rows, all blended in an illusion as instant and convincing as that of a fine Broadway stage set.

Tilson said, "Sit down. Hello, Iris. This is the only bearable spot in Government House, Paperman. The last British governor loathed the tropics, and he fixed up this room so he'd feel at home. He sat in here day and night, they say, drinking gin and bitters and nursing his gout, until the Yanks came."

"It's charming," Norman said.

The large smile on the large face of Collins faded to a mask of sorrow. "Oh, say, Norman, I want you to know how awful I feel about Tex Akers. It was inevitable, I know, but still it's a shock. What a tragedy! If you want me to line up some bids from other contractors—"

"What about Akers?" said Paperman, alarmed. "Did he kill himself?"

"Him? Oh, no! He blew the island. Said he was going to Fort Lauderdale for a week, but he'll never be back. When he sent off his family last Saturday I knew it was coming. That's always the sign."

Tilson said, "Let's see, that makes five contractors who have blown Kinja this year, doesn't it?"

"Four or five. They come and they go. I lose count," said Collins. "Tex was something special, though. He's gone bankrupt to the tune of about a hundred forty thousand."

Tilson said, "It had to happen, Crab Cove did him in."

"Strange," said Iris. "I thought those houses were lovely. I never know anything."

"They're fine houses," Tilson said. "Not at all the usual Kinja thing of crossed-up plumbing, and electric wires that buzz and spark and catch fire, and tiles that pop loose in a month. Still, they don't have jade walls and platinum plumbing. At seventy-five dollars a square foot, they should."

Collins sighed. "I'm afraid Tex was sort of a child about money. He'd already gone bankrupt twice, in Acapulco and Hawaii. He had long stories about dishonest partners."

"Oh, sure," Tilson said. "Who goes out to these Godforsaken fringe places to try and scratch a living? With the biggest boom of the century going on in the States? Freaks, frauds, fools, and failures." He gave Paperman a snarling grin. "Present company excluded, to be sure. I've lived on tropical islands most of my life. Ninety per cent of the mainlanders who come in are loonies of one kind or another, and they nearly all blow sooner or later—if they don't die of the booze."

"How about yourself?" Iris said.

Tilson held up a corded, freckled red hand. "International Nickel saw fit to post me in New Caledonia for twenty-one years. I got used to the tropics. At my age I'm not going back to snow and crowds. That's different."

Paperman was thinking, with a sick heart, of the demolished wall, of the great load of building materials, of his debts, of the ugly tarpaulin bellying across his lobby. "And there you were, only this morning," he said angrily to Collins, "urging me to give Akers another thousand dollars!"

"Well, you know, he was my client," said Collins, "I had to do what I could for him. He probably would have blown with your thousand. But then again, Tex was such a screwball that he might actually have gone ahead and put up your rooms. Of course, you did the only sensible thing, paying no attention to me."

"You were well-advised," said Tilson, with a straight face, "singularly well-advised."

"I figured you had your instructions from New York," said Collins. "That's why I didn't mind urging you. There are no flies on Mr. Atlas."

"I never talked to Atlas about it."

"Of course you didn't," said Collins, with the glassy grin that came on his face at these moments. "Of course not. Still, if I can size up people, and that's my business, you're much too softhearted to have turned Tex down yourself." There was a heavy rattling on the windows facing the lawn, and dismayed shouting and running outside. "Here we go. I said it would rain, Tom."

"We sure need it," said Tilson.

"I don't need it," said Paperman. "I've just bought seven hundred fifty dollars' worth of water."

The old man's jaw dropped and he stared at Paperman. "Are you serious? Seven-fifty? You could *float* your hotel for that."

"It does seem high," said Collins. "Was that Anatone?"

"Anatone and the garbage boat."

Collins nodded wisely, "Well, in a way it's an investment. You'll find Senator Pullman very cordial to you."

"Paperman, I have a suggestion for you," Tilson said. "Go home. Whatever you have invested here, forget it. Leave. Blow, like Akers. Pretend you had a nightmare and woke up. No matter how much you've already lost, you'll be money ahead, I promise you."

The tall door opened, and Governor Sanders came in with the senator from Nebraska. "Well," he said, waving his drink, "we do have a little company in here, Senator. But it's choice." He carefully shut the door.

"Let's leave, Norman." Iris stood. "Official business about to be transacted."

The senator trotted to her elbow, and eased her down on a couch beside him. "Not on your life, Iris. You and I are the only two Nebraskans in Amerigo. Don't you desert me."

Sanders slouched in an armchair and lit a cigarette. "What's this about that Crab Cove fellow, Chunky? Is it true?"

"Bye-bye," said Collins.

The governor shook his head. "That's the place we drove by after lunch, Senator. Those houses with the yellow pagoda roofs."

"Why, they looked excellent. I've never seen a better site than that cove."

"Well, I'm afraid the builders here suffer from a peculiar ailment," Sanders said, "the disappearing sickness."

"The defaulting trots," Tom Tilson said.

Senator Finchley smiled. "Big ideas and small bankrolls. It's the second wave in a growth area that gets rich. Somebody will pick up those unfinished houses cheap and make a bundle."

Sanders said to Collins, "True enough. I suppose the bank will auction the Cove right away for the mortgage money."

"As soon as we can get a judgment," Collins said. "I'll probably go to court on it tomorrow." He added to Paperman, "I represent the bank."

"I see," Paperman said. "Tell me, are you the undertaker here, too?"

Collins peered at him. "Pardon me? No, that's Hollis. Hollis, not Collins. My law practice is really all I can handle. But Ralph Hollis is one hell of a good undertaker."

Iris uttered a short gasping laugh, but when the men all looked at her, her face was solemn. "Norman, I think I'd like maybe one more small drink. Sort of half."

As Paperman hesitated, Governor Sanders said to him, "By the way, Crab Cove might interest your friend Atlas. He told me he intended to acquire substantial properties here."

"That's true," Paperman said, trying to talk past Iris's request for more liquor. "I'll write him about the auction."

"It's a golden opportunity," Collins said.

Tilson said, "Crab Cove has to soak up another hundred fifty thousand dollars before people can move in. If your friend's got that kind of money, and if he can send down a good builder to finish off, he can make a killing. Once those houses are finished they'll sell like hot cakes, and for twice what they'd cost in the States. That's what's so tempting about—" Tilson stopped talking, and glanced at the ceiling and at his watch. A low roar, like a far-off flight of many jet planes, was vibrating the air in the room.

Governor Sanders said in a flat calm voice to Norman, "Just sit where you are."

"What is it?"

"Earthquake," Iris said, her hands tightly clasped in her lap.

"First one in almost a year," said Sanders.

Now Paperman could see and feel the room trembling. A metal thing fell to the floor somewhere with a clang, and the glass chandelier tinkled wildly.

"How bad do they get?" said the senator, raising his voice above the swelling sound and holding the arm of the couch, but looking unruffled.

Tom Tilson replied, "Not bad here, usually. Nothing like the South Pacific."

Collins said, "I don't know, this one's going on a long time."

A harder tremor came, and a loud vibrating rumble. Paperman saw a pink-and-gold china vase topple, roll off a table, and break in pieces.

The jerking of his chair was nauseating, and it took will power not to get up and run outside. All at once Collins dived under a table near his chair, shouting over the harsh scary noise, "Better take cover, Iris! A doorway is good!"

The sound lessened and stopped; so did the unpleasant motion.

"It's over," Iris said, in the moment of total quiet that followed.

"I timed that one," Tilson said. "Fourteen seconds."

A hubbub arose beyond the closed doors. The lawyer came out from under the table, dusting his knees. "Safety first," he said.

"That stirred up the party, Senator," Sanders said. "I'm afraid we'll have to join them."

"Fun, wasn't it?" the senator said to Iris. "I once was in a real bad one in Hawaii. Some houses fell down. See you later." He went out with the governor and Collins, who said that quakes frightened his wife, and he'd better find her.

Tom Tilson leaned on his stick to get himself out of his chair. "That's the other thing about the tropics, Paperman. The Temperate Zone is a fake, you know. Go to the arctic or the tropics if you want to find out what kind of planet the Lord has put you on. It can be damned inhospitable."

Paperman said in a shakier voice than he intended, "This island is still the most beautiful place I've ever seen."

"Nobody says it isn't pretty," said Tilson. "I said it was inhospitable. It's also unpredictable. You think you're braced for the very worst that can happen, but sooner or later the island throws a total surprise at you. I've seen it happen too often, Paperman, and I'm just telling you."

"Well, I'm not blowing," said Paperman, "come earthquakes, hurricanes, or anything else that Kinja can produce."

Tilson looked at him through almost closed eyes, his red withered face tilted far back, his stringy chin thrust out. "Well, all right. I'm a hermit. Mrs. Tilson and I give one party every year, at Christmas time. Two hundred guests, champagne, caviar, chateaubriands at midnight for everybody. My house is too small for that. I've been giving it at the Francis Drake for years. Can you handle it at Gull Reef? I pay twenty-five bucks a head, that's five thousand dollars. I expect the very best of everything, and I'm a fearful bastard to deal with."

"I'm willing to try it," said Paperman, with a startled glance at Iris.

"You've got it," said Tilson. He hobbled to the door, and turned. "These tremors seldom come one at a time. You might get shaken up once or twice more this week. A real big one can produce a tidal wave. That might wash out all your problems. Check your flood insurance."

Iris said as soon as he left, "Norman, if you do the Tilson party right, you're *in*. It's the event of the island. I want another drink fast, and no arguments. Earthquakes are special. One more for the earthquake."

Paperman said uneasily, following her down the mirrored hall, "The bar's probably closed by now."

"In that case," Iris said, "there's always His Excellency's private stock."

The guests thronging through the state rooms were still laughing and exclaiming over the downpour and the quake. Many of them milled around a buffet table in the largest room, where Governor Sanders stood in an arch of the French windows, arms folded, gloomily looking out at the rain. Iris made straight for him. "Where's the bar tonight, Governor? Why not in the usual corner?"

"They closed it outside when the rain came, Iris. It was sort of late. Have something to eat."

"No thank you. I guess my credit with Terence is still good for a drink." She pushed away through the crowd.

"How many has she had?" said Sanders to Paperman.

"Two."

The governor made a wry face. "Iris shouldn't have more."

"So she told me."

Norman caught up with her in a dark narrow hallway, between walls hung with photographs, swords, and guns. "Where to now?"

"The pantry. Terence is my pal."

"Iris, I'm hungry. Let's get another drink when we have dinner. Where shall we go?"

She glowered at him. "Lay off. I'm perfectly fine, and I mean to have another drink free of charge on this f—— government before I leave." Paperman blinked at the foul word. She laughed at him and turned away. He caught her arm. "Let go of me, Norman!"

"Iris, I'm leaving now. You can stay or you can come with me, but I'm going."

She smiled, her eyes widening in a bright vicious look. "Run along, Normy, and good riddance."

Paperman had nothing to go on except Iris's own instructions to him. "Okay, so long." He walked down the hallway without looking back, into the center hall and out through the back entrance to the parking space. Rain was falling, but not heavily. He dashed to the Land Rover, started it up, and as he backed and turned around he saw her at the head of the stairway, waving. He stopped.

"You really were going to do it, weren't you?" she said, clambering into the machine. "You really were going to leave me at that disgusting brawl."

"Order from the boss," he said.

She switched her skirt angrily around her thighs. "Well, it's no more than I should have expected from a Jew. I've never known a Jew who had any manners."

"Where would you like to have dinner?"

"I'm not hungry. The food stinks everywhere on this f—— island. It's best at the Reef but I've had my bellyful of your stupid problems there, do you mind? If we eat in the patio of the Francis Drake, you can see your f—— place go up in flames, or whatever's going to happen next. There's bound to be something."

"Francis Drake." He started the Rover down the road in its snorting jerky way.

"Why in the name of your God of Moses don't you get a car," she said, "instead of this epileptic fit on wheels?"

Paperman looked straight ahead and said nothing. During the next ten minutes, as they drove through the slanting rain, Iris kept up an incoherent tirade against Jews, in a strident voice, her arms crossed, her dilated eyes fixed on him, unpleasant smiles writhing her mouth. At last, hoping to turn her off, Paperman said, "What makes you think I'm a Jew? I'm on your side. I think the Jews are taking over America, and it's a damn shame, because they're so feeble and incompetent."

"Very funny, but I happen to be serious. I can't stand Jews, I never was involved with one that I wasn't sorry afterward, and I speak with authority because Herb Tramm was one. You know, all this liberal talk is the bunk. Nobody can stand Jews. Even colored people can't stand them. You watch, people are going to stop coming to Gull Reef just because a Jew's got it."

"Okay, Iris, please shut up," said Paperman with a yawn.

"Don't tell me to shut up, you weak effeminate Jew. Scared to death by a few ants. I can probably fight you and beat you."

She said nothing more until they were seated in the patio of the Francis Drake under a striped canvas awning, having their first glass of wine with the shrimps. She drained the glass in a gulp, and then looked at him with an abashed grin, her eyes sad and friendly. "Sorry."

"Okay."

"Why didn't you throw me out of the car?"

"Well, as you pointed out, you can probably fight me. And anyway, a peeved woman is nothing new to me. I've logged about a hundred thousand hours, and I hold an instructor's license."

Iris laughed. "Henny can't be that bad. She *can't* be."

"Henny doesn't go on about the Jews, of course. And I must say she usually gets more provocation."

"Well, if it's any comfort to you, you ain't seen nuthin'. I hope you never do see me when I'm bad."

They ate in silence for a while.

"It's not my business, Iris," he said, "but since the stuff is rough on you, how about A.A.?"

Iris gnawed her lip, looking across the water at the lights of the Reef, misty in the rain. "No good. A.A. backs up to a religious idea, Norm. That lets me out. If I actually became convinced there was an intelligent God watching my antics, I'd probably cut my throat. Just to get back my privacy. It's an unbearable thought." She drank more wine. "My abiding comfort, honey, is that I know I mean no more to the universe than one of those dead ants in your wet Kleenex."

The food at the Francis Drake was not good—the meat tough and dry, the vegetables overcooked, the layer cake greasy. Paperman remarked on this, and Iris told him that he was fortunate in his cook, Sheila; the Reef offered the only tolerable food on the island. When they were having coffee, Iris patted a napkin to her mouth, and tossed it on the table. "Look, I've got to say this, and then let's forget it. I don't like anybody much, myself included, but I have a partiality for Jews, if anything.

Maybe you've noticed that. When I get ugly I say or do the worst possible thing. But I skirt an edge. If I really know I can't get away with it,
I usually don't say it. I thought you'd put up with me, and you did. Why
didn't you get angry?"

"Good question," said Norman, and he thought for a moment. "I'll
tell you a story. Way back when I was working for Loyalist Spain, before I met Henny, there was this Vermont girl in the crowd, very radical and very Gentile, which to me at that time was a tough combination
to beat. She was also not bad looking, though sort of loose-boned and
rangy, and with a wide mouth. Anyway this thing got hot and heavy
in a week or so. She was resisting a bit to prolong the enjoyment. It
was all sharply delicious, the way everything was then. Well, late one
night after going to a show, we were having coffee and cake in the
automat on Fifty-seventh Street. I was just talking at random, and I said,
'This afternoon I was to a meeting at Joe's house,' something like that.
She suddenly turned on me. 'Norman, please don't EVER say *was to*
again. You always do. It's a New York expression, and a Jewish one at
that.' I went on talking and kidding and finally took her home. I never
saw her again. What she said didn't amount to much. But you see, she
meant it." Iris nodded, looking down at her clasped hands. "How long
has it been pouring now?" Norman said, glancing up at the awning,
which sagged under the beating rain. "Two straight hours?"

"At least," said Iris. "You're not going to have to buy any more water
or chase the Guadeloupe barge for a while. Not if this keeps up."

He said, "I'm trying to decide whether to cross over in this mess
and see if the quake did anything to Paperman's Fancy, or just let it go
hang."

Iris laughed. "Paperman's Fancy is good. Let it go hang. The quake
did nothing, I assure you. Take me to the movie."

5

The narrow, dingy little marquee on upper Prince of Wales Street read
Teen-Age Corpse Eaters, but Iris assured Norman that that was the big
weekend attraction, the only title the manager ever bothered to put up

on the marquee. "The weekend is always a horror thing, or some ancient Western," she said, "or one of those Italian jobs, with thousands of Romans hacking up thousands of Christians, and raping squadrons of naked slave girls. The Kinjans like that. Tonight's an old Cary Grant."

"How did we rate the passes?" Norman said as they walked into the chilled, grimy green hall full of rows of splintery wooden seats. The little Puerto Rican manager in the lobby had waved them past the ticket taker with a bow and a sad smile.

"Oh, they know me. In my decline I did a few horror movies. The *Daughter of Dracula* is still a great favorite in Kinja. They keep reviving it."

"Really? I missed that."

"Oh, it's a honey. I'm a playful lovely girl in an old castle in the Dolomites, see?" Iris said. "Just the prettiest, sweetest young thing. Well, in due time I turn into a big bat before your eyes, and I proceed to drink the blood of a horse—what are you giggling at? It's God's truth. That's the big scene. A cheer always goes up here when the horse collapses, all pumped dry."

"You're making up every word of this," Norman said, laughing hard despite the way the slats of the wooden seat were pinching him.

"I wish I were. I'd give anything if I could buy up that negative. A stag movie is nothing in comparison. It's a favorite on TV back home, too. My silly face, the way I looked nearly twenty years ago, all fixed up with fangs and bat ears, and dripping horse blood. That's how a new generation of Americans knows me. I may have some trouble making a comeback as Candida."

The movie began after about a half hour or so of short films extolling beers, deodorants, cigarettes, whiskeys, and hair dyes. The film kept going out of focus at odd times, and turning into a sliding gray smear for a minute or two; the air-conditioning blew on Norm like a strong winter wind; the wooden seat hurt his rear abominably; but even apart from these distractions, he found the film hard to follow. It was a suspense movie, with some humor, a dramatic death, and two or three fairly passionate love scenes. During the death, the Kinjans roared with laughter. They sat respectfully silent through the comedy, and helped out the sound track of the love scenes with whistles, shrieks, hoots, giggles, and the loud sucking noises of a mule's hoofs in thick mud. "How can you stand this?" he murmured to Iris.

"Stand what? Oh, the audience. I don't even notice it any more."

In time Norman stopped noticing it too. The picture ended with a chase through Times Square at night—Broadway theatres, restaurants, night clubs, all his old haunts. Coming outside afterward was a shock. The rain had stopped. Damp, very hot air rolled through the opened steel doors of the chill theatre. The low shops and plaster arcades of Prince of Wales Street, in the dim yellow light and the steamy heat, seemed grotesquely foreign.

"Iris," he said, "you know something? We're a long way from home."

"Yes, darling. A long, long way."

The few whites in the audience—one or two hill-crowd couples, and some bearded vagabonds like Church Wagner in shorts and water-buffalo sandals, with their young slatternly wives or wenches—looked cross and sleepy, but the crowd of young Negroes was full of laughter, gaiety, and loud chaffing. The girls wore demure cotton frocks and their hair was carefully groomed; the boys, in short-sleeved shirts and tapering slacks, seemed bursting with good spirits. Norman could not understand their Calypso chatter at all, though it was presumably English; but he was struck by the good cheer of these Kinjans, nearly all of whom were not brown or yellow, but black, and strikingly handsome.

He said in the car, "What's the difference between the Kinjans and the mainland Negroes? Why are they so much more attractive?"

She looked at him with head aslant, eyes half-closed, her hand restlessly fingering her pearl choker. "Oh, you've decided that? Well, they're exactly the same people. Here it's their island, that's all, there's no place they can't get in, and the white man lives in peace on their sufferance. It makes a difference. Back to Paperman's Fancy, dear—my doggie wants his bone. I hope you've enjoyed your outing."

"It's saved me," Norman said. "The news about Akers was worse than the earthquake. I'm all right now. I'll manage."

The quake had caused no damage, and the rain had raised the water level in the cistern by three feet, Church reported. Some guests had not even noticed the tremor, and the rest had taken it as a lark. The bar was full of people, so was the dance floor. Passing through the lobby, Paperman slipped behind the tarpaulin for a moment, and contemplated the moonlight glinting on toilet stools, window glass, and the brass knobs of stacked doors. Through the tarpaulin he could hear the carefree thumping of the steel band. He walked out through the enormous moonlit hole in his hotel and went to bed.

chapter seven

The Quake

I

The second earthquake came a week later. It was not much more severe than the first. It occurred about half-past ten in the morning, when most of the guests were sailing, swimming, or playing on the beach, so no alarm ensued. Norman and Iris were going over accounts in the office, and Norman was quite pleased with his own manful calm during the trembling and the rumbling. The guest who reported the gush of water from the cistern did so casually, about half an hour later. He was a bald, dignified doctor from Indianapolis, in an orange beach robe, and he poked his head into the office just long enough to remark, "Oh, Mr. Paperman, I think you have a broken pipe or something. There's water coming out of your foundation wall pretty fast." Then this messenger of disaster went his way.

Norman put his head down on his arms on the open ledger, and moaned.

The news in the ledger was in itself bad enough. On his first week of Caribbean hotel-keeping, Norman Paperman had netted *thirty-seven dollars and forty cents*. There were reasons for this shocking figure, to be sure. The payroll was large: cook, maids, waitresses, steel band, bartender, gardener: none of them were paid much, but it added up to a lot. There had been the terrible water purchase. Money had to be set aside for the bank; and this he would have to go on doing each week, for some three hundred weeks, to pay off the loan and the notes. The revenue from the new units was supposed to balance off this drain, but they remained unbuilt. The game room full of materials stood open to wind, moon, rain, and sun, undisturbed by human hands. Bids to complete the job had come in. The range of prices was imbecile. The low bid was fifteen hundred; the high one was twenty-one thousand. Collectively, the contractors of Amerigo seemed to have as much reliability as a flock of migrant birds, and little more knowledge of construction.

But none of this was the true trouble. Even the existing rooms were not all occupied; far from it. People were checking in at a great rate, for the blizzards had started in the north. But the hotel was a coarse sieve that retained only a fraction of the arrivals. The rest leaked away complaining and cursing over one discomfort or another: electric failures, water shortage, unreliable toilets. Ever since the departure of Thor, the days had been a hell of small breakdowns.

"The cistern has cracked," Paperman said hollowly into his elbow. "On top of everything. I know it. An earthquake cracked it once before."

"Well, then, if it was cracked, it was patched, wasn't it?" Iris said. "It can be patched again."

"I know. I'll fight on," said Paperman. "I'll never quit. I LIKE the tropics." He raised his head, wiped his red eyes, blew his red nose, and threw the Kleenex into a wastebasket. "Let's go look at the leak."

Senator Pullman was on the grounds, attempting to repair the electrical failure that had darkened one third of the hotel for two days. Some guests good-humoredly took the kerosene lamps in their rooms as romantic touches. Others had checked out in rage over the uselessness of their electric razors and hair dryers. The failure was a stubborn mystery. New fuses put into the circuit gave way with loud reports, big blue sparks, and some smoke and flame. The real calamity was that the pump was on this circuit: no electricity, no water. Attempts to rewire the pump had blown out all the remaining circuits in the hotel for a while, and Norman had ordered the senator to stop trying, until he located the trouble. At heavy expense, Anatone had located and brought over a giant old gasoline generator and hooked it to the pump. It was now chugging in back of the hotel like a trailer truck climbing a mountain, emitting noise and fumes that had caused the departure of several more guests occupying rear rooms; but at least it was feeding electricity to the pump, and the pump was feeding water to the hotel.

The senator and his young apprentice electrician joined them on the beach to contemplate the long jagged cistern crack. In volume the escaping water was not yet large, but it spurted out under high pressure, in narrow sparkling arches.

"The question is," said Norman, "what to do?"

The senator scratched his head. He wore a Palm Beach suit and a narrow neat yellow tie; for, as he had explained to Paperman, he would have to leave the electric repair job at eleven to attend a session of the legislature. Paperman did not understand exactly what the senator contributed to the electrical repair work. Mostly he stood and watched his apprentice crawl into dark cobwebbed crevices to set off terrible sparks. The two usually conversed in island English, and the legislator's ability to switch at will into smooth mainland polysyllables was remarkable.

"It's a perplexing question," said Pullman. "The Guadeloupe barge came in when?"

"Yesterday."

"Then you're full."

"To the brim. We'd had the rain, so we only needed ninety thousand gallons. At Lorna's suggestion I tipped him a fifty-dollar bill."

The senator nodded. "Very thoughtful. Very customary." He turned to his apprentice and said something like, "Wha hoo hee baba de whass kum hoo ba sistom dis time ba whoa?"

To which the apprentice replied, with twinkling eyes and a jolly laugh, "Yes, I tink so. De ting wha bee ha du kistuss mak la fa berry rag de sistom whis poss. Moss du far kum."

"That's what I thought," said the senator. "Mr. Paperman, you have to let all the water out of the cistern immediately."

"What? *Why,* for God's sake?"

"Your wall here is seriously weakened. Mass masonry is very subject to shearing stresses. All that water is a tremenjus weight, and the hazard is that it will suddenly bust out the whole wall. If that happens, most of your hotel can just collapse down into the cistern and you actually will own nothing but a big ruin. You have to get the water out and repair the cistern right away."

Utterly staggered, Norman said, "But plastering it from the outside won't work?"

"Sada bee plossa wha kum loff rappa soggle ba soff de ting you tink?" said the senator, approximately, to his apprentice.

"No, de ting barra cull to de ba whada rupp ha hee sang dabee no good."

"No it will leak all around. You have to repair it from the inside out," the senator said to Paperman. He pointed to a valve like a giant faucet projecting from the bottom of the wall. "There's your emergency discharge, and you'd better open it now, if you want to save your foundation."

Paperman glanced at Iris, who shrugged.

After the trouble he had had filling this cistern, after the money he had squandered to get just a few thousand gallons in an emergency, it was hardly easier for him to open this valve than it would have been to open a vein in his wrist and let out the blood. But the apprentice, in his humble inarticulateness, reminded Norman of the lost Gilbert. This boy might know something.

"Okay," he said sadly to the boy. "Open the valve."

The corroded brass wheel did not turn easily. The apprentice straddled it, muscles bunching under his shiny black skin. All at once a glittering stream half a foot thick shot out of the valve, flying parallel to the sand for perhaps twenty feet before wavering and drooping into the beach. A pool formed on the instant, with rivulets trickling toward the sea.

Senator Pullman grinned in admiration. "There's water pressure for you," he said.

Norman pulled his eyes away from this horrible roaring waste, and studied the cracked cistern. An idea struck him. "Look, Senator. Look how far down that crack extends." He gestured at the dripping fracture. The crack began not at the ground but at the top of the wall, and extended about two thirds of the way down. Below that, the wall was solid. At least it looked solid.

"Why do I have to empty the cistern? Why can't we just let the water down to this solid level? Then there's no risk of collapse, and my guests will have water until I can line up a mason. If I empty the cistern now, I'll empty my hotel."

Iris looked at Senator Pullman, he looked at his apprentice, and the apprentice regarded Paperman with awed surprise, as though a horse had opened his mouth and spoken.

"Dat does be a good idea," said the apprentice clearly. "Dat work okay."

"I'll be damned," Iris said. "So simple."

"It's a most ingenious adjustment to an emergency," said Senator Pullman. "That is the kind of thinking that makes a successful Kinjan. I congratulate you, Mr. Paperman. As it happens, Anatone is a fine mason. Or at least he can get you one. So essentially you have no problem any more, once we locate this little short-circuit. Unfortunately I must go to the legislative session now."

Pullman departed, taking his apprentice with him, as Paperman and Iris stood watching the cistern water shower out of the valve and carve a deepening canyon in the beach sand. "I have to remember to turn this valve off," he said. "Let's see. At ten gallons a second—and we're not losing that much, surely—it'll still take a couple of hours to empty down."

"Honestly, Norm, you're getting so resourceful and masculine," Iris said. "I could fall in love with you, if you didn't keep saying *was to* all the time."

"Shut up," Norman said. "Let's meet at your cottage for a swim in ten minutes."

"Done," Iris said.

2

Lorna greeted him at the desk with a handful of letters. Most of them were local bills; he looked for airmail stamps and pulled out one letter from Henny and another from Atlas.

"De toilet overflow in twenty-six," Lorna said.

"What? That's the third one this morning."

"De lady say dey check out if it don't work by twelve o'clock. Dere be five guests you got to meet on de noon plane."

"Yes, yes, I know that. Anything else? Anything good?"

"Miss Buckley she waitin' for you in de office."

"Who's Miss Buckley?"

"She fum Immigration," said Lorna, with a peculiarly unpleasant look.

The air in the little office was somewhat more bearable now, for Senator Pullman's apprentice had hacked a hole through the heavy masonry of the back wall and had put in a rattling, screeching air-conditioner. Miss Buckley of Immigration sat in a chair directly in the line of the noisy breeze. She was a very dark young woman in a purple dress with a red jacket, quite stout, with pretty features marred by drooping unfriendly eyes, and thick magenta-caked lips set in an outraged pout. An open briefcase on the floor leaned against her chair. She had some manila folders on her lap, and in one of these she was writing with a ball-point pen. She paid no attention to the arrival of the proprietor. Since her crossed legs blocked his way, he waited for a long time, while she wrote and wrote, often sighing loudly and shaking her head.

"Excuse me," he finally said.

Miss Buckley gave him a single nauseated glance, as though he had shouted a string of filth, and moved her feet. He slipped past her and sat behind his desk. She continued to write.

"I beg your pardon," Paperman said after another long wait. "Is there something I can do for you?"

The lady from Immigration slowly turned her revolted glance on him again. "She still here," she said.

"What? Who's still here?"

The lady official from Immigration brandished a folder. "She. Who else?"

"Would you give me the pleasure of naming the person you're talking about?"

"De pregnant girl from Nevis. Dat who I'm talking about. Esmé Caroline de Quincy. She still here."

"Yes, she is. Aren't her papers in order?"

"She papers ain't de question, she condition de question. Esmé Caroline de Quincy got to leave, or she employer take de responsibility."

"What responsibility? This is all news to me."

Miss Buckley explained, with weary contempt, the problem of Esmé de Quincy.

Esmé was a foreigner, a British subject. Pregnant alien women in the Caribbean were forever trying to get to an American island to have their babies; for the law gave these children United States citizenship, providing only that they emerged from the womb on American soil. The nationality of the mother or the father, in such a case, was of no consequence. Immigration was forever trying to stem this obstetrical skirting of the quotas. The office had been keeping an eye on Esmé, and by its calculations her time was at hand, and she had to go.

Turning even more forbidding, Miss Buckley pointed out that Paperman, when he bought the hotel, had signed a paper taking on himself all the bonds of the alien employees. If Esmé did succeed in having her baby on Kinjan soil, the child would virtually have a legal father in Paperman. His duty to keep it and its mother from becoming public charges would never end until he or they died. He would become personally involved in every encounter Esmé or her child ever had with the government, forever after, wherever they went, from the cradle to the grave—welfare agencies, social security, schools, police, army—all, all, would hark back forever to Norman Paperman, who had made an American citizen of this individual.

This recital terrorized Norman. If any part of it were true—and surely it could not all be petty official bullying—Esmé suddenly loomed as the greatest hazard he had yet encountered in Kinja. He almost cringed to Miss Buckley, in assuring her that he would take action at once. The cringing cheered and brightened the Immigration inspector like a glass of wine. Her eyes cleared, her magenta-ringed smile shone. She put the folders into her briefcase; and with the pleasantest air, she told him that the Immigration Office was glad to welcome him to Amerigo, and was always at his service. She then took a flirtatious, sexy departure.

At once he called Lorna into the office, and asked her to tell him all she could about Miss Buckley. Lorna was crisp and scornful. "She don' know nothin'. She does be a troublemaker, she ignorant as dirt. Don' hoross youself. You don' have to pay her no mind, Senator Pullman he fix de whole ting."

Lorna elaborated as follows: Miss Buckley was the girl friend of Senator Orrin Easter, the chief rival of Senator Evan Pullman. Both legislators were Republicans. One led the party of Eagle Republicans, the other the Elephant Republicans. Since the election of Eisenhower, in 1952, all the senators had become Republicans. Under Truman the two parties had been the Liberty Democrats and the Freedom Democrats. There was a lot more about Kinjan politics that Norman couldn't follow, but he gathered that there were no real issues at stake; the sole question was, which of two rival clubs gave out government jobs. At the moment Pullman's Elephant Republicans were in narrow control. However, there were friendly working arrangements with the Eagle Republicans, and so Christophine Buckley had obtained the Immigration job, which had special glitter because it was a federal appointment. Lorna snarled that Christophine had been thrown out of high school for bearing twins to Senator Easter at the age of fourteen. She had then had a varied government career as a social worker, holding jobs in family guidance and mental health, before leaping to her present federal post.

There was too much female venom stirred into this farrago to convince or reassure Paperman. The only comfort lay in Lorna's scornful assertion that Esmé was at least six weeks away from giving birth to his foster-child. Paperman believed this. The girl didn't *look* on the verge of childbirth. He decided to keep a very close watch on her waistline, and to deport her after Christmas. Right now, he needed her badly. She was a good girl, the cleanest and best of the staff, and in a shadowy way she seemed to be the leader of the six Nevis chambermaids.

So he dismissed Lorna and glanced at the mail from home. Henny's letter was generally cheering. Her pain had faded, and all the doctors now tended to ascribe it to nerves. New York was unspeakably cold, crowded, and filthy in the pre-Christmas panic. Her plans for coming down with Hazel a week hence were set.

But the last page was a shocker.

I don't know how to break this to you, but with your heart history the surprise might do you in, and you'd better be warned. The Sending is coming to Amerigo for Christmas! Don't ask me why. Don't ask me what to do about it. I'm beside myself. Hazel acts delighted, but I'm very much mistaken if she isn't annoyed. Our tender little darling loves to do the pursuing, you know. She was bored by all the college boys who languished after her, and that was what sent her chasing Klug.

Oh, he drivels about finishing up his thesis on Balzac the Fruit during Xmas, and says he doubts whether he'll even see Hazel except for a swim now and then. But though Hazel may be a prize donkey, she's solid woman, and she can't be fooled. Your screwball chum down there has put a small damper on the Sending's glow. She feels it and she's let Sheldon feel it. And like every dumb cluck of a man, his ego won't allow him to take it quietly. His only hope is to pretend indifference, but no, the damn fool is going to run after her. I do believe we may be approaching the downfall of the Sending, my love, so grit your teeth. This may all be for the best.

Lester's letter was typed on the exceptionally heavy, creamy, engraved stationery of the Atlas Investment Corporation:

Dear Norman:

I thank you for your kind information about the Crab Cove situation in Amerigo. I am interested. Kindly inform the bank.

Due to exhausting negotiations on my Montana situation, including many airplane trips, I am fatigued. I will therefore spend Christmas at the Gull Reef Club. Kindly reserve the best accommodation in the hotel for me.

Kindest personal regards.

As he was digesting this double-barrelled blast of disquieting news —for Atlas and the Tilson party seemed as unpromising a juxtaposition as gunpowder and a blowtorch—Lorna put her head in again.

"Suh, you fix de toilet in twenty-six yet?"

"What? Oh, Christ, no." He glanced at his watch. "I've got to meet the plane now."

"We goin' to lose dem guests, suh. Dey a party of four."

Paperman left the office and galloped up the stairs. Eternal weeks ago, when he had first visited the hotel with Lester, this staircase had been a menace to his health, to be mounted with plodding care. Now he took it two steps at a time with hardly a thought, because he seldom went upstairs when some emergency wasn't breaking loose. His heart beat fast and angry each time he did this. But Paperman was too "horossed" to mollycoddle his heart, and with time the palpitations seemed to be getting less violent.

He ran to the supply closet, took out a plunger and a can of murderous chemical, and let himself into Room 26 with a skeleton key. The overflowed toilet and the whole bathroom were a mess, foul and malodorous beyond language to tell. Norman Paperman, the fastidious, tasteful man about Manhattan, Norman Paperman, of the "cashmere existence," Norman Paperman, who until his move to the tropics had never done anything more practical or mechanical than wielding a can opener; this Norman Paperman now sloshed manfully through the vile puddles, worked the plunger for two minutes in the splashing filth, and then emptied the chemicals into the toilet. Horrifying gurgles, steamings, bubblings, and fumings began, and these he endured, together with the stench, for the time prescribed on the can. Then he flushed the toilet and ran, halting in the other room. He heard no splash of an overflow. He returned, looked in the bowl, and saw clear murmuring water. He summoned a maid to mop up; and off to the airport he went, as pleased with himself as if he had written a sonnet.

3

It behooved him to hurry. Nothing seemed to irritate the guests more, or to get them off to a worse start, than having to wait even a few minutes at the hot airport at midday, especially if they encountered the mysterious taxicab boycott. Paperman would have gladly capitulated to the cab drivers, but there was no calling back Amy Ball's circulars with the fatal opening words: *"From the moment you arrive in Amerigo, when we personally meet you at the airport, your vacation at Gull Reef will be not a stay at a hotel, but a visit to the gracious tropical home of old friends."* This was a commitment like the Monroe Doctrine. Norman had to struggle through this season, at least, with the old policy.

He raced through the somnolent town. It was high noon. The only traffic in sight was an old red taxicab far up Prince of Wales Street, evidently making for the airport. It went out of sight around a turn; Norman came bowling after it, and saw with horror, as he rounded the turn, that the red cab had stopped short in the narrow street and the driver was happily joking with a pretty girl on the sidewalk. He jammed on his brakes, slowed with fearsome squeals, crashed into the taxi, and struck his head on the windshield.

When he came to, he was lying on the roasting hot sidewalk; he sat up, and then staggered to his feet. A dozen Kinjans ringed him, including the chief of police in his gold braid and vast pistols. "Easy, mon," said the chief, taking his arms. Paperman insisted that he was quite all right, and he seemed to be. The blackout had been a momentary stunning. Neither car was badly damaged, but it was fifteen minutes before he could quit the scene. The chief insisted on writing down all the facts. He gently chided the cab driver for stopping in the middle of the street to hold a conversation. This was a universal custom in Kinja, and Norman had observed the chief doing it himself in his silvery new prowl car. However, since the law frowned on it, and the taxi driver admitted he had stopped for a few seconds to greet his best friend's sister, the chief gave him a summons, and gave another to Paperman for negligent driving. Norman drove off down the tar highway through the green walls of cane as fast as he dared, still giddy, and thankful for the heavy glass in the Land Rover windshield, which had saved him from breaking through and cutting his throat. One more small, unpublicized hazard of Eden to bear in mind, he thought.

chapter eight

Lionel

I

"Lionel, for Christ's sake!" Paperman involuntarily yelled, clear across the terminal.

In the distraction of the quake and its aftermath, he had quite forgotten that one of the arriving guests was Dan Freed's green-faced stage manager. There he was, sitting in a shady corner with an elderly couple and two schoolteacherish women. Except for this group, the torrid airport was deserted.

"Hey there, Norm! Here's the five for Gull Reef! Say, you sure look healthy, fella!"

Lionel had been passing the time by telling theatre anecdotes, and the other guests were in good spirits despite the long wait. They kept asking Lionel eager questions about Broadway stars even when they were all in the Land Rover, jerking and snorting along the coast road back to Georgetown.

Soon, as usual, they were exclaiming at the beauty of Amerigo. Even Norman, weary and disillusioned as he was, still loved the verdant hills, the blue-green sea, the play of sun and shadow in the valleys and on the ruins. Their effect on Lionel was astonishing. It was hard to recognize in this man the phlegmatic robot of backstage. The cheese-green cadaverous face, the straight long pale hair, the pursed old-lady lips were the same. But he smiled, he laughed, he spoke in high gay tones, he pointed out wonders to the others; for he was the only one of the five who had been to Amerigo before.

"Ah, Norman, you're the smartest guy I've ever known. This is heaven. This is for me. This is for anybody with half a brain. Look, Mrs. Stegmeyer. Look, Susy! See that ruin? That's Charlotte's Fancy, built by slaves before George Washington was born. How about that ocean? Did you ever see such a color?"

Lionel's delight over the waterfront—the red fort, the arcades, the Vespucci statue amid its pink-and-purple bougainvillea, the native schooners—reminded Norman of his own raptures when he and Lester Atlas had first trod this cobbled plaza. The gondola, said Lionel, was marvellous; and as for Virgil, he was more picturesque than the beef-eaters in the Tower of London. "Tell me, gondolier, can you sing Venetian songs?" he asked, as they were rowing across.

"Fongf? No, fuh, I can't fing no fongf," Virgil said, smiling toward a spot about seven feet to the left of Lionel. "But I work two fifff."

"He does what?" Lionel said to Paperman. "Oh! Fantastic! 'Works two shifts.' How about that? Dan is going to go out of his mind about all this, Norman. Dan is going to get right up on the ceiling and stay there." He explained that the producer had sent him down for just one day to scout the Gull Reef Club; and, if he liked it, to make eleven reservations for the Freed entourage, stretching over Christmas and the New Year. "I'm sold right now," he said. "Imagine a hotel out in the harbor! It looks like a dream."

While the guests checked in, Norman went to inspect the water level in the emptying cistern, and saw that it had a long way to go. By lying on the greasy kitchen floor, and peering into the hole, he could see the jagged vertical crack down the inside of the wall.

"Take a peep down here every hour or so, Sheila," he said to the cook, "and send somebody to shut off the valve when it's about two-thirds empty."

"I do dat. Mistuh Papuh, suh, I does have de whole food list now fo' de party fo' Mr. Tilson. De cook at de Francis Drake she did help me a lot wid it. It come to a big lot o' money, suh."

"I'll bet it does. See me in the office after lunch, Sheila, and let's go over it. All right? Say three o'clock."

"I be dah, suh."

Lionel soon joined Norman in the bar. With his knack for self-efface-ment he had replaced his gray suit and red tie, which made him look like every other arriving tourist, with raucous madras shorts and an orange sport shirt, which made him look like every other guest. His legs and arms were the usual newcomer's gray-white; only his face had the strange greenish cast. This relieved Paperman. An entirely green man might have panicked the hotel's West Indian staff, with its ancestral superstitions of the walking dead.

The stage manager asked Church for a planter's punch, and stretched himself luxuriously on one of the double lounge chairs. "Ah, this is cloud nine. You know something, Norm?" he said, lighting a cigar with a sigh of pleasure. "You're still the talk of New York. I mean that. There isn't a star of a hit show who's envied the way you are. You're becoming a legend. I've been thinking about you for weeks, and I'm darn glad Dan let me scoot down here. I knew the place would be dandy, but he just wanted me to make sure. I'm actually ready to quit New York anytime myself. I've had it. I'm fed up. Twenty-nine years, fifty-three shows, is a lot of Broadway for any man. Do you know a little guest house here I could buy? Nothing this elaborate, you know, but—"

"Good lord. This isn't *Lionel!*" Iris was approaching in a frilly white shirt, blue linen shorts, and a tight chartreuse sash, carrying what looked like a Coca-Cola. Her hair was damp.

Lionel rose to his feet, staring at her, and then a delighted smile came over his face. "Why, it's Janet! Isn't it? Janet West! Jiminy Christmas, what a surprise."

She had very little make-up on, so she kissed his cheek instead of the air. "How long has it been? When was that Ibsen catastrophe? Thirty-nine? Norman, this is the greatest of all the Broadway stage managers."

"Thanks, Janet, you're prettier now than you were then, by God."

She sat on the lounge chair beside Lionel and they gossiped in the friendliest way, though Norman gathered that they hadn't seen each other in twenty years. "By the way," she said to Paperman, "what happened to our swim? I went in alone."

"I had to fetch Lionel. What do you think, Iris? He's been here an hour, and he wants to buy himself a nice little Kinjan hotel."

Iris burst out laughing.

"Why the horselaugh? I'm absolutely serious," Lionel said. "Don't you think I can afford it? I've saved my money. I'm not an actor."

"Shall we tell him," Norman said, "or shall we let him dream?"

"Tell me what?"

"Go ahead," Iris said. "Tell him."

Norman began the tale of his woes: the water shortages, the power failure, Church's sex mania, Senator Pullman, Tex Akers, Anatone, the ants, and the rest. As he got into the narrative, both Iris and Lionel started to laugh. With his raconteur's instinct, Norman was soon telling the episodes for their humor, which until now had not particularly struck him. Lionel after a while was lying back in the chair, gasping, whooping, and wiping his eyes.

"Oh, golly, Norm, stop," he wheezed, during the adventure of the Thousand Steps. "Stop, for pity's sake, or my old hernia will be opening up. Christopher! I've never heard anything like it. You're set for dinner conversation for life, Norm. That's one sure thing."

"Well, no matter how funny it sounds, I'm warning you not to be misled by some pretty scenery and the smell of frangipani. This is a rough place."

Lionel sat up, with something of his usual drawn, greenish, puckered look. "Well, I don't know, Norm. Sure, you've been having problems, but have you ever gone out of town with a show? I've done it fifty-three times. Everything is always a shambles at the beginning. You've just been having a few out-of-town troubles, fella."

"Kinja is permanently out of town," said Paperman. "Very far out."

Pulling his nose with a judicious air, Lionel glanced around at the patrons of the bar. "In what way? I admit you're kind of heavy on pansies, Norm, but aside from that—" He was looking at the fat Turk Hassim, who sat at a nearby table with two sulky-looking young men, one with long wavy bleached hair, the other with a pugnaciously masculine, but too well-groomed, gray crew cut. Hassim was being rather loud and bouncy. For a fact, Norman observed, a lot of the transient homos were here for lunch, and several resident ones had come down out of the hills today.

"I hadn't noticed," he said. "I'll admit it sort of looks like a convention this afternoon. Maybe it's Michelangelo's birthday."

"Listen, thirty years in show business," said Lionel dryly. "To me it's nothing."

Norman had caught Hassim's eye, and the Turk now left his table and danced over, arriving with something like an entrechat done by a sow. "Hello there, Norman, Iris love. Norman, you horrid old poop, what *have* you done with that *adorable* little wife of yours? I've got a shipment from Hong Kong, all full of marvellous things that I know she wants."

Norman explained that Henny would be arriving for Christmas. "Lovely, lovely, I'll be dying to see her again," said Hassim, puckering his lips most suggestively at Iris. "And no doubt you will be, too, Normie. Oh this dreary bachelor existence!" Off he slipped with a roll of his prominent eyes, in a fit of the giggles.

"Wow," said Lionel.

"He has a lovely shop," said Iris sternly. "And he's a sweetheart to deal with. I like Hassim."

Iris offered to drive Lionel around the island after lunch and show him some of the guest houses. The stage manager was delighted; and, he said, not in the least discouraged by Norman's sad saga.

"Just don't let him buy Hogan's Fancy," said Norman.

2

"Sheila, that valve—I hope the cistern isn't bone dry."

Sheila sat in the cool office, dressed in a fresh white uniform, and holding a clip board full of bills and papers. She had left off her chef's hat, she was not pouring sweat, and her usually wild hair was neatly tucked up. Sheila in repose was pretty, if far too fat, and her eyes were clever and a little sad.

"I did shut off de valve, suh, 'bout half-past two. De water gone down below de crack."

"Bless your heart. You're a tower of strength. Sheila, before we get into the Tilson party—you remember Gilbert? Gilbert once told me that after the last earthquake a man named Hippolyte repaired the cistern. You were working here then, weren't you?"

"I did work here den, yes suh."

"Do you know this Hippolyte?"

She nodded.

"Well, I'm only thinking that instead of getting somebody new who might wreck everything, it would make sense to call in this Hippolyte again."

The cook's face took on a woodenly fierce look, much like an African carving. Norman could not imagine why. Such bafflements were always arising in his dealings with Kinjans, but this time he resolved to press on. The matter was urgent. "Is Hippolyte on the island?" A bare nod. "Is he a good worker?" A shrug. "Sheila, this thing has to be taken care of." No response. "What did Hippolyte do when he was here?"

"Hippolyte he do everyting," grumbled the cook.

"Everything? What do you mean?"

"He fix everyting. Like Mistuh Thor. He fix tings."

"Well, ye gods, then why don't we hire him again? That's exactly the kind of man I need."

The African mask faced him. "Hippolyte fonny."

"Funny? How, funny? What's funny about him?"

There was a pause. "Hippolyte very fonny," the cook elaborated.

"Well, could you find him for me?"

"Don' know, suh."

"D'you suppose Gilbert could find him?"

"Don' know, suh."

"What does he do now?"

"He fish."

"Where?"

"In de ocean, suh."

"I see." Paperman held out his hand defeated. Kinjans usually won these skirmishes. "Let's look at the figures on that Christmas party."

The mask dissolved. Sheila became the harassed, good-humored cook on the instant. "It all written dah, suh. I did talk to de cook over to de Francis Drake. She tell me 'bout de tings Mistuh Tilson like."

Running his eyes down the list, Paperman saw a large red squiggle next to some items. "What's this, Sheila?"

"You does have to fly dose tings down fum New York. De rest I can get h'ah."

"Artichokes? Fresh strawberries?"

"Yes, suh. Tings like dat. And de oysters and dem big steaks. Dey does have to be de best straight fum New York. Mr. Tilson he wery particular. He does give de cook a hundred dollars tip," she said with a shy grin.

Sheila told him her plans for the party: the extra girls she would hire for the kitchen, the young men she would bring in for serving. Tilson liked his party to swarm with waiters. That was simple, she said; half the high school seniors on the island had white mess jackets and satin-striped black trousers, and they loved a chance to wear them. Moreover, Mr. Tilson was known for his generous tipping.

"Now Sheila, what about the hotel guests? We have to give them dinner that night too. We also have to get them out of the way, hours before the party."

"Mistuh Papuh, I been tinkin' about dat, dat gonna be de big problem."

"Well, I've been thinking too. Do you suppose we could have a cookout for them over at that overgrown little beach below the Blue Cottage? The one Mrs. Ball called Lovers' Beach, you know? Set up a bar, give them drinks free—sort of make a beach party that night for them? Could you handle such a setup, and the Tilson party, too?"

Sheila pushed out her lips, wrinkled her brow, and stroked her chin. "I tink dat work good, suh, dat be a fine idea for true. I got to get more help for dat, but dey plenty I know to get. Lovers' Beach way de odda side de Reef."

"That's what I was thinking."

"Yes, suh. I can do dat, suh. Dat be okay."

Norman was doing quick arithmetic on Sheila's food list as he talked. The Tilson party would require, he saw, an outlay of over two thousand dollars. He would get it back with a big profit, of course—if all went well. Meantime, it would almost wipe out the last of the money intended for the new rooms, leaving him with no margin for emergencies. He still had about eleven hundred dollars in his New York account, his last collections from clients for work performed. But this was a needed cushion for Henny and Hazel, during these uncertain weeks. The possibilities of a fiasco in this huge double party were many and scary. The chances for success rested on this black woman. All he really knew about her was that she was a good cook.

He respected Sheila. Norman could not even picture what his plight would now be if, amid the breakdowns and bad luck of these first two weeks, the feeding of his guests had also been a worry. Sheila had kept the dining room going, smooth as water. She bought the food; she managed the waitresses; she planned the menus. He never questioned the bills, though they were frequent and huge. For all he knew, she was stealing him blind, yet he believed that an audit would show she had not overcharged him by a penny. Paperman did not know why he trusted Sheila, a complete West Indian, inscrutable as any other Kinjan. But he did. For one thing, he had to.

The question was, could he rely on her to carry off this ambitious, heavy operation? He now knew his own incompetence all too well, and the bitter truth in the old saw about the cobbler and his last. He had become honest enough with himself, in these harsh weeks, to see his move to the Caribbean as an eccentric impulse of middle age, a daydream which would have faded harmlessly if not for the misleading encouragement of Lester Atlas. But he was in it now, and it was too late to make himself over. He would never regain the myriad hours he had spent joking over coffee in theatre restaurants, or fooling with forgotten women. He would never be an Atlas. He might never be much of anything. But he was what he was, and now he had to master the Gull Reef Club. What was the alternative to piling risk on risk?

"Suh, I does have to make my soup." Sheila was looking at him curiously, and he realized that he had been staring with unseeing eyes at her list. "All right, Sheila," he said. "We go ahead. We're going to do this thing, cookout on Lovers' Beach and all."

"Yas, suh." She handed him another sheet from the clip board. "De cook over to de Francis Drake she did give me dis address. She say de best ting you must cable dem. Dat de New York place dat send de stuff."

"Sheila—Sheila, it'll be a nice party, won't it? It'll all work out?"

Sheila exploded with laughter, rocking back and forth in her chair, and stood. "I do believe it be not too bad, Mistuh Papuhman."

As she opened the door he said, "How about this Hippolyte, now? Won't you try to find him? We can't operate on a quarter of a cistern very long, Sheila."

Her jollity disappeared. "Hippolyte fonny," she said with an ugly frown, and she walked out.

3

Lionel ambled into the bar just after sundown, dressed in a dust-pink jacket and light blue linen trousers, which made him blend subtly into the sunset. His green face, especially on the nose and forehead, now had a streaky sunburn. It made a queer effect, somewhat like a half-ripe apple.

"Hi, Norm," he said, "you look mighty relaxed, for a man with all those headaches!" He dropped into a chair beside Paperman, who sat at a small table near the frangipani tree, gazing out to sea and fingering the stem of his martini glass.

"Hello, Lionel. Any luck?"

"Well, Janet did show me one pretty little place over on the north side. Lots of mango and banana trees, and an unbelievable view. It's all tumble-down, and overgrown, and full of fags at the moment—"

"Casa Encantada," Norman said.

"That's it. You could do things with that one." He signalled to Church and ordered a planter's punch. "Ah, Norman, Norman, I tell you, this island is cloud nine. Cloud nine! Look at me! Only three hours in an open convertible, and look at the color I've got! A week in Miami wouldn't do it. And how about that sunset? Fabulous!"

"I know the place has its points," Norman said. "I did move here."

"Its points! You've got it *made*, Norm," Lionel said. "You're a gosh-darned genius. What an inspiration! I don't know ten fellows in New York who wouldn't change places with you. Why, you even *look* happy. You look absolutely marvellous."

Norman smiled. The fact was, he felt better than he had at any time since his arrival. He had had a bake in the sun, a good swim, and a long nap. The very cold martini in his hand had been mixed to his precise taste by Church. All the crises seemed to have simmered down; at least nobody had awakened him with pounding and a bulletin of horrible news. It was pleasant to be envied by Lionel. The big generator that fed electricity to the pump was broadcasting its Mack-truck groans behind the hotel. The pump itself was sending healthy rhythmic thuds through the bar floor. The soles of Norman's feet had become almost a second pair of ears or eyes for him. He could sense a halt in the pump, or the menacing drain of water from a faulty toilet, at once; and his soles reported all well. The bar was doing a rushing business. So was the front desk; seven people had checked in today, and nobody had checked out.

"Say, Norm," Lionel went on, "why is Janet West, of all people, holed up here in Amerigo at your hotel? Isn't that a funny one?"

Norman shrugged. "Ask her."

"I did. She sort of laughed and gave me some phonus bolonus story about getting material for a book. Ha! Iris is no writer. Is there some rich fellow up in one of those houses on the hill? Maybe keeping her, or waiting for his divorce to come through?"

Norman shook his head. He had been obtuse about Iris, perhaps, or at least too driven to think of these questions, for in the gruelling days since his arrival, he had regarded her only as a comforting presence. His fuzzy idea was that she had "retired" to Kinja, like the Tilsons, and merely talked about writing, as so many idle people did. But of course she was a puzzling woman. There were her frequent—and never explained—absences, especially at dinner and in the evenings. He said thoughtfully, "The only guy I've seen her with is a navy frogman, Lionel. He introduced me to her, in fact. But he's a youngster; why, he's sort of romancing my own daughter."

"Well, maybe he's the answer. I've learned one thing in the theatre," Lionel said, "and that is, that nothing is impossible when it comes to the old push-push. Absolutely nothing, Norman. I can't be surprised, where the old push-push is involved. Especially with a wild woman like Janet —or Iris, as you call her."

Lionel had the usual backstage relish for gossip, and he began to talk about Iris's three husbands, and her bizarre escapades, including two suicide attempts. Much of it was new to Norman. In recent years, Lionel said, Iris had tried hard with Herbert Tramm, a stuffy real estate operator in San Francisco, to live a conventional life. But her failure to have children had driven her back on the bottle, and she had completely dropped from sight. Now here she was in the Caribbean. Darn strange!

Paperman put a hand on Lionel's arm as he talked. "There she comes, and he's with her."

"Who's with her?" Lionel adopted Norman's low tone, interest glinting in his pallid blue eyes.

"The frogman."

Lionel peeked over his shoulder. "Golly, he doesn't look like much, does he? But you never know, Norm. I swear you can't tell. Sometimes these scrawny little fellows are the real tigers for the old push-push."

Iris and Cohn went to a corner table and Iris began talking rather angrily, while Cohn, who wore his gabardine suit and an overbright blue tie, leaned forward on both elbows, taking puffs at a small cigar. Since Norman kept glancing at them, he caught their attention. Iris stopped frowning, waved, and smiled. The frogman came to their table, and invited Lionel and Norman to join them for dinner. The main course turned out to be a fish Cohn had shot, a superb grouper, baked whole. Lionel was so thrilled at eating a fish with a gaping spear wound in it, that Cohn asked him if he would like to come along in the morning when he and Iris were going spearfishing. Lionel almost shouted his assent. By then three bottles of wine had gone around, and they were all quite gay; and Norman was pressed into the spearfishing party. "You're *coming*, that's all," Iris said firmly, "and for one morning, to hell with this hotel."

Norman had all but forgotten the charm of underwater scenery, one of the things that had lured him to Amerigo. Cohn paddled them next morning far out to the middle of Pitt Bay, in a rubber raft full of masks and fins. Cockroach Rock, where he tied up the raft, was actually a reef that just broke the surface. By standing on the coral, they gave the comic impression of walking on water, far out in a deep wide bay. Beyond the reef the green water turned dark blue, and the ocean floor fell off in a cliff—so Cohn said—to a chasm a mile deep.

It was a magnificent reef, with grand twisting pillars and caverns of pink coral. Groupers, parrot fish, and oldwives cruised goggling through the arches, amid moving clouds of small bright-colored fish. Lionel wasn't satisfied with this spectacle. He insisted on swimming farther out, so that he could tell his Broadway friends he had been in water a mile deep. Norman didn't like venturing out into the blue choppy gulf, but he was unwilling to turn back, with Iris gliding gracefully beside him and Lionel floundering far ahead. The deep made Norman queasy; it was like looking down from the top of a skyscraper, except that there were no cars below, no people; no fish, either, no bottom, no rocks; nothing at all but darkening blue space shafted with greenish sun rays.

They had not been out five minutes when a silver-gray shape rose from the azure shadows, making for Lionel. Cohn's brown body thrust forward and down ahead of Lionel, his fins moving fast, and he made sharp signals at the others to retreat. Norman saw a pointed wrinkled snout on the fish as it drew near, and staring ugly eyes, and slanted vents on the side of the wide head. It made a lazy rolling pass within a few feet of Lionel, and Norman also saw the unmistakable crescent mouth crammed with teeth and turned down in perpetual disappointment. He and Iris fled for Cockroach Rock, and clambered out together gasping.

Cohn shepherded the wallowing Lionel back to the reef, patrolling behind him.

"Hey! What do you know?" Lionel ripped off his mask while still in the water, exulting. "A shark! That was a real shark. Did you see? Golly, was I scared! That was marvellous. Did you see how close to me he came?" Cohn was scrambling out on the reef beside him. "Hey, why did you keep circling behind me like that?" Lionel said. "I heard you're supposed to punch a shark in the nose. Then it goes away."

"You're absolutely right," panted Cohn. "I forgot that. I have a lousy memory."

Norman said, trying to control the shakiness of his voice, "What's it doing so close to land? I thought sharks stay way out at sea."

"It's the legislature," Cohn said. "They used to bury the garbage on this island, the way I heard it. But when the Elephant Republicans last beat the Eagle Republicans, they voted along strict party lines to start dumping it at sea, and they bought that old landing craft. It's supposed to go out ten miles, but the fellow who runs it gets seasick, so he just turns in beyond Big Dog, out of sight of land, and shovels it off. We've seen him do it any number of times, and in fact I've done a lot of swimming through garbage. There's an easterly current at Big Dog that sweeps that stuff right down here past Pitt Bay."

"What they need," Lionel said, "is another captain for that landing craft."

"Our UDT commander once suggested that," said the frogman. "They told him Captain Pullman is irreplaceable."

After this Lionel was content to swim inside the reef. Cohn gave him a spear gun, and everybody stayed well clear while he made futile shots at the unperturbed groupers. Each time, Cohn retrieved the spear, stretched the rubber sling for Lionel, and got out of his way. A lot of joking went with this; but the stage manager turned the laugh at last by shooting at a parrot fish, and skewering an unfortunate grouper that collided with the spear. All the way back to the hotel, Lionel cuddled the bloody dead fish on his lap in the Land Rover, swearing he was going to pack it in dry ice and eat it that night at Sardi's, if the transportation cost him a hundred dollars.

4

"*. . . and so I say to you, fellow citizens, that at long last we have now unmasked Governor Alton Aloysius Sanders . . .*"

Norman could hear Senator Pullman's voice booming over the airport loudspeakers, as he drove up with Lionel in the Rover. This was not the only indication of something unusual afoot. There were perhaps fifty cars in the terminal parking space. Norman had noticed that the town streets seemed unusually quiet, but he had assumed it must be one of

Kinja's many obscure legal holidays—Candlemas, Transfer Day, Guy Fawkes Day, or something.

"*. . . under Alton Sanders' guise of a disinterested representative of our great President, we now know beyond a doubt there lurks a dictatorial, repressive, reactionary hypocrite who is in cahoots, lock stock and barrel, with the hill crowd!*"

Applause pattered in the loudspeakers.

The lone porter of the airport, who worked on random days when the spirit moved him, wheeled his little truck to the Land Rover, and with a groan and a flourish unloaded Lionel's one small suitcase. Lionel insisted on hugging to himself the perspiring cardboard box containing his iced fish.

"What's up?" Norman said to the porter.

"Senatuh Pullman he goin' Florida."

"Florida? With the legislature in session?"

"Dey say de senator be extrydite."

Incredulous, Norman hurried into the terminal, and saw the senator standing on a bench, holding a round microphone. Clustered in front of him were sixty or seventy laughing, gossiping Kinjans, not paying much heed to his oratory. Most of them were eating ice cream or drinking soda pop. "I pledge to you," the senator shouted, his voice reverberating in the big wooden shed lined with bright advertisements, "that despite my temporary absence, the Elephant Republicans will go on fighting the people's fight, my friends—for honest and frugal government, for lower taxes, for higher wages for underpaid government workers, for jobs for everybody, for elimination of deadwood from government payrolls, for bigger hospitals and schools, for new highways and housing projects, for free medical care and mental therapy. The unholy alliance of Governor Alton Aloysius Sanders and the Eagle Republicans are fighting to keep the hill crowd in luxury up there on Signal Mountain, friends, while the people of Kinja are crowded below in unsanitary huts. But the Elephant Republicans will never falter or procrastinate in their grandiose struggle until the people are living up in the mansions, and the hill crowd are down in the huts!"

A few listeners—those whose hands were unencumbered by food and drink—interrupted their laughing gossip to give a laggard handclap or two. Senator Pullman took the moment to puff his cigar in his usual nursing fashion, and then waved and smiled. He wore his Palm Beach suit and a mainland straw hat with a tiny brim, and his round shrewd face was serene, even gay.

Norman saw Governor Sanders leaning against the tin newsstand booth, arms folded, listening to the speaker. He appeared so unperturbed by the denunciation, that Norman ventured to walk up and greet him.

"Oh, hello there," Sanders said, a smile lighting his narrow lemon-colored face for a moment. "Come to see the fun?"

"Has Pullman really been extradited?"

"I'm afraid so."

"What for?"

"Bigamy. We put it off as long as we could, but Florida wouldn't play, and Interior finally got after me. It's just a nuisance action. The woman in Florida is greedy. She wants more money than Evan's been sending her."

"He's awfully severe on you."

Sanders grinned. "Yes, that's the style here. Lots of pepper and salt. I'm truly sorry to see Evan go. I came down just to say goodbye. He's very intelligent and reasonable." The governor lit a cigarette with an automatic motion of one hand. "I've always been able to work with him. Orrin Easter and his boys, now, are plain silly about voting pay increases and new jobs as soon as they get in. They never bother to check on what's in the treasury. Evan's very careful about that, and he's wise. Interior does get grouchy about deficits. There'll be a lot of vetoes for a while, and I just hope Evan cleans this mess up and hurries back."

"This diabolic plot of Alton Aloysius Sanders and the Democratic governor of Florida," thundered Pullman, "is a transparent maneuver to set back the cause of self-government in Amerigo—"

"Is he a bigamist?" said Norman.

"Oh, sure. It was a youthful indiscretion, one of those casual things. Evan says the woman's got another husband, too. That's how he expects to lick it. She'll probably fold up once he gets there."

Norman saw Lionel having some difficulty at the ticket counter, and he went over to help. There was a little line of passengers behind the stage manager; and among them Norman was much taken aback to recognize Lorna. She wore a tailored white linen suit and a triangular little white straw hat, with shoes and purse matched in mauve, and a little mauve nose veil. She looked like a model or a singer. When Lorna saw Paperman, embarrassment clouded her face, yielding to a radiant dimpled smile. "Hello dere," she said, with a wave of one small jewelled hand.

"Hello," Norman said. "Going somewhere, Lorna?"

"Well, I does have dis cousin in Miami, and she does be so sick, Mr. Papermon. She send me a cable to come right away. Esmé de smartest girl at de Reef. I did show her how to work de switchboard and make out de reservations and all."

"Esmé won't be with us very long."

"Well, I hope I be back by den."

Lionel's trouble appeared to involve his fish. The young man at the counter, a Kinjan in a neat pink open shirt, was objecting to the package in garbled island talk, and Lionel was loudly insisting that he had shot this fish, and nobody and nothing would stop him from carrying it on board the plane in his arms. The altercation went on as the arriving plane roared into the field. Senator Pullman came to the counter and said crossly to Lorna, "What's the holdup? —Hello, Mister Paperman."

"It ain't me. Dis man does have a fish or someting," Lorna said, flipping a wrist at Lionel.

Lionel said, "Norman, go get the manager of the airport, will you, and the customs inspector? I'll fight this thing to Washington. By golly, I've been fighting stupid regulations for forty years, that's half my job, and I usually don't lose."

The senator smiled at Norman, and rolled his cigar in the smile. "This gentleman a friend of yours?"

"A good friend, yes."

The ticket-counter man said, "I don't see no regulation does allow him take a dead fish in no passenger cabin, Senator. It does be unsanitary."

"Didn't he tell you it's a glass fish?" said Pullman. "It's a Chinese glass fish from Hong Kong. That's why he wants to carry it, Aubrey. They're tremenjusly breakable. He got it in Little Constantinople."

The counterman blinked at Senator Pullman. "I see. A glass fish. Well, dey ain't nothin' wrong wid no glass fish." He stamped Lionel's ticket, and the stage manager swept the package off the counter and hugged it. It was covered with a white deposit like hoar frost, and smoking. Lorna stepped up to the counter.

"Thanks," Norman said to Pullman, "and good luck."

"Always glad to oblige," smiled the senator.

Norman shook Lionel's free hand. The stage manager's red-streaked green face was agleam as he patted his package. "Golly, can you picture the boys in Sardi's tonight? See you Christmas, Norm. Keep an eye on Casa Encantada for me."

Governor Sanders, standing in the sunshine in front of the terminal, gestured toward a long black limousine with two American flags on its fenders, as Norman came out. "Can I give you a lift?"

"I have a car, Governor, thank you."

"Not at all. I wanted to ask you, is it true that Mr. Atlas is coming down to bid on Crab Cove?"

"So he wrote me."

"Fine. I'm delighted."

Norman was emboldened by the governor's mellow manner to say, "Why? What difference does it make to you?"

The governor raised his grizzled eyebrows. "I'm interested in the island's development. Crab Cove will give things a big lift here."

"So what? You're not a Kinjan. Chances are you'll be gone before it gets finished."

Governor Sanders' thin lips twitched. "You think we'll have a Democratic President next?"

"I don't know about that. You strike me as a man on the way up. You're just touching base in Kinja."

Sanders chain-lit a cigarette. "Thank you. Right now this is my job, and everything goes on the record, you know." The chauffeur opened the rear door, and the governor gave Paperman a little mock salute and climbed in, saying, "How's Iris? Staying off the booze?"

"Pretty much. We were swimming out at Cockroach Rock this morning and a shark made a pass at us."

The governor's face darkened. "I'd close Pitt Bay if I thought anybody would pay attention. —Well, here I go for a jolly session with Senator Easter. If you get tired of hotel-keeping, Mr. Paperman, try Caribbean politics."

chapter nine

The Bayfins

I

Virgil came skimming across the water like a scull-racer, ribbons streaming in the breeze. "Forry fuh," he panted, helping Paperman aboard. Norman had waited twenty minutes, and then telephoned the Reef; others on the dock claimed to have been waiting almost an hour. "Feela did fay I fould clean de bayfinth, fuh."

"What? Hey? Bayfins? What on earth are you talking about?"

"Bayfinth, fuh. Bayfinth for water."

"Oh. *Basins?*"

"Yeffuh. Bayfinth. Fikty of dem. I did have to crawl in de fellar and pull out all de pailth and de bayfinth. De bayfinth awful rufty. Feela fay fine 'em up."

Paperman by now could transpose by ear the Old English typography of Virgil's talk. "Bayfins" was a tricky one that had thrown him off. For some reason Sheila had Virgil polishing up sixty basins. Paperman had seen in the crawl space, where the pump stood, enormous cobwebbed stacks of pails, basins, and jugs. Why had Sheila gotten them out at this juncture? He stood up in the bow of the gondola, leaped as it drew near the dock, and ran up to the hotel.

The soles of his feet told him, as he entered the lobby, that something was amiss. The floor was dead. There was no vibration from the pump. Nor could he hear, from behind the hotel, the groaning and thumping of the generator that drove it. The pregnant Esmé, perched in her green chambermaid's smock on a stool behind the desk, with headphones awkwardly framing her bashful, pretty, coal-black face, somehow seemed an omen of fresh troubles. Three chambermaids emerged from the passageway to the kitchen, each carrying two full pails, slopping water as they came.

"Amaranthe! Faith! Where are you going with that water?"

As usual, the girls averted their eyes. The Nevis chambermaids were all silent, impassive, and shy as wild animals in his presence, though he often heard them giggling and shrieking happily to each other in their West Indian babel-language. Amaranthe, the ugly one with pink patches on her face, muttered, "Sheila she say take dem upstairs," and hurried sloshing past him. Two more chambermaids appeared with four more pails, and the procession marched up the stairs.

Paperman hastened to the kitchen. The floor over the cistern had been lifted. Millard, dripping sweat under his paper-bag hat, was hauling out of the cistern a brimming five-gallon paint can on a rope. Church caught the can as Millard swung it away from the opening, and began filling a row of pails. Pails stood outside the kitchen door in dusty stacks. Sheila, posted in the doorway in her chef's hat, was making supervisory remarks.

"Sheila, what's happened? What are you doing?"

"Dese de only way, suh, till de pump get fix. We puttin' a basin an' full pail in every room."

"What happened to the pump? Have you called Georgetown Plumbing?"

"It ain' de pump, suh. It de generator. Dey done take it away."

"What? *Who* did? How dare they? I rented it from Anatone for two weeks. I paid him a fortune to get it over here!"

Church was moving the full pails into the hall, and lining up another row of empty ones along the cistern hole. "Sir, it turns out that the machine was the emergency generator of the East End hospital. I don't know how Anatone got hold of it, but the hospital sent over a gang of workmen and a barge an hour ago and just hauled it away. I tried to argue, but . . ."

"Senatuh Eastuh he did send dose men for de generatuh," said Sheila, her eyes heavy and sad with old island experience. "Dey ain' nothin' to do suh, but use de pails and de jugs and basins, like we done when de whole island didn' have no powuh. Like after de hurricanes, and de time de powuh plant blow up. De people does wash in de basins and flush wid de pails. Dey get use to it."

The gravity of his new predicament now hit Norman Paperman with full force. To an extent that he could not yet even guess, the Gull Reef Club had been leaning on the prop of Evan Pullman's influence. It had been a powerful prop, enabling Anatone to perform even this amazing outrage of borrowing and renting to him the emergency generator of a hospital. But Anatone was no more the magician able to solve all problems for a large fee. The prop had been yanked out, and he was just another Kinjan. These thoughts were running through Norman's brain, leaving a red-glowing trail of alarm, when Amaranthe, carrying an empty pail, put her pink-patched face into the kitchen. "Dah does be a telephone call for you, Mr. Papuh."

The empty headphones were abandoned on the front desk. There was no sign of Esmé. In the office, the telephone lay off its hook.

"Hello?"

"Mistuh Papuh-mon?" The severe official female voice was unmistakable.

"Yes? Miss Buckley?"

"Dat right. You better come down here to Immigration right away."

"I'll be glad to. As it happens I've got some serious problems in the hotel, Miss Buckley. If it can wait till morning, I'll be grateful."

"You got a serious problem in dis office, Mistuh Papuhmon. You let it go till tomorrow, dass all right wid me, but you be regretful when it too late, I do believe."

"I'll be right over."

Paperman rolled a sheet into the old typewriter and rattled away for a minute or so. He dashed to the kitchen and thrust the paper on Church, whose red-white-and-blue shirt was soaked black with sweat. The chambermaids were lined up receiving full pails from Sheila and Millard. Church glanced at the paper and gave Norman a winsome exhausted smile, his perfect teeth gleaming in the oval of neat beard. "Wonderful! That's an inspiration, sir."

"Can you find a few minutes to letter this on a poster?"

"I guess so. Certainly, sir."

"Post it in the lobby as soon as you can. Who's tending bar?"

Church's eyes rolled in his head, and he grinned wearily again. "Well, I sort of dash back and forth, sir."

"Good boy. I think it's time we got in a boy to assist you. The busy season's upon us. I'll do it tomorrow. Esmé seems to be gone, I don't know where. Put her on the switchboard again, and try to convince her never to leave it untended, will you? I ought to be back in an hour."

2

The Immigration Office was on the second floor of an ancient building behind the church, at the top of a very steep, very decaying brick staircase slippery with moss. In the anteroom dejected Negroes, ill-clad but neat, sat around on hard chairs, all with the puzzled, sad, wistful eyes of "garrots"—off-islanders. A Kinjan girl, in a starched blue smock with a saucy bouffant hairdo, took Norman's name and wrote it at the bottom of a long list on her desk. "Miss Buckley said she wanted to see me right away," Norman remarked.

The girl nodded. "Dat be okay. Just take a seat."

Norman sat. He sat for a long time. Every now and then a buzzer sounded, the girl called out a name, and the garrots marched turn by turn through a door crusted with old green paint, emerging after a while with sadder faces than when they went in. To vary the monotony, Norman got up and wandered about, reading flyspecked government bulletins on the cracked gray wall about immigration rules, social security, and control of aliens. When this palled, he sat again and leafed through the book he had snatched at random from the mildewy lot on the shelves of the hotel lobby. He had dealt in his time with many minor officials. This wait did not surprise him.

"Mr. Papuh-mon?"

The girl pointed to the door. A mournful, muscular Negro in ragged shirt and trousers came out looking at a paper and scratching his head, and Norman went in.

The large room had thick-walled brick windows opening on Prince of Wales Street, and a rickety floor of wide, splintered old boards. Steel files lined the four walls. Near the windows, at a small steel desk, a girl was typing, and Miss Buckley sat writing at a large desk of mahogany, dressed in a dark gray suit that magnified her capacious bosom. It was some time before she showed awareness, with a heavy-lidded glance, that Paperman was standing at the door. She pointed the end of her pen at a chair beside her desk, and resumed writing. Paperman walked to the chair, the boards yielding and squeaking under his feet, and sat. The Deputy Chief of Immigration—so her desk sign identified her—wrote. Paperman opened the book in his lap and began to read.

"Mistuh Papuhmon, dis office does not be de public liberry." The Deputy Chief was glaring at him, her magenta mouth pursed in an offended pout. "You here on official business."

"Of course," said Paperman, "but if you're occupied I don't want you to feel pressed. I'm quite happy with my book."

"What dat book?"

"*Moby Dick.*"

"Let's see dat book!"

She inspected it, riffling the pages as though looking for packets of heroin. "Dat be a long book. You like long books?"

"Well, I like that one. I've read it before."

"Oh yes? Den what for you read it now?" said Miss Buckley, pouncing on this obvious self-betrayal.

"Just to be doing something. Did you want to see me about Esmé, Miss Buckley?"

With an exasperated sigh, and an irritated thrust of her pen into its holder, Miss Buckley rose, marched to one steel file and another, opening and shutting drawers, and returned to the desk with several folders. Stacking these before her she informed Paperman that the bonds for his alien help would come up for renewal within a week. They had to be renewed each December and June. These renewals were granted only when the employer was law-abiding and responsible. It wasn't a law-abiding or responsible act, she said, to help alien women get their children born on United States soil.

Norman offered to get a doctor to certify that Esmé was many weeks away from delivery. Miss Buckley sneered at this notion. Doctors couldn't understand the tricks of Nevis girls. They used belly bands and other queer things, and were built funny anyway. Esmé was about to pop. Immigration knew that, and if she didn't go within forty-eight hours the Gull Reef Club's application for renewing its bonds—here she rattled the sheaf of folders—might well be forwarded to Washington for review. This process took six months, and meantime no aliens could work at the hotel. Did Mr. Paperman know, she inquired, about the shortage of Kinjan labor?

"Look, may I speak freely and off the record?" Norman said.

"It don't make no difference. Go ahead," sighed Miss Buckley.

"When I bought the Reef, you know, a couple of weeks ago, Lorna was already there. From everything I hear, Senator Easter is a great statesman who will do a magnificent job of leadership, and—"

Miss Buckley's eyes opened wide and snapped fire. "Evan Pullman goin' be put behind bars in Florida fo' ten years. Dat Lorna never come back. If she do come back, she soon see who de boss now on dis island."

"No doubt. What I'm saying is, I feel that the Gull Reef Club has inadvertently been caught in some sort of cross-fire of politics, and if there's anything I can do—"

"Politics? What politics?" Miss Buckley hit the buzzer with a thick thumb. "We all federal appointees in dis office. Politics! Come in, come in," she said to a melancholy young girl who sidled through the door with hanging head. "Sit down, sit down. Politics!" She pointed in the direction of Paperman's lap, and resumed her scrawling and groaning.

Norman took all this as a hint that he had permission to withdraw, and he got out of there.

3

Church Wagner's poster dominated the lobby on the center wall: red cardboard five feet high and a yard wide, lettered in elegant black brushwork:

> *Gull Reef Club Regrets*
> *Water Difficulties. Bear With Us.*
> *Everything Will Be Fixed Tomorrow.*
> *(We Think!)*
> *Meantime There's Tonight. Let's Live.*
> *Champagne Party On the House. All You Can Drink, Free!*
> *If the Water Can't Flow, the Wine Can.*
> *Music! Laughter! Hubbub! Wassail!*
> *How's That? We're Trying!*
> *See You after Dinner at the Party!*
> *Gull Reef Club.*
> *Norman Paperman, your host.*

Ornamenting the words was a fantasy in gold ink of bubbles, bottles, flying corks; also pails, basins, toilets, and a large faucet yielding one meager drop. Norman was amazed at Church's facility. Obviously, whatever this young man did, he did fast. It was his idiosyncrasy.

Guests crowding around the poster greeted Paperman with great good humor. In the bar he found that the champagne party was the talk of the hotel. The guests were a motley lot, old and young, from the East and from the Chicago area, mostly Gentile, with a sprinkling of young adventurous New York Jews bored with Miami. The grumpy, easily dissatisfied ones had already departed. The party announcement had welded the rest into one gay and stimulated company. Church Wagner avowed that the party was the best idea he had ever seen created on the spur of the moment; that Mr. Paperman had a genius for running a tropic hotel. "Why, you've turned a disaster into a fun thing, sir. It's just wonderful."

"Fine. Now Church, where's Esmé? I still don't see her at the switchboard."

The bartender's glowing face turned sober and a little sneaky. "Sir, I couldn't find her. The girls say she went home. She wasn't feeling good. But I've got the board fixed so the calls are coming in here, sir. It's no problem."

"The hell it isn't. I must find Esmé, Church, and right away. It's imperative. You know where she lives, I daresay?"

"Why, a place called the Thousand Steps, I believe, sir."

"Oh, Lord, her too? Okay. I'll tend bar for an hour. Go and fetch her."

"Mr. Paperman, that really wouldn't be advisable." Church looked appalled. "She lives there with the fellow who—with the father, as you might say. He's six foot two and he's very jealous."

"Is he from Nevis?"

"No, no. He's a Kinjan. He has a job in public works."

"He *does?*" Paperman laughed out loud with relief. "Well, for Christ's sake, let her marry him then! God, what a simple solution. How marvellous! I'll pay for the license. I'll give her a *dowry.*"

Church shook his head. "Sir, he's been trying to marry her for months. She won't do it. She can't stand him. He's a religious fanatic, she says, he reads the Bible all the time out loud, and mostly he eats mangoes and carrots."

"Why the devil is she living with him, then?"

"Sir, rents are high in Georgetown. Esmé has to economize."

Paperman clutched his head, feeling the old Kinjan vertigo coming on him again. "All right. All *right*. I'll get Esmé. I'll go there right after dinner. I'll go up and around the Jewish cemetery."

"Sir?"

"Sorry. I'm talking to myself. What about the water arrangements? What if people use up their pails?"

"Millard is staying on till midnight. He'll keep drawing water and delivering it to the rooms. Sheila arranged that."

A ragged fork of lightning, at this moment, plunged down the eastern horizon, which was a solid bank of low dirty clouds. Norman had noticed weather building up in the east ever since Lionel's departure. This was no straggle of thunderheads; it was a wide storm. But it was far away. The thunder did not come for perhaps fifteen seconds, and it was a mere rumble.

"Look at that, sir," Church said.

"I know. Just when we have a third of a cistern and can't use it."

"Millard says we can use some. His bucket is starting to hit bottom."

"In that case, there's no problem. It'll pass us by. Give me a scotch on the rocks, Church. I'm going to take my rest before dinner."

The rain began just as Norman was getting into bed. Seldom in his life had he heard a sweeter sound than the sudden thick drumming on the galvanized-iron roof of the main house. He now lived in Amy Ball's apartment on the second floor. The White Cottage was far too good an income producer to house him; at the moment a family of six occupied it, at fifteen dollars a day per head. Amy's apartment was small and dingy, and he expected Henny to complain, but he thought a look at the ledgers would end her protests. She could redecorate and brighten it.

He lay back on the bed in his silk Chinese robe, smoking a cigarette, sipping at his scotch, and listening to the heavy rattle overhead. This was no teasing sprinkle, good only to wash spiders and bird droppings into the cistern. This was rain, real rain. It was deeply reassuring; it seemed an augury of better things. He put out the cigarette and allowed himself to be lulled into a delicious drowse. He lay in a sagging wrought-iron bed caked with cracking white paint, under a slanted wallpapered ceiling, a riot of sun-faded roses big as basketballs.

chapter ten

Champagne, Si—Agua, No

I

Governor Sanders was in the bar when Norman came down, and with him was his wife. Norman had not heard that the governor's lady was back in Amerigo. He lingered near the doorway, watching them talk over their drinks. Reena Sanders, though black as she could be, was unmistakably not a Kinjan. Her pseudo-Egyptian coiffure, her elegantly tailored black suit with large white buttons, were only part of her difference. The rest lay in the way she held herself, the assurance in the tilt of her head, the straight glance of her eyes, the controlled, sharp moves of her hands. She was all Washington–New York sheen. Norman approached them with a word of welcome, and they invited him to join them.

"No, no. I'm sure you two have a million things to talk about."

The governor's long hollow face creased in a bitter little grin. "Reena's just telling me the same old thing—that she can't stand Kinja. At this point you're probably on her side."

"Not yet."

Mrs. Sanders was on her way to Caracas for a United Nations conference on housing. She had routed her trip to include an overnight stay in Amerigo, she said; one or two days on the island was about all she could stand. The place gave her the creeps. She wanted to know what Norman's troubles had been. Having already broken in this monologue on Lionel and Iris, Norman rather eagerly began to perform. He loved nothing more than making people laugh at a table, over drinks or coffee. It had been his life's work, pretty much. Reena Sanders was soon uproariously amused, because he was tickling her own prejudices against Kinja. After a while even the governor began to laugh in a strange high neighing way, as though laughter came hard to him. People in the bar turned to look and to whisper.

During the tale of the Akers wall, Mrs. Sanders held up both hands. "Oh, dear, Norman, stop. I'm hungry as a wolf, I want to eat right now, but I absolutely must hear the rest of this. Join us for dinner. Please!"

The rain was thrumming on the awnings of the crowded dining terrace; but the kerosene flares, and the orange-flaming oil lamps of the tables, hardly flickered. The wind blew from the other side of the hotel, and the terrace was in the lee. Slanting rain hissed into the floodlit green shallows. "If there's anything I like on this island," said the governor's wife, looking out at the hazy waterfront lights and the dim sparks of homes on the hills, "it's this terrace and this view. I've never seen anything more beguiling."

Norman went to the kitchen for a moment and talked to Sheila about the governor's dinner. The menu at the hotel was strictly table d'hôte, and Sheila rotated her menu day by day in a pattern she had not varied in seven years. Still, for a special guest, or for the proprietor, the cook was reasonable about making exceptions. Millard, the gardener, sat sweltering in a corner on an inverted pail, in his ragged dungarees and brown paper hat, gnawing on a pork chop.

"You're putting in long hours, Millard. I'm sorry. You'll get paid overtime."

"I does praise de Lord, please," said Millard, with a sweet and happy smile, "dat I does be helpful to you, and to all dese nice people."

Returning through the lobby, Paperman saw the tarpaulin bellying taut in the wind, making a singing noise and flapping at an upper corner. He had not realized how much slack there was; the dirty brown canvas swelled halfway across the lobby. Evidently the wind tonight was blowing straight into the hole made by Akers. He called Church out of the bar to show him this unsightly thing, and they heard tumbling sounds behind the ballooning tarpaulin.

"I don't want to look," Norman said. He had had three drinks and was feeling good, and was determined to go on feeling good. "There's nothing we can do back there anyway, right now."

"The wind can't hurt any of that stuff, sir," Church said. "Just shuffle it around a bit, maybe."

"But our party's going to be ruined," Norman said, "with this gruesome thing bulging half across the room like an elephant's backside."

Church pulled at this and that rope of the tarpaulin. "It just needs to be secured, sir. Please don't worry about it. One thing I can do is handle canvas." He hauled on a rope, and the flapping stopped. "I'll fix this up right now."

"Good lad."

Sheila sent out excellent steaks to the governor's table. Paperman ordered one bottle and then another of Beaune, the best wine he had, and resumed his tale. He was in good form; the governor and his wife were entranced. Sanders even remarked once, between high-pitched guffaws, that Paperman ought to keep notes, and one day write a book.

At what seemed to be the right moment—just after signing the check for the dinners with a flourish, over Sanders' protest, and ordering brandy and coffee—Norman told them about Miss Buckley and Esmé. He was hoping, of course, that the governor would offer to intervene. This had been the point of his whole effort to charm. His picture of Miss Buckley's habit of ignoring him, while writing and groaning for minutes on end, convulsed the governor's wife. "Oh, mercy, a puffed-up little bureaucrat and a *Kinjan,* rolled into one," she said. "What a combination! Sheer Frankenstein."

"You'd be amazed," said Sanders, "how nice Christophine Buckley can be. Just laughing, pleasant, and obliging all the time. A real sweetheart, whenever I've had anything to do with her."

Reena Sanders put a cigarette in a long ivory holder and Paperman swooped a flaming lighter to it. "Thank you, dear. —Of course she's nice to *you*, Alton."

Norman said that once dinner was over and the champagne party had started, he was going to borrow a raincoat and spend the night hunting down the pregnant fugitive in the jungle of the Thousand Steps.

"In *this?*" Mrs. Sanders made an abrupt gesture at the lashing rain. "On the Thousand Steps? With your heart condition? You'll drop dead and nobody will ever take notice. The dogs and the rats will eat you."

"I don't know what my alternative is. If I lose my chambermaids and gardeners, I fold and go back to New York. It's the end."

"Alton, surely you can do something. I mean, to me this is ridiculous, I mean, even for the Caribbean! Mercy! Make Buckley take a literacy test, and get rid of her. Just threaten it and she'll cave in."

"She's federal," the governor said with a shrug. "Nothing to do with the local government."

"Oh *please*. I mean. Who're you kidding?" Mrs. Sanders blinked at her husband with a dangerous, exasperated look in her wine-brightened eyes, "This is what I hate about Kinja, Norman. It's all low-grade vaudeville and burlesque, it sickens me, and in other words I'm afraid Alton is going to become just like them if he stays here much longer, and to me I'm being a good wife by staying in Washington and keeping the children out of *this*." She flung a hand at the island of Amerigo, and Norman noticed that the charm dangling from her gold bracelet was a Phi Beta Kappa key.

The governor was slouching more and more, glancing about and dragging continually and deeply at a cigarette, drumming fingers of one thin hand on the table. "Ordinarily I'd be glad to put in a word to Buckley," he said in a low voice. "This is a sticky time, that's all. I'm trying to get along with Orrin Easter, and Buckley is his pet. That's why my predecessor got her a federal appointment, out of the way, out of the local civil service. Reena, maybe we'd better go back to Government House."

Mrs. Sanders gave a short barking laugh. "Hah! Civil service! Alton, it doesn't take the guts of a rabbit to slap down such types, and I think you should do something."

Paperman quickly stood. "I have to see to my water-shortage party. Please stay and have a glass of champagne or two with us."

"I will if he won't," said Reena Sanders. "To me that should be fun. Thank you for a splendid dinner."

The governor said, "Yes, thank you very much," smiled mechanically, and lapsed into slouching silence. As Norman walked away, the governor's wife started to talk again in cutting tones.

2

Champagne, Si—Agua, No.

Church had somehow found the time to cut out this motto in red cardboard letters a foot high, and to string it across the straining tarpaulin. The canvas hardly bulged any more. It hummed powerfully, like a close-hauled mainsail, but Paperman could see that it was secure. The party was already under way; the lobby furniture had been pushed to the walls and the straw rugs rolled back, leaving a broad bare red-tiled floor for the dancing couples. The steel-drum music, which outdoors had a mournful thin quality, thundered and reverberated in the lobby like musical tom-toms, with doubled excitement. Church and two waitresses, standing between a pair of tables lined with wineglasses in the center of the lobby, were dispensing pink champagne punch from huge bowls, and the dancers swirled around these tables, many of them drinking as they danced. Because of the rain, not many outsiders had come to the Reef tonight. There was the usual sprinkling of young Kinjans who liked to dance to the Gull Reef music, and a small, self-conscious knot of sailors in whites from a submarine staying overnight in Amerigo. Norman had ordered Church to give the free champagne to everybody present, hotel guests or not. If noise, movement, and laughter all through the lobby, and crowds around the champagne tables, were an indication, the party was off to a good start. Norman took a glass of punch from each of the two bowls, in the line of duty, and found the drink sweet but passable. It was being drunk in large quantities, and that was what mattered. Again in the line of duty, he picked out the least attractive guest he could see, a fat, young schoolteacher from Yonkers with a terrible double chin, and asked her to dance. He was determined to make this party a success.

The governor and his wife soon came strolling in. Paperman hurried to them, dragging along the Yonkers girl, and took a glass of punch with them. The governor agreeably toasted the success of the Gull Reef Club, and an end to water shortages. Most of the guests knew who the skinny grizzled Negro in the black suit was, but few had met him. Paperman began introducing the governor, a handshaking line formed, and Sanders responded with the affable grace of any politician. This novelty put the party into high gear. Stragglers came crowding in from the bar and the dining terrace to shake hands with the governor of Amerigo. He sealed his little triumph by asking the Yonkers girl to dance, and wobbling off in a stiff rickety merengue to loud applause. This put Mrs. Sanders into Paperman's arms. She danced clumsily, her eyes darting about in amused curiosity at the guests, the poster, and the tarpaulin. "This place has a real nutty charm, you know? I gave friend husband holy hell about your pregnant chambermaid," she said. "I mean I pointed out in other words that if the best hotel on the island gets closed down by an idiotic female bureaucrat who just feels like making trouble, that won't look too good either when Interior finds out. I guess maybe that penetrated."

She saw the sailors, standing in a corner by themselves. She said it awakened her old USO hostess blood, and she went over and asked one of them, a tall, powerful Negro boy, to dance with her. He hung back, grinning in embarrassment, but his friends, thrilled by this gesture of the governor's lady, pushed him into her arms. Later Paperman saw Mrs. Sanders dancing one by one with the other sailors, to all appearances having a fine time. Sanders himself made a shadowy withdrawal. After a while he just wasn't there.

Norman asked various lady guests to dance, and in time the one truly good-looking girl at the Reef, a tall skinny blonde, with slanting brown eyes ringed in black paint, was in his arms. She had been posing on the Club grounds and in scenic spots of the island in breath-stopping bikinis and sun clothes, for a bald gnome of a fashion photographer. The man was clearly indifferent to her, except as an object to put on film; he emerged from under the black drape of his camera to push her naked limbs here and there like a dummy's, while men gathered to gape and envy. This girl at work, striking her angular poses, was as solemn as though she were doing algebra. Norman had noticed her, of course, but in his driven state he had never even bothered to find out her name. He now learned that it was Delphine. She had drunk a lot of punch, and she treated Norman with instant marked warmth. She knew of his friendship with Dan Freed. Obviously she thought him a man of glamour, and Norman perceived almost at once that something was doing here. In the Broadway argot of the moment, Delphine was a "swinging chick"; that is, an unfettered sort, reasonably available for fornication.

This discovery delighted him less than it might have some years earlier. Nowadays he found swinging chicks a bit oppressive. There was little excitement in conquering an easy girl; at his age it was a stale small chore. With the onset of middle-aged health problems, moreover, the question as to who his dirty or diseased predecessors might have been loomed large. Most of all—though this was not the point he dwelled on—Norman no longer had quite the energy to service a swinging chick.

The effect Delphine had on him was to make him think of Iris. Why wasn't she at the party? Norman thought he would just go and have a look in the Pink Cottage. He turned Delphine over to a hot-handed bachelor with a peeling red nose, who had been following her around the dance floor like a bloodhound. He borrowed Church's raincoat, swallowed another glass of punch, and ran out into the heavy rain.

The Pink Cottage was dark. As Paperman came to the door he heard growling and snarling; and the hurled thuds of the dog's body against the door indicated that he was unchained. It was a stout door, but Paperman reversed his steps and was leaving hastily when Iris's sleepy voice called, "Anybody out there? —Meadows, for Christ's sake, shut your big face. —Who's there? —See stupid, it's nobody. You were dreaming. Shut *up!* I'm trying to sleep."

Paperman shouted, "Iris, it's me, it's Norman."

"Norm? Are you out of your mind, wandering around in this weather?"

"I want you to come to the party. I miss you."

"You sound drunk. Go away, will you? I look unspeakable."

"Have you got on your bat ears?"

He heard her laugh. "Just about. Wait a second, Norman. I can't go yelling through a door in a storm."

Paperman huddled under the streaming overhang, listening to the rich pleasing gurgle of water down the spouts. The entrance light snapped on and the door opened a crack.

"Still here? Come in for just a second and be cured of me for good. Shock treatment."

She wore her green silk robe, her hair was close-tied in a net, her face was pink and oily, and her eyes seemed smaller and less brilliant without cosmetics, but she looked desirable enough, Norman thought. Only one red-shaded floor lamp was lit. Meadows crouched in the cone of light, ears cocked, tongue flickering over his nose, curses rumbling in his throat.

"My God," she said. "You're half-drowned."

Norman dashed the rain from his face. "Listen, come on to the party."

Iris yawned. "Are you crazy? It would take me two hours of hard labor to make myself fit to be seen. And for what?"

"Don't be difficult. Put on lipstick and some powder and a dress. We're having fun up there."

She shook her head, yawning and yawning. "I just took two sleeping pills. You trot yourself back up there and dance some more with Reena Sanders." She grinned at him and wagged a finger in front of her nose. "Spies. I've got spies. Surprised you, didn't I? Heh heh."

"Were you having dinner on the terrace? I didn't see you."

"Oh, no, you were too busy convulsing His Excellency and the first lady. Cute, isn't she?" Iris yawned again. "I'm about to pile up on this floor in a heap of old bones. Anything I can do for you first? Wanna drink?"

Norman buttoned up the raincoat. "Well, if you're full of happy pills, it's no use arguing. I'm off to the Thousand Steps."

"You're off *where?*" Iris's heavy dimming eyes opened wide and glistened at him.

He told her about Miss Buckley and Esmé. She shook her head groggily. "You're cuckoo, I swear. How much champagne have you had? Don't you *dare* go sloshing around on those steps tonight, do you hear! Don't you dare! Go back up to the hotel and get stoned. It'll do you good."

"Iris, if Immigration doesn't renew those bonds—"

She shook a fist at him. "You're *not* going up to the Thousand Steps, Norman Paperberg! I mean Paperman. Jesus, what a name. Listen, Amaranthe does sewing for me. We talk. We're real old pals. I'll track down your Esmé myself, first thing in the morning. Leave it to me." Her voice was becoming thick and trailing off. She put her arms around his neck. "Promise? No Thousand Steps?"

He embraced her soft body in the smooth silk robe. Iris was no photographer's object like Delphine; she had the blurred used figure of thirty-nine; but she was an attractive woman, not a swinging chick. She yielded against him, inert, sagging, heavy. "Don't you go raping me now, you unprincipled cad," she murmured. "I'm dead to the world. It'll be—it'll be—necrophilia."

The cover was off the divan, the pillow was crumpled, and the thin blanket was thrown back. He had to lead her only a few steps. The crouched dog did not interfere, but the bright brown eyes never left him. She let Norman take off the robe, moving her arms with drowsy limpness, like Hazel in her baby years. Iris's gauzy, peach-colored short nightgown made him regret her remark about necrophilia. It had put him on his honor. He tucked her into bed, turned out the light, and when she reached a hand toward him with a meaningless mutter, he leaned over and kissed her once. Then he went out into the whipping rain.

3

The party was in a jolly roar. A surpassingly noisy business was going on at the far end of the lobby. Two sailors held a long stick parallel to the ground, and a line of guests, sailors, and Kinjans were dancing under it face upward, or trying to. This "limbo" had been in progress for some time, for the stick was low, and most of the white people who attempted to wriggle under, with knees bent and spines arched backward, were sprawling one by one on their backsides, each time raising fresh bawls of mirth. The Kinjans were undulating beneath the pole without trouble, and two of the sailors also edged under, less fluidly than the natives but with practiced speed. The star of the antic, how-

239

ever, was certainly Delphine. Her dress, a tight beige linen sheath, allowed little room for the necessary knee work. The swinging chick solved this difficulty, when her turn came, by sliding her skirt up on her hips; and as she went inching under the stick, head and body thrown back, legs bent double at the knee and spread apart, she displayed to one and all her naked thighs clear up to their natural junction, imperfectly veiled by a wisp of pink nylon. She passed the barrier to a cheer, and shook down her skirt, only to raise it again in a minute or so to repeat the performance under the lowered stick. The sailors and guests, of course, were goggling and applauding, the women hardly less than the men. But the Kinjans glanced uneasily at each other, and mostly averted their eyes from Delphine's free show.

It was a new sensation for Norman Paperman to be ashamed of the white race. Whatever one might say of the Kinjans—and he had already endured much from their taciturn primitiveness and odd ways—their modesty was austere. The one Negro girl left in the limbo line, a Reef waitress, was thrusting her full orange cotton skirt far down between her thighs as she took her turn; moreover, as Delphine made another pass, Norman saw this girl wrinkle her nose, whisper something to a Negro boy, who was the best dancer of the lot, and walk off with him.

Norman went to the punch bowl and drank three glasses, one after the other. All at once, returning from Iris's cottage to the rollicking party, he had been hit hard by loneliness, by homesickness, by certainty that his ownership of this grotesque hotel in the Caribbean, where a crowd of strangers were jigging, writhing, haw-hawing, and guzzling to crude music, was an insanity. Norman Paperman had in his time taken part in many a steamy brawl, and had seen much lewder displays than Delphine's. Unmistakably, he knew now that that part of his life was over. He was as disgusted by the chick, almost, as if he were his own synagogue-going father; and this knowledge threw a chill of evening on his once jocund Broadway spirit.

But the champagne worked. His mood hovered in blue gloom for a few minutes, while he looked at the cavorting, sweaty dancers and thought of the vanity of all things, the frailness and brevity of human existence, and such liverish profundities. Then, slowly but definitely, the world—or at least the lobby of the Gull Reef Club—began to assume a brighter hue. Paperman drank some more, and—why, there was the good old world again, looking quite all right. In fact, this was a hell of a party, and Paperman regretted that the limbo was finished, and that Delphine was now doing only a mild twist with the red-nosed bachelor, to a most inexpert whumping of the steel drums. He was restored to a normal, even hearty, interest in a display of her underwear, but alas, the moment was gone. He gulped another glass for good measure, and asked one of his waitresses to dance.

His memories of what happened after that were unclear. He did a lot of dancing, and drank a lot of champagne, and said a great many enormously funny things, because everybody he talked to kept laughing and laughing, and he was continuously laughing too. This was the first time since his purchase of the Club, he realized, that he was having any fun at all. The party was a marvellous idea, he decided, and he'd have a champagne party in the lobby once a week, water shortage or no. He danced with Reena Sanders, and while he couldn't remember anything he said, the governor's exotic lady laughed so hard she could scarcely keep time to the music. At one point, he was dancing the merengue with Hassim, in the center of a ring of clapping and cheering merry-makers, and the effete Turk in his orange slacks, far from being offensive, struck him as a killingly amusing parody of a fat lady. There was even another limbo after a while, and he got into line and fell flat on his back the first time he tried to go under the pole, which caused a new climax of hilarity. Delphine generously showed her underpants time and again, with the roguish zest of a little girl playing Doctor, and some of the less appetizing women guests were emboldened to imitate her; and so all was laughter, champagne, jokes, shouting, and voyeur delights, when the tarpaulin tore loose.

It was a total surprise. One moment there was the limbo, and a gay joking crowd; the next moment a writhing brown wall sailed across the lobby, battering down in its path musicians, steel drums, guests, chairs, and both punch tables in a bedlam of shrieks, clatters, yells, and the crashings of overthrown glass. The huge canvas fetched up against the opposite wall and collapsed, still flapping and tumbling about, and the wind and warm rain of a tropical thunderstorm came boiling into the lobby, through the hole that had once been a wall, and through the chaos and ruin of the old dining room. All of Akers' building materials —the windows, the door frames, the plywood panels, the washstands, the crates of tiles, the venetian blinds—lay in toppled, tangled, sodden heaps. Some crates had burst open. There appeared to be forty toilet seats scattered about, and a thousand brass doorknobs, and crisscrossing in all directions were unrolled fluttering yards and yards of streaked, soggy red-and-silver wallpaper. The wind, coming in gusts of perhaps thirty miles an hour, clattered the aluminum blinds, careened the plywood panels, and pelted the victims of the tarpaulin in the lobby—who were picking themselves up and dazedly staring around—with flying rain, green leaves, paper scraps, and wet excelsior.

The destruction and the mess went almost unnoticed at first, because the tarpaulin, piled up against the far wall and trailing halfway across the lobby, was continuing to writhe in a peculiar way not ascribable to the wind. There were several lumps working under it, and the lumps were making muffled, discontented sounds.

Church, the sailors, and Paperman went to the rescue, and after much hauling and heaving of the incredibly heavy, soaking brown canvas, they liberated three guests, including the red-nosed bachelor and the Yonkers schoolteacher, who was laughing and crying at once. Then the tarpaulin began to work again and out crawled a very small sailor in filthy wet whites. On his hands and knees, peering around with a glassy smile, he said in a young Southern voice, "Jesus, Ah never did *see* such a wing-ding. Is the bar still open?"

This brought a shout of laughter from most of the guests. They had drunk enough to regard mishaps and destruction as funny. Norman, who had been laughing almost without cease since the tarpaulin's brief mad flight, was inspired to yell, "You bet it's open! Everybody into the bar! All drinks on the house, from now till dawn!"

With a cheer and a rush, the entire party went funnelling into the bar, musicians, guests, waitresses, sailors; Mrs. Sanders too, arm-in-arm with Paperman and Hassim, the three of them bawling in raucous song,

> *"Carnival is very sweet*
> *Please*
> *Don't stop de carnival—"*

Church tactfully closed the doors on the lobby and the old dining room: on the crumpled tarpaulin, the overturned furniture, the broken glass glinting from every tile of the wet slippery floor, the piled-up tan-

gled wreckage of unused building materials; on the wind, still coming
in gusts to knock and slide things around; and on his red-lettered sign
—*Champagne Si, Agua No*—swimming in mid-lobby in a puddle of
blown-in rain.

> *"Carnival is very sweet*
> *Please*
> *Don't stop de carnival,"*

sang Paperman, and the Turkish homosexual, and the black governor's
lady, as the door closed on them.

It rained all night, and the water level in the cistern kept rising. Norman was not thinking about such matters. Mine host was having a good
time at last.

4

He did not in the least recall going to bed, but obviously he had, since
he woke up in bed; in his own bed, on the second floor, under the slanting ceiling of hyperthyroid roses. He woke with what presented itself
at once as the worst headache of his life, a headache like a big object
with many razor-sharp edges inside his skull; with a filthy taste in his
mouth; with a terrible quick pounding of his heart; with a scary numb-
ness running all down his left arm to cold trembling fingers; and with
a general sinking sense of ill-being, compared to which death seemed no
great threat. He had a champagne hangover. He knew, he had known
for thirty years, that this was the worst of all hangovers; what on earth
had possessed him to drink all that mediocre champagne doctored and
made deadlier with grenadine and sugar? The very memory of that taste
drove a wave of nausea through him.

He sat up with an awful moan, his head in a whirl, his eyes throbbing
in pain from the white sunshine at the window. The knocking on the
door came again, louder and more urgent. He now realized that he had
been awakened not by his own physical misery, but by the usual reveille
of the Gull Reef Club, knuckles on the door rapping out the alarm.

"Who—ah, who is it? Wha' is it?"

"Sheila, suh. I does have to talk to you, suh. I wery sorry to hoross you, suh."

"Give me two minutes."

A hair of the dog was the only thing at such a time, medical theory and warnings notwithstanding. Norman staggered to the bathroom and choked down a tumbler of tap water and scotch with one of the mighty oval yellow pills which Henny took to fend off migraine, and which, he had accidentally discovered long ago, acted for him as a sure head-clearer for about four hours, at a cost of perhaps twenty-four hours of the shakes. He knew, from the very sound of Sheila's knuckles on the door, that this morning would require an alert mind and a strong heart. Ye gods, that pink slop he had drunk by the gallon! He brushed his hair and his teeth, flushed his mouth violently with full-strength mouthwash, and dizzily opened the door.

The leading bulletin in the cook's evil tidings was that all six chambermaids had quit. Amaranthe had sent this word by Virgil; no explanation. Insatiable demands for water had been coming from all the rooms since seven in the morning. It was ten now, Millard was half-dead with running up and down the stairs, Virgil was helping him, and still the guests were in an angry uproar and some were starting to check out. It had been impossible to do anything about the party wreckage as yet; the lobby and the old dining room still looked, as Sheila put it, "like Noah's flood done go troo de hotel." Immigration had telephoned three times. There was a cable from New York, requesting an eighteen-hundred-dollar check for the Tilson party provisions before they would ship anything. That, Sheila said, was about all.

"Sheila, I badly need food," Paperman said, clutching his brow. "Make me—make me a mushroom omelet. Right away."

"Yassuh. De maids does be de serious ting, dey ain' no maids to get in Kinja. I tink dey does be concern for Esmé."

"Can't the dining-room waitresses make the beds, just for today?"

"No suh, de union dey does be very strick about dat."

The upheaval in the lobby was so appalling that Norman hurried through with averted eyes to the dining terrace. Many guests were still at breakfast, a glum, silent, red-eyed lot. Iris Tramm sat in the slant sunshine of a far corner table, in a blue silk shirt with large gold polka dots, and tailored white shorts, looking fresh and radiant; or perhaps she only appeared so to Paperman, through the kindly screen of his dark glasses, and the glow of the scotch and the yellow pill, which were commencing their work of uplift. Meadows sat beside her, tightly leashed to a table leg, and she was giving him bacon scraps.

"Don't say it," she greeted Norman as he approached. "No dogs allowed on the dining terrace. We're just leaving. I sneaked him in because it's his birthday."

"Don't go." He fell in the chair opposite her, with a groan. "I need company."

"I can imagine. What on earth hit the lobby last night?"

"Just let me eat something. Then I'll talk." Paperman rested his face in his hands.

"You didn't go to the Thousand Steps, did you? I woke up worrying about you."

"The Thousand Steps? No. God knows I should have."

His mushroom omelet came. The sun was warm and comforting on his back, and the whiskey and the pill took firm hold as soon as he had eaten a few bites. He began to feel much better. It wouldn't last, he knew, but the relief was wonderful. While he was recounting the misadventures of the night and the morning, Church appeared, rather gray in the face, and told him that a fourth couple had just checked out. "I tried carrying water up for a while, sir, but so many of them are in the bar, trying to get over last night—"

"Stay in the bar, Church. Sweat it out till I find Esmé. I'm going from here to the Thousand Steps. Once she comes back the others will."

Church gnawed his lower lip, and pulled at his beard. "Sir, I'm afraid you'll be wasting your time. I think she's disappeared into the brush. She always said she would. I'll get at the lobby as soon as I can, I know it's a mess." The bartender shook his head, and walked off scratching his beard.

Iris untied the dog from the table. "Just let me put Meadows away. I'll do the rooms."

"*You?* Don't be fantastic."

"I was a hospital volunteer in the war. I can make up ten rooms in the time these Nevis girls do one."

He said, "Look, if it comes to that I can make the rooms."

"Well, maybe you'd better work with me, Norm. Two people go fast,

making beds. And when they see the poor hung-over proprietor cleaning the rooms, it may stop the check-outs. Sympathy."

"Iris, you're a paying guest, not a chambermaid."

"It's just for this morning. Once we've done the rooms, I'll hunt down
Amaranthe and she'll herd the girls back. Get yourself a mop and pail,
and never say die."

As often happens, this unthinkable business of cleaning rooms with
Iris became a sort of lark, once Paperman fell into the swing of it. They
joked about the luggage, the photographs, the clothing they saw. Paperman had never before pictured the breach of privacy that went with a
chambermaid's access to one's room; nor how guests characterized themselves with the state of a bathroom, the way clothes were hung, the
books, magazines, and more intimate objects littered about; nor, most of
all, what pigs most people were. He soon recovered the knack of making
beds, something he had not done since his boy scout days, and he and
Iris made swift progress down the hall. They had been at this for half
an hour or so; they were shaking out a bedsheet, laughing over the lady's
flimsy pajama bottoms that went floating to the floor, when the building
trembled under them, and they heard a distant noise like the dumping
of large stones down a chute. They froze, looking at each other, still
holding the extended sheet.

"Not a quake," Iris said in a low nervous voice. "That's not a quake."

"Sh!" Paperman said.

A heavy vibration was coming up through the floor, unlike any usual
operating noises of the hotel. Paperman flung his end of the sheet on
the bed, ran out of the room, trampled down the stairs, and rushed
through the chaotic lobby to the dance terrace. There was a jagged
break in the red tiles at the edge, and a section of the rail was gone.
Leaning over the broken rail, Paperman saw green water spouting out
of the foundation like blood from a cut throat. The cistern had broken
wide open, and was losing water in a torrent four or five feet wide.
Guests lined the beach, watching the novel sight, shouting at each other
and laughing.

As Paperman stared down at this visible death of his Caribbean enterprise, motionless, his hands gripping the rail, tears starting to his eyes,
he felt Iris's warm hand clasp his. He was ashamed to look at her, or to
try to talk.

"I'm sorry, Norm," she said, in a sweet, husky tone, full of undisguised affection. "I'm awfully sorry."

This note of feminine despair gave Paperman strength. He cleared his throat. "Well, let's go and see just how bad it is, shall we? The hotel hasn't fallen down yet, you know. Neither has the sky."

It took the water about five minutes to pour out of the broken cistern, gouging a deep canyon in the beach. Paperman stood on the sand, to one side of the rushing water, with Iris, Church, and Sheila. He had plenty of time to review the totality of his defeat—the wreckage in the game room, the vanished wall, the unsolved electric failure, the stopped pump, the departed chambermaids, the empty bank account, the unpaid debts, the certain departure of most of the guests after this new disaster. Nor could he accept any more incoming guests. To run a hotel, he needed water.

The escaping water slowed to a murky trickle. The hole, now visible from top to bottom, was a ragged, lop-sided V in the wall. One side was almost vertical, the other slanted and zigzagged up to the break in the terrace. Chunks of masonry lay tumbled on the beach, and big blue and brown stones protruded all along the broken edges.

The guests, clustered behind Paperman, were not laughing any more. They stood silent or whispered, with the embarrassed long faces of people at a funeral. Sheila was at Paperman's side, weeping and dabbing at her eyes with her apron. "I didn't tink dey be so much rain," she said. "So much rain, so much rain, so much rain—"

Paperman patted her shoulder. "Sheila, it wasn't your fault. I should have thought of it, if anybody should have, and opened the valve. I didn't, and it happened, that's all."

He stepped up to the broken wall, unmindful of the wet sand and muck squirting over his shoes, and peered into the cistern. A shaft of sunshine illuminated the big space, and the wet rocks glittered on the far wall. The bottom was inches thick in brown slime.

"Hello," he shouted, and the silly word resounded and boomed. He walked back to Iris, Church, and Sheila, who stood together, a little apart from the rest. "Just as I thought," he said. "Empty." He turned to the guests, and threw his arms wide. "Champagne, anyone?"

Nobody laughed. Nobody said anything.

Sheila had stopped crying, and her fat face had hardened. "Mistuh

Papuh, I be back one o'clock. De lunch on de stove, you just tell de girls start dishing it up." She started to waddle off, putting the back of her hand to her eyes.

"Where are you going, Sheila?" called Paperman. "I need you here."

The heavy black mask turned and looked at him with blank eyes. "I comin' back. Tings does be too confuse in de hotel, Mistuh Papuh. Dey ain't no oder way no more. I going to get Hippolyte."

Part Three

CARNIVAL
IS
VERY SWEET

chapter eleven

Hippolyte Lamartine

I

Within ten days, a striking change had come over the Gull Reef Club.
The cistern was repaired. The dance terrace was tiled over and the
rail was repaired. The pump was working. There was plenty of water,
and electricity was restored in all the rooms. The chambermaids, including Esmé, were back on the job. There were no further telephone
calls from Christophine Buckley. The lobby was straightened up, shining and clean. Most surprising of all—so very strange that Paperman
blinked every morning when he saw it—the old dining room was
being transformed into bedroom units. In the place of Akers' destroyed
wall stood a raw cinder-block wall with four louvered windows. Most

of the partitions for the rooms were up. The plumbing was going into place, and the estimate was that the rooms might be ready by Christmas Eve. All this was the doing of the man named Hippolyte Lamartine and his strange crew.

Hippolyte Lamartine was a broad-shouldered fattish fellow, perhaps five feet nine, with a round, pale, red-patched and somewhat scaly face, and thick straight black hair growing low on his forehead. He always wore a heavy khaki shirt buttoned to the throat and wrists, khaki pants, and a high-crowned straw hat with an enormous ragged brim turned down in front. He went barefoot. His feet and toenails looked horny as a beast's. He had small brown eyes close together, and his face was set in a puzzled squint, with deep worry lines on the forehead converging to the bridge of his thick short nose. His mouth was a line, pulled down at the corners, the lips out of sight. When he spoke—which was not often—he disclosed irregular dirty teeth. He always carried a long curved machete with a red wooden handle, which he called a "cutlash." If he was doing nothing else, he was usually whetting his cutlash on a smooth square stone, with little shrieks of sharpening iron. At the end of his day's work, he retired to the gardener's shack behind the kitchen; crawled onto a wooden bunk which he had hammered up over Millard's bed the day he came; and fell into slumber with the cutlash at his side. He was at work again before dawn.

He repaired the cistern in a couple of days, aided by two white men who were dressed like him, who looked enough like him to be his brothers, and who talked to him in barbaric guttural grunts. When Paperman, in an early effort to be sociable, asked Hippolyte whether they were in fact his brothers, the man just shook his head, and went on grunting to the others in a language that was not Calypso. Nor was it French to Paperman's ears, though that was what Sheila told him it was.

Sheila hated to discuss Hippolyte. When Norman pressed her, she said that he was a Frenchman from Guadeloupe; that there was a settlement of these white Guadeloupe natives at the west end of Kinja off beyond the sugar fields on the rocky coastal slope; that they mostly were fishermen and construction workers. Norman tried addressing Hippolyte in French; the man just squinted peculiarly at him, as though he were gibbering. He understood English, but often he gave Norman much the same kind of uncomprehending, surly squint when Norman asked a question or gave an order. Hippolyte paid very little attention, in fact, to anything Paperman said. He returned to the Gull Reef Club like an owner who had been away for years, and was setting to work with a will to fix the long decay due to incompetent caretakers.

He never explained what the electric failure had been. In his first hour on the premises he disappeared beneath the hotel, and when he emerged some time later, all sandy and greasy, the circuit was fixed, the lights were on all through the hotel, and the pump thumped healthily, drawing on the emergency tank. Paperman was working on the ledgers in the office when he felt through the floor the life-giving pulse of the pump. He rushed down to the beach to salute his rescuer, who came out of the crawl space brushing off sand and wiping grease from his hands on a rag. Hippolyte listened to Paperman's joyous congratulations with an impassive, worried squint, then picked up a shovel and walked off. Norman followed him but halted when Hippolyte marched through the gap in the cistern, splashing ankle-deep with his bare feet, and began shovelling out the vile brown muck.

"Look here, Hippolyte," he called into the echoing cave of the cistern, "I want to talk about your wages. What were you getting paid in the old days?"

"Hunnerd a mond."

"I'll start you at a hundred twenty-five."

"Okay," the Frenchman grunted in a dissatisfied tone.

"If things go all right I'll do better than that."

"We see."

Later—that same first day—Norman saw the two other men arrive at the beach on a barge carrying a cement mixer, a wheelbarrow, piles of rock, and stacked cinder blocks and bags of plaster. He became concerned about money, and tried to discuss with Hippolyte the costs of the materials and the barge, and the wages for his helpers. But he found it very hard to get a word in. The three men fell to unloading the barge, exchanging their coarse grunts, and shoving him out of the way. At last he planted himself directly in Hippolyte's path, as the Frenchman was tottering up the beach under two bags of plaster.

"Look, Hippolyte, I'd like to have an idea of what all this is costing."

"Dunno yet." Hippolyte tried to shoulder past, but Paperman held his ground.

"Don't you want money for the barge? For the materials?"

"No."

"What do these men get by the day?"

"We see."

Coming downstairs next morning, Paperman found seven other men cleaning the old dining room, stacking up the scattered panels and toilet seats, and laying out paint-stained cloths and power tools. There were several whites like Hippolyte, and the rest were burly Negroes. Norman thought he recognized them as members of Akers' crew, but he wasn't sure. Again he went after Hippolyte, who was well along with his new cistern wall. This time when Hippolyte merely squinted at him, Paperman lost patience and shouted, "Look here, how do those men up there know what to do? They haven't got the sketches, the blueprints, the specifications, nothing! Have they? Who's supervising? Who's the contractor? What's the price? I mean I appreciate the fine work you're doing, Hippolyte, but I want to know what the hell's going on here."

"I come de offus."

About two hours later Hippolyte came to the office, covered with plaster dust and sharpening his machete. "Where de plans?"

Paperman dug into his desk and brought out Akers' roll of sketches and folder of specifications. The Frenchman put his machete on the unrolled plans to hold them flat, and inspected them sheet by sheet, running his thick filthy fingers along the wiring schemes and the plumbing diagrams, looking very worried and working his nose like a rabbit. He rolled the plans up, and tucked them under his arm with the folder.

"You got two hunnerd dolla?"

"Yes, I've got two hundred dollars."

"I need two hunnerd dolla. Later more."

"Are you going to try to do this job yourself?"

"Last year I foreman Mr. Akers."

"Well—what's your estimate for the whole job?"

"Not too bad."

"How long do you think it will take?"

"Not too long."

Then and there Paperman had to make a key decision; either to trust this sullen, squinting, impenetrable, unhealthy-looking djinn, or throw him off the grounds. It was clear that Hippolyte did things on his own terms. He gave him the two hundred dollars. The Frenchman grunted and went out, putting on the hat with a flourish. Next day the construction job was under way; and, so far as Paperman could see, going well. Meantime the cistern was finished; another good rain fell, and the water problem was, to all appearances, over.

As for the chambermaids, they appeared, the day after Hippolyte did, at work at eight as always. Esmé took up her post at the switchboard, avoided Paperman's eyes, and said nothing about her disappearance. Norman tried to find out how Hippolyte had achieved this wonder, but Sheila would talk even less about it than about the other deeds of the Frenchman. "Hippolyte he does find people," was her surly explanation.

The cessation of Christophine Buckley's persecutions was a mystery. Paperman did not know whether Mrs. Sanders had finally persuaded the governor to intervene, or whether Hippolyte's occult efficiency extended even into the Immigration Office. Norman made the firm decision to ask no questions, to let well enough alone.

2

About a week after Hippolyte's coming, when Norman was still wavering between delight at his change in luck, and incredulous uneasiness over it, he at last learned some hard facts about the Frenchman. Church telephoned the office to say that Tom Tilson was looking for him in the bar. He found the old man and his wife sitting in deep armchairs by the frangipani tree, drinking their unvarying morning refreshment of double white rum and tonic water.

"Hello there! Come join us for elevenses!" Tilson rasped.

"Certainly. —Beer, Church."

He sat in an armchair facing Tilson, who leaned forward, gnarled freckled hands clutching his protruding kneecaps, and studied Norman's face. "Paperman, you look a bit the worse for wear."

"I'm fine. All I need is a couple of carefree weeks on a tropical island."

Tilson winked at his wife, a little woman with gray, beautifully groomed, upswept hair, a very red face, and several petrified dimples. "What about my party? Is it still on?"

"On? Of course it's on. I've ordered everything from New York."

"I just wondered." Tilson spoke in his usual abrupt loud way. "I didn't hear from you. Where are you getting the steaks? How about the oysters?"

He nodded and nodded at Paperman's description of the party plans. "Well, it all sounds pretty good, if it comes off that way. Have you laid out a lot of money? Do you want an advance?"

"Money? Ah, I don't know. I guess I can manage." Norman didn't want to disclose how nearly broke he was, but he regretted the answer as soon as he said the words.

"Well, all right. I'm not going to force money on you. I was just figuring that you're probably in for a couple of thousand or more at this point, and—"

Mrs. Tilson jumped half out of her chair, exactly as though a gun had gone off behind her, and clutched her husband's arm. "Lovey—lovey, look there. By the bar." She spoke in a low, shaky voice. "It's him, isn't it? It can't be anyone else."

Paperman and Tilson both looked in the direction of her glance. "My God!" Tilson wrinkled up his face so that he looked like a mummy. "Now when in the Christ did *this* happen?"

"When did what happen?" said Paperman.

"When did you hire Crazy Hippolyte?"

Mrs. Tilson said, "I didn't even know he was out of the madhouse."

"Neither did I." Tilson turned and shook his stick at Norman. "What the hell, Paperman? Do you have to recruit your staff out of lunatic asylums? Don't you even know better than that? —Hippolyte! Hey, there, Hippolyte!" The Frenchman, with his back to them, was working at the fuse box on the wall behind the bar. He squinted over his shoulder, then came, removing the straw hat, and running his fingers through his thick hair. "Well, Hippolyte, how goes it?"

The man put a finger to his forehead, and fumbled with his hat. "How do, Mist' Tilson. How do, Mistress."

Mrs. Tilson said, looking straight at him, "So, Hippolyte. Back on the old job."

"Old job. Yah." Hippolyte shuffled his feet.

"How are you these days?" Tilson said.

"Not too bad."

"We heard you weren't well there, for a while."

"Not too good."

"You're all better now?"

"Yah."

"Well, do a good job for Mr. Paperman, you hear! He's a friend of mine," Tilson shouted in a severe tone, as though addressing a deaf child.

Hippolyte smiled. It was the first time that Norman had seen the Frenchman's face perform this particular evolution. All the features seemed to fall away, into the crinkly, sweet vacuous grin of a baby six months old, with a mouthful of large bad teeth. "Good job. Yah."

Tilson uttered some disjointed noise, to which Hippolyte responded with a silly heaving laugh and similar noise. This time Paperman discerned fragments of French in the sounds. Hippolyte put on his big hat and went back to the fuse box.

"How did you get hold of him?" Tilson said. "Did he come around looking for work?"

"No, Sheila fetched him."

Mrs. Tilson giggled and a number of transient dimples appeared around her permanent ones. "Sheila! Didn't she tell you about him?"

"Not much. Just that he was 'fonny.' "

This tickled the Tilsons exceedingly; they laughed and laughed, looking at each other and throwing back their heads. The old man began to cough, and his eyes watered.

"Fonny, hey? Well, so long as you get him off the Reef on the night of my party, I don't care. But be sure you do."

Paperman told them how Hippolyte was mending the Club's troubles. Tilson pounded the floor with his stick to attract Church's attention and pointed to the empty glass. "Oh, sure. Hippolyte's a great worker when he's right in the head, and he knows more about the Reef than anybody. He dates back to Tony and Larry, in fact he brought Sheila here. He was living with her then. Two of her kids are his. —Or is it three?" he said to his wife.

"I don't think Sheila really knows, lovey."

"Is that usual?" Paperman said. "I mean Frenchmen mixing with colored?"

"Nothing is too unusual in the Caribbean," Tilson said. "Mostly the island French interbreed, that's how come they all look like each other. But you get one like Hippolyte, and he'll do any old thing that occurs to him. That's why I had to get rid of him. It was too bad, he's a good gardener and handy man. But he tried to rape our maid, and he chased her up a tree."

"He did *what?*"

"It was awful," Mrs. Tilson said, smoothing her back hair, "that poor girl shrieking up in this lovely mango tree, and Hippolyte chopping away at the trunk with his cutlash. Luckily I was right there in the kitchen. I got out there in time to save the tree."

Not knowing whether to believe any of this, Paperman said, half jocularly, "Weren't you afraid of him? That machete's like a razor."

"My dear, scared stiff. But that was my best mango tree. Anyway, these island French aren't too different from the ones that worked for us in Nouméa. We had our house way back in the hills near the mines. You learn how to talk to them. You've got no choice, you know. There you are, and there they are."

"Is that why he got committed? For molesting your maid?"

Tilson grunted. "In Kinja? If that were grounds, you couldn't build enough asylums. I couldn't have even gotten a policeman to caution him for that. No, Letty telephoned me, and I came home fast. I paid him off, told him he'd been a bad boy and not to come back. He didn't. I've got a shotgun and he knows I'd use it." Tilson turned to his wife. "Why did they put him away?"

She frowned thoughtfully. "Not on account of the policeman?"

"The one whose throat he cut? No, he came to us after that, didn't he? I seem to remember—"

Paperman, more and more appalled, burst out, "What is this? Are you pulling my leg? He cut a policeman's throat, and nobody arrested him? And then you *hired* him? You expect me to believe that?"

"Well, nobody ever proved he cut the cop's throat," Tilson said, rather patiently for him. "This cop was out around Frenchman's Point a lot, either after some fellow's wife, or trying to catch the fishermen smuggling. The story was never clear. He got into a fist fight with Hippolyte in a bar, and arrested him. Hippolyte spent a week in the jug. Then two weeks later this cop didn't report for duty. After a few days, the other cops went poking around in the brush in Hastings Estate and they found him, sort of minus an Adam's apple. In fact, his head generally was kind of loose. They pulled in Hippolyte, but they never could hang it on him, and they let him go. I needed a gardener, and one's as crazy as the next on this island, so I took a chance."

Mrs. Tilson swallowed a deep drink. "I had a fit when Tom hired him. But he was just a lamb for months and months, until the tree thing happened. Best gardener we ever had. The only one who ever did grow decent lettuce for me in that miserable soil up on the hill."

"And now you've got him, Paperman," chuckled Tilson. "Crazy Hippolyte! Well, good luck. Just pick out your tree now, in case he ever blows a fuse. Haw haw."

Norman said bitterly, "I might have known. Anything good that happens on this island has to have a big fat catch to it."

"Oh, he's probably okay now," said Tilson. "That's a pretty good madhouse they have in Guadeloupe. I don't think they'd have let him go if he weren't all right. Of course," the old man added with a one-sided leer that showed a gap in his worn-down teeth, "he might have escaped."

"Why did he go to a Guadeloupe asylum? Isn't he a Kinja citizen?"

"Oh, sure. The thing is they've never built an insane asylum here." Tilson poured the rest of his rum and tonic down his throat in one gesture. "I guess they didn't want to get into the ticklish question of who goes into the nut house. That would be a hell of a hot potato on this island."

"Why? Nothing to it," said Mrs. Tilson sweetly, with a grand display of dimples. "When the Eagles are in power the Elephants go behind the fence. When the Elephants get voted in, everybody changes places. That way everybody's always either on government salary or on government support."

"Jesus Christ," Tom Tilson said, "why haven't they thought of it? It's the solution to Caribbean politics."

They heard snarling, yapping, the jangling of a chain, and a woman's shrill angry voice. Iris Tramm came into the bar, dragging Meadows on his chain leash. Rearing and plunging every inch of the way, the dog was straining toward the lobby. "*Stop* it, you son of a bitch!" Iris shouted, slapping the dog so hard that dust rose from its black coat. "Stop it this minute, I say! Oh, god damn you!"

"My goodness, how the dust accumulates in the tropics," Mrs. Tilson said. "Iris, you want to vacuum that creature."

"I'll vacuum the son of a bitch," said Iris, flailing away. "I'll kill him! Down, I say! Down!" The dog was beginning to subside, but it still growled and pulled toward the lobby door.

Tom Tilson said, "My dear, it's no insult to call Meadows a son of a bitch. That's what he is."

"What's the matter, Iris?" Norman said.

"Oh, he's got this silly hate on for Hippolyte. He was that way about poor Millard, too, for months. He hates new men. He's going to get himself hacked in half, and it'll serve him right. Lie down, damn you. That's right. Lie down and stay down. Whew." Iris dropped into a chair. "He's so strong! He's got me sweating like a mule-skinner."

"Hippolyte won't hurt him," Mrs. Tilson said. "One thing about Kinjans, they're all scared to death of dogs. We keep four Great Danes, and to hell with the police force."

Tilson said, "Blazes, yes, I wouldn't have a Kinja cop on my land. They've got these damned six-shooters, and there isn't one of them can hit a cow standing sideways right in front of him. You're not safe within a mile of a Kinja cop."

"Have a drink, Iris," Paperman said.

"I don't want a drink, thanks. Look at you, though! Elevenses for mine host! Things have by God changed around here."

Paperman gave her a halfhearted smile. He was still digesting the news that the wonderful Hippolyte had been a mental case, probably a homicidal one; and that there was no assurance he was cured, except for the dubious fact that he was at large.

Iris looked out at the beach, yawning. "What a sublime day! All blue and gold again. If only there were something amusing to do—I'm supposed to get my hair done, and it seems such a crime on a day like this. However—"

Tilson deliberately put on his sunglasses, pushed himself erect with both hands on his stick, and looked out to sea. "I don't know, Iris. Is it too late to crank up the old stinkpot, Letty, and have lunch out at Big Dog? All four of us? Is there anything in the galley?"

"There's always sardines and crackers and things. Nobody'd starve." Mrs. Tilson looked at her watch. "Can you come, Mr. Paperman? Just a short boat ride, for a change?"

"I'll go if you will, Norm," Iris said. "Come on, it'll do you good."

There was a little pause.

"Well, I'll tell you what," Paperman said. "I can't think of a single reason why I shouldn't go. I've been to the bank. I've talked to the accountant. I'm even caught up on my reservation letters. How about that? You're on."

3

An hour later, Tilson's boat was rounding the eastern end of Amerigo. It was a sixty-foot white cabin cruiser named *Rainbow II,* built in Hong Kong; Tilson had hired it for the season upon selling *Moonglow.* It had two baths, a bedroom with full-sized beds and an electric fireplace, two other cabins, a large bar, and appointments of leather, brass, and teak. At twenty knots, it murmured along on high swells with scarcely a vibration or a roll. Norman, in swim trunks, lolled in a red leather fighting chair at the stern, taking in the scenery like a tourist. He had not seen this wild, craggy, roadless part of Kinja except in glimpses from a wheeling airplane. It was surpassingly beautiful: red broken cliffs rising out of clear turquoise water, green valleys tufted with palms; and here and there the white smooth scallop of a deserted beach shaded by palms and sea grapes. A strong scent of flowers mingled with the salt wind. He gave a tremendous, luxurious yawn. Iris, sitting in the other leather chair in her fetching black jersey swimsuit, yawned at the same instant, stretching out her legs. They looked deep in each other's eyes and laughed. A black-skinned hand took away Paperman's empty glass, and placed in his grasp a full cold one. He drank. This was his third or fourth. He didn't know which, and didn't care.

"I have an announcement to make," said Norman. "It's not earthshaking. Maybe you'll all think it's of no consequence. But I mean to make it."

Iris put both fists to her mouth and did a fair imitation of a sounding trumpet.

"Thank you," said Paperman. "Ladies and gentlemen, I am the happiest man in the world."

"Jesus, you're easily pleased," said Tilson. "Just a little ride on a stinkpot. I wish it did that for me." The Tilsons lounged between Norman and Iris on a couch of bamboo and red leather.

"This thing you call a stinkpot, which as you know is a snazzy yacht, is all very well," Norman said. "But it's the least part of my happiness. For the first time since I came to the accursed rock called Kinja, I see the Caribbean really looking like the Caribbean, and its beauty moves me to tears. Opposite me is a lovely, famous, witty, and sweet woman. We sit in warm sunshine on the gently rolling deck of a private yacht, with a perfumed sea breeze cooling us. Our hosts are clever, unusual, interesting people, who've been everywhere and done everything, and that, too, is what I always expected of the tropics, and never found until today. A Frenchman who is a genius or a maniac or both is solving all the problems of the Gull Reef Club, so that I can go for a spin in the Tilson's palatial stinkpot if asked. Last, this is the best rum punch I have ever drunk. I'm the happiest man in the world."

"He's very nice," Mrs. Tilson said to her husband.

"He's plastered," said Tilson. "What's unusual or interesting about me? I'm just a retired mining engineer who hasn't enough sense to get his arse out of the tropics."

"You are unusual. You're distinguished. You've lived in Nouméa, wherever that is, you've been to Africa and I don't know where else—"

"A Japanese prison camp. Which is one reason I can stand Kinja," said Tilson. "I've really seen a place to which this island compares favorably. Not many people can make that statement. —Lucien! Let Francis take the wheel for a moment and come here."

The captain, a Frenchman who looked like Hippolyte, with a pleasanter and brighter face, came aft, pushing his yachting cap back on his brown forehead. He wore hacked-off tan shorts and a long-sleeved white shirt, and like all the island Frenchmen he had sideburns down almost to his mouth.

"Lucien, you know Hippolyte, don't you? Hippolyte Lamartine?"

"Hippolyte? Yah, I know Hippolyte." Lucien smiled and scratched his thick hair with a hand holding the hat.

"Why did the doctors send him over to Guadeloupe? What happened? Do you know the story?"

"Yah. I was dah when it happen. Hippolyte he sort of my cousin, like."

The story he told was that Hippolyte had been having bad headaches, and had gone to the waterfront to try to get passage on an island schooner to Guadeloupe for treatment. A boat captain haggled with him about the price and got him angry. Hippolyte took out three hundred dollars in cash, tore the bills to pieces, and threw the scraps in the captain's face. Then he tore up his passport and papers and threw them at the captain, and followed this by ripping off his clothes piece by piece, in broad daylight on the busy waterfront, and pelting the captain with them. He announced he was going to swim to Guadeloupe, dived into the harbor naked, and started on his way. When the coast guard caught up with him, he was a mile and a half out and going strong, with sharks circling and darting all around him.

"Hippolyte he a very powerful fella. Good fella," Lucien concluded. "He just fonny."

Tilson said, "I don't see what's funny about taking a man's head half off with a machete. Even if it's only a Kinja policeman."

"Oh, Hippolyte never do dat," the boat captain said with a peculiar grin, his small eyes crinkling shut.

"Well, what do you say happened to that cop they found out there in the bushes in Hastings Estate? Did he cut himself shaving?"

"I tink maybe he have a fight wit anudder cop."

"What I want to know, is Hippolyte going to start chopping people's heads off at the Gull Reef Club? You know he's back there now."

The Frenchman shook his head, his expression very solemn. "Oh, no, suh. Hippolyte all better now. In Guadeloupe dey give him electricity." He put one finger to each side of his head. "*B-z-z-z-z! B-z-z-z-z!* It hurt like hell, Hippolyte say, but he all better. So dey let him go."

4

Rainbow II anchored in a bay on the seaward side of Big Dog, out of sight of Amerigo. The white yacht was the only work of man in a world of sea, sky, sand, and green brush, except for a crazily leaning ruin on the beach. The sun was high and blazing, and the Negro mate was rigging an awning over the deck.

"How hungry is everybody?" said Mrs. Tilson, speaking now a little more slowly than before, but without slurring. "I mean we can have just heaps of cheese and tuna and such, and so forth, or the boys can go looking for lobsters."

"Lobsters!" said Iris and Norman, to which Tilson put a postscript, "And maybe one more drink all around to stave off those hunger pangs."

"No, thanks," Iris said. "We're going exploring. Come on, Norm. Over the side."

"Right behind you." Norman was putting on his mask and fins.

"Ah youth, youth," said Mrs. Tilson, accepting another white rum on the rocks from the captain. After the noon hour the Tilsons always discontinued tonic water. Tom said that in excess it harmed the liver.

The cool water, clear as air, felt wonderful on Paperman's heated skin. Far down on the bottom, pink conch shells abounded, foolishly smiling parrot fish grazed on brain coral and sea fans, and a turtle darted by in alarm, its greenish-white flippers working hard. The captain looked very strange, diving past them toward the reef, in his white long-sleeved shirt and ragged tan shorts.

Iris made straight for the shore, swimming easily, and they soon climbed out on a powdery white strand.

This was the first wild beach on which Norman had ever set foot. Big Dog had no human inhabitant. The ruined house, half hidden by climbing vines and sea grapes, was a mere pile of rotten slanted timbers painted a faded yellow. The iron sheets of the roof lay curled and rusting nearby on the grass or out on the beach—ripped off, Iris said, by a hurricane. Nobody knew who had built the house or lived in it. Some said a French fisherman; some, a Negro religious fanatic; and another story had it that a beautiful white woman from Canada had lived there alone for three years and drunk herself to death.

"Follow me. Just watch out for thorns," Iris said, walking straight into the green tangle of brush. There was a half-obliterated footpath of sandy soil and dry leaves meandering through the trees. In the silence, the scuttling of lizards among fallen leaves was loud and scary. Iris turned here and there where the path branched, always moving down a slope. "Here we are," she said after a while. "How about this?"

The clearing they came into was carpeted ankle-deep in soft grass. It was almost circular, perhaps fifty feet across, and at one end was a tumble-down stone fireplace full of ash heaps and charred wood. The air was soaked in a penetrating sweet perfume; a dizzy humming of bees sounded everywhere; stunted trees, overgrown by vines and heavy with white flowers, ringed the clearing.

"What on earth?" said Norman, sniffing the air.

"Orange blossoms. Whoever built that house planted an orange grove. They've gone on growing wild. They're sheltered from the wind, and the rain drains down in here. Like it?" Humming the wedding march, Iris went to a tree and plucked two small, scrawny oranges. "They don't look like much, but they taste all right," she said, holding out the fruit. "Try it."

Norman bit off rind and sucked the pale, seed-filled pulp. A wild bitter taste within the orange sweetness puckered his mouth. "Well, Big Dog will never be a threat to California," he said, "but this is sure as hell an orange."

"Of course it is. The UDT boys love them. Bob Cohn says the Israeli orange tastes like this." Iris sucked her fruit with gusto.

Norman broke off a sprig of orange blossoms and handed it to her. "What for?" she said.

"Oh, a lot of things. For helping me make the beds at Gull Reef."

As she was tucking the sprig in her hair, he took her in his arms, and they kissed. Iris pushed herself a little away; he still held her waist. "Norman, when did you say Henny was coming?" she murmured, her eyes brilliant and melancholy.

"Day after tomorrow, Iris."

She broke free. "I call this place Dingley Dell. Don't ask me why. Feel this grass. The wild goats keep it eaten down. There's just this fresh soft new grass, all the time. What are you doing tomorrow, Norman, anyway?"

"Who, me? Not a thing, not a thing, to speak of. Thanks to Hippolyte."

Iris said, with her strange awkwardly curved smile, "Don't you suppose we could borrow a boat, maybe Church's catamaran, and have a picnic here tomorrow? Just the two of us? Nobody else waiting in the boat and wondering why we're so long about it, and all? Don't you think we might do that?"

5

All was serene at Gull Reef when Norman and Iris got back; serene and busy. Church said that the people who had checked out during the water crisis were coming back from the Francis Drake, Casa Encantada, Hogan's Fancy, and Apache Marina, annoyed by primitivisms they had encountered there, and lured by the food, the location, and the beaches of Paperman's hotel. "There's no beating the Reef," said the bartender. "Sooner or later they all discover that."

Norman was uneasy at finding Church not on his feet behind the bar, but sitting at the large center table amid seven twittering white girls in smart mainland sun clothes. Church blandly introduced them to Paperman one by one: daughters and granddaughters of hill-crowd families, home from school for the winter recess. They were a sort of informal sorority, it appeared; they had all grown up together in Amerigo, and they called themselves the Sand Witches. These pretty young Sand Witches were visibly fascinated, one and all, by the bearded, tanned bartender in his clam diggers and striped shirt; and Church, after several weeks of chastened conduct, unmistakably had the old stallion look in his eye.

"See me in the office in about five minutes, Church," Paperman growled, turning to go.

"Yes, sir." The slight mockery in the doleful tone set the seven girls into a chiming chorus of giggles, and Norman hastened off, embarrassed at being so old.

He glanced behind the lobby tarpaulin. The workers had left for the day. Hippolyte was padding around, inspecting exposed pipes and wires, and honing his machete as he went. The job had progressed so far that Norman could see now what the new units would be like: six rooms on a new corridor off the lobby, narrow but comfortable chambers, each with a window, a bath, and a large overhead fan.

"It's moving along now, Hippolyte."

The Frenchman squinted at him from under his hat. "Not too bad."

"When do you think it'll be done?"

"Next Tuesday, Wednesday."

"So soon? Have you any idea of the cost yet?"

"Tousand. Maybe a little more."

"A *thousand dollars?* For the whole job?"

"Maybe tousand, tree four hunnerd. Labor. De materials was all here already," said Hippolyte, in an exceptionally long oration.

"That's wonderful. It's terrific. I'm going to give you a handsome bonus, Hippolyte."

"We see," said Hippolyte, whetting and whetting the cutlash, and crouching to peer at a maze of pipes. "Dis work not bad."

"I'm sure it's fine."

Norman was thinking that Henny would know tricks with wallpaper, and mirrors, and fabrics, to make the narrow cubicles seem like luxury suites. Twelve more beds a night to rent, at fifteen dollars a bed! It came to more than a thousand dollars a week, more than fifty thousand dollars a year. What a wise old thug Lester Atlas was, after all!

Iris was leaning against the front desk, still in her bathing suit, reading what looked like a lawyer's letter. "Hi. Esmé says there's an urgent message for you."

The black girl shyly handed him a blue envelope, hand addressed and unstamped. The flap opened at a touch, showing an embossed Cartier's trade-mark. On the flap was a single word engraved in blue: *Broadstairs.*

"Iris, who's Bunny Campbell?"

"Bunny Campbell? Gosh, is that from *her?*"

"Yes, some drivelling apology for the last-minute stuff, and will I come to her house this evening for cocktails and a buffet dinner."

"Good Lord, Norman, you've arrived in Amerigo. You really have." Iris looked amused and surprised. "Go, by all means. Don't miss it."

"Is she hill crowd?"

"Baby, the Campbells are *so* hill crowd they don't even live on the hill. They have their own bay, their own beach, and a mansion to match, right on the water. Broadstairs. I've only seen it when I've gone by on a boat."

"Are you invited?"

"Me?" Iris laughed and shook her head. "Hurry and shower. Don't overdress. Hill crowd, week night, is sport shirt and Bermuda shorts. Water buffaloes are all right."

"Iris, I thought I'd have dinner with you."

"I have a dinner date, dear. Heavy business." She waved her letter. "Go ahead. You'll tell me all about it tomorrow in Dingley Dell. I'll talk to Church about borrowing the cat."

"Look, Iris, can you sail a catamaran? I can't, any more than I can fly a B-52. If you want me to hire a motorboat—"

"A cat sails itself, more or less, sweetie. Getting it to come around can be sticky and beating upwind is rough, but I've had some practice. We'll have a marvellous time. Motors are so smelly and noisy."

"God, I'm looking forward to tomorrow, Iris."

"So am I, Norman Paperman."

6

It was dark when he set out for Broadstairs. Hassim, who was at the bar entertaining a young man in a cerise jacket without lapels, told Norman he had furnished every stick in Broadstairs, and gave him explicit directions. But Norman got lost in the dirt roads crisscrossing downward toward the sea, about five miles west of Georgetown, and only found the place by heading for a twinkle of far lights, amber and green and yellow in the starlit wilds. An arched stone gateway between poled flares, clustered about with Volkswagens, appeared just around a turn of the rutted road. He parked the Rover amid tall pipe cactus, and descended a grand stone staircase with elaborate curving balustrades, which, in the light of amber lamps set at knee height, looked like marble. A round-faced woman with unruly blond hair, a shapeless tub of a body and spindle legs, wearing a white shirt and yellow shorts, appeared at the bottom of the staircase. She held a large crystal tumbler in one hand and a spray can in the other. "Hello, there. You must be Mr. Paperman. I'm Bunny Campbell. Are you anointed? The sand flies are beastly tonight. Joys of waterfront property."

"They don't seem to bother me."

"Bless me, are you one of those lucky souls? I'm so sorry you can't see the gardens, it's so black dark. That's more or less the whole idea of our humble abode, the staircase and the gardens, but you'll have to come again by day, very soon." As Mrs. Campbell rattled on hoarsely in upper-class tones—Boston, or possibly Philadelphia, to Paperman's limited discernment—he followed her through a terrazzo-tiled foyer lined with paintings, including an unmistakable Degas, across a wide oblong room furnished partly with antiques and partly with good rattan furniture, and walled with paintings and oversize leather books. The far wall was all folding doors to a terrace facing the floodlit beach, tall palms, and the dark sea.

"Norman darling, you *did* come. How enchanting of you!" Imposing in a bottle-green evening dress with a very low neck, her red hair piled high above her head, Amy Ball came forging out of the crowd of drinkers on the terrace and sailed toward him. A powerful arm went around him, thickly painted lips smacked the air, and he smelled rose perfume and scotch.

"Come get a drink, love. I hear you've been having sheer bloody hell for weeks, and now Hippolyte's back and everything's humming. How marvellous that you've got Hippolyte! He's the jewel of the island. If that utter bastard Thor hadn't fired him, I'd probably still be here, running the Gull Reef Club. I didn't know when I was well off."

She took a fresh sizable tumbler of scotch at the bar, linked an arm in Paperman's, backed him into a corner of the terrace, sat him down, and poured out her woes. Mrs. Ball was drunk, but clear in her speech, although wide jolly smiles kept coming and going on her face with no relevance to what she happened to be saying. Also as she slumped toward Paperman for confidential passages of her tale, the neck of her dress fell away, and so far as he could see, there was nothing under the dress but Amy Ball, sagging, bare, and large. It made him nervous.

Thor, according to Amy Ball, was a brute, a horror, a deceiver, a vampire who had sucked her dry and cast her off. Once aboard *Moonglow*, she said, her two-year affair with him had come to an abrupt end. He loved the boat. He loved it as he had never loved her, as it was impossible for him to love any woman. He had pushed her bodily out of his cabin one night—Mrs. Ball said with a quick smile, "Of course

269

we were lovers, dear, you knew that, I made no bones about it"—and he had humiliated her to the core by saying, "Dat stuff's no good on a boat." In Panama he wouldn't come off *Moonglow*. He made one excuse and another, always painting, hammering, sawing, or tinkering. When finally she had dragged him to a hotel one night, he had drunk himself senseless, lain like a log all night in his clothes, and returned to the boat at dawn.

"He never loved me," said Mrs. Ball, smiling and looking tragic in the same second, "never, never, never. He pretended for two years, just to get me to buy that boat. And I fell for it." She raised her glass. *"Lycka till!* The utter bastard."

"Why don't you fire him and sell the boat?"

"Oh, darling, don't you *Suppose* I've thought of that? *Dreamed* of it? The utter bastard talked me into buying the boat in both our names. Some kind of tax gimmick it was, or he said it was. I adored the monster so, I never thought twice about it. And now every penny I have in the world is in that filthy abominable scarlet horror of a boat, and he's through the Canal and heading for Hawaii. And here I am. *Lycka till!* Let's have another drink. The utter bastard."

Tom Tilson was getting a drink at the bar. He did not appear to have changed the shirt, shorts, and sandals he had worn on the boat. Amy threw her arm around him, and kissed the air beside his ear. "Oh, Tom, how enchanting of you to come! I'm a defrauded, cast-off old bag, and Thor's turned out to be an utter bastard. Let's find a little corner and have a chat. Where's Letty?"

"We had a big day, Amy. She stayed at home."

Norman sat alone on the stone rail of the terrace, sipping his drink, and wondering why he had been invited. Amy Ball appeared to be guest of honor. She was clad more formally than the rest, and her return to Amerigo seemed the occasion for the dinner, if there was one. Possibly Mrs. Ball had been curious about him and the Reef; but she had had him alone for half an hour, and she had talked entirely about herself. Broadstairs was beautiful, to be sure, and this awkward glimpse was worth while in any case. At the center of the terrace a small fountain plashed. Begonias and geraniums grew around the fountain pool in a circular planter covered with blue-and-white tiles, where several guests sat with their drinks. Another wide balustraded staircase descended to the beach, and to a flagstone path leading to an enormous illuminated blue swimming pool.

Though the totally Gentile look of the party rather intimidated Norman, he nevertheless felt a peculiar relaxation here in Broadstairs, a new sense of being almost at home, or at least on familiar, non-Kinjan ground. He wondered whether it might not stem from the fact that the scene looked so much like a hundred *New Yorker* advertisements for rums and cigarettes, presumably consumed in such glamorous tropic settings. But, sitting there by himself, he puzzled out the real reason. Except for the two bartenders, and the servants setting up the buffet dinner, there was on the entire crowded terrace not one Negro face.

When dinner was announced Norman lined up with the others at the long oak table, and filled a plate with lobster and rice, a slice of smoked turkey, and another slice from a bright red roast beef. Tom Tilson, on the line right behind Norman, walked with him to the terrace rail, and they sat together and began to eat.

"What a magnificent place they have here," Norman said.

"Ya-a-as." Tilson wrinkled up his face at Norman. "No doubt this is also what you had in mind when you moved to the Caribbean. Only to have this you need to be a Campbell of the Columbus, Ohio, Campbells. You've heard of Campbell Ball Bearings?"

"Of course."

"I like your Reef better, anyway. You've got the town view and the lights at night. Freddy's got nothing out front but sand and ocean. He has to take to the hills if there's a hurricane. When the wind's wrong the seaweed drifts in thick, the beach gets disgusting, and the flies can carry you off. Then he needs a squad of gardeners to clean up. Of course, it's nothing to Freddy. Campbell Ball Bearings pays him a quarter million a year just to stay the hell away from Columbus, Ohio. He's an awfully decent boy, Freddy, but not bright."

"I had an idea Amy Ball was rich, too," Norman said, "and now she tells me she's broke."

Tilson said, "Hah!" and ate a large bite of roast beef. "Amy's going to take a while building up enough cash for her next foolishness, that's all. Her husband left her a bundle, but it's in a trust, and all she gets is the income, though she's had half the lawyers in London try to bust through to that capital. —Amy! Sit down, old girl. Tell us more about that utter bastard."

Mrs. Ball giggled and sat in a chair facing them. "You know, it's the most marvellous relief to cry on people's shoulders? I think if I tell it about four more times it's going to start seeming funny to me, and then I'll be fine." She ate some food voraciously. "I want to know what's going on at the Reef. Is Hippolyte really as clever as ever? That man knows every inch of the Club, Norman, every wire and valve and hole and conduit. Why, he *is* the Club. He's its soul. Don't laugh. Something went out of the Club when that utter bastard fired him, just because Hippolyte took one teeny swipe at him with a cutlash."

"That wouldn't bother me in the least," Paperman said. "Hippolyte can do no wrong, and I don't care how many headless policemen I find on my lawn."

"It's all nonsense," Tilson said. "Hippolyte Lamartine is a fair maintenance and construction man. In the United States there are twenty million of them. It's just that he's on Kinja. By contrast with what's available here, he looks as though he's jetting around with flames shooting out of his behind."

"Never mind, you stick to him," Mrs. Ball said to Norman. "He's docile as a schoolgirl if you just let him have his way. What I want to know is"—here she dropped her voice—"how about lovely Iris? How is she?"

"She's fine," Paperman said.

"Dear Iris. She's such a sweet thing, and she's so attractive, isn't she, Norman?" Mrs. Ball gave a loud sigh, and smiled, and stopped smiling, and smiled again. "It's such a pity about her. Isn't it, Tom?"

"Well, we're all peculiar here, Amy, and one peculiarity's as good or as bad as another. Talk doesn't help."

"Yes, but such a lovely woman, and an actual film star once, and still very pretty, actually—I mean don't you think it's sad, Norman?"

Paperman knew that this was his chance to find out whatever there was to know about Iris Tramm. The drunken woman was pushing him to ask one question; then would come the spill. He was about to ask the question (though ashamed of doing so) when a crowd of youngsters came cascading on the terrace with a great noise. Giggling, whispering, chirping, shouting, they swarmed up to the buffet. Most of them were girls, in yellow, white, and pink; some in flounced dresses, some in narrow pants that were mere stretched films over their blossoming behinds. They had three baby-faced boys with them, all over six feet tall, in dark suits with absurdly short trousers, and great growths of hair. These girls were the Sand Witches, Norman perceived, a bit the worse for their evening hairdos, but still unquenchably pretty with the prettiness of seventeen. Amy Ball leaped up when she saw them. "Great day, just *look* at those children! Aren't those the Sand Witches? Isn't that Maude Campbell? Why she's a *woman,* and a year ago she was an *infant.* Maude! Don't you remember your Aunt Amy? And isn't that Gloria Collins?" Mrs. Ball strode to the youngsters, and they swirled around, hugging her.

"The children's hour," Tilson said, flipping his cigarette stub from his holder to the sand below. "Bedtime for me, Paperman."

"I'll go too." Paperman put his plate down hastily. He made his farewells to Mrs. Campbell. She briefly expressed her desolation at his having to leave, and turned back to her little knot of gossipers. Norman was halfway up the wide stairway when he heard a voice from below, "Norman! Norman, love! Do wait up, there's a dear," and Amy Ball mounted the stairs on a rather weaving course. "Love, I abhor talking business at a party, but I'm so glad Bunny asked you, because there is just this one teeny thing."

"Perfectly all right."

"It's those silly old promissory notes, lover. I'm such a boob about money, but as I recall they're dated so that you don't start paying them till you've retired the bank loan, and that'll be a couple of years at least. Am I right?"

"Yes, Amy."

"Well, the point is, lover," said Amy, snuggling his arm to hers and teetering so that Paperman had to brace himself to keep from toppling down the stairs with her, "the point is, lover, two years from now I may be dead, do you know what I mean? Or you may be, or the nasty old Russkis may have blown the world to smithereens. You know? I mean ten or fifteen thousand dollars cash would look a hell of a lot better to me right now than some silly little bits of paper that promise thirty-five thousand after I'm dead."

Paperman had drunk very little; and though he was no businessman, he realized that here was a sudden chance to cut the price of the Gull Reef Club almost in half. He also perceived why he had been invited to Broadstairs. "Well, Amy, that's something I have to think about."

"Of course, darling. I just want you to give it some thought, you and that enchanting man, Mr. Hercules, the one who was on the *Time* cover—"

"Atlas, you mean."

Mrs. Ball swayed and laughed. "Of course. Atlas. What did I say, Hercules? How silly of me. Anyway I absolutely adored him he's so clever, and if you and he are interested in that notion, well, so am I, love. Good night."

chapter twelve

Dingley Dell

I

Norman and Iris set out for Big Dog in high spirits, at seven in the morning of a perfect day. Norman was almost prancing in his eagerness for the promised delights of Dingley Dell. They loaded the catamaran, hoisted sail, and skimmed out of the harbor, running before a fresh north breeze.

While they sailed down the south shore of Amerigo, the catamaran went like a train through calm green waters. But at Hog Point, the western end of the island, they saw swells from the north rolling by, throwing up thirty-foot showers of spray on the naked red spires of rock. As they passed the point, the catamaran picked up speed and began to toss in the wind and swells. Coming about was an ordeal; the two-hulled craft wallowed, the sails rattled and flapped, and waves broke over Iris, Norman, and the picnic hampers. But the water was warm, and they laughed off the soaking. They were in swimsuits, and getting drenched was part of the fun. Iris doubled the point with Norman's awkward help, and the catamaran went foaming and hissing up the north shore, over a heaving blue sea. The speed was good, but they were making little way toward Big Dog, though as close-hauled as possible.

There the island sat, green and beckoning in the morning sunlight, due northeast, and straight from there the wind blew. Iris tacked again and again, losing some of her good spirits each time she had to bring the catamaran about, and gradually disclosing a rich store of obscene imprecations, mostly heaped on the unlucky direction of the wind. At the end of several hours of this, the orange blossoms of Dingley Dell remained three good open sea miles away, straight to windward. The sun was high and blistering. The wind, grown stronger, was clipping whitecaps and plumes of spray from the dark blue swells. Norman and Iris were so wet they might as well have been swimming to Big Dog.

Trying to come about once again, Iris slipped and fell on the pitching deck, and the free-swinging boom hit her head. She lay there swearing till she was breathless. Then she took another breath and bellowed over the flapping of the sail and the slosh of the waves, "This was the dumbest idea I've ever had! *Screw* Dingley Dell, Norm! I can't make it. I'm sorry."

"Whatever you say, Iris."

Norman was relieved when she quit. In theory love-making in Dingley Dell (which he had counted on as part of the picnic menu) was worth any hardship. But in fact he was soaked, burned, chilled, and a bit seasick; and also scared, out there in the wild sea, in a balky boat with an angry, exhausted woman.

One extended run to the west, and they sailed into the quiet lee of the south shore, dripping sea water, grumpy, silent. It was a straight long slow sail back. As they turned into the harbor, the noon whistle blew from the fort. They unloaded the hampers, the snorkelling gear, the sodden blankets, towels, and clothes, and they brought everything to Iris's cottage.

"Let's see what we can salvage," she said, ripping open a hamper. "We'll have our picnic down on my beach."

But though she had wrapped the lunch in a waterproof cloth, the sea had gotten in. The food was a gluey mess of salt water, bread, vegetables, and meat tumbled together, unfit even for Meadows. Iris dug down farther, saying "Hell, let's drink the martinis anyway," but she stopped with a cry of pain, pulled out a bleeding thumb, and sucked it. The glass jar of martinis had broken.

She and Norman were standing in her kitchenette, in their damp swimsuits, their skins dry, burned an angry pink and crusted with salt. Norman's hair hung on his forehead in salt-stiffened gray ringlets exposing the bare place on the crown of his head. "Oh damn!" She sounded as though she would weep, though her eyes were bright and she was even smiling a little, as she watched blood well from her finger. "This does it, Norman. Doesn't it? A stinking, total, unmitigated bitch-up, complete with spilled blood. And I thought it would be one of the nicest days of my life. Wait a minute while I bind up my wound."

She went into her bathroom. Norman dropped on her divan, his bare white-crusted shoulders slumped, his chin dropping on his chest. Soon she came out in her pink robe, securing a Band-Aid on her thumb. She glanced at a round mirror on the wall. "Look at me, will you? The daughter of Dracula, to the life." She made comic fangs of her teeth, and said to Norman's reflection in the mirror, "Poor Norman Paperman. A little whipped down too, no doubt."

"I'll be fine," he said. "All I need is a shower and something to eat."

She turned and came to him. "Take your shower here. I'll fix you something."

"Thanks, Iris. I need clothes and all. I'll drag myself up to my room."

He stood, and since she was so close to him, he put his arms around her. She embraced him willingly enough. "Honey, I'm so sorry about the disaster. It was that damned north wind. A cat just won't beat to windward. We should have taken a motorboat, after all."

"It was fun, Iris. It was an adventure."

"Oh, sure. But this isn't exactly Dingley Dell, is it?"

"Why, no. But it would do."

"Do, dear?"

"Yes, do." He did his best to produce an eager smile, and he kissed her. There they stood, to a certain extent holding each other up, and kissing. They were both very tired.

Iris took her palm from his naked back, and licked it. "Jesus, Norman, you taste like a pretzel," she said. "Go take your shower."

"What about you?"

"Well, I'm for a long sleep. Then I'll try to put the old hulk back together again. I may actually fail this time, and they'll just find the pieces scattered around the bathroom."

"You're having dinner with me tonight," Norman said wearily but firmly. "If you have any business or other mysterious shenanigans, they're cancelled. You're dining with me. Understand?"

Her eyes lit up with affectionate mockery. "Why precious, you're so masterful. I'm not doing a thing. I'd love to have a nice date with you. They say Hogan's Fancy has a new French cook who's marvellous. I find it hard to believe, but shall we try?"

"Dinner at Hogan's Fancy it is," Norman said. "And then a long, memorable night of it. We are going to paint Kinja red."

He staggered out.

2

Despite its tiny bathless rooms and its pervading moss, mildew, and rats, even Hogan's Fancy was crowded at this time of the year. All the tables of the terrace were taken, and guests lined the ornamental iron rail, watching the sun go down. Gilbert, in a new white mess-jacket and satin-striped black trousers, came out from behind the bar to greet Norman and Iris, laughing and offering his hand. He placed them by the rail at a small wrought-iron table, brought in a hurry by two colored waiters, with chairs. Gilbert didn't touch these objects, but he minutely supervised their placing, glancing at Norman in open pride of executive status. "No, mon, not dah, dey can't see nuttin' fum dah, mon, put it hyah—dat bettah, mon—yazzuh, Mistuh Papuh, I does miss de Reef. Aha udune nassaba dungda." Paperman noted with pleasure that his ear for Calypso was improving. He could transpose readily: "I hear you're doing not so bad down there."

"Not so bad, Gilbert. We'd do better if you'd come back."

Gilbert laughed and laughed, slapping his hands together. "You does have Hippolyte now. He okay 'cep' when he fonny."

He took their order and went back to the bar, still laughing. The lawyer Collins now appeared in brown Bermuda shorts, brown knee stockings, and a butter-yellow jacket with a sort of green leprosy all over it. "Hello there, stranger!" he bawled, treating Paperman to a bear hug and a strange whiff of a masculine perfume with a name like Brawn or Thuggee, which Paperman particularly detested. "You've really picked the evening for it. Look at that horizon! A razor edge. It's that north wind that's been blowing all day. You'll see a green flash to end all green flashes. Say, do you realize you're about to get some competition?" He pulled up a chair and sat, his huge jaw dropped, his eyes popped in a sly, glassy grin, his tongue stuck far out.

"Competition?"

"You know that your friend Lionel Williams is coming next week with the Freed party."

"Why, sure. He'll be staying at the Reef."

"For a while, yes. Then he'll be staying at Hogan's Fancy, since he'll own it."

"Lionel?" said Norman, astonished. "I thought he wanted to buy Casa Encantada."

"Well, yes. As a matter of fact, I represent Casa Encantada. I did try to put over the deal, but there were all kinds of crossed signals, and now he's buying Hogan's Fancy. So there'll be *two* Broadway producers running Kinja hotels. You see? You've started a trend, by George." He jumped up, pointing out to sea. "There it goes, folks! The sun's just touched the horizon!"

Several guests left their tables and joined the watching crowd. It was a remarkably clear evening. The sun, its lower edge already sliding below the purple horizon, was bright as gold. The shiny disk sank to half its size, reddening and dimming. It went lower, turning orange-red, shrinking moment by moment. Soon there was only a glistening orange fragment poked above the ocean—and at that moment Paperman saw it. In the instant of its vanishing, the last bit of sun turned green.

There was a wave of chatter along the rail. Some had seen it, some hadn't, and everyone was talking at once.

Oddly stirred, he said to Iris, "It's really true. I saw it this time."

"Yes, so did I. I've seen it three or four times. It's the strangest thing."

A waiter set their martinis before them. Norman extended his glass toward her. "Well, Iris, darling—to our green flash at sunset."

Iris's eyes misted, and her face grew taut. She looked long at Norman, then raised her glass. "Watch me on these tonight, please."

"Watch yourself. Don't you want to have fun? I do."

"Yes, I do, Norm. I very much want to have fun." Iris took a small sip, put the glass on the table, removed her hand from it, and clasped her hands in her lap. "I'm no damned good, you know. I'm sorry that Henny's coming tomorrow, and I'm sorrier yet that I ever met her." She stared at her drink, her lips sulky and tight. She wore her diamond earrings and a light low-cut gray dress. Her thick hair was pulled back behind her ears, which gave her something of her old look of Janet West. Her face and bosom had an afterglow of the morning sunburn. She looked more fetching to Norman than she had in his first glimpse of her, sitting at the Gull Reef bar with Bob Cohn. At that time it had been an insubstantial attraction, a vagrant wistful pulse such as any man can feel for a lovely strange woman glimpsed in an airport or on a train. Now he knew her.

She was shaking her head, as though trying to clear it. "Tell me something, Norm. What's it like to have kids? I mean really, all sentimental gop and double-talk aside. Is it a mess? Is it a bore? Is it nice? Is it painful? Has it been very important to you?"

"I only have one daughter, Iris."

"I know that."

Norman drank and thought for a moment. "How is it? Well, I'll really try to tell you. Of all the years of my life, and I mean childhood, and then playing the field as a guy on the town with the show girls, and then marrying a woman I still love, and having a million laughs with some of the nicest and smartest people in New York—of all that time, what I liked most, what I can hardly bear to think about because it was so sweet and now it's all gone, was the years from the time Hazel was born until she was five. It was heaven, every moment of it. It was heaven just changing her wet pants. It was heaven making her laugh and telling her stories while I fed her puréed carrots. Even the pain when she would spike a fever, was all right, because it was about her. There's been nothing else like that love for me—not ever—and I don't even know if I'm peculiar or if it's common, because you don't read much about it. Maybe that's because there's no adventure in it. It's just pure whole love permeating your body, and I'll tell you something, I'm a very big fan of sex, but to me it's minor-league fun compared to that love. And that's all I can tell you about having kids. I'm not very experienced."

Iris's eyes were glistening. "Well, that's quite a report. How do you feel about her now?"

"Hazel? I still love her, naturally, though I don't idolize her in that way. She's half the reason I came to this lunatic island. Watching her grow up and throw herself away on a puking fat phony was unbearable. I cut and ran."

"Well! How about that green flash? Worth the price of admission, hey? Only at Hogan's Fancy!" Mr. Collins bounced himself into the vacant chair, all swollen with gay excitement. "Yes siree Bob, I'm going to miss this place. I'm going to miss all of Kinja, but this little terrace at sunset I'll miss most of all."

"Oh!" Norman said, as graciously as he could. "You're leaving?"

"Well, Norman, frankly yes. I've been waiting for this opportunity for quite some time. It's just been a question of getting my capital out of Hogan's Fancy. We're moving to La Jolla, California. I mean this is the finest little island in the Caribbean, but there comes a time when you start thinking of those mainland amenities, you know? Like decent roads, movie houses with good movies and seats that don't tear up your fanny, shops with real food in them, courteous service, mechanics that can fix things, you know, I mean a plumber, an electrician, just normal workmen who show up on time and do things fast and right. You know? You simply start hankering after the good old U.S.A. And I also mean" —he winked—"seeing a few pale faces as well as sunburned ones now and then. Do you follow me? Don't misunderstand me, the Kinjans are marvellous people, but the five-hundredth time you can't get the telephone operator to answer up, the thousandth time a taxi driver mashes your fenders and the cop gives *you* the ticket, you get a wee bit fed up, you know?"

Iris said, "Chunky, I thought you were this island's biggest booster, and the black man's friend."

"Why, I am. I mean locals and continentals come and go in my house, it doesn't mean a thing, and there isn't a white man on the island who can speak Calypso like me. Kinja is Paradise, but Iris, let's face it, here's Norman, and now Lionel's coming. New York has discovered Kinja. You know what *that* means. Oh, great for real estate prices, maybe, but the charm will go fast. In five years they'll be selling bagels and lox on Prince of Wales Street. No, I think I've had the best of it, and it's time to skedaddle."

Collins went off to the bar.

"There is only one word for Chunky Collins," said Iris, "and I over-used it this morning."

"Best lawyer on the island," said Norman. "Maybe we should eat somewhere else."

"No, we're here now, and Bob raved about the new chef. Norman, you must stop Lionel from buying Hogan's Fancy."

"Lionel is smarter than me about such things."

"He has island fever. It's mentally disabling."

They ordered sole *bonne femme,* the dish Cohn had praised, and Chablis. Twilight drew on fast. The clear orange glow in the west dimmed, lights blinked on all over Georgetown, and Gull Reef twinkled on the dark harbor. They talked, in the deepening shadows, of old times, of the show for Loyalist Spain in which Iris had performed, of their radical pasts. Norman had never joined the party—out of mere cautious instinct for self-preservation, he said—and he had held Henny back too, though she had argued that they were being soft cowards. She had almost won out. They had been on the verge of joining, when the Nazi-Soviet pact had disillusioned them.

"You were sissies," Iris said. "I joined. I hung on until after the war, too. What the hell else was there to believe in, then? In the long run it was the Russians who beat the Nazis. We sent them the stuff to do it with, and Normandy was a big help, but they lost twenty times as many lives as we did, and killed maybe twenty times as many Germans. You're still not supposed to say that out loud, but I don't give a good goddamn, it's the truth. I believed in the whole Communist thing for a very long time. Then I stopped believing in it. I realized it was just one more religion, and phonier than the rest, and that was that. Nobody scared or bullied me out of it."

"What do you believe in now, Iris?"

"Me? That I have a good dog. That I was young and enchanting, and am old and fat. That sitting opposite me is a lovable Jewish nitwit with handsome hair, and that his nice wife will be here tomorrow."

The sole *bonne femme* came: leathery yellow slabs of dry thick fish, under a dump of lumpy flour paste. "My God!" Iris said, turning up her nose. "This is nothing but their old seafood special—jerked grouper, I think Bob calls it. But what's this white filth all over it? Sole *bonne femme!* Waiter! I want to speak to Mr. Collins."

The lawyer appeared, rubbing his hands and grinning. "Hi, folks. Enjoying your din-din?"

Iris said, "Chunky, is this the French chef's night off? Do you *have* a French chef?"

Collins looked sad. "I had a wonderful one. He was from Panama. But he turned out to be a fugitive, some funny business about diamonds. The FBI in San Juan sent a man here to talk to him, and the next day François blew. He lasted five days."

"God, that's short even for Kinja," Norman said.

"Well, the felons usually don't stay long," said Collins. "The nuts do, sometimes. Some of them just settle down. But isn't the fish good? François did show my new cook just how to make sole *bonne femme* before he left."

"It's divine. Is it too late to get a couple of steaks?" said Iris.

"I guess not. You won't want Chablis with a steak." Collins cheerfully carried off the dripping bottle.

"Well, so far today not one thing has gone right," Iris said. "Nothing. Don't you think we'd better call this date off and go our ways? I have a feeling you'll run your car off a cliff tonight if I stay with you."

"We are going to have fun tonight," Norman said, "if we go over a cliff trying."

"Okay. You're a brave man."

"I hunt the red fox of remembered joy," Norman said.

Iris's face lit up. " '*To tame or to destroy*'—Norman were you a Millay man? I once knew whole volumes of Millay by heart. Let's go! '*Mine is a body that should die at sea—*' "

"No, no. I've forgotten it all, Iris. I haven't read a poem of Edna Millay in twenty-five years. I don't know where that line came from, suddenly. Henny didn't like Millay, she said it was slush. Henny was a zealot. She read the *New Masses,* and novels about strikes in coal fields."

"She doesn't seem like that now."

"Well, until she met me, all mankind was Henny's personal problem. After that, I was."

Iris began to recite.

> *"Wine from these grapes I shall be treading*
> > *surely*
> *Morning and noon and night until I die . . ."*

She spoke the whole poem in a harsh even voice, looking out to sea, and glancing once or twice into Norman's eyes. A fragment of a poem came to him. When he had said as much as he knew, she picked it up and finished it. They began to toss off stanzas, tag lines, isolated couplets of Edna St. Vincent Millay, vying with each other. Norman was surprised at how much came back to him. They both avoided the threadbare verses: the ferry, the candle burning at both ends, the shining palace. The sweet pipings of the dead poetess of the twenties, her elegies over brief Village amours, her young defiance of convention and time, her nostalgia for nature, her dirges fluttering always between death and sex: these old words, dormant in Norman's memory for decades, awoke. The frail music wove a spell, a ghostly simulacrum, of young love. He had utterly forgotten what it was like to be in love at twenty-three. Now he remembered. The spell was on Iris Tramm too. She was looking at him the way a girl in love looked. And to him, Iris was Janet West again, the dazzling star he had hopelessly admired backstage at the Follies for Free Spain.

Whether the steaks were good or bad, whether the wine was mediocre or passable, he could not tell. He was on a date with a beautiful actress and he was twenty-three, and everything tasted marvellous. They exhausted Millay, laughing. They talked about old shows, about the actors and actresses of the thirties, the duets of Ethel Merman and Bert Lahr in *Du Barry Was a Lady,* Ed Wynn's crazy inventions in *Hooray for What?,* Leslie Howard and Humphrey Bogart in *The Petrified Forest.* Night fell. A crooked late moon came up red.

3

The blank-faced waiter was clattering down coffee between them. Iris scooped her purse from the table. "Norm, let's have our coffee somewhere else."

"Sure. Where?"

"Come. I'll drive. It's a birthday party down in town. I said I'd look in for a minute and bring you."

"People I know?"

Iris shook her head. "Locals—as Chunky calls them. They know who you are. You're a curiosity in Kinja."

Paperman was willing, indeed interested, to visit a party in a native Georgetown house. Iris drove the Rover through the sloping maze of lamplit streets and alleys, downhill at first and then up again. A policeman stood in the middle of one cobbled lane, and here Iris stopped. "Hello, Ray. Is there any parking space left up there?"

The policeman touched his gold-crusted tan cap. "I tink so, Miss Tramm. A car just come dung."

"Lovely."

She turned the Rover into a stucco gateway and drove up a very steep cement alley, lined all the way with canted cars, to a round driveway before a big white building, square as a blockhouse. Norman recognized it. From the Gull Reef Club this house stood out on Sugar Hill, halfway up, dominating it as Government House did the higher hill.

"Who lives in this place, Iris, for crying out loud?"

"The Turnbulls. Old family."

Norman heard music—not a steel band, but a good jazz ensemble—and the voices of a crowd. Large doors with ornate bronze grillwork stood open, and they passed into and through gigantic rooms with marble floors, furnished in a mixture of colorful modern mail-order things, and heavy dark Victorian pieces. It was not artfully done—as the New York decorators touch contemporary with Victorian—but in a jumbled way. Still, the effect was lively and opulent. There were many people in these rooms, nearly all Negro, with a few whites here and there, whites

Norman had not seen before. The band was playing in an archway leading to a vast terrace strung with colored lights. Dozens of couples danced in the inside foyer and on the terrace.

Iris led Norman to a very fat black woman in orange satin, with a complicated high coiffure of iron-gray hair, sitting in a redwood arm-chair on the terrace, leaning on a cane and surveying the dancers. The woman smiled at them. "Hello, Iris."

"Happy birthday, Mrs. Turnbull. This is Norman Paperman."

"Oh, yes. The gentleman from New York. Welcome."

Norman, not knowing what the manners were in this group, awk-wardly put out a hand, and Mrs. Turnbull gave him the limp brief clasp of an islander. She was happy to meet a Broadway producer, she said, and proud that he had chosen this little island as a place to live. Norman didn't contradict her. The two misconceptions—that he was a producer, and that Atlas had been on the cover of *Time*—were imbedded beyond recall in Kinja folklore.

While he and Iris were having coffee and luscious coconut layer cake at a little table in the foyer, Norman saw and waved to several Negroes he knew—the banker Llewellyn, Anatone, the accountant Wills, the doctor and the dentist who treated ailing Reef guests. Others came drifting past, obviously wanting to meet the Broadway producer; not thrusting themselves forward, but waiting until Iris caught their eye and beckoned. Norman shook hands with the Commissioner of Educa-tion, the Director of the Budget, the editor of the Amerigo *Citizen*, law-yers and bank executives, shop owners, and more "old family." He was struck by the calm good humor of these upper-class colored people, some black, some yellow-light; a friendliness tinged with reserve, but free of subservience, or arrogance, or hostility. They made him feel, most of them, that great warmth was there, waiting and wanting to break through, but held back for age-old reasons. He had never known such Negroes. In their assurance, ease, fine dress, and old-fashioned manners they were a dark mirror image of the hill crowd at Broadstairs, but there were differences. They were not supercilious, and they were all sober—though they were drinking—and they gave him no unease at being either Jewish or white.

"I don't know anything about this island," he said to Iris. "I'm just realizing that. I've been a prisoner on the Reef since the moment I came here. That hotel is a loony bin with a steel band. This is Kinja."

She smiled. "This is the best of Kinja. These are the ones who keep it going somehow despite all the low slapstick. Of course the hill crowd helps with its income taxes. I'm glad you got to see this. There's more to see. Game? This seems to be our night out."

"Lead on."

Iris took him on a round of Kinja's night spots. They were few: a shabby undecorated hall at the top of the Thousand Steps, full of gay young Negroes dancing under blazing electric lights, or drinking beer or soda pop; a dark pseudo-Greenwich Village dive on Prince of Wales Street lit by kerosene lanterns, offering the usual noisy espresso machine and girl folk singer using foul words, sparsely peopled by bearded barefoot white boys and stringy-haired girls with huge backsides bursting out of dirty pants, also a few black youngsters, and white women with black men; next a roadhouse far out in the sugar-cane fields, with one dusty disused bowling alley, a shrouded piano, an empty dance floor, and some middle-aged whites drunkenly muttering and cackling around a red-lit bar; and out beyond the airport the Frenchmen's place, a yellow shack called Montmartre, where blue bulbs dangled on long electric cords, a jukebox played, and a nightmare group of Hippolytes gathered: fat, thin, tall, short, young, and old Hippolytes: with some blatant white and Negro whores in cotton dresses and gaudy city hats.

"That's about it," Iris said as they left this den after merely tasting their beers. "You've seen the night life of Kinja. Gull Reef's much the best, that's why you do all the business. Some of the guest houses have bars, but the whole island closes up like a cemetery at half-past ten. Except for Casa Encantada, of course."

"What happens there?"

"Oh, that sort of hells along all night. But it's solid fags, Norm."

"We're on our way."

A piano bar, surrounded three deep by men, stood in a wide curved bay window in the shabby mountaintop guest house called Casa Encantada. The view was a thrilling one of crags and sea in moonlight, but the room was so jammed and smoky that Norman caught only a glimpse of it. Cries of friendly greetings to Iris rose from the men around the bar. A lean handsome white lad, hardly twenty years old, was at the piano, playing the score of a new musical with nervous skill. He wore a buttoned-down tieless pink shirt and tight chino trousers, and he had an intense, troubled look. A paunchy barefoot man in sagging shorts, with a gross red face, bulging bloodshot eyes, and an absurd flat-top haircut, emerged from a knot of men and embraced Iris. "Hello, love. Where's your UDT boy?"

"On duty, Felix. This is Norman Paperman."

"Oh my *gawd*. The competition! Well, a belated welcome to paradise! How long has it been? Three weeks? Being measured for your strait jacket yet? Ha ha ha! Isn't it a gas, playing mine host in the glamorous Caribbean? Isn't it *heaven!* Everyman's dream come true."

"When are you going to play, Felix?" Iris said. "We can't stay long."

"Oh, soon, poopsie. I just got off. Isn't he good? That's Arthur, from Minneapolis. Just loaded with talent, and his folks want him to run an electric-appliance wholesale business. Ain't it *awful?* Sit down here, Iris. Sit ye down, Norm."

He ordered drinks for them and a double brandy for himself.

Iris said, "Well! And when did you fall from grace?"

"Why, about four days ago, love, when that butch lawyer of mine, Chunky Collins, gave me the shaft. I thought he was selling the Casa to Norman's friend Mr. Williams from New York, and what do you know? By some silly accident he sold him Hogan's Fancy instead!" Felix giggled, showing large yellow buck teeth. "Of course, it's a mistake anybody could have made. But me, I was all set for the health kick, can you bear it? I was going to go home to Toledo, dry out, lose eighty pounds, get my old job back, yes sir, my poor old mother had my room all fixed up, she's always kept the candle burning in the window—ah me! But it's just as well, dearie. It gets damn cold in Toledo, and let's face it, the health bit is so dull, you know? I mean for *me*, honey, at this point, health would be a sort of neurosis."

He soon displaced the boy in the pink shirt at the piano, sang two ribald numbers, and changed to a solemn, husky manner for a few folk songs. Then he played tunes from old shows. This was his specialty. He appeared to know a hundred scores from the thirties and forties by heart. Somebody would throw him a title, or just a line, and he would say,

"Yes, aha, *Band Wagon*, 1931," and he would play and sing it without an error, his eyes agleam with lewd mischief even when the song was innocuous. Iris delighted in the performance; she knew many of the songs herself, and sometimes she and Felix improvised little duets, to giggling applause all around the bar. Norman found the proprietor amusing, and he was enjoying the songs of his youth. But the Casa Encantada made him uneasy. Men were flirting with each other all around him; some were cuddling like teen-agers in a movie balcony. The boy in the pink shirt, biting his nails and constantly looking around in a scared way, sat at a small table with one of the rich pederasts from Signal Mountain, a pipe-smoking gray-haired man in tailored olive shirt and shorts, with young tan features carved by plastic surgery, and false teeth. Norman was glad when the proprietor finished a run of Noel Coward songs and left the piano, so that he and Iris could politely get out of the place.

"Home?" he said, starting up the Rover, and taking gulps of sweet air scented with night-blooming jasmine to get the fetid Casa Encantada atmosphere out of his nostrils.

"No place else to go, sweetie. We've done Amerigo. Paris it ain't."

After a silent downhill ride of a few minutes he said, "The cops don't bother them? I mean, that kid in the pink shirt—and then, some of those native boys there looked like high school kids. Nobody cares?"

"There was a fuss here, I understand, about five or six years ago," Iris said. "Some gay boys staying on the third floor of the Francis Drake had a brawl, and one of them fell naked off a balcony, and sort of spattered all over the cobblestones."

"Good God," Norman said.

"Yes, some senator introduced a bill in the legislature to run 'em off the island. Then when they got to analyzing it, the trouble was that if just half a dozen of the queens up on Signal Mountain were included— just five or six of the richer ones—Kinja would lose about half a million a year in income taxes. Now, Norm, how do you go about writing a nice moral law that exempts local tax-paying citizens? Cooler heads prevailed, and the only thing the cops ever care about to this day is sailor boys. The navy's been in here once or twice raising hell with the government, and the word is really out on that. No sailors. I've never seen one in the Casa."

"How about Bob Cohn?"

"Oh, the UDT's never in uniform off duty. Anyway, Bob's with me when he comes."

Iris said after a glum pause filled with the Rover's rattling, "I'm getting dismal waves from you. What's up, darling?" She sat with folded arms, regarding him with wry, knowing amusement, her hair tossing in the breeze from the open window, her face lovely in the moonlight.

"I don't know, Iris. Too many songs of the thirties. Or too many queers."

"I'm having the only good time I've had in months, maybe in years, so please stay happy, Norm."

"Truly?" He looked at her again, and she was not smiling.

"Really and truly."

Her tone dispelled his mood, and warm excitement ran in his veins.

4

When they came to the Pink Cottage, Iris opened the door, and with a look and a smile invited him in. One floor lamp burned by an armchair. Norman was reminded of the first time he had entered this room, more than a month ago, and had been surprised by the smart furnishings, the mass of books, and the long table with the amateur sculptures. The distinctive odor—exquisite woman tinctured by doghouse—was strong tonight, but Meadows himself was not in evidence. In the silence Norman could hear the steel band thumping away on the terrace, *Boom-da-boom-boom.* . . .

"I'll be damned," he said, pausing just inside the door and looking around.

"What, dear?"

"Dingley Dell."

Iris broke into a wonderful female laugh, deep, intense, and rich. "I've been a very good girl all evening. You will now fix me a light Bombay gin and tonic, with a slice of lime."

"With pleasure, and I'll make it two."

In the kitchenette, he heard her putting a stack of records on the phonograph. The power hum of the big machine started up, followed by the loud high surface hiss of an old recording. He was slicing a large aromatic lime.

> *"By yon bonny banks*
> *And by yon bonny braes*
> *Where the sun shines bright on Loch Lomond—"*

The high sweet voice, slightly muffled by the obsolete recording, shocked him like the voice of a dead person once dear to him, and needling thrills rippled down his backbone. It was the Negro singer Maxine Sullivan, who more than twenty years ago had had a bright vogue, among young lovers in New York night clubs, with her jazz arrangements of Scottish songs. It startled Norman to perceive how thin and antiquated the instrumentation was; but Maxine's voice was unchanged. A flood of old sensations broke on him. He could feel the pressure of a girl's soft thigh jammed beside him at a table in a smoky crowded cellar; he was drunk, young, happy, totally alive, vibrating with appetite and with hope. Dazed, he walked out of the kitchenette, holding the knife and the cut lime. Iris was not there. He sank on the divan and listened.

> *"You take the high road, and I'll take the low road,*
> *And I'll be in Scotland afore ye.*
> *But me and my true love*
> *Will never meet again*
> *On the bonny banks*
> *On the bonny, bonny banks—"*

The song ended. It was astonishing how short the old records were; had it played more than a couple of minutes? The machine clicked, slammed, crackled, and another record began to play, an old show tune that meant nothing to him. He sat there, smelling the sharp perfume of the lime in his hand, tears trickling down his face. He was not thinking of any girl he had ever slept with. He was thinking of Hazel, standing up in her kiddie bed in a pink sleeping suit, smiling at him. The record had touched the spring in his mind, whatever it was, that released the pure absolute impulse of love. His tears were for Hazel, and for the passing of time, and—with no self-pity, quite unbidden—for young Norman Paperman, and what had become of him.

"Norman, sweetie, for heaven's sake what's the matter?" The phonograph stopped. Iris strode to him, and brushed his cheeks with light fingers. "Ye gods, you're worse than I am. Does Maxine do that to you?"

"Got caught unawares," Norman said very hoarsely.

She took the knife and the lime from him and put them in the kitchenette, then came and sat beside him, scanning his face. "Want a drink?"

"I don't think so. Not this minute."

"Neither do I."

He took her in his arms, and they lay on the divan and kissed. She was not responsive.

"What is it?" he said after a while.

"I don't know, Norm. Tears—really, a big boy like you—" She smiled up at him, compassionate, willing, pretty, and terribly melancholy.

"It just happened to hit me that way."

"Who were you reminded of?"

"Nobody."

Iris leaned up on an elbow. "I have a feeling, somehow, all of a sudden, that this is one hell of a lousy idea."

"It's a great idea," he said, pushing her shoulders down. "It's the only idea."

"You're sure, now? The last thing I want is to make you miserable."

"Then stop talking."

"Norman Paperman," she murmured, and she put her arms powerfully around him. "Honestly, what a name."

It was exquisite, kind, peculiarly familiar love-making. It was Iris instead of Henny, a larger woman with some different ways. It was as shockingly, unexpectedly familiar and poignant as the old record; and like it, too brief, too soon over.

Iris left him, and after a while she came back wearing a white silk robe trimmed in green. She brought two tall gin and tonics with slices of lime.

"I want mine now. Do you?" Her voice was low and vibrant.

"Sure."

"How are you?"

"Great. Marvellous. Very happy. A little sleepy."

She laughed. "Big night out. Conscience?"

"No. I have a large callus where that used to be."

She sat beside him on the divan, leaning against the black cushions; put up her feet, tucked the robe around her thighs, and took a long pull at the drink. "The hell with it. I'm happy too. I'm truly happy, tonight, completely, deeply happy for once, and there's only the present moment. That's the simplest idea in the world, and the hardest to grasp and hold on to. I don't know why." She drank again, and looked slyly at him. "Why should Henny be bothered? How have we hurt her? One more slice off a cut loaf, they say."

"It won't hurt her if she doesn't know."

"God knows *I* have no conscience pangs about Alton," Iris said. "I don't owe him a damned thing, and as a matter of fact I think I'm getting some of my own back, and high time— What's the matter now? Why the funny face?"

"Alton?" Paperman said.

"Of course. His Excellency himself, damn his tricky hide." She stared at Paperman and he stared at her, and she laughed. "Oh, look here, Norman. I've appreciated your delicacy, really I have, but at this point I guess you can drop it. You know I'm the governor's girl friend, and I know you know it, and I really don't mind any references to it, if they're not ill-mannered. It's a very old story to me, after all, dear."

"Alton Sanders' girl friend? Honestly, Iris?" Norman stammered, too dazed to be smooth.

"Of course, dear, and of course you know."

"Why, no, Iris. I didn't. I suppose I've been stupid or blind, but I actually didn't."

Iris's face changed. It became tense, serious, and guarded. "You're not being polite? Because truly, Norman, that's unnecessary and even a little embarrassing, and I'd be happier if you wouldn't keep it up."

"I'm not kidding you. To tell the truth I sort of thought that Bob Cohn—maybe"—Iris's eyebrows shot up, and she smiled most incredulously—"well, Iris darling, take my word for it, I didn't know *anything* about you. I met you for the first time with Bob, and—" Paperman was growing rattled and shaky, trying to maintain a light tone over his shock, and the dizzying ugly sickness at his heart—"and if I've ever seen you with a fellow it's been with Bob, so—"

"But darling, Bob is a *boy*. He's clever and wonderful, he's been a lifesaver, a shoulder to cry on, Bob Cohn couldn't be nicer, but—gee

293

whiz, Norm, did you really think of me as one of those old bags who screw boys?"

Paperman said, "Well, let's take it that I'm some kind of world-beating fool, and let it go at that, Iris."

"No, let's not." Iris put her drink on a side table, folded her arms, and looked at him intently. "Norman, now listen. Everybody on this island, everybody without exception I think right down to your Virgil the boatman, knows about me. Why, I came here with Alton. I used to stay nights in Government House. He was going to marry me, or he said he was, he still says so in fact, and I didn't give a damn what anybody thought. I never have. Now how in God's name, Norman, has it happened that nobody told you? Didn't Tilson? Didn't Collins? Didn't *Lorna*, for Christ's sake, the fresh little tart?"

"Nobody ever did, Iris. Maybe like you they assumed I knew it. Or— I don't know. Nobody ever told me."

He was thinking how unbelievably dense he had been. Everything was falling into place; her odd conduct on the first night when Reena Sanders had beckoned to him; her bristling hostility to Sanders in Pitt Bay, her demonstrative affection to himself under the governor's eyes, and the dog's friendliness with Sanders; a glimpse now and then of Iris with Sanders, her decidedly strange way of talking about this Negro, and about all Negroes. There are none so blind, he thought, as those who will not see. Iris Tramm had been for him the embodiment of the magic of Kinja, the glimmering blonde at the core of the island dream, and he had not wanted to see that she was the Negro governor's mistress, and he hadn't seen it.

Iris's searching eyes on his face made him uneasy. "Are you sure it doesn't make a difference to you? Be honest now. It must be a sort of shattering idea, Norman, if it's actually news."

"Why? I like Iris Tramm, the woman I know. Your love life is your own."

"But I love a Negro, dear. Let's get that very straight. I've been in love with him for two years, and it's been beautiful. For a while it was the most beautiful thing that had ever happened to me. Nevertheless, a Negro he is."

"I know he is, and it doesn't make the slightest difference, I swear that to you."

Iris heaved a sigh, never taking her eyes off him. "Doesn't it, though? Honestly, now, Norman—all the Broadway and all the Marxism never got three inches below your skin, did it? You're a nice middle-class New York Jewish liberal, and you're shocked to the core. Obviously you are. I just hope you're not disgusted, too. Because really that's how things are."

Paperman, thoroughly demoralized, said the first thing that came into his head. "Look, Iris, I've slept with a colored girl."

Her face stiffened into a smile, and she said in a hard bright tone, "Have you? Tell me about it. Was it fun? Is it true what they say about them?"

"All I mean is, to me they're just people—"

Iris got off the divan, and stood looking down at him. "Poor Norm. You're floundering, and you're reading your lines very badly. I didn't mean to stagger you like this, baby, God knows. Nevertheless this makes our score for the day perfect, doesn't it? We're over the cliff, after all."

He stood, and tried to put his arm around her. She deflected it with no ill-humor, went to the kitchenette, and took a bottle from a cabinet.

"How about dragging your bruised and broken body up to the main house?" she said. "You're having important company in the morning."

"You're building this all up, Iris. I don't want our evening to end."

"I believe you sweetheart, but how do we get the car back up the cliff?"

"What are you making there?"

"Bourbon and tap water. That's what one drinks when one drinks. No fussing with limes and ice cubes and such."

He took the full glass from her and poured the brown contents in the sink.

"Why, thank you," she said. "With that simple gesture, you've saved me from my worst enemy."

"Iris, listen—"

"Norman, *go away.*"

The pulse of sudden power in her voice stopped his protests.

He managed to kiss her once. She did not object. She stood straight and endured the kiss. Then Norman left the cottage named Surrender.

chapter thirteen

Return of Atlas

I

The corrugated iron shutters were still down over the wide entrance arches of the terminal when Norman drove up at eleven. He wanted to catch the manager of the air-cargo office early. Peculiar customs regulations existed for fresh foodstuffs arriving by air, and he had a sheaf of official papers with him. But there was nothing to do but wait. No live thing stirred outside the airport except a stray donkey trailing a broken rope across the entrance walk in the beating sun, and browsing on a border of red lilies.

Bob Cohn came driving up in a small gray navy truck a few minutes later. Cohn had unofficially volunteered the truck, with his commanding officer's unofficial permission, to transport Norman's two hundred chateaubriand steaks to the Georgetown freezer. Norman had asked this favor, and Cohn had cheerfully arranged it. The fact that Hazel was coming on the same plane as the steaks had gone unmentioned.

"Hi," Cohn said, squatting beside Norman, who was sitting on the hot tarry-smelling driveway, in the shade of the Rover. The frogman's leg muscles stood out stringily under the red-brown skin. "I told you eleven was too early."

Norman looked at him for a moment and then said baldly, "So, Iris Tramm is Governor Sanders' mistress."

Cohn's eyes widened, and his smile faded away. "What? What makes you say that?"

"She told me."

"She *told* you?"

"Yes."

"When?"

"Last night."

"I see. Were you surprised?"

"I was stupefied. And that got her angry."

A little lizard stood on the roadway staring at them, pulsing out its throat in a grotesque red loop. Cohn caught it with a rake of a hand. "What else did she tell you?"

"Not much. She sort of threw me out."

Cohn opened his palm on the ground, and the lizard leaped free and ran. He grinned at Paperman, his teeth white and regular in his hawkish sunburned face. Cohn wore a T-shirt, very brief khaki shorts, and heavy dusty shoes with white socks. "She got that angry, eh? She got angry at me, too, when I once said I didn't think you knew."

"The way I had it figured, you were probably the lucky man," Paperman said.

Cohn laughed out loud. "I'm the guy Iris tells her troubles to. Back in October the governor asked my C.O. to check her out in an aqualung, because she was wild to try it. I drew the assignment and so we got friendly. The lung gave her claustrophobia, and she made only two dives. She's a good swimmer, though, and a game woman."

"You never even made a pass at her? She's smart, and she's very pretty."

Cohn shrugged. "Iris has always treated me like an eighteen-year-old, Norm. —Well? Did you mind?"

"Mind what?"

"Finding that out," Cohn said, looking him in the eye, and Paperman felt that the frogman understood what had happened the night before, in all its main points.

He hesitated, then spoke stoutly for the record. "Not in the least. But she didn't believe me."

Cohn nodded slowly, and thought for a few moments, head down, juggling pebbles in one hand; and then began to talk about Sanders. He was a California Republican, a minor professional politician whose chief asset—so Cohn said—was that he was a Negro. Aside from that, Alton Sanders was a typical career bureaucrat, perhaps brighter than most, hard-working, knowledgeable, alert, and bound to end as a congressman, or an undersecretary in the Cabinet, unless he made a bad mistake; such as, for instance, marrying a white woman who was a former film star notorious for drunken collapses, and an ex-communist to the bargain. Iris's real problem wasn't loving a Negro, Cohn said, it was the more common one of loving a married man, who wouldn't break up his marriage and career for an unsuitable woman he'd fallen in love with.

"You came along about the time she was facing up to that," Cohn said. "Reena was down here, you remember. For a showdown, supposedly, but nothing was happening. When you came into the bar that night for the first time, with all your jokes and Broadway talk, you were a lifesaver. I'd never seen Iris spark the way she did to you. I thought she was working up to try to drown herself, and maybe she was, but you diverted her. She's been worrying over you and your hotel ever since. Iris likes you."

Paperman said, not too steadily, "I liked her. I mean, I still do."

Cohn nodded. "This needed no force reconnaissance to find out. But Norman, why were you so shocked? If you stopped to think about it, what could a smart, beautiful woman like her be doing all alone on a West Indian island? It could only be that her life was such a lousy mess, she'd be strictly nobody to get involved with."

The entrance shutters began to rattle and screech upward. Paperman said as he stood, "You're wise beyond your years."

He had forgotten how small and slight Henny was. She was the first white person out of the plane, after several natives descended the little ladder. She eagerly waved at him, with the smile that he loved, and came toward the gate in a fast walk just short of a scamper. She wore a small beige hat, a tailored black suit, she carried a fur on her arm, and she proclaimed New York as a tiger proclaims jungle. Atlas emerged from the plane right behind her, in a blue brass-buttoned jacket and white flannel pants, hoarsely bawling over his shoulder. He carried a small canvas bag with a bottle sticking out. So much Paperman saw, and here was Henny, running the last few steps and embracing him, with the desperate hug of a lost child that has been found. The smell of her perfume was as welcome and as novel as her kiss.

"My God, you look marvellous," she said.

"Where's Hazel?"

"Oh, still pulling herself together. She's been doing a heavy make-up job for the last half-hour on that bumpy rattletrap. Hi there, Bob! Jesus, the men look good down here. What a ride! Murder! We've been dodging through thunderstorms. It's so clear here!"

"HEY, NORM! HAVE THEY GOT A BAR YET IN THIS SHITTY AIRPORT?" roared Atlas, halfway to the gate. "I'm shaking like a leaf. I need a drink!" He grasped Norman's hand in a damp huge paw. Atlas was pale, and unshaven, and the dark bags under his red eyes were appalling, but otherwise he was the same, complete to the bourbon reek.

"Welcome back, Lester. I'm sorry there's no bar. We'll rush you back to the Reef and you can tank up."

"Doesn't the son of a bitch look healthy and happy?" Atlas said to Henny. Even when he wasn't shouting, he had the voice projection of a hog-caller, and after his first remark, everybody in the airport was staring at him. "Look at that relaxed face. Why, he's dropped ten years. This can only come from laying all the women who register at the Gull Reef Club. It tones up the system."

"Oh, shut up, Lester," said Henny.

"Why? Listen, if Norman's giving that extra service it ought to be advertised. I might pitch in to help him handle the Christmas rush. HAW HAW HAW!"

"What the devil, where's Hazel?" Paperman said. "They're starting to unload the luggage."

A motor-driven wagon was beside the plane, and men in overalls were slinging suitcases and parcels out of a hole in the plane's side. Cohn said, as two frosty oblong paperboard boxes were handed out smoking, "There comes your meat, Norm."

"What meat?" Henny said.

"And there's Hazel," said Cohn. "We're all set."

The girl stood on the top step, one white-gloved hand resting in the doorway, posing for invisible news photographers. Her light clinging pink silk suit displayed a voluptuous figure; she wore no hat, her dark hair fell to her shoulders in an old-fashioned charming way, and at this distance she looked fresh and dewy as a primrose. With a queenly little wave that might have been for Norman, for Cohn, or for everybody in the airport, she came down the stairs, and behind her the Sending emerged from the doorway, carrying Hazel's fur-collared coat, and her hatbox, and her make-up bag, and a typewriter, and a tennis racket, and his own coat, and two cameras.

Hazel gave her father a brief hug and an offhand kiss, looking over his shoulder at Bob Cohn with immense startled eyes. "My goodness! It's you!"

"Sure."

"What on earth are you doing here? Why aren't you off somewhere a couple of hundred feet underwater, strangling an octopus?"

"The navy's discharged me for arteriosclerosis, Hazel."

"Oh yes, no doubt."

The Sending came to the gate, panting, perspiring, and tourist-white. "Hazel, I looked under every seat," he said. "That eyebrow pencil is gone."

"Oh, well, I'll buy another one. You remember Bob Cohn."

Klug looked Cohn up and down and said, "Oh, yes. The frogman. Are you meeting somebody?"

Atlas was herding together the six passengers who were guests of the Club. "Here's our gang, Norm! They had first preference on my booze while it lasted, by God. Gull Reef hospitality this time began right in San Juan, didn't it, folks?"

"In Idlewild Airport for me," giggled a gray-headed woman, whose feathered hat was askew over one ear. "My, there's always a first time for everything, isn't there? I think I like straight bourbon out of paper cups."

"You're a swinger, Millicent," said Atlas, throwing his arm around her waist. "Us two are going to make beautiful music together. Let's go, sexpot. We're in the tropics now." He chanted unmusically,

> *"Down de way*
> *Where de nights are gay*
> *And de sun shines gaily on de mountain top—"*

while he waggled the woman around in a revolting parody of a Calypso dance.

"That's right. Keep everybody amused, Lester, for one minute," Paperman said. "I've got to check on the meat."

"What meat?" said Henny. "Where are you running off to?"

The air-cargo manager, a plump Kinjan in a business suit—named Elias Thacker, according to the plate on his desk—waved a wad of papers as Norman entered the office. "All fix. You got you meat. It all pile in de shade by de cargo depot. You drives you car right on de field troo de next gate and picks it up." With great relief, Norman paid the charges and signed the papers. He found Cohn waiting outside the office. Norman asked him to load the meat in the station wagon, and take it back to town.

"Sure thing," Cohn said. "Say, your Hazel looks pretty good."

Norman shrugged. "She always does. Her boy friend seems a bit haggard."

"Why, no. He's full of the old fight. He wants to go down in an aqualung right away. Today. Says he swam for Chicago University."

"Can you find him a lung with a slow leak?" said Paperman.

Cohn laughed and went off. Norman returned to the Gull Reef party, which sat now on benches in a huddle, the only people left in the terminal. Atlas, hunched and sagging, glowered at Norman as he came. "Norm, what's the holdup? You got a bunch of hot and tired people here, including me."

"What's this meat that's causing all the trouble?" Henny said.

"No trouble. Everything's fine."

Norman started to tell them about the Tilson party and the chateau-briands.

"Hey, Norm!" Cohn was calling to him from the field, on the other side of the locked plane gate about twenty feet away. "You did say steaks, didn't you?"

"Of course. Chateaubriand steaks. Why?"

"Come and take a look. Better hurry."

Norman ran to the gate, clambered up the hinges, and vaulted the high wire fence.

"Norman!" shouted Henny. "Who do you think you are, Tarzan? Stop that."

"What *now*, for Jesus' sake?" bellowed Atlas. "We're dying here!"

Norman followed Cohn at a trot to the cargo depot, where eight frosty wire-fastened paper cartons were stacked on the porch, oozing blood. Large green labels on each package read *San Juan Wholesale Meat Supply. Highest Grade Chicken Necks and Wings.*

"Look here." Cohn squatted, pointing to shipping labels pasted to the side of each carton, with typed addresses:

> *Grosvenor House*
> *Barbados, B.W.I.*
> *Rush—Perishable.*

"I would guess there's been some mistake, Norm," he said. "They probably took off the wrong shipment."

"It's a nightmare," said Paperman, clutching his head. "What gibbering lunatic in Barbados wanted eight cartons of chicken necks and wings air freight, for Christ's sake?"

A loud growl of revving motors startled him.

"That plane! Bob, my steaks *have* to be on that plane. The cargo office has the airway bill!"

The airplane was swinging around for take-off, far down the runway. Paperman ran out into the knee-deep grass of the field, thrashing his arms in the air. The plane roared past him, lifting off the ground, and dwindled away into the sky. He came back to Cohn, and said with a deathly grin, "Maybe there's another pile of cartons somewhere. My pile. Let's go to the freight office."

There were no other cartons. Mr. Thacker blamed the pilot. He had been in a hurry to take off again, and had rushed the cargo boys. This was always happening, he said. That particular pilot was a very unpleasant man. Probably the steaks had been under the pile of luggage bound for Barbados, Trinidad, and Caracas, and the pilot certainly should have given Mr. Thacker's boys a chance to have a good look. But no, hurry, hurry, hurry, and naturally the boys, seeing packages of frozen meat, had assumed that this was the Gull Reef shipment.

"Yes, yes, but what's going to happen to *my steaks?*" exclaimed Norman. "They're off to Venezuela, defrosting as they go."

"God knows," said Mr. Thacker. "It is an unfortunate confusion."

Lester Atlas barged into the office. "Norman, what the hell? They're closing the goddamn doors of this terminal."

Norman told him in great agitation what had happened. Atlas gave the cargo manager a grossly charming smile. "Where's the next stop for that plane, Mr. Thacker?"

"Barbados," said the manager.

"Barbados," Atlas purred. "Now how about telephoning Barbados, Mr. Thacker, and telling them to take off those steaks, see, and put them in a freezer, and send them back on the next plane. Don't you think that would be a nice idea?"

The cargo manager said cordially that this was irregular procedure, and out of the question. There would be the matter of the freezer charges; the Barbados people needed the airway bill before they could take the meat off the plane; he had no authority to make overseas calls; it was all the fault of Windward-Leeward Airways, but unfortunately their agent was gone for the day by now; and he himself was late for lunch. As he said this he started to walk away from his desk.

Atlas charged and blocked him, his smile turning to a horrid glare. "Listen, *mister!* This airport operates on a federal subsidy and I just happen to have a few connections in Washington," he thundered. "I swear to Christ that Federal Aviation Agency men will be down here next week checking into the competence of a certain ELIAS THACKER" —he spat out the name like a curse—"if anything happens to those steaks. You hear me?" He ripped the telephone off its cradle. "Now, who do I talk to in Barbados? *I'll* handle this, and then I'm calling my Washington attorney, right from this telephone, *mister.*"

Thacker rolled white-rimmed eyes at Paperman. "Dis de porson what on de cover of *Time?*"

"That's the person," Norman said.

The cargo manager sadly took the telephone. "I see what we can do. —Ovaseas?"

Atlas stood over the cargo manager as he put the call through. Norman meantime found Cohn, and asked him to take the guests to the Reef in the Land Rover; he would drive back the navy truck, he said, as soon as this business was wound up. "Okay," Cohn said, "I guess we can get everybody into the Rover, all right, except maybe Hazel's friend. There's quite a mess of luggage, and all."

"Splendid. I'll bring him," Norman said.

The Barbados call took a half hour to get through, and somehow Thacker arranged the return of the steaks, or said he did. Norman drove Atlas and Klug to Georgetown along the back road down the coast, which usually elicited raptures from newcomers to Amerigo; but Klug was not impressed. "The *filth* of this place," he observed several times, mopping his face. He also said things like, "Don't they have trash collection on this island?" and, "What's the incidence of diseases like cholera and leprosy? I should think every other native would have *something.*"

It struck Paperman that, in truth, Amerigo was a damned dirty place. He had long ago stopped seeing the empty beer cans, sodden cartons and newspapers, and broken boxes that lined the roads, but now he saw them again. The Kinjan drivers habitually drank beer or fruit nectar as they went, and disposed of the cans with a cheerful toss through the window. Every half mile or so there was a large iron trash bin, heaped to overflowing or wholly invisible under a garbage mound. Rusting wrecks of cars dotted the wayside. When a Kinja automobile expired, its corpse was dragged off the road and in a day or two was picked clean to the chassis; there it lay where it had fallen, oxidizing fast in the sun and sea air, but still requiring a few years to rot to earth. Cars in all stages of decomposition were part of the island scenery.

In his first days of enchantment, Norman had seen only the lovely views of hills and sea. In time he had noticed, and been repelled by, the refuse and the wrecks; then these had become a vague annoyance, just one more of the tropical irritations like the sand flies and the power failures. On balance he still thought Amerigo was a pretty place, if not exactly Eden. Klug obviously didn't, but Norman had a feeling that Klug would never like the tropics. He was a perspirer. He was perspiring in streams, his shirt was streaked black, and his handkerchief was wet and gray.

2

Norman found Henny in his apartment, freshly combed and made up, wearing a brand-new, sheer creamy lace negligee, and nothing else. She had lost a bit of weight. "Oh, hi there," she said, casually tightening a blue silk sash around her slim waist. "Is the meat crisis solved? I thought I'd go on ahead and get a shower before lunch. This is a nice little apartment. Airy, anyway."

Norman took her in his arms.

"Really, Norm, what's this bottle of champagne on ice here for? And all these gardenias and red lilies? I mean, brother, how corny can you get?" He was kissing her, and these sentences emerged between kisses. She went on, "Aren't you hungry? I'm famished. Let's have lunch. Norm, really, if I go drinking champagne before I have something to eat I'll never make it down the stairs. Norman, for pete's sake, it's been all of three weeks. Don't overdo it or I'll get suspicious."

"How's your pain?" he mumbled into her hair.

"Pain? What pain? Oh, the pain. Funny, I had it like mad all the way down on the jet, but then it went away in that bouncy ride. The doctor says—*Norman*. Ye gods. Mr. Hot Hands."

"I'm glad to see you, Henny."

"That's good," Henny said, and she sighed deeply. "Oh, well, go ahead. Open the champagne."

Cohn, Hazel, and Klug were finishing lunch at a large round table when Norman and Henny came out on the dining terrace considerably later, looking gay and somewhat silly. Hazel sat with her chin on her fist, yawning. The two men appeared to be arguing volubly. "What happened to you? Sit down," Hazel said to her parents. "These fellows started on courage, and got on to bullfights, and I'm about to pass out."

Klug gave an ironic little smile to the Papermans. "Grace under pressure is the topic. It all began with aqualunging, and branched out—"

"Let me finish and then I'll shut up on this, Hazel," Cohn said. "Sure, I admit that I'd be too scared to try to stab a wounded bull to death with a sword. I said that ten minutes ago. But I just don't know if the act is courageous. Isn't it just a cruel, dangerous form of commercial entertainment? I guess those fellows show grace under pressure, whatever that is, doing all the stylish dancing close to the horns. But I think the only courageous thing to do in a bull ring would be to try to stop the bullfight."

"That's not bad, actually," Klug said, with a small reluctant smile, and an instructor's approving nod. "You insist on a moral content to courage, then. You're not content with an abstract, lovely arabesque of death and risk. I think you might develop that point of view in an article. It would have thrust, coming from a man in a hazardous occupation."

"Me? I can barely sign my name," Cohn said.

"Oh, come, come," said Klug. "In any case, to get back to the point, will you, or can you, take me out for a dive in an aqualung? Or is it against regulations, and will I have to rent a lung somewhere? Because dive I will."

"I guess you can make a dive with us if you want to," Cohn said. "We're going lobstering tomorrow morning on Cockroach Rock, and my commanding officer is pretty non-regulation."

"Perfect," said the Sending.

"Gosh, can I come?" said Hazel.

Cohn said to her with an affectionate light in his eye, "Want to make a dive, Hazel?"

"Horrors, no. I just want to see Shel go down and come up."

Henny said, "Well, you'll certainly see him go down."

"The rest," Norman said, "is a question of grace under pressure."

Klug stood. "Do you have any idea where I can lay my head tonight? I want to get unpacked and into some cool clothes."

"The island's pretty tight," said Norman. "Why don't you telephone Casa Encantada? They might squeeze you in."

"Casa Encantada—Enchanted House," said Klug. "Sounds delightful. Bye, Hazel. I'll be back here for dinner." He leaned down and gave her a proprietary kiss, which she seemed to relish, her immense slanted eyes sparkling on the frogman.

"Casa Encantada?" Cohn wrinkled his forehead at Paperman, as Klug walked off. "I really think you're guessing wrong, Norm."

"What's the matter with that place?" Hazel said suspiciously to her father. "You're so mean. I know you. Has it got rats?"

"Birds," Norman said. He glanced at his watch. "Do you know where Atlas is? He and I have an appointment at the bank soon."

"He went swimming," Hazel said. "What a horrid man! All night long I kept pretending I didn't know him. Then he'd come and paw me and kiss me and call me his niece. His niece! *'Haw, haw, Hazel, give Unkie a kiss! Con permisso!'* And him smelling like an old high-ball with a wet cigar in it."

"You have to understand Lester," Henny said. "Lester is very lonesome."

"I'll bet. The lonesomest man in town."

Cohn took Hazel off for a ride in a navy boat—an LCP, he called it—to see the harbor and the submarine base. Henny declared she was too excited to eat; and while Norman devoured a hot roast-beef sandwich with great appetite, she went roaming around the hotel. She returned full of enthusiasm for the new rooms. "Why, they're all but done, and they're fine! You won't know those rooms when they're decorated. But golly, Norm, who's that menacing creep with the tiny squinty red eyes? The one that keeps sharpening a big machete? He gave me one look and I got the chills. You ought to get rid of him."

"I'll get rid of you first," Norman said. "That's Hippolyte. You be nice to him. He's a little eccentric, but he's a genius. He's our handy man. He built those rooms. He can fix anything. He can do anything. He's a savior. He's irreplaceable."

"I'll take your word for it," said Henny. "Where's Janet West? Is she still in that same cottage?"

"Who? Iris? Well, yes, I suppose she is. I mean of course she is. I only mean I don't know whether she's there just now."

"I want to ask her if Hassim got all the stuff I asked for," Henny said, looking at Norman—so he thought—a shade appraisingly. "How is she? Has she been on any benders?"

"Janet? No, no, she's really very sedate, at least around here she is. She keeps very much to herself, you know."

"What do you call her? Janet or Iris?"

"Well, Henny, here on this island everyone calls her Iris. It's just that you said Janet."

Atlas appeared, looking unusually dignified in a gray featherweight suit and a dark tie. "Get a move on, Norm. We're due at the bank."

"Coming." Norman drank up his coffee.

Henny said, "Can I phone Janet at her cottage?"

"Well, I guess so," Norman said with elaborate lightness. "You might disturb her if she's napping, that's all. She generally shows up at the bar around five or six."

"Oh, I'll just give her a ring," Henny said.

3

In the banker's small, chilled office, increasingly choked with cigar smoke, Atlas and Llewellyn pored over large real estate maps and blue-bound accounting statements, and talked financial cabalisms, while Norman worried about a meeting between Iris and Henny. Iris would be discreet, if she were sober, but he didn't think she was sober; and he feared Henny's anger. It was not beyond her to get on an airplane and go straight home. She had given him notice after his coronary that she would endure no more of that nonsense. The warning had rung like iron.

Atlas rapped fat knuckles on a large blue-inked map. "Can I take this along for now, Llewellyn? Norman and I want to drive out and look at the property."

"Naturally, Mr. Ot-loss."

"Are there going to be any other bidders?" Atlas said, rolling up the map.

"I know of two others."

Atlas looked down at the small banker sitting primly at his desk. "The property's going to go for three," he said jovially. "Maybe three and a quarter."

The banker smiled. "I'm afraid it will not go then. The bank advanced three hundred and fifty thousand dollars. Of course we must recover our princi-pal, at least."

"How in the Christ could you lend so much money to a goofball with a balance sheet like that?"

Llewellyn danced his fingers together over his little potbelly. "He had syndicate financing of a quarter of a million from Florida, after all, which was all spent here."

Atlas said, "Yes, and which those misguided Florida clucks will never see again."

"I fear not. But you see, meantime Crab Cove is almost built, isn't it? And somebody is bound to finish it. Then it will be an asset to our is-land."

Lester grunted. "Jesus Christ, of course. What a setup! You're sitting here like a croupier, aren't you? Bring the suckers in, clean them out, and play the game again tomorrow. The house never loses."

The banker spread his hands upward. "We exist to serve our expand-ing little community."

"You're all right, Llewellyn. We're going to get along," Atlas said. "Let's roll, Norm."

Crab Cove looked terrible to Paperman when they went walking on the property. Seen from the road, the rows of pagoda-like homes had quaint charm. Up close, the houses were visibly incomplete, abandoned in mid-construction as though the workers had fallen in a plague. Dirt-streaked toilets and bathtubs stood in the middle of living rooms; entrails of wire burst from walls; rubble of wood and plaster was everywhere, and the muddy paths between the houses were aswarm with mosquitoes and flies. Atlas squished from house to house, exclaiming with delight, sinking to his ankles in mud, leaving filthy tracks on the tile floors. A silent black caretaker trudged behind them, with a silly short-haired Kinjan dog, all bones, sores, and fleas; the animal never stopped leaping and barking.

"Norman, this thing is a gold mine," Lester said, inserting his usual obscenities of enthusiasm in suitable places, "Three-fifty! Why, there's twenty-five houses here. They're finished. A hundred thousand cleans this place up and makes a park of it. All right, say a hundred fifty thou-sand. *Can't* go higher. For half a million you've got yourself twenty-five Caribbean houses to sell, and these houses have got to go for forty each.

Why, there's three big bedrooms and two baths in them, patios, barbe-
cues, and they've got beach rights. What am I talking about, forty? You
know the thing to do, Norm? *Furnish* half of them. Get some smart
faggot down from New York, you know, to fill them with that stylish
crap from Japan and Denmark that comes in here duty-free. Then you
got class. Norm, think! We're talking about a profit of half a million
dollars here, I swear. All we need is a selling job. Find families in the
States who want to own a home in the Caribbean. There's *millions* of
them. Florida's all finished. It's cold and rainy, and full of those goddamn jellyfish."

Paperman was unimpressed. Atlas didn't know Kinja; he couldn't
picture the horrible possibilities, nobody could without having lived on
the island. The unfinished plastery-smelling houses of Crab Cove
seemed to Norman full of the vengeful West Indian jumbies that had
nearly ruined him at Gull Reef, and that had bankrupted Akers. He
started to say that he was too busy to handle real estate, but Atlas cut
him off. "Norman, will you wait till I buy the thing before you start
arguing? If I bid it in, you've got yourself a finder's fee of five thousand
dollars. Is that bad for a start?" He looked at his watch. "Holy mackerel!
Can you get me back to the Club in ten minutes? I've got a red-hot call
coming in from New York."

He told Paperman as they went jouncing back to town along a broken
tar road heavily lined with rotting autos, that his Montana deal was
coming to a head. It was the biggest thing he had ever touched. But as
usual, he was in for a fight. Other operators had gotten wind of the
situation, and had also started buying stock and lining up proxies.
He was going to win out, but it would be a close thing. His real
problem had been to find out who his opponents were. They were acting
through a dummy, an obscure St. Louis lawyer, and it had taken Lester
several weeks to figure out that a syndicate of rivals of his from Phoenix
were the competition. He knew their money resources. They would back
down before he did, so the temporary run-up of stock prices didn't
bother him, though he was rather extended now. "You can't lose your
nerve in this business, Norm," he said jovially. "I've been in situations
when I was hanging on by my teeth, and I was once damn near busted.
This one isn't half bad."

Norman left him at the telephone in the office, and went to his apartment. The afternoon sun had heated it up as usual, despite the open windows. Henny was sprawled on the bed in her slip, fast asleep. A note was propped against the vase of flowers on the bed table:

> *Had some drinks and am passing out. Wake me up. I want to talk to you!!*

This was an innocuous note, except to a guilty man. Norman thought it was charged with rage and menace, and he considered sneaking off. But that was pointless; he took heart, and shook her. Henny moaned, rolled on her back, and opened her eyes; and by the look in them Paperman knew that for the moment he was safe. She held out her arms sleepily.

"What's all this?" he said, waving the note.

"Oh, yes." Henny sat up and yawned. "Listen, Norm, did you say she wasn't drinking? That woman's going to be in bad shape if we don't get her out of her cottage. She's on a real toot. Empty bottles are all over the place. She drinks bourbon and water, then switches to a beer, and then has more bourbon and water, and I mean not that much water, you know? So far she's all right, just a bit fuzzy in her talk maybe, but her mind is clear. She says this is how she loses weight, isn't that ridiculous? She just drinks and takes it easy and reads for a week or so, she says, and never eats, and ten pounds melt off. She's got dusty yellow Marxist books piled around her bed, Strachey and Mike Gold and all that, and a stack of old seventy-eight records on her phonograph. It's sort of eerie, Norm. She just talked on and on about her first husband, and Hollywood and the Party. She's completely back in the thirties. It was all kind of wild, but fascinating. I asked her to have dinner with us but she said she didn't want to intrude, and anyway she's not eating. How about you calling and urging her? She likes you, though she thinks you're sort of ridiculous, the way I do. I died laughing when she told me about the ants. Why didn't you write me about the ants?"

"Did she—why is she on the booze? Did she say?"

"No. Has she got a boy friend here? She must have. I'll bet she had a fight with him. That's how she's acting."

"I'll try to get her to come to dinner."

Atlas was smoking a cigar in a lobby armchair, leaning forward with one elbow on his knee. His face was sagging and gray. His eyes looked straight ahead, unseeing, as two pretty girls went laughing by in bikinis, their billowy white flesh aquiver.

"Everything all right, Lester?" Norman ventured to ask. "Did you get your call?"

"Eh? What? Oh, sure, Norm. I got it. Everything's going to be fine. It's one of those things. Come on and I'll buy you a drink. I need a drink or four."

"Sure. I'll be with you in a few minutes."

Norman went to the Pink Cottage, and halted outside. On the phonograph Ethel Merman and Bert Lahr were blasting out *Friendship*. Meadows began to bark, and after a moment Iris opened the door.

"Well, bless my soul if it isn't Joe Hill," she said, "alive as you or me."

Paperman was relieved to see that she looked all right. He had feared to find an unkempt stumbling wreck, but Iris was well-groomed and erect in a charming flowered housecoat he hadn't seen before. Her eyes were too bright, her speech was too emphatic, and she was holding a drink that was too dark.

"Hello, Iris."

"Come in, come in. What are you drinking? You're smack in time for the cocktail hour. Where's Henny? She's looking yummy, isn't she? Thin as a rail. That's for me, boy. I'm not eating again until my scale's down ten pounds. What did you say you were drinking? Shove a couple of those books aside and sit down. I've been looking up a few things."

"Iris, all I wanted to say—do you mind if I turn that phonograph down?"

"I'll do it, honey. I'm a nut, I like it to shake the walls." She jabbed a button. The sudden silence in the cottage was more oppressive than the loud music. "Yes, Norm? What can I do for you?"

It seemed absolutely incredible to Norman Paperman that last night he had made love to this woman. She was a sad, worn stranger.

"Iris, that's nonsense about not eating for a week. You'll get sick as a dog, you know that, and you'll end up in a hospital."

"So will you, Norm, whether you eat or not. As a matter of fact you're just out on a short parole, aren't you, dear? But don't worry, Meadows needs looking after, and I'm not going to the hospital on this bloody rock. I can take very good care of myself, Norm. I'm an old hand at that, and if I get to feeling at all bad my doggie and I will head right out on a plane back to San Diego, where my folks will take care of us. All right?"

"Henny is worried about you, and so am I, that's all."

"Henny's a good scout. Do you want me to get out of the cottage? Do you think I'll embarrass you? I really won't, but I don't want to add to your problems, Norm. I'll get out if you'll feel easier that way. I can find another place."

"Good God, Iris, are you trying to make me feel like a bastard? You needn't work at it." He put his hand to his brow. She was standing near him, and she caught the hand.

"Darling, no! No! Of all things! Why, you fool, what have *you* got to feel bad about?"

"Iris, come to dinner with us. Really, on all counts, it's the best thing for you to do."

She let his hand drop, and smiled, and looked drunk. "Take my word for it, Norman, I can't eat."

He got up and went to the door.

"Norman," she said in a different, bashful tone.

He turned. "Yes, Iris?"

"Well, it's just— Oh, hell, look here, I sort of thought you didn't know. I was almost sure anyway. After all, I was playing it that way right along. I was putting you on the defensive last night, dear, women do that, but it was lousy. I'm sorry."

Paperman was unable to answer, because his throat swelled shut. He went out.

chapter fourteen

The Sending Goes Down

I

Next morning the reunited Paperman family was breakfasting on the sunny terrace of the Gull Reef Club, when Sheldon Klug appeared in very short, conspicuously virile white bathing trunks, a gray sweatshirt, new water-buffalo sandals, and a perky little straw hat. He looked lumpy under his new sunburn, and he diffused a strong pungent smell yards ahead of him.

"Hi, sorry I stink. Insect repellent. Have you ever heard of creatures called sand flies?" he asked Paperman, after kissing Hazel's cheek and dropping in a chair. "You can't even see them, and they give the most ferocious sting!"

"I've heard of them," Norman said.

"Oh, you have. I hadn't. I thought I was breaking out with the small-pox. It seemed quite logical on this pestilential island."

"Amerigo really isn't pestilential," Paperman said. "The sun sort of sterilizes all the loose garbage. Everyone's pretty healthy."

"That's reassuring. I see you're still eating. I only had coffee. That proprietor at the Casa is charmingly frank, he said his food is lousy and yours is excellent, so here I am."

"Well, order something quick, dear," said Hazel. "Bob is expecting us in Pitt Bay at nine."

Henny said, "You'd better not eat much before diving. Some dry toast, maybe."

"I discussed that with our frogman friend last night. He said it's a superstition, and I should eat a normal meal." A waitress answered his wave, and Klug ordered cantaloupe, oatmeal, scrambled eggs, pork sausages, toasted English muffins, and Sanka coffee. "Ordinary coffee speeds up my heart," he explained.

"How do you like Casa Encantada?" Norman said.

"Splendid. Thanks for suggesting it. It's wonderfully typical. I'm going to get a *New Yorker* short story out of it, I know, at the very least."

"Typical of what?" Henny said.

"Any exotic milieu. Homosexuals invariably flock to the periphery of a society. Actually I got insights last night that will feed straight into my thesis. It's a perfect place for me to finish writing it."

Klug ate his breakfast with dispatch, getting more cheerful as the food went down. He didn't like Amerigo, he said, but the scenery was full of interest, and so were the people, natives and whites alike. He was delighted at having come. He even had a kind word for Cohn. "We got into quite a discussion last night, Hazel, after you went off to bed. He's an intelligent fellow."

"You'd *been* in quite a discussion for an hour. That's why I gave up," Hazel said. "I wanted to dance."

"But it's curious," Klug said. "After you left, his manner changed. You know he likes to pose as an ignoramus, and he keeps up the façade very carefully, but last night after a few drinks he began quoting books. It's a stereotype that he affects, of course, the existential hero that Hemingway popularized, the intellectual confining himself to the vocabulary and reference frame of an inarticulate roughneck. It's all a pastiche of *Huckleberry Finn*, actually, which is central to the American anti-intellectual ethos—the suspicious dislike of culture and the glorification of pragmatic action, of plain talk, of getting your hands dirty and enjoying danger. It's very chic, but it sits peculiarly on a Jew. Anyway all poses are a little silly. A man should be himself, even if he happens to be an intellectual. Cohn knows his Dostoevsky and Joyce very well, and his range of awareness is wide, and I actually think he could almost teach literature, the way his brother does at Brandeis. This man-of-action stuff is just a pretense."

Henny said, "Well, he does swim in and out of submarines at night, a hundred feet down. Isn't that carrying affectation a bit far?"

Klug beamed. "Men die for a pose all the time. Look at Lawrence of Arabia."

"It's a terrific insight, Sheldon," Norman said, "but you ought to finish up those sausages, you're late."

The Sending said placidly, "I'm ready. I suppose I can phone for a cab."

"I thought I'd drive you out," Norman said.

"Oh? That's very cordial of you."

"I'm coming too," Henny said. "I want to see this."

Lester Atlas was in the lobby, talking to the two bikini girls. Norman went over to him and offered to take him along to Pitt Bay.

"No thanks, Norm, you go ahead and have your fun. I'll mind the store," Atlas rasped. "The senior partner's here, and you can take it easy now. You've earned a little vacation."

One of the girls chirped at Norman, "Does he really own this place, and was he written up in *Time?*"

"You can believe anything Lester Atlas tells you," Norman said. "Look at that face."

Both girls broke into giggles, and Lester joined with loud haw-haws. "Go on, enjoy yourself, Norm. This hotel is in good hands now. Relax."

2

Whatever its drawbacks, the old Land Rover was fine for crashing past the cactus and thorn trees down the dry stone gully to Pitt Bay. A navy truck was parked at the beach, and near it a fat grizzled man in a wet T-shirt and bathing trunks, and a younger man in green fatigues, lounged on the sand beside upright gray air tanks with dangling straps. "Hello there, Mr. Paperman, remember me? Bob's C.O., Lieutenant Woods," called the man in green. "We met the first night you came to this island."

Norman recalled a formidable person in a white dress uniform rainbowed with battle ribbons. This was a round-faced, bristle-haired, cheery young man. "You're the same one?"

"Same one. Bob's gone out with the fellows. Chief Eller will take your friend out."

The Papermans sat on the sand, listening fascinated as the chief explained the workings of the regulator mask, and showed Klug the functioning of each valve and lever on the tanks. "I've read up on all this," Klug said with a slightly impatient smile, but the chief plodded right on with his memorized recital to the last word. "Any questions?" he said.

"What depth will we go to?"

The chief glanced at Klug's large, somewhat fat, pasty white body, with a coating of new pink sunburn on face, chest, and knees. "Forty feet, sir."

"What? I've been down to forty feet in Long Island Sound, Chief, with a face mask. I don't need a lung for forty feet."

"You can get an air embolism in ten feet of water," said the chief. "You'll be breathing compressed air, sir. This is our procedure for a first swim."

"Watch." The Sending ran to the water, dove in, and didn't surface for several minutes. He popped up at a great distance from shore, waved, swam back with beautiful form at high speed, and came out not breathing very hard. "Honest, I can swim," he said.

The chief shrugged at his commanding officer, who reclined on the sand. "That's really impressive, sir," Woods said, "but you'll be using navy equipment, and we're responsible for you. If you rent a tank at the Sea Shop after this, I'm sure Bob Cohn will go down with you to a hundred, a hundred fifty, whatever you want."

"Okay, let's go," Klug said shortly to the chief.

They donned the clumsy gear, waddled into the water, submerged, and were gone.

"I'm scared stiff," Hazel said.

"They're still close by," said the lieutenant. He took from the truck a blown-up black inner tube, and coils of cord. The chief broke to the surface a few feet away, and Woods tossed him the tube. Klug rose out of the water, removing the mask. "Why, it's superb, Hazel," he cried. "You're a fish. You're down there, and you're breathing. It's indescribable. I want you to do this before you go home. It's an existential must."

"Let's see you make me," Hazel said.

The chief now buckled a six-foot length of cord between himself and Klug, who protested loudly, "Really, Chief, I'm all for the buddy system, but won't we be kicking each other in the face?"

The chief paid no attention. He checked Klug's straps and valves and fussed with cords a bit more; then both men vanished beneath the water. The tube began to glide along the surface, out toward Cockroach Rock.

"They're off," Woods said.

Hazel sighed heavily, "Well! That's that." She was wearing a loose cover of chartreuse linen. She now stood and lazily took it off. Norman heard a slight hiss from the lieutenant. Two wisps of yellow were stretched across Hazel's naked pink-and-cream breasts and round hips. She had Henny's tiny waist, her dark hair billowed to her shoulders, and altogether she was ridiculously luscious.

Norman said, "Hazel, what's that you're not wearing?"

"Oh, please, Dad. You should see what some girls wear. This is nothing but a semi-brief."

"Ah! For nuns, and such?"

"Pooh. I want to look for shells. I've got to do something until he comes back, or I'll go nutty." She went off down the beach, Henny with her.

"Are you married," Norman said to the lieutenant, "and do you have daughters?"

"Affirmative. I have three."

"This Bob Cohn, Lieutenant—do you mind talking about him? What do you think of him?"

"Bob?" The lieutenant pushed his crumpled fatigue hat back up on his head. "He's sort of an individualist, as you might say, but in this outfit we run to those. He's right in there when it comes to the work. Why?"

"Hazel's nineteen, and Cohn's playing up to her. How about that?"

The lieutenant grunted. "Twenty-twenty vision, I'd say." He ran sand through his fingers. "Bob's a funny one. Actually he's kind of a scholar, sir, he reads all the time. His main trouble is, he thinks he's a gambler. It's against regulations and I'm not supposed to know about it, but every payday, from what I understand, the petty officers take him to the cleaners."

"Not a provider," Norman said.

With a laugh, Woods said, "Well, his father has this import-export business, you know. Bob's going back to Israel, once he finishes his navy hitch, to handle it from that end. I think Bob'll provide, all right, if he doesn't blow in the whole business one night playing stud poker."

A red inner tube came skimming toward the shore, and six masked tank-laden figures broke the surface, several of them holding clawing crayfish. Hazel and Henny came hastening back, and Hazel pretended panic when Cohn offered her an enormous mottled langouste still whipping its tail. She caused a real panic among the swimmers. When she ambled off down the beach again to search for shells, she had five muscular assistants, and she was dispensing startled looks and V-shaped smiles on all sides. Cohn dropped on the sand and talked with Henny, Norman, and the lieutenant, glancing to sea every now and then. So half an hour passed.

"How long will they be out?" Henny said edgily. Norman had told her about the sharks around Pitt Bay. She had little use for the Sending but she wished him no harm.

Woods said, "The chief can stretch his air to an hour and a half, but a beginner usually gulps it in thirty or forty minutes. They should be showing up soon."

"How do you tell when you're out of air?" Norman said. "You don't start to drown."

The lieutenant smiled. "Hardly. You get a very clear mechanical warning. As soon as the tank—"

"There's the chief, sir," Cohn said. "By himself." His tone was a shade too easy.

"Yep. All right, Bob. Suppose you get on out there? I'll come with a couple of the fellows." The lieutenant slipped out of his green shirt and trousers, disclosing short khaki trunks and a knife on a belt. He took an air tank and flippers from the truck as he spoke, moving without seeming haste but getting everything done remarkably fast. He shouted "Hey!" down the beach and Hazel's five escorts left her at a trot.

"Is there anything wrong? Was the chief making a distress signal?" Norman said. Cohn was already in the water in mask and flippers, speeding out to Cockroach Rock with scarcely a splash.

"Probably nothing," the lieutenant said, strapping on the tank. "Fisher, Davis, there's two full tanks on the truck. Chief's gotten separated from his buddy, looks like. He surfaced, and then went down after him."

"Yes, sir."

The lieutenant waddled to the water, and submerged, followed in less than a minute by the other two men. The remaining three stood at the water's edge, hands on their hips, looking out toward the reef.

Hazel, when she came up, was unable to talk. She looked at her parents with eyes dilated, for once, in true alarm.

Nobody spoke for what seemed a very long time.

"There's the chief," said one of the men, waving.

Another, a very tall, lean boy with a shaved head, said, "And there's Bob." A pause. "Bob's bringing the fellow in."

"What is it?" Hazel said. "Why is he bringing him in? I can't see anything. Is something wrong?"

The boy with the shaved head glanced at Hazel and smiled. "Why, miss, your friend probably got tired, is all. That often happens the first time. You keep losing body heat and you're not aware of exerting yourself, but then all of a sudden—"

Another man said, "I think he's out." He dived into the water, heading toward Cohn, whom the Papermans could see now, bobbing shoreward.

When Cohn reached shallow water the other swimmers helped him bring Klug to the beach. Klug's tank and mask were gone, his reddish hair hung over his face, and his head rolled.

"My God," Henny muttered. Hazel clutched Paperman's arm.

The men put Klug face down on the sand, his head turned to one side. The shaven-headed boy straddled him and began pressing rhythmically on his ribs. Klug's eyes were closed; a little water ran from his mouth.

Cohn panted to Hazel, "He unbuckled himself from the chief and wandered off."

The lieutenant and the other swimmers came out of the water. Without taking off his tank or fins, Woods knelt beside Klug, and pulled up his eyelid; nodded, and glanced up at the Papermans. "I'm sure he'll come out of it."

"He slipped away," the chief said. "I turned around and there was the empty cord."

"Where'd you find him?" said Woods.

"Hung up on the reef at sixty-five feet. I guess he caught an air tube on the coral. His mask was off."

The lieutenant said to Paperman, "When he comes to, we'll want to take him to the hospital. Just for a routine checkup. I can make better time in your Rover, if you don't mind coming back with the boys in the truck."

"Of course. Anything," Paperman said.

Cohn said, "His lids moved."

"Right. See if he'll breathe," said the lieutenant.

The man on Klug's back ceased pushing. After a moment Klug took a gasping noisy breath, and another. He moved his arms and legs, and opened his eyes. "What?" he murmured. "What did you say?"

"Get off him," said the lieutenant.

The swimmer obeyed. Klug stirred restlessly, rolled over, and sat up with two men holding his elbows.

"Easy," Woods said to him.

"I'm all right," Klug said, hoarsely and thickly. "Did I pass out? I'm okay. There was this big fish I was following and—" He looked around, comprehension brightening in his eyes. "Did they have to pull me out? What a nuisance."

One of the men was holding a small flask of brandy. "Here, sir. Just take a swallow."

Klug's recovery was surprisingly quick. He stood up almost at once, wavering only a little, and objected strongly when Woods told him he was going to the hospital.

"But I'm fine. Really I am—I want to finish that swim—honestly, this is completely unnecessary."

As he spoke, the men propelled him to the Rover, supporting him on either side. He climbed in still arguing. "Hazel, why don't you—" he said, poking his head through the window, and then the Rover shot away in a spray of sand and a grinding roar.

3

After driving the rest of the UDT men to the submarine base, Cohn took the Papermans back to the Gull Reef landing. Hazel wanted to get off at the hospital, but he wouldn't stop.

"You can't see him yet, Hazel, I'm sure. My C.O.'s still with him. He's going to have to file a report. I'll go and get the dope, and then I'll come straight back to the hotel, I promise. Your friend's all right, I know that. I'll bring the Rover, Norm."

"Will your commanding officer be in trouble?" Norman said.

"Nothing he can't handle."

"It wasn't his fault in the least," said Henny. "Sheldon did his best to knock himself off."

"Everything is always the commanding officer's fault," Cohn said. "I'll be right back."

By the time they changed their clothes and came down for lunch, Cohn was waiting for them on the dining terrace, dressed in his fatigue uniform. "They've got him in an oxygen tent, but that's routine. He's fine, the C.O. says. He could walk out now. In fact he's full of fight and hollering to get out of there. But it may take a little while. How about a drink all around to quiet our shattered nerves?"

"Why can't Sheldon get out if he's all right?" Hazel said.

"Well, you see, Hazel, there's always the remote possibility of brain damage in a water accident, when the man's been out cold. Your friend revived much too fast for that. But this hospital's very fussy, that's the problem. They let a tourist go last year after an incident like this, and then he sued them for neglect. Claimed he developed headaches and whatnot. The chief of the hospital says he's not discharging Klug until he's absolutely satisfied there's no brain damage."

"Holy smoke," said Norman, "the boy is in for life."

Henny said, "Goodness, yes. Any time he opens his mouth he'll get in deeper."

"Oh, stop, Mom," Hazel said.

"I mean it, dear. These people are bound to take his ordinary conversation for wild ravings. Why, I do myself."

"Really, Hazel," Norman said, "can you imagine when the doctor asks him what he's doing these days, and he says he's writing a book to prove that Balzac was a fairy? They'll put him in solitary."

Henny said, "And suppose he starts giving his views on the thanatos urge? Honestly, dear, your friend's going to get sent off this island in a bag."

"Old Sendings never die," Norman said, "they just get sent away."

Hazel said to Cohn, "I have the two most heartless parents alive."

Atlas's vague hoarse bellowing sounded in the lobby, and he came in sight leading Virgil and Millard, each carrying a large frosty cardboard package.

"Hey, Norm! Here's your meat, by Jesus, eight packages, ice cold and hard as rock. All right, boys, take those on back to the kitchen and bring over the rest."

He came charging to their table, clad in something known as a cabana set, shorts and a matching shirt, vertically striped pink and blue; sweaty, wrinkled, and indistinguishable from slept-in pajamas. He fell in a chair with a crash, and pulled out one of his torpedo cigars. "Yes, sir, Norm, the senior partner saved the situation this time, hey? Tell Henny. Did I or didn't I? Where would those steaks be now if not for me, hey? Stinking up the whole city of Caracas. Waitress! Double Old Granddad on ice."

Norman said, "I told Henny, Lester. We're both grateful to you."

Atlas chuckled. "Well, I only hope this little incident teaches you a lesson. You're a sweetheart, I know, and I'm a son of a bitch. In this world the sweethearts have the friends, Norman, and the sons of bitches give the orders. The thing is, you're giving orders now, mister. You're trying to run a hotel, and you've got to become a little bit of a son of a bitch. You'll never be a real one, that's a matter of talent, but you've got to work at it anyway."

"I resent all this," Henny said. "My husband is too a real son of a bitch."

"She knows," Norman said. "She's called me that any number of times."

"She was just building up your ego. Haw, haw! Henny, you know I'm telling the truth. He's a sweetheart. He's nice to people. He trusts them. He puts up with all kinds of horse manure. He probably wouldn't sleep at night if he fired somebody. This won't do Norm, I'm warning you. I've been checking around here this morning. How on earth could you tolerate for even one *day* that barefoot slob with the big straw hat on? The one with the machete? That's not the kind of personnel for a hotel, Norm. You've got to start thinking of your image. I fired the bastard. I mean, pleasant appearance is absolutely the first thing you have to—what's the matter? Bone in your throat? Want me to slap your back? Catch me eating those goddamn trout, they're a menace—"

Norman stopped gasping and choking long enough to articulate, "You did *what?* You FIRED Hippolyte? What do you mean? How could you do that?"

"How? I told him to get his ass off the grounds. I didn't intend to do that at first. I just told him to put on his shoes, take off his hat, and put away that machete if he wanted to keep his job. But he gave me some kind of dirty sass in a foreign language, and do you know, he made a sort of pass at me with the chopper? I don't think he meant it, he was trying to scare me. Heh! Norman, I was taking knives away from guineas on Longfellow Avenue before that character was born. I wasn't scared, but I was annoyed. I told him to get the hell off the island and stay off before I threw him off. He gave me some more sass, but then he went. You've seen the last of him, and good riddance. What did he do here, anyway? He looked pretty useless, just mooching around the lobby."

Norman slowly got to his feet, drawing a deep breath to ease the terrible tightness in his chest. He started talking in a tone of exaggerated soft calm. "Now listen, Lester, maybe we should get one thing straight. You don't own the Gull Reef Club. You know? *I own it.* You're not a senior partner. You're not a junior partner. You don't have a dollar in this hotel. You have no right to do anything here but ENJOY YOURSELF. You're a *guest*. Is that clear? Maybe I'll die here trying to make this hotel work, but for God's sake, I'm going to do it *my way!*" Norman was now pounding the table and shouting.

Lester said not unkindly, "Norm, you own the place because I put my name on a piece of bank paper. I'm only trying to be helpful. Maybe I had no right to rescue those steaks for you either, but I just did it. I'm that kind of guy."

"Go ahead and finish your lunch, everybody," Norman said. "I've got things to do in a hell of a hurry. That man was my best employee, and I've got to get him back, if it means crawling on my hands and knees."

"Well, go ahead, go ahead, but you'll regret it. Nobody loves a truth teller, Henny," Atlas said plaintively. "And that's all I am, an old truth teller, and that's all I've done here, and Norman doesn't like it. Okay, Norm, I wash my hands of this hotel. If you drop dead, I'm out twenty thousand dollars. It's perfectly okay. Do things your way from now on."

Atlas's maundering self-pity made Norman feel better, it was so laughable. "We all love you just as you are, Lester," he said. "Don't ever change."

Millard and Virgil, each with a package of frozen steaks on his head, stood in the doorway of the kitchen. Sheila was showering them with abuse. When she saw Paperman she came plunging out at him, and he was hard put to it to stand his ground.

"Mistuh Pape'mon! Tell me one ting. *Who de fot porson?* He make so much confusion ron' hyah, we ain' goin' be able do nuttin'. De fot porson he hoross Hippolyte. Hippolyte say he goin' away, he don' want to kill de fot porson. You know dat?"

Paperman assured her in the strongest terms that the fat person would not bother anybody, ever again. She began to calm down. But when he asked her where he could find Hippolyte, she exploded.

"NO SUH, Mistuh Pape'mon. You wants Hippolyte, you does have to send away de fot porson. We goin' have a wery bad accident in de hotel if Hippolyte come back now. Hippolyte he come talk to me before he go, and he talk plenty fonny." She turned on Millard and Virgil, standing dumbly and dropping sweat, and she shouted, "You crazy, mon? I *tole* you take de meat by de freezer dung tung. What for you stand dere like jumbies?"

Virgil smiled in a pitiable effort to please. "De fot porfon, he fay bring de meat heah."

"Dis my kitchen, an' de fot porson he ain' nobody! You heard de boss!"

"Do as Sheila says," Paperman told the men. "Never mind the fat person. Never mind anything he says after this."

They trudged away with relief.

Norman begged Sheila to rush to Hippolyte with his apologies, and an urgent request to return, and a promise that Atlas would never interfere with him again. The cook would not go. Nor would she even tell him where Hippolyte could be found. "Mistuh Papuh, you gone be wery sorry if he come back before de fot porson go. You best hope he don' come back *widout* you ask him. Hippolyte plenty mad."

"Sheila, Mr. Atlas will be here for at least two weeks."

"Dey ain' nuttin' to fix now. De confusion all fix, we got 'lectric, we got water. I tell you someting, suh. Leave Hippolyte be."

4

Miraculously—as it seemed to Norman—the Gull Reef Club did survive the departure of Hippolyte, day after day. It was true, as Sheila had said, that all the serious troubles were over, and for the moment no fresh ones were cropping up. Hippolyte's queer mute crew stayed on the job and finished the new rooms, glumly accepting Henny's supervision of the last touches. The work seemed good. The toilets flushed; taps flowed; lights burned; doors opened and shut; the green-and-gold Japanese wallpaper stayed on the walls. Henny furnished the rooms out of Hassim's shop with stuff from Hong Kong and India—wicker chairs, brass or porcelain lamps, Chinese scrolls and water colors—none of it very costly and all blending in exotic charm. Smaller than the old rooms, these were nevertheless the best accommodations the hotel now offered. Dan Freed and his party grabbed them when they came. Lionel, who arrived greener than ever in the face, but happy as a boy, announced that he was going to hire Henny to redecorate all of Hogan's Fancy in exactly this style.

Freed's Broadway entourage, a laughing fast-talking group of eleven that included two well-known actresses, filled the Club with chic clothes and New York chatter. The other guests were thrilled and awed. Islanders crowded the bar day and night to stare at the celebrated performers and the pasty little producer of four current Broadway successes. The delight of the New Yorkers with Kinja and with Paperman's hotel was complete. They swam, they sailed, they danced, they drank, they roared around the island in rented jeeps, they made friends with Kinjan field workers, bartenders, and policemen; and they all said they had never had such fun in their lives. Norman became tired of being told how brilliant his idea had been, and how lucky he was. The main thing was that, with these finicky people, the Club had scored a success. There was little doubt that next year it would have a Broadway vogue.

And as it was, the Club glittered with sudden prosperity. The Christmas jam was on. Norman turned away dozens of people begging for any kind of place to sleep, even a cot in the lobby. The reservation list for lunch and dinner was closed each day by ten in the morning. Two extra bartenders were assisting Church, who was now spending most of his time ringing up money and keeping records. The accountant, checking the books three times a week, reported that Church was accurate and honest, and that earnings were sharply up. Altas, scrutinizing the books every day despite his pledge not to interfere, told Norman that he was over the hump at this point, and set for life, if he actually wanted to stay in the Caribbean. The extra rooms had been his salvation, Atlas said; the hotel would smoothly pay off its purchase price now, while giving him a living of ten thousand a year or so; and once the debts were cleared, Norman would be swimming in profits.

None of this reassured Norman much. He knew all too well how quickly a calm situation in Kinja could explode into chaos. Each day the absence of a mechanical breakdown seemed to him almost too good to be true. His hope was that the rickety structure would stand until Atlas left, when he could get Hippolyte back; and his prayer was that a collapse, if it did come, would at least occur after the Tilson dinner party on December 27th. Norman now had nearly three thousand dollars sunk in that venture alone. For all his temporary prosperity, he was working with a chokingly narrow margin of cash. If the Tilson affair failed to come off, or ended in disaster, he would not only be in permanent bad odor on the island, he would collapse under his debts. He pointed out these hazards to Atlas, who merely laughed. Norman was like a child afraid of the dark, he said; what could go wrong with a dinner party? The old truth teller's optimism about the hotel was now boundless.

When Norman told him about Mrs. Ball's offer to settle her promissory notes for cash, Atlas became almost as excited as he usually did at seeing a bikini girl. He wanted to find Mrs. Ball and wind up the matter at once. "She'll take five thousand, don't give her another nickel," he exulted. "She's got herself a new stud already, that's what. She wants to buy him diamond cuff links and such garbage. Five grand instead of thirty-five! Norm, that's fourteen cents on the dollar! Jesus, you should have made the deal right there."

Norman mildly pointed out that he hadn't had five thousand at the time, and still didn't. Atlas told him to find Mrs. Ball; he would arrange for Norman to get the money. But she was off the island that day, and with all he had on his mind, Norman didn't immediately follow it up.

For one thing, Iris was a continuing worry. She remained immured in her cottage. Once Norman glimpsed her swimming near her beach; she answered his wave with a wrist flick, and turned her back on him. Esmé reported that she never answered the telephone, and that the governor was calling often. Sheila told him Iris was not allowing the chambermaids into the cottage, and that no food was going down there from the kitchen, not even for the dog. Walking by the cottage, Norman could hear the phonograph and the barking dog, and he could sometimes see Iris shadowily moving inside. On the fifth day of this siege, Iris did admit the cleaning girls. When they left, she asked them to bring table scraps for Meadows. The girls carried back to Norman such an ill report of Iris's looks that he nerved himself to telephone the governor. It was a miserably awkward little conversation.

"Governor, I'd like to talk to you—in private—about Iris, about Mrs. Tramm. She's not quite well."

"I see." The brisk voice became guarded. "Here, or at your hotel?"

"There, I think."

"Come on over."

Sanders was at his desk in his shirt sleeves when Norman arrived. He shut off his telephone and intercom, locked the door, and sat in his chair with arms folded, smoking, while Norman told him about Iris's collapse. Norman talked as though she were the governor's sister or ex-wife, about whom no preliminaries were necessary. Sanders accepted the tone. The governor's face showed no emotion as Norman spoke. His fingers, when they weren't drumming softly on the desk, strayed to his thin mustache or his kinky grizzled hair.

"Do you think she should be hospitalized?" he said when Norman paused.

"She should be brought out of there somehow, Governor. I've tried and failed."

"I can see that it's awkward for you. After all, there she is, and you have a hotel to run."

"That's not the idea. She's been kind and helpful to me. She's not creating trouble, but I think that at this rate she's going to become dangerously sick. If you could persuade her to go back to her parents in San Diego—" The governor winced and grimaced. "Governor Sanders, I'm well aware that this is not my business, but—"

"Perfectly all right. However, telling Iris to go back to San Diego, I assure you, isn't the best idea you ever had." Sanders left his desk and paced the room, swirling the layers of smoke. The air-conditioner rattled away; it was the noisiest one on the island, Paperman thought. Sanders half-sat on the edge of his desk, very close to Paperman, and said with a bitter little smile, "She's talked to you about us?"

"Only a very little."

"Well, I guess there's no point in presenting my side. Possibly I have no side, but since you seem to be saddled with the problem—the long and the short of it, Mr. Paperman, is that I was given this post instead of something in a big city, or even in the Virgin Islands. Iris wanted to come anyway. I couldn't resist letting her come because I'm in love with her, Mr. Paperman, but in this tiny place she's been living in a glass bowl. It's no good. That's why after a while I, too, suggested San Diego, just until I could get another appointment. It caused an explosion such as I hope you'll be spared, and she went into a spin like this one. Things have been bad since." Sanders lit a cigarette and paced; and as he talked, a Negro quality, more attractive than his studied speech-class diction, came into his voice. "You see, Mr. Paperman, here's how it is. If I were a night-club entertainer, I could marry a white lady and go right on performing—even an unusual white lady like Mrs. Tramm—but unfortunately I'm not a very amusing fellow. I'm strictly government. If we got married I'm afraid she'd find herself with an inexperienced porter or bellhop fifty years old on her hands. Do you follow me? I have no answer to that, and if you could think of one I'd be truly obliged."

The two men looked at each other. Norman spread his hands, and stood. "I thought I had to tell you."

"Thank you. Iris is an unbelievably strong woman, I can assure you. She's probably healthier right now than you or me. The psychoanalysts have called her a self-destroyer, yet the fact is she has one hell of a will to live. She pulls out of these things. I've been through this. The less you interfere, usually, the better. If you keep an eye on her and inform me of anything real bad I'll appreciate that, but I think it's going to be all right. As all right as it can be. —Well! And so your Mr. Atlas is here again," he said, turning on his speech-class voice. "And he is bidding on Crab Cove. And at the Reef, I hear, everything's going as merrily as a marriage bell." He held out his slender cool hand, yellow on the back and white-palmed. "Thank you for coming."

5

Hazel had been visiting the Sending daily in the hospital, sometimes twice a day, and had found him most unreasonably peevish; so she told her parents. His bitterest complaint was about an intelligence test the hospital had given him. It had been so insultingly elementary, and he had been so irritated and bored, that he had filled it up with the most comically wrong answers he could think of, depicting himself as an illiterate with an IQ of perhaps thirty or forty. Unfortunately the hospital had taken the results quite seriously; it closely agreed with the kind of scores they often got in their large ward of mentally disturbed Kinjans. His frantic efforts to convince the staff psychiatrist that it had all been a hoax, and to let him take the exam again, had been to no avail. The chief of the hospital, Dr. Tracy Pullman, had ruled that this would be cheating.

It had, therefore, really begun to seem that Klug was in for a long confinement in the Amerigo Hospital, as a brain-damage case, capable of lapsing now and then into a human vegetable. He was in a foaming rage about this, and claimed to have already written to the Ford

Foundation for a grant on which to live while composing a scathing play about the low state of Caribbean medical science. But an unexpected turn set Sheldon free before the week was out.

From the first day he had maintained that he must have wrenched an arm and a shoulder in his underwater struggles, because he had pains in the right shoulder, elbow, and wrist, and in the right knee joint too. A doctor from a visiting submarine, brought to the hospital by Lieutenant Woods to check on these pains, announced after thoroughly examining Klug that he actually had a mild case of the bends. Nitrogen bubbles had settled in his joints, when he had ascended too fast from a hundred and ten feet to the point where he had hung up on the coral. The bubbles were still there. He would continue to be in pain until he was decompressed; moreover, if he weren't decompressed soon, he might become a chronically gouty sort for life. The nearest decompression chamber was at the navy base in San Juan. The Sending, beside himself with frustration and ill-humor, elected to fly back to New York instead, to get himself decompressed at the Brooklyn Navy Yard. On this basis the hospital released him.

Norman, busy as he was, insisted on driving Klug to the airport himself. Hazel came along, of course, as sweet and gay as the Sending was acid and morose. Her display of affection at the plane gate was touching. She kissed him several times, and clung to him, and put a handkerchief repeatedly to her eyes. "I wish you'd change your mind," she said as the loudspeaker announced the plane's departure. "Please, Sheldon. Promise me you'll come back after you've been decompressed."

"I don't think I can afford it. A round trip down here costs a fortune, Hazel, and to tell the truth I'm just sour on the West Indies." He put an arm around her and groaned. "God, this elbow. It feels like it's full of broken glass. Goodbye, darling. See you in New York."

And so the Sending departed. It was the day after Christmas. Norman watched the plane snarl off the runway, and sighed and smiled. "Nobody will ever convince me after this," he said, "that there isn't a Santa Claus. The thing is, Santa moves in a mysterious way. But he grinds exceeding small."

"I never heard such nonsense. I hate you," Hazel said, putting away her handkerchief. "My vacation is ruined, and I'm heartbroken."

"Where did you say you're meeting Bob? The sub base?"

"No, he said he'd have the boat at the Old Mill landing. It's closer." Hazel glanced at her watch. "My gosh, we're late, let's step on it."

Norman turned Hazel over to Cohn and four other brown swimmers in a navy boat tied up near the airport, and returned to town. He was driving along Prince of Wales Street in an unusually happy mood, when a few feet ahead of him on the crowded narrow thoroughfare, a taxi abruptly stopped; and the driver poked out his head to discuss life with a passing girl. It was second nature to Paperman by now to watch for this general Kinjan custom; he jammed on his brakes in good time, and silently waited. Blowing the horn in such circumstances was considered rude.

"Mis-ter Paper-mon. Well, this is luck-ee." The banker Llewellyn halted on the sidewalk, putting his hand on the window of the Rover. "Here you are, and I've been trying for an hour to call you and Mr. Ot-loss at the Club."

"Why, Lester is there."

"So they told me, but he was on the long dis-tance phone for ever so long, and then I couldn't reach him. I want to congratulate both of you. You are the proud owners of Crab Cove."

"We are?" Norman was nonplussed by this news, Crab Cove being the furthest thing from his mind.

"The bids were opened this morning. Mr. Ot-loss is a clever man. He bid three hundred and sixty-five thousand. The closest bid was only twenty-five hundred less. I was sure he would bid at least four hundred thousand. The property is worth far more than that. Very shrewd, very able."

Cars were lining up behind Norman. Ahead of the cab, the traffic lane was empty all the way to the waterfront, but the driver's chat with the giggling girl seemed to be just getting started. Norman ventured a honk, and was rewarded by two glares. However, the driver shifted gears, and talked a little faster and louder.

"I'll tell Lester, of course," he said to the banker. "He'll be pleased."

"You might tell him that it would be extremely practical to come in tomorrow to execute the papers. It is Thursday, so we'll only be open till noon."

"How about today? There's still time."

"Ah, but today is Boxing Day. Friday is Carnival Parade, Monday and Tuesday are New Year, Wednesday is Columbus Day, and it'll be a whole week to wait if he doesn't come in tomorrow morning."

"Columbus Day? Right after New Year? It's in October," Norman protested.

"We have an old Kinjan tradition," said the banker, "that Columbus stopped here for fresh water on the second of January."

Norman could still hear the banker's jolly laugh as he drove off, leading a long procession of cars.

It was lunch time when he got back to the Club. Atlas wasn't in sight on the dining terrace. He didn't answer a room call. Norman went to the bar and there Lester was slumped on a stool with his head on his arms, naked except for flowered swimming trunks.

"What's this?" Norman said in a low voice to Church.

The bartender scratched his beard. "I guess he's asleep, sir. Or—or passed out, you might say. He's just had four double bourbons in a row. He drank them sort of fast."

Norman put a hand on his shoulder. Atlas smelled rankly of whiskey, cigars, and locker room. "Lester? How about having some lunch with me? There's good news, and we ought to celebrate. Maybe open a bottle of champagne?"

Lester raised his head and looked at Paperman, his bloodshot eyes half closed, his jaw hanging, his lower lip pulled in, all the heavy lines on his gray face creased and sagging. "Good news? There's no good news. What good news?"

"You bid in Crab Cove."

Atlas stared, then an understanding light flickered dully in his eyes. "We did?" His voice was hardly more than a croak. "What was the next lower bid? Do you know?"

"It was twenty-five hundred dollars under yours."

"Son of a bitch." The old truth teller haggardly smiled. "Really? And I was *this* close to bidding four hundred thousand." He pulled himself erect. "I *knew* there was nobody with enough brains around here to make a sensible bid, Norm. It's a steal. I took a chance and saved us thirty-five thousand dollars. And you'll get your finder's fee and you can buy off old Amy Ball with it. You're right. It's good news." He nodded his head heavily, and his melancholy smile faded. "Good news.

Real good news. Let's have a drink. —Boy! Bring us a couple of drinks over there." He seized Norman's arm and stumbled with him to a corner table. He fell in a chair, lit a cigar with wandering gestures, then put his head on his arm on the table again.

Paperman had never seen Atlas in this state; and he had more than once seen him drink a whole bottle of bourbon in an evening. When the drinks came Lester sat up, took a small sip, and sighed piteously. "I'm getting old, Norm. I don't know. I guessed right on Crab Cove. But I sure guessed wrong on that Montana situation. Norm"—Atlas leaned forward, putting his arm around Paperman's shoulder in a feeble parody of his usual charm routine—"I told you about Montana, didn't I? How I was buying stock, competing against another outfit for control, Norm, and the price was going up and up?"

"Sure, but you said you had no problem because you were stronger than your competitors."

"That's what I *said,* and that's what I *thought,* and Norm, let this be a lesson to you, Norm. Those Montana bankers and politicians were either awfully good at playing dumb, or awfully dumb, or the biggest liars in the world, or all three. Norm, do you know who I was fighting against for control of that company?"

"No, I don't."

"Norm, I was fighting the Anaconda Copper Corporation." He gave Paperman a clumsy hug and released him. Atlas was smiling like a dazed boxer on the floor. "Ever hear of them? The snotnose from Long-fellow Avenue was taking on Anaconda Copper. That's what I just found out from St. Louis. I've been had, Norm."

"How bad is it, Lester? You're not in trouble?"

Atlas laughed harshly. "Me? Listen, mister, if my whole structure collapses, if everything goes sour, every single thing I've got a hand in, I dust myself off and walk away. I've got a company in North Carolina that makes kids' clothes, and an electronics outfit in Oregon, small corporations you never heard of—these I never touch, and on these I live and can go right on living. No, Norm, I'm kind of clean right this minute. But if I die tomorrow, what does it amount to? Three or four million less to leave to a couple of daughters who are set for life anyway, and who can't stand me. So what? I haven't been hurt. I've been had."

"Will you go ahead with Crab Cove?"

"Hell, YES." Atlas brought his big fist down on the table, and the glasses jumped. "I took a licking like this in 'fifty-two and I came back. One of the ways I'm coming back is with Caribbean real estate, and by God, we're going to be a winning team, Norm. We're starting out lucky with Crab Cove. That's the sign. This Caribbean's one big uranium lode and we're still in ahead of the mob. —Boy! Double Old Granddad."

chapter fifteen

The Tilson Party

I

Paperman opened his eyes on the morning of Thursday, December 27th, excited and anxious, without knowing why; as a man will wake on his wedding day in a boil of emotions, before the reason for his turmoil dawns on him. This was the day of the Tilson party. It was eight in the morning. Henny lay beside him in blue, lacy baby-doll pajamas, sound asleep. Even in repose her face had the humorous, satirical, slightly bitter cast that had captivated him two decades ago. He considered romantic overtures, here and now. Henny often voiced sleepy objections in the morning, but could be persuaded to forget them. Norman didn't want to go downstairs and face the oncoming Tilson party. He had double-checked all arrangements the night before. So far as he knew, everything was in order. Supplies and personnel were converging on the hotel by now—chairs from the undertaker, tables from the Eagle Republican Club, steaks and other fragile New York delicacies from the freezer plant, extra kitchen maids, waiters, and waitresses from all over Amerigo—an operation like the invasion of Normandy, already in motion beyond recall. It was a tempting notion to blot out an hour or so of this portentous day with a little love-making. But Norman got himself out of bed, and shaved and dressed, leaving Henny in peace. Sheila might need him for some small thing. Downstairs he went.

He had only to step into the lobby to see that this was no ordinary day at the Gull Reef Club. The red-and-gilt chairs from the undertaker, two hundred of them, towered in stacks along one wall. Negroes with unfamiliar faces paraded through the lobby toward the kitchen, shouldering cases of beer and champagne, or boxes of rattling soda bottles, or smoking freezer cartons, or baskets of fresh vegetables; coming back, they chattered, laughed, and wiped their perspiring faces. On the wide center wall, a poster blared in Church's flamboyant style, red script letters on gold:

Now Hear This!
COOKOUT AND DANCE ON LOVERS' BEACH!!
(Northeast Side, Gull Reef Club)
Exclusive for Club Guests Only Tonight
From 5:30 P.M. until ——?
Steel Band, Drinks, Charcoal-Broiled Chickens
and Steaks with All Fixings
Everything on the House!
Dress: No Shoes, No Ties, No Shirts, No Nothing
(Well, maybe trunks or bikinis. Police, you know.)
EXTRA ADDED ATTRACTION!!
Death-Defying Leap of Six Intrepid Navy
Parachutists!! From an Airplane at 10,000 Feet,
Directly into the Waters off Lovers' Beach!
Promptly at 6:30! Be There!

> *Talk to the Daredevils afterward. Get their*
> *autographs! They're the Honored Guests of the*
> *Gull Reef Cookout!*
>
> > Your host,
> > Norman Paperman

Below all this, in very small black print, were these words:

> *(Regular bar and dining terrace reserved tonight for private party. Hotel service at cookout only.)*

Tom Tilson sat in an armchair, stooped and red-faced, reading the placard.

"Hello there!" he shouted, waving his stick at Norman and then at the poster. "Paperman, I used to have my doubts about you, but so help me I'm beginning to think you've got a flair for running a hotel. This is inspired."

"We had to do something," Paperman said.

"It's great! How in the devil did you get the UDT to put on an air show for you?"

"Well, my daughter—she hangs around with them—told me these fellows were planning a water jump this week. I called the commanding officer and said if they'd jump at Lovers' Beach tonight, I'd give the team drinks and a steak dinner. They're delighted and it sort of saved us. The main problem of your party was getting the hotel crowd out from under foot."

"Of course. And they'll be out there to the last man. Damn keen thinking! I've been talking to Sheila, and I must say I've never seen a better-organized affair. You've thought of everything, Paperman. This is going to be the best damned party anyone ever had on this miserable island. I'm thoroughly pleased."

"Well, thank you," Paperman said. "We haven't had the party yet."

Tilson wrinkled his face at him. "By the bye, who's 'the fot porson'?"

"Eh? What? Who talked to you about him?" One of Norman's worries about tonight was that Lester Atlas might erupt into the Tilson party and scatter it like a crazed elephant. Lester had been drinking without cease since the Anaconda Copper disclosure, and there was no telling what state he was in by now.

"Why, Sheila just told me that a 'fot porson' threw Hippolyte off the place. I've been hearing rumors from the Montmartre bar, too. My gardener does his boozing there. He says Hippolyte's been drinking himself blind night after night, and telling everybody he's getting ready to kill 'the fot porson' at the Gull Reef Club."

"He's Lester Atlas," Norman said, trying to put a calm face on his alarm. "You remember, the fellow I came down with originally. He's here for Christmas."

"Oh, that one. The big tycoon. The fellow they wrote up in *Time*. I sure do remember him." Tilson pushed himself out of his chair with a grunt, leaning both hands on his stick. "Ha! Quite an encounter. Diamond cut diamond. I'd like to see it, but not tonight, please. The ladies won't appreciate it."

"Has Hippolyte talked of coming here *tonight?*"

"Well, I didn't hear that he specified a time."

"Maybe I'd better ask for police protection," Norman said.

"From Hippolyte?" Tilson laughed. "A Kinja cop? He'd simply warm up by whacking off the cop's head, then he'd look for your friend. Just make damn sure your people have orders not to let Hippolyte across in the gondola, if he shows. The other idea might be to put Atlas over on the shore, and let Hippolyte chase him around Amerigo all night. That would keep Hippolyte out of our hair. Give it some thought. Hee hee!"

Tilson stumped off, uttering senile chuckles. Norman, not at all amused, went to the kitchen, where Sheila stood amid scampering scullery maids and new-hired male helpers, issuing orders right and left. She was strangely calm and cheery amid the chaos flooding the kitchen and spilling out into the hallway: bottles, bloody meats, cases, cartons, tumbled fruits and vegetables, giant gleaming new pots, all piled along temporary tables set up on sawhorses. A lunch with a savory Italian smell was already steaming in the old saucepans and cauldrons.

"It look like one big confusion, don't it, Mistuh Papermon?" she said, laughing. "It all gon' come out not bad. We just layin' everyting out. We start de canapés when de girls clear off de lunch, and den—"

"Did the grill come for Lovers' Beach?"

"Yassuh, de Francis Drake cook, she did send it over first ting. We gettin' a Carnival boot', too, for de drinks at de cookout. Everyting okay, only I don't know where is Church. Church say he come six o'clock dis morning. He ain' come yet. Church he suppose start fixin' de bar down to de beach. I got him tree helpers, dey just waitin'."

"I'll hunt him up."

Church was nowhere in the hotel. Esmé hadn't heard from him, she said, but the hospital had telephoned three times this morning. Dr. Tracy Pullman urgently wanted to talk to Mr. Paperman. "He say someting about a bartender, I tink. I din' understand good," said Esmé, fluttering her eyes away and down. The subject of Church somewhat embarrassed her.

"Call him back. I'll talk to him in the office." It occurred to Norman that the Nevis girl now looked very, very pregnant. Without fail he would send her home tomorrow. Once past the Tilson party, he could clean up all these matters.

"Yes? Dr. Tracy Pullman speaking."

"Hello, this is Norman Paperman at the Gull Reef Club."

"Ah yes. Mr. Paperman, I've been trying to reach you." Dr. Pullman had a powerful baritone voice, and sounded much like his brother, the absent senator. "Tell me, did you have in your employ a young fellow named Church Wagner? Good-looking white boy, with a beard?"

"Did I? I still do. Has something happened to him? He's missing this morning."

"He is, eh? Ah—Mr. Paperman, are there any ladies present there with you?"

"Ladies? I'm alone in my office."

"Good. Now you know about this little group of girls, seven of them, from our finest families, who are home for the holidays—the Sand Witches, I understand they call themselves?"

"Yes."

"You do? Ah. Well! Not to put too fine a point on it, Mr. Paperman, the plain fact is, that Church Wagner has given six of the seven Sand Witches the clap."

Paperman groaned as though he had been stabbed. "The clap? The *clap?*"

"The accurate term is gonorrhea, Mr. Paperman, but that's how the young people refer to it. We are still testing the seventh girl. She is being very frivolous and uncooperative, I must say. Now we're most anxious to get hold of this Wagner fellow. First of all he needs treatment, and then the police may want to have a chat with him for his own protection. The fathers are all angry, understandably. I think the Health Department inspectors will be talking to you, too."

"I didn't know about this, Doctor!"

"He's your employee. In any case, if the young man appears at the hotel, you'd better bring him right down here."

"All right," Norman said. The old heartsickness of his first weeks in the Gull Reef Club was coming upon him again, and his nasal passages were tickling and swelling.

"Now of course," the doctor said, "you'll keep this in strict confidence. For the sake of the families."

"Sure. Naturally." Norman sneezed violently.

Dr. Pullman sighed, "God bless you. I'm afraid the worst trouble will be with the girls. They don't mind talking about it at all. They giggle, and make jokes, and say it's no worse than having a cold. I'm afraid the morals of our island young people are becoming very deca-dent. The finest families! Goodbye."

Norman hung up, stunned and shaken. Church Wagner was no great loss. Since Henny's arrival, they had been talking of rearranging things so that the bartender would merely mix drinks, while they took over the handling of the money. Such bartenders were plentiful; Norman had hired three just for the Tilson party.

What hit Paperman so hard was the dark reminder, on this tense morning, that life in Kinja teetered always between the dreadful and the ridiculous. This episode, far from being curious, was an abrupt return to normality. It struck Paperman as a harbinger of evil things. He had never forgotten—though he had tried to bury out of mind—Tom Tilson's warning that sooner or later the island was going to throw a catastrophic surprise at him. This haunting fear for weeks had been that this fatal surprise was going to erupt out of the dinner party. Church Wagner's defection, coming just at this moment, seemed an ominous, absurd, utterly Kinjan prelude.

Norman began to sneeze. He sneezed until his eyes streamed, his nose swelled up aching and red, and his breath came in rough wheezy gasps.

The old dusty clock read quarter to nine. It was starting out to be a long day.

2

Lovers' Beach, little used because it was far from the main house and hemmed in by thorny brush, was almost as pretty as the main beach, and not much smaller; but its view was only the open sea, and so the first builder of the Club had wisely placed the hotel on the town side. Virgil and Millard had hacked broad paths through the brush, and a charming party site was springing up on the beach during the day. Strung Japanese lanterns, a grill, a bar, chaises of aluminum and red plastic, and gaily painted tables and chairs enlivened the newly-swept white sand. The weather continued excellent. One of Norman's many worries was that rain would drive the wet and sandy hotel guests stampeding in their bathing suits back into the hotel, at the height of the formal Tilson party. But at six o'clock in the evening, when the airplane was scheduled to begin its climb with the parachutists, there wasn't a cloud in the sky, and guests were already lining up for free drinks, full of eager chatter about the parachute jump. The cookout struck the guests as a great treat, and nobody showed the least resentment at being herded away from the hotel for the evening.

At the Club, a platoon of handsome Kinjan boys in satin-striped black trousers, white mess jackets, and white gloves waited to go to work. The bar, the dance terrace, the dining terrace were festooned with flowers; and so was the enormous hors d'oeuvre table that stretched the length of the dance floor, covered with platters of cold meats and canapés, great odorous cheeses, jars of Russian caviar, and mounds of fresh fruit. The fried shrimps and the cocktail frankfurters, hundreds of them, were on trays in the kitchen, hot and ready. Tubs full of ice and champagne bottles lined the hallway. An improvised bar stood in the lobby, another on the dance terrace, and these and the regular bar were stacked with myriads of glasses. The new young bartenders in red jackets manned the three posts, cheerfully jittery as horses before a race. Sheila had caused an immense charcoal pit to be dug in the main beach and covered with iron grills, offering space to cook dozens of large steaks at once. Sheila herself, lording it over the kitchen in a new white smock and chef's cap, was less excited than Norman had ever seen her, despite all the newcomers taking her orders, and the amazing pile-up of food in every corner of the kitchen, overflowing into the hall. "Everything does look not too bad, Mistuh Pape'mon," she said, after patiently answering a few of his nervous questions. "Dey ain' nuttin' to worry about, it be a wery good party."

"Achoo! Achoo! Thank you, Sheila. You're a godsend." Norman blew his nose, and hurried back to Lovers' Beach for the parachute jump, more than half-convinced, in his nervous state, that his disaster was at hand in the death or maiming of a parachutist.

Hotel guests crowded the strand, holding drinks and craning their necks up at the sky, amid a bedlam of laughs, shouts, jokes, snatches of song. Splendid pink sunset clouds billowed across the light blue sky. Lieutenant Woods, wearing brief khaki trunks and a T-shirt, watched the sky, calm and smiling, but his flippers lay on the sand beside him, and the tenseness of his folded arms showed he was ready to plunge in. Some of his men were circling offshore in a gray navy boat.

"Hi, there's the plane," Woods said, pointing almost overhead. "I think they've reached their altitude. This may be the run-in for the drop."

Paperman saw the tiny aircraft, a black cross against a pink cloud. It disappeared, came in sight, and disappeared again, moving through cloud streamers. "Ye gods, that's high."

Hazel and Henny emerged from the crowd. Henny said, "I've never been so scared in my life. Jumping from way up there! Imagine!"

Woods said, "They've done it often, ma'am."

"THERE HE GOES!" It was a general shout.

High, high up a red streak was sliding downward across the pink-and-blue sky, like a mark made by a giant, slow-moving crayon. "TWO!" everyone on the beach yelled. "THREE! FOUR!"

And in a moment six streaks were lengthening down the sky; thick, puffy, parallel scarlet lines.

"They free-fall with flares," Woods said, his eyes intent on the streaks.

Soon a brilliant orange-and-white parachute blossomed at the base of one red streak, about halfway to earth. Another appeared; a third, a fourth, a fifth. The last red streak kept sliding downward, far below the irregular line of five parachutes drifting in the sunset. It fell and fell.

"Who's that last one?" Henny said shrilly.

"Don't know," Woods said, with a slight note of anger, and as he uttered the words the parachute opened. A relieved cheer rose along the shore. The jumpers floated down. The one who had free-fallen so low struck the water long before the others, about fifty yards out from the beach. "Cohn," Woods said, though Norman could only see a brown, nearly naked body in the parachute harness. "Wouldn't you know." The men in the boat, speeding to the jumper, recovered the parachute as it crumpled. He swam ashore and made his way through the applauding crowd to his commanding officer. "Sorry," he said.

"What the hell?" said Woods. "I said no hairy falls."

"You won't believe this," Cohn said, dripping, and panting a little. "I got interested in the scenery, believe it or not. It's pretty, with the town lights coming on and all. I was only a couple of seconds late."

"You came near boring a hole in the ocean," Woods said.

A second and a third parachutist settled in the water. Hazel said furiously to Cohn, "They shouldn't let you do that. You're too old, and anyway, you're plain crazy."

"See? I told you I'm too old, sir," Cohn said to Woods. "I want out of this outfit."

"You damn near made it," Woods said, watching the boat speed from one parachutist to another. All were down, all bobbing and waving.

In a little while, excited guests were bunching around the UDT men at the bar, making jokes and asking questions. The eyes of the women shone as though these brown, shy, almost naked young men were film stars. Satisfied that the Lovers' Beach cookout was well launched, Norman left with Henny to dress for the Tilson party. Hazel was staying at the beach, of course, in her new role of queen bee to the swimmers, which she much relished. She paid no extra attention to Cohn, at least not when Norman and Henny were around. She made big eyes at all the frogmen in turn, and they appeared devoted to her, to a man.

"It's going to be hard to interest that girl in a nice substantial doctor or lawyer after this," Henny said as they crossed the lawn. "Or a businessman."

"Or an English professor," Norman said.

His wife laughed. "Well, that's the good part, but they're not all like the Sending. A college professor would be fine with me. Sheldon was just a sickening fraud. But I'm not too happy about this frogman business, you know. I mean, the action thing is glamorous, and I could eat those boys up myself, old bag that I am. But it's strictly a lousy living. People think you're nuts, and what's more, you can get hurt."

"What do you propose?"

"I'm not proposing anything. What good would it do me? I'm making anxious mother noises."

As they entered the lobby a bellicose shout echoed out of the bar, "Listen, mister, I *own* this place and you're telling *me* I can't have a drink? Now, get your black ass moving, and—"

Norman bolted to the bar, which was empty except for the new bartender, Atlas, and the two bikini girls—schoolteachers from Maine whom he had adopted. Atlas wore a white yachting cap, a red-and-white striped T-shirt such as Church had affected, and new vast blue jeans rolled up to the knees. The girls were in their bikinis. All three were horribly sunburned. Atlas's fat face looked swelled and boiled, and he had large white rings around his eyes in the shape of Polaroid glasses.

"Lester, take it easy. The boy is just obeying orders," Norman exclaimed. The new bartender was glaring at Atlas, his lips sucked into a scowling line. "This place is set up for the Tilson party tonight. I *told* you about that. You can get all the drinks you want over at Lovers' Beach."

"Who the hell wants to go way down there? We're just off a sailboat. The goddamn captain ran out of beer, he ran out of booze, he damn near cooked us in the sun. Poor Hatsy and Patsy are ready to pass out. We want three planter's punches, and goddamn it, we want them now and here!"

"Give them three planter's punches," Norman said to the bartender.

"Oh, thank you," said one girl faintly.

The bartender sullenly assembled the punches, sullenly served them, and turned his back.

"Well, here's lead in your pencil, Norm," Atlas said, tossing off half the drink. He embraced the two girls around their waists, and fondled a scorched breast on each. "Ah, that's better, hey, girls? Put us in shape for the big party."

"You're going to the cookout, Lester, aren't you?" Norman said anxiously. "Free steaks, free drinks, free everything?"

"Free love?" giggled the girl called Patsy.

"No, no. *That,* Norman has to charge for," Atlas said. "He's in such demand we've had to put a meter on him. Haw haw! Con permisso!" He dandled the two fiery breasts. "Sure we'll be there, Norm. Hatsy, Patsy, and Atsy, the three musketeers. Grease up the old meter, boy, and maybe get one ready for me. Con permisso!"

Norman went upstairs to dress, somewhat relieved. At least the drunken monster would be as far removed from the Tilson party as he could be, on Gull Reef.

3

By ten o'clock, the Tilson party was going strong. People had been arriving since about half-past seven, and more than a hundred of them had come in a cataract a little before nine. Paperman had hired three large motorboats to ferry the guests, so Virgil wasn't overwhelmed. Norman had not yet seen such a turnout in Amerigo, not even at Government House. Tom and Letty Tilson evidently bridged the two societies of Kinja. The hill crowd was there; Norman did not miss a face of those superior whites he had seen at Broadstairs. The grave, dignified natives of the Turnbull party had also come, and the two groups were mingling in the bar and on the dance terrace in an amiable mass, from which there arose the rich, pleasant noise of a good party. The orchestra— musicians in silver coats, not a steel band—were playing prim jazz, and many couples were dancing. The formal dress of these people could hardly be faulted, even to the finicky taste of Norman and Henny Paperman, who were used to New York first nights. It might be that some of the white women's dresses were a season late; that some of the Negro women had gone further with color than Henny would; that a few of the men—the white more than the black—had permitted themselves eccentricities in their dinner jackets. For all that, this was a rare scene of West Indian society in a gala mood, on a broad terrace lined with kerosene flares, under a beaming white moon and innumerable stars, with the lamplit black hills of Amerigo as a backdrop across the shimmering water of the harbor.

Into this scene, almost on the stroke of ten, came Iris Tramm.

She wore purple; a floor-length draped silk dress of deep purple, with a heavy Mexican silver necklace. She stood in a doorway of the dance terrace, looking around, not moving. Her hair was swept up in negligent disorder, and as Norman approached her, he could see the pale puffiness of her face, the glitter of her eyes, and the slight trembling of the hand that held her silver purse. She walked to meet him, and once she put a leg to one side instead of straight ahead. But she held herself well, and she did not stagger or weave.

"I was invited," she said. "Ask Tom Tilson. He invited me weeks ago."

"Good God, of course you were, Iris. I can't tell you how glad I am to see you."

"Are you?" Iris moved her head heavily here and there. "Magnificent brawl. Where's Henny?"

"Somewhere. Look, there's still lots and lots of hors d'oeuvres. The steaks won't be along for a while. Come on."

"Well, Your Excellency. How do you do?" Iris said, with a mock little curtsy that she was not quite up to making, despite her clear speech and taut self-control. She staggered sideways, and Governor Sanders caught her elbow.

"Hello, Iris," Sanders said in a warm but pained voice. "What will you have? A drink? Something to eat?"

She looked at him through half-shut eyes for a long time. "Well, get set for a big surprise, Alton. Something to eat." Iris achieved her clear speech by excessively careful and exaggerated motions of her lips.

"Good," the governor said. "I'm famished myself, I just got here. Let's go."

She was glancing around again. She turned to the governor and took his arm. "What the f—— is everybody looking at? Is my fly open? There's no fly in this dress. There's no flies on *me*. Period."

"It's a beautiful dress. That's why everybody's looking," said Sanders. "The table's over here. They have drinks, and caviar, dear."

"Bye, Norm. I want to see Henny later," Iris said, as Sanders led her off. "I want to see her dress."

This arrival of the governor's mistress in a sodden but functioning state sparked an already successful party into a blaze. The Sand Witches scandal had already been well chewed over (so far as Norman could tell, everybody in Kinja knew about it); a new topic was needed, and here was Iris. The noise level rose. Eyes gleamed, heads leaned together, as Alton Sanders moved to the hors d'oeuvres table with Iris, holding her arm, his face set as though he were at some grave ceremony.

Amy Ball, breathing a fishy smell, came and draped a big arm around Norman's neck. Her long, black, beaded dress had a very high neck, which Paperman counted a mercy.

"Isn't it a pity, Norman dear?" she said through her teeth. "I mean, really it's almost a tragedy, don't you agree? I mean fifty years from now nobody will think anything at all about such things. The world's all going one way, lovey. But meantime poor Iris and Alton are trapped in nasty, backward old 1959. Doesn't it upset you?"

"It's not really my business, Amy."

"Well, no, but we all love Iris so. You do adore her, too, don't you? I mean like the rest of us, when the poor girl is herself? Of course, it's awful when she gets like this. I had to put up with it a couple of times. Ghastly! How long has she been at it this time?"

Norman said abruptly, "Amy, Lester Atlas is here now, you know. I've talked to him about your promissory notes, and I'm ready to give you five thousand dollars for them."

Mrs. Ball's beaming smile contracted at once to an artificial look, a small painted smile on a big serious face. "Oh! Five thousand? I said ten, you know, dear, and at that I was just maundering, I was half-tiddly. I did say ten, didn't I? I know I did, love. On the staircase at Broadstairs. And even at ten it's a shocking steal, Norman. You know it's a shocking steal. I mean you do owe me thirty-five thousand dollars, precious."

"I'll pay you thirty-five thousand, Amy, when the time comes, if we're both still alive. I thought you wanted cash now. I don't have much cash."

"But Mr. Atlas does."

"You saw Mr. Atlas in a discussion of money once."

"So I did," Mrs. Ball said with a husky laugh. "I did indeed. Oh, Douglas, how kind of you! Thank you. Douglas, you've met Norman Paperman, haven't you?"

Douglas was a tall heavy man with bushy, sandy hair, a big sandy mustache, a red handsome face, and bulging veined eyes. He carried two full champagne glasses. Amy had introduced him before as Commander Something-Something—Scott-Gresham, or Marple-Twayde—Norman didn't recall the name. The commander had talked at length to Norman about Amerigo, in a crackling British accent, using the words *actually, tremendous,* and *fantastic* in much the way Lester Atlas employed obscenities. He was looking into the possibilities of starting a new airline in the West Indies, he had told Norman.

"What do you think, dear?" Mrs. Ball said, accepting a glass of champagne and draining it. "Horrid old Norman here only wants to give me five thousand dollars for all those notes. Isn't that mangy and beastly of him?"

"Very beastly. However, it's five thousand more than nothing at all, pet," said the sandy man. "Actually."

"Douglas is my new business partner." Mrs. Ball took the commander's arm and snuggled. "We may start a brand-new island airline together, Norman. I mean wouldn't it be fantastic if we had some decent planes and pilots flitting about the Caribbean, instead of the lunatics we've got now, in those frightening old kites?"

"It would be an improvement, yes."

"The growth possibilities are tremendous, actually," said Douglas.

"Of course, if I did take Norman's miserable, insulting offer, love," said Mrs. Ball, "we could charter that Cullen yacht next week after all, couldn't we? And just muck about the Greek islands for a while. It would be a lovely change. We could take off any time."

"Actually, when you think about it, promissory notes are promissory notes," said Douglas, "and money is money."

"Just so." Amy Ball put out a hand. "Do you want to make it a deal, Norman? It's kind of funny at a party, but still—"

He shook her hand at once. She looked sly and burst out laughing. "Well, that's that. Funnily enough, you know, I've buggered you and your fearsome Mr. Atlas very royally. I paid Tony and Larry four thousand for the whole lease. Not six, as he said. I've made my money back half a dozen times over. Not bad."

"Tremendous," said Douglas, squeezing her waist. "She's got a fantastic business head on her, actually."

Henny came up and said she wanted to visit the cookout to see how Hazel was doing. Mrs. Ball complimented her on her dress, a pink-and-gold sarong from Hassim's shop. Henny looked charming, indeed. She had a rosy tan, and she glowed with the excitement of the party and the pleasure of wearing a new, beautiful dress, a size smaller than usual. The mysterious pain, which had quite disappeared since her arrival, had forced her into dieting, and she was slimmer now than her own daughter. A few drinks had softened the satiric lines in her face and put sparkle in her eyes.

Norman went with her to the Tilsons, who sat in state at the grand center table of the bar, ringed by friends, Negro and white.

"Paperman, everything's wonderful. Marvellous. What do you say, folks? Doesn't this beat my Francis Drake parties?"

There was vigorous agreement around the table, and a little applause. Llewellyn, the banker, said, "Mr. Paperman, you have made the Gull Reef Club a much greater asset to our island. You and your charming wife. Everybody in Kinja admires you both, and we are all grateful to you."

"Well, you're very kind." Norman turned to Tilson. "All I really wanted to ask was, don't you think we might put on the chateaubriands now?"

"I'm in your hands," Tilson said. "It couldn't be going better. You just keep doing it your way."

The long charcoal pit in the sand glowed yellow-white in the moon-lit gloom; little flames of blue and garnet danced on the coals. The steaks lay wrapped in thick sheets of foil on a table nearby.

"I think it's that time, Sheila," Norman called from the top of the beach stairs.

"Yassuh. Dass what I been tinkin'. Dey got to cook 'most an hour, dey so tick. Girls! You hear de boss. Put on de steaks. If you drops a single one on de sand, start runnin' an' don' never come back."

Wielding long forks, the girls plopped the heavy purple meat slabs all along the grills, to instant sizzlings and delicious aromas.

"We does have to keep turning dem, dat fire plenty hot," laughed Sheila. "Dey come out real good, suh. I stay right here and watch."

"My God, how marvellous that smells," Henny said. "Honestly, you've done an unbelievable job, Norm."

"I've got Sheila," Norman said. "That was luck."

As they passed through the thronged lobby, jovial party guests, clustered here and there with plates of hors d'oeuvres and drinks, called compliments at Norman and Henny.

She said when they came outside, "Listen, is that true about our cute little bartender? What everybody's been saying?"

"Too true."

"Good lord. The clap? All seven of them?" Norman nodded. "Where is he? What's happened to him? Have they arrested him?"

"He's just gone, Henny. They watched the airport, but he never showed. His catamaran isn't at our pier, and it isn't in the marina. My guess is the girls warned him, and he got into his little boat and sailed away. Just sailed off into the sunset, our handsome sailor lad, to start all over in some other island Eden, no doubt. Guadeloupe, Barbados, St. Croix, Nassau, who can say? A good-looking young white bartender is welcome anywhere. Church was born for the Caribbean."

"He was so—so *sweet,* somehow. So shy."

"He was a fire-eating sex maniac. I knew it. I just had to make do. That's the first lesson you learn down here."

Henny glanced at him as they walked along the lawn, a gloomy place of quiet between the dins of two big parties. "These people I was talking to were awfully gabby. The Campbells. They also said Iris Tramm is that governor's mistress. Is *that* true? Is it possible?"

"Why not? He's a pleasant, clever man, and not bad-looking."

"He's COLORED, Norm."

"Spoken like a liberal, Henny."

"Well, is she, or isn't she?"

"Yes, she is."

"Did *she* tell you she was?"

"Yes, she told me she was. —Watch this brush in through here. Once you get past the flare, it's catch-and-keep."

They could hear the steel band bang-de-bang-banging on Lovers' Beach, amid confused hilarious noises.

"I swear, Norm," Henny said, "once you're down here a little while, you begin to feel you've turned over a rock."

"That's the second lesson of the Caribbean. And there are always more and yet more rocks, kid, with more ugly little surprises always scuttling out from under them. Never a dull moment."

She clasped his hand. "What's the matter, honey?"

"Nothing. I'm nervous. And to tell you the truth, when I saw Iris I felt like crying."

"She's in bad shape. I don't think she'll make it through the evening."

"Neither do I. Keep an eye on her, Henny, will you, when we go back, if the governor gets sidetracked?"

"Sure I will, Norm."

4

"Wow," Henny yelled—she had to yell—when they came out of the newly hacked path through the brush onto Lovers' Beach. "This brawl looks better than the other one!"

A gigantic bonfire blazed in the middle of the beach, showering red sparks skyward. In the blazing firelight stood the steel-band boys, stripped down to red shorts, thumping and slamming away, eyes prominent, foreheads dripping, big white teeth gleaming, shiny dark bodies reflecting the flames. All around them were writhing, wriggling, almost naked bodies, mostly white, but with a sprinkling of Negroes, among whom Norman recognized some of his prettier chambermaids. Many of the dancers held drinks that splashed and spilled. Girls were shrieking along the beach in the moonlight, chased by baying men. People were splashing in the sea, too, jumping on each other, standing on shoulders, cavorting and wrestling, all this to an obbligato of protesting happy feminine screams. Some of the older guests were sitting at tables, drinking; but many gray or bald heads were among the thronging barefoot dancers on the sand.

Lionel Williams rushed up to them, crowned with a wreath of scarlet hibiscus blossoms, which in the firelight set off his red-streaked green face most engagingly. "Norman, this is the greatest! I've never had so much fun in my life! *Nobody* has, in our whole crowd. Dan just told me to be sure to book us all in right away for three weeks next Christmas. Dan's gone right through the top of the tent, Norm. He's in orbit. You've got it taped, boy, with this hotel. It's fabulous. It's the end!"

Lionel shouted all this hoarsely above the music, the singing, the laughter, and the shrieks.

"I'm glad," Norman said absently. He was looking for Atlas. Hatsy, the larger Maine schoolteacher, was close by, naked to all purposes in a bikini that looked like two white strings, joyously undulating her blistered loins at a UDT man.

Lionel seized Henny's hand. "Come on, kiddo, tonight's our night to howl. Give your little self a shake-shake-shake."

"Well, why not?" Henny kicked off her gold slippers and they danced away.

Now Atlas's other schoolteacher, Patsy, went wiggling past, in the arms of one of the black bartenders hired for the evening. "Patsy, where's Lester?" Norman called.

"Who knows? Who cares? I haven't seen him. Golly, I love dancing on sand." And she was gone.

At this moment Norman saw Atlas—at a far table, sitting alone, an elbow on a knee, his head cocked sideways and sunk low, watching the dancers. "Hi, Lester. Having fun?" Norman said, hurrying to him.

The heavy look on Lester's face gave way to a tired smile. "Why, sure, Norm. This is a swinging party. I just haven't got that old pep tonight, you know? Ate too many spare ribs, I guess." With a shrug of his fat shoulders, Lester fumbled for a cigar at his naked hairy chest, in the place where his shirt pocket usually was. "Every now and then I think about Anaconda Copper, too. It makes me feel kind of run-down and anemic. Lot of blood to lose, Norm. How's the other party going?"

"Well, it's not as gay as this one."

"Maybe that's what I need. Too many happy people here. Maybe I'll come over to the hotel." He drained his tumbler of whiskey, and while Norman was still seeking a tactful way to head him off, Atlas groaned. "Oh, hell, I don't want to get dressed. I'm okay here. Hatsy and Patsy are having fun."

Henny came up dishevelled and giggling, holding her slippers. "Well, I found Hazel. She's in the middle of that mess, and honestly, the girl should be arrested for the way she's dancing."

"Who's she dancing with, Cohn?"

"It's hard to say. She's sort of throwing it in all directions. Cohn is standing by, looking nonplussed. How goes it, Lester?"

"Oh, I'm swinging, Henny," said Atlas. "Swinging."

"Well, I just wanted to be sure Hazel hadn't been eaten by a shark or something," Henny said. "But if there's a shark around, I think its mother is the one to worry."

The Tilson party seemed stately and stiff after the saturnalia on Lovers' Beach, but it had grown even larger, and it was lively enough. It filled the lobby, the bar, and the dance terrace. Most of the people were standing, all had drinks in their hands, and everybody seemed to be talking at once over the dulcet jazz played by the five men in silver coats.

"Hi, Iris," Norman said, as she approached him in the lobby. "Enjoying yourself?" She went straight past him without turning her head or moving her eyes. She was walking in a stiff, straight-legged way, bent slightly forward, hands hanging down, making for the bar. Norman's first thought was that she was snubbing him. Then he realized that she hadn't seen him. She bumped into one man, and other people got out of her way, whispering to each other.

Governor Sanders, he perceived, was watching Iris as she went, leaning in a doorway with folded arms. The governor looked gaunt and forbidding in his narrow white silk jacket and ruffled shirt; his face was grim.

Norman came to him and said in a low voice, "Can't you help her? What she doesn't need is a drink."

"There's only so much I can do," Sanders said, with an empty little smile. "She just said to me, 'If you don't want me to take this place apart, stop following me, you son of a bitch.'" Sanders twisted his mouth. "It doesn't mean anything, the abuse. That's what you have to realize."

"What's she likely to do? I mean, what's the worst? The place is a little too well built for her to take apart, really."

"Oh, that depends, Mr. Paperman. Iris can break up a party by just getting loud. I've seen her do it. She has a voice like Charles Laughton, you know, when she wants to use it, and the vocabulary of a marine. It's very disconcerting, especially to the ladies. They tend to pick up their purses and leave."

"I've heard her."

"Or she can lift her dress to her navel and dance around. Or maybe punch a few people. Iris is very strong. I gave her a plateful of food, you know. But she just put it down and went and got a glass of bourbon." Sanders glanced around at the party. "I'm awfully sorry about this. Tom Tilson's a fine fellow. Maybe she'll be all right. The fact is, she's trying to behave."

Iris was coming back, walking in the same unseeing way. She seemed scarcely aware of the drink in her hand; she held it at an angle, and it spilled as she walked, leaving a wet trail on the tile floor. A dark stain was streaking down the bosom of her dress.

This time her dulled eyes rested straight on Paperman. "Hi, Norm, great party," she said, writhing her lips around each word. "First goddamn time in a year I've had any goddamn fun. Let's dance."

"Sure, Iris," he said, holding out his arms, but she walked straight by him and Sanders, sat in a chair, and drank.

He felt a tap on his shoulder.

chapter sixteen

Return of Hippolyte

I

It was Sheila. She did not say a word. She beckoned.

"Excuse me," Norman said to the governor. He followed Sheila through the lobby, through the bar, down the beach stairs, past the charcoal pit blanketed with sizzling, snapping steaks, along the shore to where the beach ended in pebbles and an outcrop of rock.

"Look dah," she said.

Her outthrust arm pointed to the shadowy stretch of water between the fort's floodlights and the hotel glow. Norman saw what appeared to be a straw basket floating on the water. "That?" he said, pointing.

"Yas, suh."

"It's a basket."

"No, suh."

"No, you're right. It's a hat, isn't it?"

"Yas, suh."

It was, in fact, the kind of hat that the island Frenchmen wore. Norman looked at Sheila. "Well, what about it?"

"I tink dat Hippolyte."

"Hippolyte? Swimming in the harbor with his *hat* on, for crying out loud? At midnight?"

"Hippolyte fonny. He swim all de time wid he hat. He don' like de sun."

"There's no sun now."

"No, suh."

"I mean it's absurd, it's idiotic, swimming with a hat on, especially in the middle of the night."

"Yes, suh."

Norman watched the moving hat. "You really think that's Hippolyte."

"I tink so, suh."

"Sheila, can you do something for me? Can you go to Lovers' Beach, find Lieutenant Woods, and bring him here kind of fast?"

"Suh, if I go away, dem girls dey gone ruin dose steaks. Dose steaks dey half done. I got to go back now."

"Can you send a girl, then? Send the smartest one, and tell her to hurry. Send Delia."

"Yas, suh. I send Delia. Lootenant what?"

"Lieutenant Woods. He's a navy lieutenant. From the UDT."

"Lootenant Woods from de UDT. Yas, suh. Mistuh Pape'mon, where de fot porson?"

"At Lovers' Beach."

"I send Delia right now, suh. Lootenant Woods."

Alone in the gloom, Norman kept his eye on the hat. He could now see a face under it. The man was swimming with a side stroke, bringing only one hand out of the water. Norman began to climb along the rocks in the gloom, toward the point where the swimmer would be landing. Out here on the rocks there was only moonlight, patched with shadows of old thorny trees. He sat on a rock in the shadow and waited. His mouth felt as it had in former days when he had smoked three packs of cigarettes in a night: parched, sandy, aching. Breathing was an effort, because of the rapid, heavy beat of his heart.

Hippolyte came stumbling out of the water, glancing about with an ugly scowl. He looked most ridiculous—and at the same time most terrifying—in the big straw hat, brief bedraggled cotton shorts, and nothing else. The machete dripped in his hand.

"Hello, Hippolyte."

The swimmer turned around and peered at the shadows. Hippolyte's face seldom showed much expression, but now it did. He was very surprised.

"De boss?" he said.

"Yes, the boss."

Norman came out into the moonlight, picking his way on the rocks. He wore a crimson linen dinner jacket, black tie, black trousers, and patent-leather pumps, an interesting contrast to Hippolyte's array.

"Well, Hippolyte, how've you been?"

The Frenchman wrinkled his brow. "Not too good. I got headaches again."

"Did you go to the hospital? They can give you stuff for that."

"Yah. I go. Dey give me injection, too."

The two men stared at each other.

"Well, Hippolyte, what can I do for you?"

The Frenchman looked vacant and sheepish, and scratched his nose with the handle of the machete. After a pause, he said, "I came for de clock."

"Clock? What clock?"

"I leave my alarm clock by de gardener shack."

"So? You came for your alarm clock."

"Yah."

"All right. Come along. Let's get you your alarm clock."

He motioned to Hippolyte to go first. Norman was showing a lot of grace under pressure, for a peaceable middle-aged New Yorker with a coronary history, but he wasn't up to walking ahead of the Frenchman and presenting his back to the machete. Hippolyte docilely obeyed, scrambling along the rocks, and then striking up a path through the brush. It was an almost black path, but Paperman followed him, and in a minute or so they were on the rear lawn near the gardener's shack,

well away from any of the hotel lights; a stretch of level grass surrounded by thick dark shrubbery, and lit by the high moon.

"That's quite a short cut," he said.

"I go down by dere to fish, some time."

They came to the closed door of the gardener's shack, where they
could hear Millard's loud, regular, peaceful snores.

"Millard sleep," Hippolyte said. "I come back de next time."

"No, no, as long as you're here, let's get you your alarm clock, by all
means." Norman rapped at the door. The snoring went on. He knocked
again.

"Ugh. Ugh. Who dah?"

"The boss. Open up, Millard. Hippolyte wants his alarm clock."

"Yes, please."

Stumbling and thumping inside; the door opened. Millard, naked to
the waist, and wearing his ragged gardening pants, stood there yawning, holding a cheap tin clock, with no glass over its bent hands and
yellowed face.

"Wha' Hippolyte?" Millard handed Norman the clock, showing no
trace of surprise or annoyance.

"Why, he's right here. He's come for his clock."

Norman gestured and glanced at Hippolyte, and uttered a startled
gasp. There was only moonlit air where the Frenchman had stood seconds before. In the nearby shrubbery there was a rustling sound.

"Hippolyte!" he shouted. "Hippolyte! *Hippolyte!* —All right, Millard.
Thanks."

Norman handed back the clock and ran to Lovers' Beach.

Almost the first person he noticed in the mill of the merrymakers on
the sand was the kitchen maid, Delia. She was easy to spot because of
the new yellow-and-white smock that Sheila had put on all the maids
for the party. "Delia!" He pushed through the dancers to her. She was
cavorting with Lionel Williams, and she wore his hibiscus wreath.
"What are you doing? Where's Lieutenant Woods?"

"Couldn't find no lootenant, suh," the girl said with a furtive giggle,
her hips working like a flywheel.

"Go away, Norm," Lionel said. "Delia's my girl now. No cutting in.
Jiminy crickets, what a bash!"

Norman worked his way along the beach, and saw Woods sitting at a table with Cohn, drinking beer.

"There you are," he panted, shouldering through to them.

"What's up?" said Woods genially. "You look 'horossed.' Sit down, and have a beer."

Norman started to explain. He had not spoken half a dozen sentences when Woods, smiling but alert, held up a hand and turned to Cohn. "How long ago did the fellows leave? Can you still catch them?"

"I can sure try." Cohn got up and loped away.

"Yes, sir," Woods said. "Go on. Skivvies, and a straw hat, and a machete, you say? I'd like to see that. And where's your fat friend? The one he's after?"

"Here on this beach somewhere."

"Well, maybe to start with you'd better collect him, you know?"

"All right."

Norman circled the beach and cut through the dancers once, twice, and a third time. When he came back to Woods's table, Cohn was there with three other UDT men. Woods was slapping a long flashlight against his palm as he talked to them.

Norman said, "I can't find him. He's not on this beach. He's not at this party. Not now. I'm certain he isn't. But he was."

Woods said, "He probably toddled off to his room to sleep. You better check that. Most of the fellows just went back to the base, sir. It's too bad, because all of us working together could find your handy man fast. This is a tiny island. Us five can round him up, too, but it'll take longer."

"This man is dangerous," Norman said. "He's supposed to have killed a policeman. Don't you think I should notify the police?"

"Well, I don't know," Woods said. "They sort of have a losing score with him, don't they? We've had a lot of training in disarming a man. Why don't we try first?"

"If you want to, I'll be desperately grateful. But shouldn't I warn my guests now?"

Woods looked thoughtful. Cohn said to the lieutenant, "Sir, I think somebody's more likely to get hurt if they all start panicking around, and talking about a maniac on the loose, and all that."

Woods nodded. He said to Paperman, "Let's first see how we make out. All right? I'd guess he'd stay where it's dark, and not bother anyone.

Except your fat friend, of course, if he finds him. Just keep *him* out of the way." He gestured to the four frogmen. "All right. You all know where to go. Shove off, and we'll join up at the hotel steps."

The men trotted away in different directions.

2

Hastening back across the lawn, Norman saw Governor Sanders and Iris leaving the main house. Sanders had his arm around her waist and was holding her elbow. As she put her foot on the top stair her legs collapsed under her, and Sanders was caught off balance. She tumbled free, pitched all the way down the stairs, and sprawled face down on the gravel path. Norman ran to help. Her face was scratched and bleeding when they raised her to a sitting position, and her torn dirtied dress was pushed up above her skinned knees. She looked from Sanders to Norman, her head lolling, her eyes hardly focusing. "Norman, y'ole Jewboy, I felt sorry for you, that's why . . . take the f—— place apart . . ." She fell dead asleep in Sanders' arms.

Sanders pointed to her purse lying on the grass. "Get the key of her cottage, please."

Norman retrieved the purse, saying, "Can you carry her?"

"I've done it."

Sanders raised her to her feet, and swung her up awkwardly in his arms, staggering. "Just open the door for me. I'm glad we made it outside. She really didn't do anything very bad in there."

Norman opened the Pink Cottage door. The governor plodded in with the limp, hoarsely breathing woman. "Her dress is ruined, anyway," Sanders said, putting Iris on the divan. "Might as well leave her as she is for now." He went to a closet, took out a knitted red-and-black comforter that Norman hadn't seen before, and covered the unconscious woman. He got a damp towel from the bathroom and sponged her face.

Meadows was whimpering, scratching, and clanking his chain in the porch. Norman said, "How about turning him loose?"

"Why?"

"Well—just to take care of her. Just an extra precaution. There's a lot of drunks around tonight." Norman was in a tremendous hurry to look for Atlas, and he didn't want the governor to know about Hippolyte—not yet, anyway. He was hoping to avoid an alarm.

"I guess so." Sanders went to the porch, and a moment later Meadows bounded in and licked Iris's face.

"There's nothing more to do," Sanders said. "She'll sleep for hours. She may wake up in a very bad state. You'll let me know?"

"I'll send my wife in, early in the morning, and then I'll call you."

Sanders looked down at the swollen, paint-smeared, scratched face of Mrs. Tramm, and then at Norman, with a disturbingly penetrating glance. "What did you think when you first met Iris here? Tell the truth. The blond goddess of the island paradise?"

"Something like that, yes."

Sanders regarded Iris for a moment, smiling without amusement. He brushed hair out of her eyes. "I suppose I should get back to the party, and keep the talk down. Meadows, take care of her."

Emerging from the cottage, they saw Woods, Cohn, and two other swimmers talking in a huddle near the steps to the main house; four muscular brown men, almost naked in the warm night.

"Hello, Lieutenant," the governor said, "leaving the party so soon?"

"Well, sir, pretty soon now."

"I hear your boys made another fine jump. Well done." The governor went into the hotel.

Woods said to Paperman, "No sign of him, but Thompson is still beating along the rocks on the north side. Find your fat friend yet?"

"I'm just going up to his room."

"Well, unless Frenchy's better at getting himself into solid thorn brush than we are—and we're not bad at it, and he's as naked as we are —he's probably in some crawl hole, or maybe he broke into one of the cottages. We didn't want to search them without your say-so."

A squat round-headed UDT man came trotting into the light, signalling lack of success with upturned hands.

"That does it. Nothing to do but keep looking," Woods said. "Better locate your friend, though."

"If he isn't already dead," said Norman nervously.

Woods smiled. "I really don't think Frenchy's got him this fast, sir. The question is—"

"Wait a second." Norman held up his hand, and listened. He was hearing hoarse guffaws and shouting in the hotel, coming from the vicinity of the bar or the dance terrace. The words were indecipherable, but the noise was as characteristic as the call of a moose. *"Waw baw graw ror wah haw haw,"* came the voice. Then, somewhat more clearly over the party noise, *"Con permisso!"*

"That's him," Norman said.

"Fine," said Woods, "now we know where *he* is."

"Not so fine," exclaimed Norman, feeling greatly relieved and much more frantic, all at once. "He's in there ruining my dinner party! Don't you realize that? He's absolutely fractured. And Hippolyte's lurking around somewhere, that's for sure, and he'll hear him, too, sooner or later. Suppose he comes charging among all those women in his wet drawers, swinging the machete? What then?"

"Well, we can keep a pretty good watch out here, sir—"

"Yes, but he *knows* this place! Suppose he slips through? He'll start a riot. Tilson's guests will all be swimming for the shore in their dinner clothes. I'll probably go bankrupt. He may behead a couple of people in sheer playfulness as they run around screaming. I'm just mentioning a few small possibilities here—"

Woods put a hand on his arm. "Sir, you keep your friend in there. Frenchy won't get past us, and we'll find him."

"In fact, this will probably bring him out of hiding," Cohn said. "Make your friend holler louder."

"That's something that's never been necessary," Norman said.

"Before we check the cottages," Woods said, "can you tell us of any hole where he might be hiding? Some place he'd know about, and we wouldn't?"

Norman bethought himself, after a moment, of the crawl space beneath the hotel, where the pump was. He described it to Woods.

"That sounds real possible. Bob, why don't you volunteer to take a look in that hole?" The lieutenant handed Cohn the flashlight. "You've got sort of a stumpy neck, it's less of a target."

"I unwillingly volunteer," Cohn said. "Where's this death trap, now, Norm?"

363

Paperman led him around the back of the hotel and pointed down the sandy embankment. "Through the trelliswork there. You'll see the hole in the wall. Good luck, Bob. Be very careful, please."

Cohn said, "You know, I don't like this one bit. I'm too short for Hazel as it is." He went down and disappeared in the gloom.

The Atlas noises were definitely coming from the dance terrace now, and there was handclapping too. Norman dashed through the kitchen passageway and the lobby to the terrace, and saw Atlas dancing the merengue with Sheila, in a ring of laughing, applauding guests. Atlas now wore a brown silk dinner jacket, with his blue television evening shirt, and black trousers. A big cigar was in his teeth, and Sheila's chef's cap was on his head. The cook seemed both amused and annoyed; at any rate, she was dancing, and they made a monumental pair.

Norman found Henny and Mrs. Tilson in the ring, giggling together. "Ye gods, Henny, why didn't you stop him? This is so awful."

Letty Tilson, all dimples and diamonds, in a knee-length bouffant black dress, said, "Oh, pshaw, Norman, he's funny. Let him be."

Henny said, "Have you ever *tried* stopping Lester?"

Lester and the cook danced by them, and Sheila rolled her eyes at Paperman. "Suh, de fot porson *make* me come and dance," she cried. "De steaks dey all ready."

"Steaks, shmakes," roared Lester. "Hey, Norm! What does your meter read now? Haw haw!" And he spun away.

Mercifully the music soon stopped. Sheila snatched her cap off Atlas's head and retreated in grinning embarrassment, shaking her head at all the jokes the guests shouted at her. Atlas rolled up to the Papermans, sweating. "I'm telling you, Norm, your fancy party was dying," he panted hoarsely. "I was just doing my duty as senior partner, here, stirring things up a bit."

"Well stirred," Mrs. Tilson said. "It's my party, Mr. Atlas, mine and my husband's, and I'm much obliged to you. You're a real live-wire."

Atlas at once put on his company manners: the straight back, the softened voice, the ingratiating smile. "Well, hello! I'm not aware that I was invited, and I'm off to Lovers' Beach now, but I just thought I'd look in."

"Of course you're invited. Don't you dare go away, now."

Norman said hastily, "No, don't go, Lester. Don't think of it. There's an extra place at our table. Come along, they're going to serve any minute."

"Well, how nice of you all," Lester said.

Norman's table was one of the outer ones, at the edge of the dining terrace; and Lester dropped himself in a chair with his back squarely against the low terrace wall, before Norman or anyone else asked him to. After this, all Norman could think of was that it was now possible for Hippolyte to climb the rough fieldstone wall and kill Atlas with a blow. It was not only possible, it seemed to Norman the next event of interest that was going to occur. Atlas's shiny red skull was a terribly recognizable and visible target. He sat right under a flare. Norman had a vision, almost a hallucination, of Hippolyte rising up and shearing off Atlas's head so neatly, with that razor-sharp machete, that it would remain sitting on Lester's shoulders, not even bleeding; and there would be no immediate way of knowing what had happened, except that Atlas would at last shut up.

With this gruesome fantasy strong in his mind, Norman made a poor show of accepting compliments on all sides for the massed flowers decorating the terrace, the individual place cards that the depraved Church had done in water colors before sailing away, the gardenias at each lady's plate, the orchid centerpieces, and all the other touches on which he had labored. So restless was he that he excused himself as waiters began bringing in bowls of salad and steaks on wooden boards, while others passed around the tables pouring Burgundy; and he went out to talk to Woods.

The lieutenant stood as before at the entrance to the main house, with one other frogman. "Hi," he said. "No luck yet. The boys are making another sweep all around. Then if you give us the okay, we'll try the cottages. He's got to be hiding, if he didn't swim off."

"I take it Cohn came back alive."

"Greasy, but alive, yes."

"Do you know where Atlas is sitting?"

"Yes," Woods laughed. "He doesn't have a worry in the world, does he?"

"Nobody does," Norman said, in a flare of irritation. "They're all having the time of their lives, they think everything's peachy. And I'm hovering between a heart attack and a nervous collapse."

"Well, now, Mr. Paperman, why don't you go on back and have a good time yourself? If he shows, we'll get him for you."

Norman went back, endured Henny's growl at him for letting the wonderful steak get cold, and did his best to eat. But he could hardly choke down a few mouthfuls. He would not drink wine. He had drunk nothing since Hippolyte had appeared. Atlas, of course, ate enough steak for three, and drank wine to correspond, all the time joking in his foghorn voice. Norman thought that Hippolyte, even if he were blind, could home in on that voice to strike and kill.

A round of pink champagne came with the dessert. Chunky Collins stood, glass in one hand, silver spoon in the other, and began to lead the guests in serenading Tom Tilson with *For He's a Jolly Good Fellow*. Midway through this song, bawled gaily by two hundred people, Norman saw—far down the terrace, at the end in shadow—Cohn's head, and his brown waving arm, poking through the doorway. At once he left the table, ignoring Henny's peevish challenge, "Norman, *will* you stop jumping up every two minutes? Come *back* here! What now?"

Cohn was streaked with black grease and plastered with sand. He seemed in an excellent humor. "I guess we've got him," he said. "He was hiding under the pier all the time. That telephone operator of yours came down to get the gondola, and he popped out at her. Almost scared her to death. She screamed, and he took off into the brush, and the fellows are after him now."

"How about Esmé? Is she all right?" Norman said, with a pang of worry and guilt. He had prevailed on the girl, with a promise of overtime pay, to stay at the switchboard until midnight, though she had said she was very tired.

"Well, she's sort of hysterical. She's still on the pier. The C.O. says for you to go have a look. Frenchy is boxed in now, in the brush between the Blue Cottage and Lovers' Beach, and I've got to get back there. We'll be fetching him out."

"Watch yourself!"

"Oh, sure."

Esmé sat in the gondola moaning. Virgil was trying to comfort her. Her eyes were starting from her head, and she clutched both hands over her stomach. "He have nuttin' on," she said. "Jus' a hat, de crazy mon. He jump out wid a big cutlash, he all naked like a don-key. He crazy."

"Esmé, how do you feel?" Norman said.

"Mistuh Papuh, I got bad pain," said Esmé, rocking back and forth. "Bad pain start."

"You stay right here with her, Virgil," Norman said. "Dr. Tracy Pullman is at the party and I'm going to bring him down here, right away."

"Yeffuh, I ftay heah."

"Esmé, I'm going to bring you the doctor who's the head of the hospital. You just be calm, now."

"Tank you, suh," the girl moaned.

Norman rushed back to the hotel and made his way across the dining terrace, dodging among the waiters with their baked Alaskas, looking for the doctor. Henny called at him as he passed, "Norman, what the hell is the matter with you?"

"Nothing, nothing."

"Then why do you keep popping in and out like a lunatic? It's a perfect party. Just sit down and *enjoy* yourself, for Christ's sake."

"I'll be right back."

Atlas said, "Norm, a boss has to look relaxed. He has to look on top of the situation, Norm. You're creating the wrong image."

"Okay, okay."

Espying Dr. Pullman at Mrs. Turnbull's table, Paperman hurried to him, and whispered in his ear. Dr. Pullman pushed back his half-eaten portion of baked Alaska, threw down a napkin, and rose with a discontented sigh. He wore a splendidly cut tuxedo; he was taller and heavier than the senator, with the same round dark face and shrewd eyes.

"Busman's holiday," he said. "Excuse me, folks," and he went along with Paperman to the pier. On the way Norman told him about Esmé's alien status, and forlornly asked the doctor whether he could "give Esmé something" to arrest the course of nature until he could bundle her on a plane to Nevis in the morning.

Pullman laughed. "Man, that's a pill nobody invented yet."

"Well, then, what shall we do? Move her to the hospital? I mean, we have no facilities here—I'll pay—"

The doctor patted his shoulder. "Suppose I just take a look first."

The round-headed frogman, Thompson, came jogging up to Paperman as they approached the pier. "Sir, the C.O. thinks we've got him, and says for you to come along. You might be able to talk to him."

Norman followed the young man as he trotted tranquilly down the lawn toward the Blue Cottage, the last cottage in the row. Woods and Cohn were pacing, and peering into the brush. "Hello, Frenchy's right in here," Woods said. "He was quiet for a while, but then he started to move, and we heard him. We surrounded him and he stopped again." Woods directed his flashlight at the thick brush; the leaves looked a bright artificial green in the cone of light. "That's about where he is— somewhere between there and the water. Try talking to him."

Norman thought for a moment, and raised his voice. "Hippolyte? Hippolyte, you come out and go home."

No response.

"Nobody's going to bother you. I haven't called the police, Hippolyte, you can just go home and forget about all this. Come back tomorrow and I'll give you the clock." He paused. The only sounds were the loud party noise from Lovers' Beach, and the faint orchestra at the main house. He glanced at Woods and shouted, "I'll give you the clock, and the money I owe you, Hippolyte. You know you have about seventy-five dollars coming."

From the brush, not a sound.

Woods said to Cohn, "I guess maybe we'll have to go in."

"Are you sure he's there? Maybe he's down on the rocks," Norman said, "working back to the main house behind the cottages. Hippolyte knows his way around this place."

"Davis is down at the water," Cohn said. "He won't get past Davis."

"No," Woods said. "How about passing the word, Bob? Tell the fellows we'll go in now. I'll give them a yell to start them."

"Wait a minute! I'm going to call the police," Norman said. "There's absolutely no reason for your men to take these chances any more."

"It's kind of late at night to telephone the police, isn't it? You'll only wake the man on duty," the lieutenant said. "This is not a bad night exercise. Go ahead, Bob."

Cohn went into the brush, making little noise; Norman could barely hear him moving. The moon glittered almost overhead in a clear black sky, paling out all but the brightest stars. By contrast with the muffled jollity at Lovers' Beach, the lawn seemed quiet as a graveyard. After a minute or so, Woods, softly tapping the flashlight on his palm, said, "Okay, here goes. You just stay here, will you, sir? We'll bring him out this way, and you can—ye gods, what's *that* now?"

Far up the lawn, in the Pink Cottage, the dog was bursting forth in crazed, furious, hate-filled barking and snarling.

"*That's* where he is, Lieutenant," Norman shouted. "He did slip past your men. I told you he could. He's at the Pink Cottage. He's there right now!"

Norman ran up the lawn. Woods called quick orders at his men in the brush, then sprinted after Norman, overtook him, and plunged out of sight on the far side of the Pink Cottage, heading down through the shrubbery toward the water. Cohn came up behind Norman. The dog yapped, howled, barked, and as they neared the cottage they could hear the beast hurling himself against a door.

"I guess this is it," Cohn said. "The C.O. says for you and me to stay out here on the lawn."

They heard confused shouts from down below the cottage. "There he is! I see him. Hey, Fred, he's heading your way! No, no, he turned—this way, *this* way, Tommy—up the bank—"

There was a loud crash on the seaward side of the cottage—a splintering, tearing sound, a breaking of wood, and a skittering of wood and metal on stone. Hippolyte at the same moment came out of the shrubbery into the moonlight, moving clumsily but fast. He stopped when he saw Norman and the swimmer, showed his teeth, and made a disgusted, wordless noise—"Aaagh!" As he did this, Meadows came snarling and bounding from behind the cottage, straight for Hippolyte's back. The Frenchman heard the animal, turned, and raised the machete. Meadows leaped for him, Hippolyte swung hard, and the dog fell to the ground with a piercing yelp. In this moment when Hippolyte was distracted, Cohn ran at the Frenchman, shouting for the others; and Norman Paperman, entirely without forethought, charged Hippolyte, too.

Cohn caught the man's arm as it swung up again, Norman clasped him around the middle, and the three went thrashing down on the dewy, sweet-smelling grass. Hippolyte's knee caught Norman painfully in the stomach, and he tore at one of Norman's ears. The Frenchman smelled rank as a zoo animal. This frightening tangle on the wet grass lasted a very short time. The other frogmen came trampling up, there was a grunting scrimmage, and Norman was pulled free and helped to his feet. Woods captured the blood-streaked machete, and three of the men raised Hippolyte, keeping a tight hold on him. But the Frenchman, his head bowed, didn't resist. For the first time, Norman noticed that Hippolyte had a large bald spot.

Meadows was limping in circles, uttering cries of agony; then he sank to the grass, whimpering, licking his fur. Woods approached the dog carefully. "That's a bad gash," he said with a cautious pat on the dog's head. Blood was welling from a slanting cut on Meadows' left haunch, extending all down the leg. "It has to be sewed up right away. Red, where does that vet live? Red's got a dog," he said to Norman.

The tall shaven-headed youngster, who was standing guard on Hippolyte with the others, said, "He lives out near the dairy farm, sir. The heck of it is, he doesn't have a telephone."

"Isn't this Mrs. Tramm's dog?" Woods said, kneeling and patting the dog's drooping head. "I guess somebody should notify her. We can get him up to the vet in our truck, but—"

"I'll tell her," Norman hastily put in. "Please go ahead right now, and just take him to the vet. She's somewhere at the party, and I may be a while finding her. Go ahead, and I know she'll be grateful."

"Well, all right. And I guess we'll turn our friend here in at the fort," the lieutenant added, with his hands on his hips, regarding Hippolyte with a wry smile. "And then cease present exercises."

"Boss, you get me my clock?" Hippolyte spoke up without rancor, even with a simple smile, his face asquint as usual. He had never given the dog a second look.

"You really want that clock?"

"It my clock."

"All right."

Norman went around the back of the Pink Cottage first, and entered through the screen door that Meadows had smashed open. He found Iris lying on the divan in the same position as before. The puffed, scratched face was wet with perspiration, and she was breathing hard. The dog's wild commotion had evidently not roused her at all. He dried her face with the towel Sanders had used, left her undisturbed, and hastened to the gardener's shack. Millard, hammered awake, handed over the clock again, displaying not the slightest annoyance.

Hippolyte sat in the stern of the gondola between Lieutenant Woods and another frogman. The boy with the shaved head held Meadows on his lap in the bow, stroking him and murmuring to him. Meadows, his fur matted with blood, lay with hanging tongue, looking beaten and doleful. Cohn and the bullet-headed swimmer Thompson stood on the pier. Norman said to Virgil, "Where's Esmé? What happened to her? Where's the doctor?"

Virgil reported, in a great cascade of *f*'s, that Pullman had ordered him to send Esmé immediately to the hospital in a taxicab, and had returned to the party. Esmé was surely at the hospital now. "Fee in bad fape," Virgil commented. "Fee fcared."

Norman handed the clock to the impassive handy man. "Hippolyte, you've been very bad tonight."

"I got headaches," Hippolyte said, with a puzzled squint.

"I suppose that does it," Lieutenant Woods said. "Bob and Tommy are staying on for a free beer or two, if that's all right, sir. We'll shove off."

"All right?" Norman said. "Lieutenant, your team has permanent total free bar privileges in this club. I mean that."

Woods laughed. "You don't know what you're saying. I didn't hear that. We enjoyed the drinks and the steak dinner, we're more than even, and thanks."

"Well, how in God's name can I thank you?"

"What for? It was a good drill. The boys did all right, I thought—and say, so did you, sir. Let's go, Virgil."

The gondola pulled away. Meadows, on the lap of the frogman, raised his head, panting, and watched Norman's face. The frogman stroked him as they went.

"Poor pooch. Did you tell Iris?" Cohn said.

"I couldn't find her. I will."

"I'll get back to the brawl, I guess. Hazel must think I ducked out on her. Coming, Tommy? Thanks a lot, Norman."

"What the devil are you thanking *me* for?"

"Well, there was only one bad moment in the whole business there, really," Cohn said, "when he came out on the lawn. You were a help. If the truth be known, Norman, you're an ugly customer."

The two swimmers went off, in the elastic lope which seemed their normal gait.

Norman encountered Dr. Pullman in the hotel lobby, hanging up the desk telephone. "Well, right on time. Congratulations," Pullman said. "I've just been checking. It was quite close. She had the baby on the floor of the admissions room. A fine boy. Come down to the hospital tomorrow morning, Mr. Paperman, and I'll make out the birth certificate for you. Any time after nine o'clock—"

"Dr. Pullman, what do you mean, for me? I'm not the father."

"I'll take your word for that, but he's an American citizen now. She's in your employ, and there are the customary formalities." Dr. Pullman gave him a knowing smile and a wink. "In a way, I suppose you should pass out cigars. It's a real addition to your family. By the bye, this is the best party I've ever been to on this island. You really have the touch."

Numbed, bemused, Paperman returned to the party. He still could scarcely believe that the crisis was past, that the catastrophe had not occurred, and that tonight it would not occur; that for once, in this grim test of the Tilson party, he had beaten the island of Kinja at its sullen eerie game. The dining terrace was emptying, but some guests still lingered over their coffee and liqueurs. Henny sat alone at Norman's table, her face clouded and mean.

"Well, hello there, beautiful," she said to him. "I decided I was just going to sit here until you remembered to come for me, or until the sun rose. Where in the lousy hell have you been? Making time with some floozie at the other party?"

Norman sank into a chair. "I'm sorry, darling. There were a couple of small things I had to look after. Where's Lester?"

"Off boozing, naturally. Small things! What small things? Everything was going smooth as oil, only *you* kept flapping around like a demented albatross. I've never been more aggravated."

"Did it really go all right? Really? Nobody was disturbed by anything?"

"What was there to disturb them? Iris's dog barking once? And how did your jacket get so rumpled and damp? What on earth *have* you been doing?"

A hand fell on Norman's shoulder. Letty and Tom Tilson were standing there. Tilson offered his hand, and Norman wearily rose and shook it.

"Thanks, Paperman," said Tilson, looking him in the eye. "Thanks for an incredible success. It's been marvellous. Not a hitch, not a slip-up. In Kinja! I'm impressed, I swear to you."

"Everyone is. If you're interested," Letty said, "you and your Gull Reef Club are *in*. There's nobody worth mentioning on this island who doesn't think you're great."

"I'm glad. Very glad. Of course the party isn't over. There's more music. The bars will go till three—and then there'll be late snacks—"

"I know." Tilson was still holding his hand, and looking keenly at him. "Tell me something, Norman. Has it been all that hard? You seem a little tired."

Norman did not miss this switch to his given name, the first time Tom Tilson had used it.

Norman took a moment to reply. "Well—yes, Tom. It's been a bit hard. But that's this business, you know."

"Listen, man," Tilson said, "the important thing is, you've licked the Caribbean once. It'll stay licked now. You're all right, Norman."

He squeezed Paperman's hand, smiled, and walked off.

"Come on, Henny," Paperman said. "I'm sorry I neglected you. I'll never neglect you again. Let's have some fun now. Let's dance."

chapter seventeen

Carnival Is Very Sweet

I

A few surly breakfasters were on the dining terrace when Norman came down, and half a dozen guests were already in the bar, starting the day with the most popular if not the wisest hangover remedy. He had been awakened by a call from Cohn. Meadows was all right, and the veterinarian had said the animal's leg would heal, though with a bad scar. The frogman had first tried to talk to Iris, but she had not answered her phone.

In the lobby, the undertaker's assistants were stacking and carting away chairs. The chambermaids were sweeping the floor and rearranging the furniture, and the waitresses were taking down chains and

374

wreaths of wilted flowers. It was a beautiful morning, even for Amerigo. The sky was pure clear blue. A fragrant breeze hardly ruffled the
quiet sea, as it lapped at the beach in small crisp ripples. The sunlight
was white and very hot. When Norman walked where the sun shone,
the warmth on his tired body was a tonic. He had hardly slept, elated
as he was with his unlooked-for triumph. A good bake in the sun, he
decided, a beer or two, and a swim would fit him for the day. He returned to his room and put on trunks, tiptoeing about so as not to wake
Henny. Coming back to the bar, he was surprised to see Hassim there
with a blond, curly-haired, broad-shouldered sailor in whites, not more
than nineteen, with an innocent tough pink face.

"Norman, you wonder man, you," Hassim squealed. "That was the
best party I've ever been at! What a do! They'll talk about it for years!
Meet Hennessy, sweetie. Hennessy's just off that sub that came in this
morning. They'll only be in port till noon. He bought an *adorable* watch
for his mother from me, and I'm standing him to a beer. Let Mr. Paperman see it, Hennessy."

The sailor with bashful pride took out a Little Constantinople box,
and showed Norman a tiny French gold watch set with small diamonds.

"Isn't it *heaven?*" said Hassim.

"Ye gods, can you afford that, boy?" Paperman said.

The sailor put away the box, blushing. "Well, sir, it's like this, the
other fellows play cards and Ah don't. And well, you know, Ah don't
spend mah money on some other things like they do. Mah mom's about
all Ah've got, and well, this is mah pleasure, sir."

"Isn't he nice?" Hassim purred. "Only Southerners are like that.
Real gentlemen."

Norman could see that Hassim wasn't making a play for this sailor.
Such a boy would be dumfounded if Hassim made one of his odd pro-
posals, and would just laugh at him, if he didn't knock him senseless
with a blow. Hassim was wistfully enjoying Hennessy's sunny presence
for an hour or so, as a lonesome ugly old man will take a beauty to
dinner with no hope of sleeping with her; as, indeed, Lester Atlas entertained actresses, who put up with his crudity for the sake of dinner at
the Colony or the Four Seasons. Norman wasn't happy about having
Hassim at the Club this early in the morning. The Turk was such a
blatant old queen; colorful and exotic, no doubt, with his quacking

voice and bouncy manners, and adding much Caribbean authenticity to the scene, but a bit oppressive. There was nothing to do about it, however. He left Hassim to entertain the sailor boy, and went down on the beach to enjoy the sunshine and his beer.

He had been lounging on a chair for perhaps half an hour, oozing sweat and beginning to feel drowsy and good, when a call from the new bartender roused him. "Mistuh Papuhman, suh! De police heah. Wants to axe you about last night."

A rookie cop by the name of Parris stood at the top of the beach stairs beside the bartender, his khaki uniform ablaze with gold braid, pistols and bullet belt prominent around his slim middle.

"Hello, there, Parris. Shall I come up?"

"If you please, suh. It kind of hot out dah."

"Coming."

Parris said as he approached, "Dat Frenchman still in de fort. De chief send me to get a full statement."

"Good. Something to drink?"

"I just have a Seven-Up, tank you very much."

"Right. Another beer, please, Cecil."

Norman knew Parris and liked him: a tall, bony, slightly jittery Kinjan, not too many years out of high school, with a toothbrush mustache that made him look younger, perhaps, than he was. Parris took himself and his uniform most seriously. He was one of the pleasanter Kinja cops, punctilious and obliging, and quicker than most to answer a call, or to untangle a traffic jam without excessive shouting and bullying.

Parris pulled out a large leather notebook and began writing down Norman's narrative, often asking him to stop while he painstakingly scrawled. He hardly touched his soft drink. He seemed distracted, and more nervous than usual; he kept glancing at Hassim and the sailor, who were now on their third or fourth round. The sailor was flushed and boisterous, and Hassim was putting on a rather strong performance. All at once Parris snapped his book shut. "Excuse me a minute, suh," he said, and he went over to the other table.

Norman was well aware of the unwritten rule in Kinja protecting sailors from the gay crowd. But Hassim's intentions toward Hennessy being so obviously innocent, Norman hadn't thought of it before, and he imagined it might not even have occurred to the fluttery Turk. After all, a mere drink in the morning!

Parris spoke to them in low tones, and Norman saw the disconcerted look on both their faces. Hassim said something placating and jolly. The sailor also answered the policeman with a joke. Parris spoke louder. The sailor retorted sharply, and the policeman grasped his shoulder. The sailor knocked the dark slender hand off his white uniform with such force that Parris staggered back.

"Now, mister policeman, hands off me. Ah'll drink a bottle of beer with anybody Ah please. This gentleman's mah friend, and whah don't you get lost? We ain't bothering nobody."

Parris fell back a few more steps and drew a large pistol. "You resistin' an officer!" he exclaimed. "You realize dat?"

The sailor opened very round blue eyes, and stood, swaying a step or two toward the policeman. "Now listen, mister policeman, take it easy, heah? That there's a *gun*. Whah, Ah bet it has real live bullets in it. People can get hurt by them things, honest."

"You keep away from me. You coming wid me to de fort," Parris said shrilly, brandishing the pistol.

Norman was too startled by all this to interfere, but Hassim got up and seized Hennessy's arm just as the boy started to move toward the policeman, smiling genially. Parris walked backwards three or four steps, and fired his gun twice. The two explosions sounded thin and fake in the open air of the bar. Norman smelled gunsmoke. Nothing happened to the sailor, but Hassim put his hand to his chest, with a shocked, pained look. "Oh, Parris, you *fool!* Now why did you do that? This is so ridiculous—this is absolutely *ridiculous.*" So saying, he toppled forward on his face. Norman jumped to his side. Hassim rolled over and turned his head toward Norman. "I don't believe this, Norman dear, you know?" he said with a grimace and a cough. "I simply *don't* believe it. It's too silly, and besides—" He said nothing more because he died. The light went out of his eyes, he gave a gasp, he stopped breathing, and his mouth fell open. Norman had a corpse on his hands, and Hassim looked every inch a corpse. His chest was still, and so was he; quite still, and limp, his open eyes fixed. A stain discolored his mauve shirt.

Parris dropped his gun on the floor, fell into a chair with his hands over his face, and started to sob.

The sailor stood, legs spread as though he were on a heaving deck, looking at the dead man and then at the weeping cop, his square face as puzzled as an animal's.

Norman telephoned the police at once. The agitated desk sergeant promised to come over, and to bring the chief of police if he could find him. The trouble was, he said, that the Carnival Parade down Prince of Wales Street had already started, and the chief was out in a patrol car to help keep things moving.

There was nothing to do but wait. Parris pulled himself together and told everybody not to touch Hassim—who was looking deader by the minute—because the police had to record the details of the incident exactly as it had occurred. He took the names of the half-dozen other people in the bar who were sitting around in somber stupefaction, told them to remain, and closed off the door to the lobby.

Hassim's death seemed to Norman not tragic, not serious, hardly real. There the storekeeper lay on the red tiles, his last whiskey sour still unconsumed on the table, a sea breeze fanning him, a beautiful tropic scene as his background, with eight Christmas vacationers as unwilling stunned watchers over his cadaver. Norman's thoughts were fragmentary and stupid—what would this do to the lunch business? Could a pretense be carried off that Hassim had had a stroke? How loud had the shots sounded? To Norman they had seemed no noisier than two big firecrackers going off.

Fifteen minutes after Norman telephoned, the chief of police appeared in his sunburst of gold braid, accompanied by three other cops in the usual bullet belts and pistols. Norman knew the chief as a jovial sort given to flirting on the street, but now he was all business. He marshalled the witnesses one by one, got a coherent story in short order out of them, and hurried along the photographing of the scene, and the taking of measurements. Two men from the undertaking parlor arrived with a long brown basket—the same ones who had been removing chairs an hour earlier—and stood waiting for permission to carry off Hassim to his last home. The usual procedure in Amerigo, except for people who had family plots in one of the old cemeteries, was to bury them in weighted sacks at sea.

It was now wearing on toward noon, and people were beginning to knock at the closed door of the bar. A few also tried to come around by the open terrace, but the chief posted a man there to send them back. At one point the hammering at the door became insistent, and a policeman came in to whisper to his chief, who nodded, and beckoned to Paperman. "Ah, suh, de lady who stay here, Mrs. Tramm—ah, de governor's, ah, friend, you know—she want to know what become of her dog. She can't find him and she very upset."

"May I go out and talk to her? I won't be long."

The chief nodded.

The lobby was about half full of murmuring guests, who glanced at Paperman with alarmed curiosity. Lionel, standing right at the door, buttonholed him. "What is this, Norm? Some people say there was a shooting, others say a fellow dropped dead. A lot of folks want a hair of the dog, you know, and they're all wondering what the hell about the cops and everything."

"Tell them the bar'll be open in about ten minutes, Lionel. We're having a bit of trouble. It's one of those things." Norman broke away, seeing Iris at the door of the lobby, staring out at the lawn.

"Iris, I know where Meadows is. Don't worry," he said, coming up to her.

"Do you? Thank God. He broke the screen door and got out. I could swear I had him chained. But I was so damned drunk!" When she turned to talk to him, she shocked Norman with her battered unpainted face, her bloodshot eyes in sunken brown sockets, and her wild look of fear. She wore a shapeless house dress of gray. "Where is he? Is he all right?"

"Yes. He will be."

Norman gave her a rapid account of what had happened, starting his story with Cohn's reassuring report. Iris's face contorted when he described the wounding of the dog. She pressed him for details about the injury to Meadows. Norman did his best to minimize it.

"Well, there's only one thing to do, and that's go and get him," she said. "Dr. Keller is fine, Meadows likes him, but the poor beast must be horribly sad and lonesome." She started down the stairs, then halted halfway.

Iris was sober, her walk was steady, but she was suffering a storm of nerves, Norman judged. The broken door, the vanished dog, had been a shock for which she was ill-prepared. She seemed oblivious to the trouble in the bar, to the gathering crowd in the lobby.

"Norm, what day is this? Thursday or Friday?"

"It's Friday, Iris."

"Hell and damnation, then the Carnival Parade's on. I'll never get my car out of the garage. It's right up there on Prince of Wales Street. You'll have to lend me the Rover." She ran up the stairs, holding out a shaky hand. "Please give me the key."

"If you wait a while, Iris, I'll drive you."

"But when will you be free? Don't you have a tourist with a heart attack in the bar, or some damned thing?"

A policeman came to Norman at this moment and said, "The chief axe to talk to you now, suh. He got papers you must sign."

"I'll be right there."

Iris followed Norman to the desk in the lobby. "How can you drive out past the parade?" he said. "Isn't the whole waterfront shut off by the judges' stand? You're better off walking to Back Street and getting a taxi."

"No, no. There's a way around the back of the judges' stand. I've done this before. All the damned taxi drivers will be watching the parade. Not a one of them will want to drive me way out in the country, not for love or money. Give me the key, Norman. Please. I'm perfectly all right and I want my dog."

Norman gave her the key.

She sighed. "Darling, did I do anything very terrible last night? I remember nothing except getting dressed and coming over here with every intention of wrecking the joint. Don't ask me why. I woke up and found my evening dress still on me, and all messed up. What went on? Did I rape somebody? Or get raped?"

"You were fine, Iris. You fell asleep and missed the dinner. The governor and I put you to bed. You sort of slipped and fell on the gravel at one point. You didn't do anything."

"Thank heaven. How was the party?"

"Everyone says, the biggest success ever on this island."

Her looked brightened. She leaned over and kissed his cheek. "I'm glad. Norman, don't ever tell Henny, and let's not do a thing about it, for heaven's sake, but I do believe I fell in love with you, a little bit. But now I'm going to get my dog and go back to San Diego, on the first plane I can catch. I've had the Caribbean. I've decided on that."

"That's wise, Iris. We'll miss you, but it's the thing to do."

"We'll stay in touch, though, Norm, won't we? I'd like to know how you and Henny make out here. And listen, no matter what, let's go on exchanging postcards, just a couple of times a year—say on Yom Kippur and Easter, how's that? Till we're both old and gray. And whenever you hear a Maxine Sullivan record, why, you can think of me, your young love that you had when you were fifty."

"Forty-nine, for God's sake, Iris," Norman managed to say. "That's bad enough."

"Bye, Norman Paperman." She glanced around the busy lobby, then touched his face with her hand. "Let's have another incarnation some time soon, why don't we? And next time let's do it right, okay darling? Let's make it to Dingley Dell. God, I've felt better. And looked better, I daresay." She gave him a crooked smile, and hurried out of the lobby.

The door to the bar was open and guests were streaming in. Where Hassim's body had lain there was only the red tile floor. Norman saw the two undertaker's men moving clumsily off down the dance terrace with the shut brown basket. The policemen were following the basket, and Hennessy was going with them; only the chief remained at a table, writing. Norman had to sign a green form and a white form, and the chief told him that later a policeman would return and the witnesses would be asked to sign typed transcripts of their stories.

"What's going to happen to Parris?" Norman said. "Was this murder, or manslaughter, Chief, or what?"

The chief shrugged, putting his papers into a briefcase. "Dat be for de judge, and maybe for a jury, to say. Parris a good officer, and Mr. Hassim a fine gentleman, but"—the chief rolled knowing eyes at Norman—"his unfortunate peculiarity cause de trouble, you know! Mrs. Tramm find her dog all right?"

"Yes, that's taken care of."

The chief closed his briefcase and stood. "Well, I'm sorry dis disagreeable incident mar your holiday sea-son."

"Excuse me, Chief." The new bartender was hovering nearby. He pointed to the table where Hennessy and Hassim had sat. "Is it all right —can I move dose now? Parris say not to touch dem."

On the table stood Hennessy's empty beer glass, and the whiskey sour that Hassim had not managed to drink.

"Oh yes. Dat be all finish."

The bartender took up the glasses and swept a rag over the table. Four guests immediately fell into the chairs, clamoring for drinks.

The chief shook hands with Norman, in an embarrassed way. "Could you stop by de fort some time today and give us a statement on Hippolyte Lamartine?"

"Yes, of course. How's Hippolyte?"

"Oh, not too bad. He got plenty friends in de jail."

Norman's fear that the death would cast a pall over the hotel was groundless, he soon saw. The bar became as crowded as ever, and unusually animated. The shooting was a topic for talk, and since almost nobody knew just what had happened, there was much room for jovial improvising. Hassim had in fact, with his absurd demise, provided the needed antidote for the general hangover after the Lovers' Beach party. The questions thrown at Norman grew tiresome, and he went down to the beach, where he found Henny and Hazel in bikinis in the sun, both looking tense and worried. He started to tell them what had happened, but he had not gotten far when the bartender called to him again from the head of the stairs. "Mistuh Papuhman, telephone for you in de office."

"Oh, no!" he groaned. "Not now, Cecil. Get the name and I'll call them back."

"It be de chief of police callin', suh."

Norman gave his wife and daughter a weary look. "I suppose this thing will haunt me for days. Be right back."

He dragged himself to the office, closed the door, switched on the wheezing air-conditioner, and picked up the telephone, seating himself on the disorderly desk.

"Yes, Chief?"

"Sorry to boddah you again, Mr. Papuhmon. We givin' you kind of a bad time today, I guess."

"Quite all right. What is it?"

"Mr. Papuhmon, dat green Land Rover, license 1674, dat belong de Gull Reef Club, don't it?"

"Yes," Norman said. "Yes, it does."

The chief's heavy sigh rattled in the telephone. "Well, it bust up pretty bad on Back Street, near Pomegranate Alley. Just around de turn by de Big Bamboo Bar. —You still dere, suh?"

"I'm still here. Was Mrs. Tramm hurt? She was driving it."

"She a little hurt."

"How bad?"

"She went troo de win'shield. She hit a cab dat stop in de middle of de street. Dat same old ting."

2

The Amerigo Carnival was a torrent of merry Kinjans, parading down Prince of Wales Street to a steady blare of clashing music from many bands. Thick ranks of applauding tourists and natives lined the sidewalks, drinking pop and beer out of cans, and cheap wine out of bottles strung around their necks. Floats jutted up along the line of march, and banners of schools, clubs, and churches swayed over the marchers' heads.

The ideas in the parade were the usual thing; but the troupes were remarkable for energy, elaborateness, and sheer size. Norman saw a Wild West show with cowboys and live horses on the float, and dozens of Indians in war paint and feathers prancing in the street; a company of perhaps fifty red satin devils, and another of as many gauzily clad harem girls; an enormous Chinese display, including a gold-and-red pagoda with a real waterfall, and a horde of black Chinese marchers pounding gongs; tumbling white-masked clowns doing a springing dance with sharp-cracking whips; space men in bubble helmets and silver suits pulling a papier-mâché rocket topped by a five-year-old Negro space child waving an American flag; Gay Nineties and Roaring Twenties dancers; also, at intervals, men on high stilts in women's dresses gyrating in burlesque obscenity fifteen feet in the air, while people in the upper stories of the houses shouted encouraging jokes at them.

Norman Paperman was in no mood to enjoy this bright, huge, noisy pageant; he was trying to get to the hospital. But perforce he had to elbow his way upstream under the arcades, against the drift of spectators toward the waterfront grandstand; and so, whether he wanted to or not, he saw a lot of the parade, because the hospital was three blocks up from the harbor. He was impressed, despite himself, by the outpouring of decorative labor and skill, and by the tide of jubilant high spirits. At noon the temperature in Prince of Wales Street, where a breeze seldom penetrated, was perhaps a hundred and ten degrees. On an ordinary day this avenue, at this hour, was deserted. But today, here were the Kinjans cavorting and tramping in force under the high fierce sun, perspiring in streams in their gaudy costumes; the musicians dripping sweat as they marched along blowing on glinting tubas and trumpets or hammering and clanking at their steel drums; the onlookers cheering and fanning themselves; the dancers pausing every hundred feet or so along the line of march to repeat the entire antic they had learned. It seemed to Norman that the Kinjans, marchers and onlookers alike, were exulting in the terrible heat, in the color, in the sweat, in the bray of many discordant melodies, in the crush of costumed leaping dancing hot bodies; they were tireless, they loved it, they were capable of going on forever, their indolence had vanished, they had come wholly to life.

The parade had no meaning. That was another peculiarity. Lent, the actual occasion of Carnival, was months away. Ten years ago the legislators had instituted this parade for the last Friday of the year (so Tilson had told Norman), to please the tourists and incidentally to make the Christmas week an almost continuously workless one. For want of a better name they had called it Carnival. The custom had caught on, and now Carnival was as hallowed as Christmas itself; perhaps slightly more so. But Norman Paperman, seeing the Carnival Parade at close range, thought that there was a meaning to it which the islanders did not put into words, yet which made it the authentic supreme day in the Kinjan calendar. Africa was marching down the main street of this little harbor town today; Africa in undimmed black vitality, surging up out of centuries of island displacement, island slavery, island isolation, island ignorance; Africa, unquenchable in its burning love of life. Carnival was Africa Day in Amerigo.

"Carnival is very sweet
Please
Don't stop de carnival—
Carnival is very sweet
Please
Don't stop de carnival—"

Band after band after band played this refrain, a lively Calypso melody endlessly repeating the one couplet, the traditional song of the parade; and whenever musicians went by performing it, the spectators and marchers took up the words:

"Car-nee-val is very sweet
Please
Don't stop de car-nee-val."

Paperman reached a point on the sidewalk opposite the hospital, but he had to wait for the passing of a troupe in Shakespearian costumes with Macbeth's witches on the float, stirring a steaming caldron over a real fire, then a brass band led by a gigantically fat black tuba player in a battered straw hat, smiling and sweating and shuffling, and blasting out earth-shaking *oomph-oomph-oomphs*. Norman scuttled across the street ahead of oncoming Roman slave girls and into the hospital.

The branching corridors were gloomy, cool, and almost empty; the smell was the universal hospital smell. He saw a door labelled *Emergency Ward,* and at a venture he went in. A very young oriental-looking doctor—Philippine or Korean, Norman judged—was tying a splint to the finger of an unhappy-looking Kinjan in an orange sport shirt and black slacks, whose face was patched with bandages stained bright red.

"Yes, I took care of Mrs. Tramm a little while ago," said the doctor, with a marked accent blurring the *l*'s and *r*'s. "She's resting in Room A-42, and I'm going to get some X rays as soon as the technician comes back from the parade. This is the cab driver she ran into."

"How is she?"

"Well, she's had a shock, no doubt of that, and she's had a head injury and some bad cuts. I'd like Dr. Pullman to look at her. I think she'll do fine."

385

Paperman said to the cab driver, "It's really a bad idea to stop your car in the street to talk, you know? I hope you believe that now, and you'll pass the word around."

"I on'y stop for a minute," said the driver. "She goin' too fast, she breakin' de speed limit. Dey give *me* a ticket and it all *her* fault. But she de governor's friend. Dey ain' no justice arong heah, it all depen' who you knows."

Room A-42 was on the ground floor. Norman had to find it himself, and it took a while, because there was nobody at the main admittance desk. When he came on the room he thought at first that the doctor had mistaken the number. A stout Frenchwoman lay in a bed near the door, and two men and three children, all with faces that were minor variations of Hippolyte's, sat on the bed, talking loudly in their occult jargon. Then Norman saw the two other beds. The one in the middle was occupied by a shrunken white crone, sleeping on her back with her toothless mouth open. In the bed near the window Iris lay. The room was clean, large, and airy; only crowded. Sunlight blazed on Iris's heavily bandaged face and head. Her eyes were closed. One bandaged arm lay outside the blanket, badly swollen.

"Iris?" Norman said gently, approaching her bedside.

She opened her eyes and smiled, a weary vague smile. The skin around her eyes was puffed and discolored. "Oh, Norm, hi. Sorry about the Rover."

"How are you, Iris?"

"Pretty fair, considering. Those silly cabs again . . . be out of here soon enough. Doctor even said none of the scars would be permanent —maybe a little mark on the bridge of my nose—" Iris's speech was thick and drowsy.

"Can I do something for you, Iris?"

"Well—I don't want to bother Alton, he's judging the parade—maybe afterward—"

"I think I should tell him right away, if nobody else has. For one thing you should have your own room, until you feel a little better."

Iris glanced at the other occupants of the room, nodded, and yawned. The lively chatter of the French people was going on as before.

"Norm, I'm awfully full of dope, I may pass out on you. Thanks for coming."

> *"Car-nee-val is very sweet*
> *Please*
> *Don't stop de car-nee-val,"*

came a crowd chant through the open window, to the tuneful rattling of a steel band, *boum-di-boum-boum.*

"Listen," Iris said. "Sounds like fun, at that."

He took her hand and kissed it. It was all wet. "I'll be back very soon, Iris."

She blinked at him. "You're a sweetheart. You always have been."

Norman hurried to the emergency ward, and told the doctor he would pay any charge to have Iris moved at once to a room by herself. "I think she's in bad shape. She needs quiet."

"It would certainly be preferable, but I don't have that authorization. Dr. Pullman has to approve it."

"Where's Dr. Pullman?"

"He's one of the judges of the Carnival."

"Mrs. Tramm is a very close friend of the governor, Doctor."

"Oh, is that so? Well, that will expedite the authorization, I'm sure. I'm sorry I can't take the action myself."

Norman found he could walk much faster in the direction the parade was moving. He went out into the street with the small boys, hastening alongside the marchers, and in this way he reached the waterfront in a few minutes. Getting to the grandstand was harder, because the troupes were piled up at the plaza, waiting to perform in the cleared space before the flag-bedecked grandstand. At the moment the Chinese troupe was doing a song, and a mincing dance with fans. Norman began working his way through hilarious devils, angels, Indians, and clowns, who were mostly drinking beer, Coke, or whiskey, or eating ice cream. Though he wore only a cotton shirt, shorts, and open sandals, he was as wet from the heat as if he had fallen in the harbor. The policeman guarding the narrow wooden steps into the grandstand was flirting with a harem girl, and Norman slipped past him and ran up through the full benches to the top row where the three judges sat alone: Sanders, Dr. Pullman, and Senator Easter. He slipped along the back of this top bench and in a minute, baldly, he told the governor and the doctor about Iris.

"How bad is it? You say she was talking to you," Sanders said in a low voice. "I mean I'll go now if I should, but if it can wait another hour —it would be very awkward for me to leave just now, you can see that."

Pullman said, "Did Dr. Salas ask for the governor to come? Or me?"

"No, he didn't."

"Well, he's a very competent young fellow." Pullman turned to the governor. "I'm sure you can wait until after the parade, sir."

Sanders stood. "Well, I don't like this, Tracy, but I'd better go. I'll see to the separate room, anyway, and I'll probably be back in ten or fifteen minutes." He had been holding the coat of his Palm Beach suit on his lap; now he put it on and headed for the stairs.

The troupe of harem girls in blue sequined bodices and pink gauze trousers were moving into the performing space, bells jingling on their ankles, dark arms undulating, hips gyrating.

> *"Car-nee-val is very sweet*
> *Please*
> *Don't stop de car-nee-val,"*

they sang as they came, flashing white charming smiles.

"Too bad we have to miss this," said Sanders, and he went plunging ahead of Norman through the throng of performers, and up Prince of Wales Street. People made way for the governor, when they recognized him, and the two men reached the hospital in a short time.

Far down the hospital corridor, Norman saw three nurses clustered at the door of A-42. He was finding it hard to keep up with Sanders' long strides, and he was gasping from the heat and the fast pace. "Well, how is she?" Sanders called as he drew near the nurses. He was walking so fast that he was entering the door when one nurse, a stout Negress with a kindly face and gray hair, put her hand out and stopped him. "Governor, I sorry, de lady she die."

"*Died?*" Sanders stopped short and swayed, staring at the nurses. "Died, you said?"

"She go into a coma and die fast."

Sanders shook his head and pushed into the room, and Norman followed him. Dr. Salas bent over Iris's bed. "Oh, hello," he said, desultorily pulling a sheet over Iris's bared pink nipple. "I've been trying heart massage, governor, and I gave her adrenalin, but she's dead, sir. I'm sure an autopsy will show a massive brain hemorrhage. The clinical picture of shock was mild and not clear at all. It had to be a hemorrhage. There's a probable skull fracture, and—"

The French people were all still in the room, talking, and the occupant of the middle bed was still asleep with her mouth open.

"Isn't there anything to do?" Sanders interrupted in a rasp. "Shall I get Dr. Pullman? He can be here in no time with a motorcycle escort."

"Sir, she's been dead several minutes. She's gone, sir."

Iris's sweat-beaded, bandaged face did not look alive: greenish-blue, sad, sunk on her chest. She looked as dead as Hassim had; indeed it crossed Norman's mind that she resembled the shot storekeeper now, in the family look of the dead.

Governor Sanders fell on his knees beside the bed, clutching Iris's hand and kissing it. Norman put his hand on the governor's shoulder. Sanders glanced up at him, with an expression in his large brown eyes of a boy badly hurt. "She the only woman I loved," he said in a choked voice. "And she dead." There was no trace of the speech class in his words.

Another brass band was going by outside, and the crowd was taking up the chant:

> *"Car-nee-val is very sweet*
> *Please*
> *Don't stop de car-nee-val!"*

3

Henny was worried about Norman. More than an hour had passed. She sat at a beach table with Cohn, Hazel, and Lionel, having a lunch of hamburgers and beer. Lester Atlas was in the water not far from them, disporting with Hatsy and Patsy in great showers of spray and bursts of guffaws, giggles, and shrieks. The beach was unusually crowded. All the guests seemed to be wanting a waterside snack today, instead of a full lunch. Lionel was volubly reassuring Henny that the

389

Hassim death would do the Gull Reef Club no harm. By now the handful of guests who had seen the killing had told the story over and over,
and everybody had it fairly straight, except for the point of Hassim's
innocence. The impression was that the Turk had been carrying on
lewdly in broad daylight with the sailor, that the policeman had tried
to stop it, and that in the ensuing fracas Hassim had accidentally been
shot dead. People thought that this was a bit hard on Hassim, but that
the cop after all had only been doing his duty, and that one queer the
less in the world was no grievous loss.

"As a matter of fact, Henny, I feel sorry for the poor bugger," Lionel
said, munching on his thick-piled hamburger. "I've known thousands
of those guys, and there's no harm in ninety-nine out of a hundred of
them. It's just a sickness and it's their own business. Though gosh
knows, when I was a kid working backstage, I sure got some surprises.
Yes ma'am, it was darn near worth my life to bend over and tie my
shoelace, I tell you." He laughed salaciously. His once green face was
burning to an odd bronze color like an American Indian's, and he looked
very relaxed and happy. "Actually, Henny, I almost hate to say this,
but I think this thing's going to prove a break for the Club. I bet the
nances stop coming to Gull Reef after this."

"There's Norman," Henny said. She had never stopped watching the
beach stairs. He stood at the top now, looking around at the merry
beach scene, his hair disordered, his face drawn. "Norman!" she called.
"Here we are!"

He turned his gaze to her, waved tiredly, and came down the stairs.
"Hi, Bob," he said, dropping in a chair. "Hello, Lionel. I'm glad you're
here, I wanted to talk to you."

Hazel said, "Shall I get you a hamburger?"

"I'm not hungry. Maybe a beer, Hazel, thanks."

He sat slouched, looking around at the others with haggard, shocked
eyes.

"Norman, what *is* it?" Henny said.

"I've been running around a lot, Henny, and it's hot in town, you
know."

"What did the chief of police want?"

Norman stared at her, and then his gaze wandered to the wallowing, frolicking Atlas. "Lionel, you're still bogged down on your deal with Chunky Collins, aren't you?"

"Yes. He's getting a little too cute on small things, furnishings and such. Our deal was for twenty-five thousand, and he's inched it up to almost twenty-seven. I can't say I appreciate that."

"How would you like to buy the Gull Reef Club?"

Lionel laughed. "If I could afford it, and if you were crazy enough to sell it, why—"

"Can you afford thirty thousand dollars? I'd rather not lose money, and I'll let you have it for that. That's what it cost me." Norman said this in such a colorless offhand way that neither Henny nor the others knew what to make of it. Hazel now brought him a bottle of beer and a glass. "Thanks, Hazel. What do you say, Lionel, is it a deal? I'm ready to shake on it, right now." And he stretched forth a hand.

Lionel scratched his long chin and looked at the others. "Well, golly, Norman, this is certainly from left field. Are you serious? What's the matter, are you upset because that poor fag got shot? I was just telling Henny that's not going to hurt you. I mean this is something you better think about. You've got it made here."

Norman put down his hand, and turned to Cohn. "Iris Tramm is dead, Bob." Amazement and horror showed on all their faces. "She was going to get the dog in my Land Rover, you know? And she ran into one of those stopped cabs on Back Street, and she fractured her skull. She's lying in the hospital, dead. I've just come from there."

"Good God," Cohn said slowly. "She's *dead?* Iris? Dead, Norman?"

Norman nodded. "I guess Sanders will take care of sending her body home. I left him there with her. He's very broken up."

Henny said, holding her hand to her chest, "Jesus Christ, Norm! The poor woman. Was she drunk?"

"No, she was sober, Henny. These Kinja drivers just have a way of stopping short and chatting any time, any place. They mean no harm, they're like heedless kids, and you learn to watch out for them. I once got knocked cold myself. But poor Iris was anxious to go to her dog, you see, and I guess she forgot." He turned to the frogman. "What'll become of the dog? I've been worrying a lot about that. I guess because Iris would worry about him, more than almost anything."

Cohn said hoarsely, "Why, I'll be glad to take Meadows, Norm. Or any one of the fellows will. That's a good dog. My God, Norman! Iris is *dead.*"

Lionel shook his head. "That's a darn ridiculous and pointless way to die."

"I know, like Hassim," Norman said in the same matter-of-fact, weary tone. "It's kind of funny, two deaths like that in one day."

"Funny? It's awful," Hazel said, her face almost ugly with horror. "It isn't funny in the least."

Norman looked at her and smiled. "Is that what you think? Then we agree, Hazel. I've been surviving here on my sense of humor, and I know these deaths are ludicrous, but I can't laugh at them. I tried here, I tried hard, and it's been a real experience, but now I want to go back to New York." He turned to Henny. "Will you mind very much? If you'd rather stay on—the thing is, I don't. That isn't going to change."

She scanned his face anxiously. "Norman, are you absolutely sure? This place is a success now, and it's fun, and all that. It's everything you wanted when you came down here."

"She's right, Norm," Lionel said. "Give yourself at least a week to calm down. It's awful about Iris, sure it is, but you forget these things, I swear you do. My Lord, life is so full of them! I mean I'll hold off on Hogan's Fancy, for a week, or even longer, as far as that goes."

"There's a four o'clock plane all through the Christmas season, Henny," Norman said. "I want to get on that plane today. I've called, and there are seats. I want to leave Kinja today." He held out his hand to Lionel again. "Thirty thousand dollars, Lionel? Twenty for the bank, five still owing to the last owner, and five I put into it. Is it a deal?"

"It isn't a deal, Norm, it's a steal." Lionel was staring at the outstretched hand, eagerness and reluctance comically mingling on his bronzed face.

"I'll call it a favor if you'll take it," Norman said.

Lionel suddenly reached forward and clasped his hand. "Well, what the heck! If you honestly want it this way, Norm. This is a dream place, and I'll jump at it. I'd be crazy not to."

"Wonderful," Norman said. "Thank you. Now, Lester Atlas is the businessman in this setup. I'll explain it all to him. He'll handle the details better than I can. He'll be staying on for a while, he's got a real estate deal going."

Hazel said abruptly, "Dad, can I stay?" They all looked at her, and she blushed and stammered, adjusting the almost nonexistent bodice of her bikini. "I mean, that is, do you mind if I don't go with you today, and just come back for school next Thursday? I mean as long as I'm down here already. I mean for me this is still my vacation, Dad, and I love it here."

Cohn, his face sallow and drawn as though he were ill, said, "If it means anything, I'll look after Hazel."

Norman glanced at Henny, and something like his usual grin broke through his expression of wan shock. "No doubt. Any objections, Henny?"

"Objections? Me? Have fun, Hazel. —If we're getting out of here in two hours, Norm, I better start scrambling around and packing."

"I'll help," Norman said. "I've gotten a little handier, down here."

They talked about Hazel and Cohn while they hauled luggage from closets and started putting in clothes helter-skelter. They dwelled on the topic, as though avoiding other matters. Norman said that Cohn was bound to go into his father's import-export business, once his navy hitch was up, so that it would work out well enough, if he and Hazel were really getting serious.

Henny said, "Gosh, we may end up going to Israel to visit our grand-children. Won't that be something?"

"As a matter of fact," Norman said ruefully, "this fellow comes along in the nick of time. I fully expect him to support you and me. Somebody's got to."

"You'll support us, never fear."

"How? My clients can't come back to me for five years, no matter what. That was the deal I made, and I have to honor it."

"Well, it's a lousy trade, I've always said so and I always will," Henny said, "but you're the best man in it, and you'll get other clients."

She was putting her jewelry away in a velvet-lined box. "Norm, I'm not trying to argue about this, but I hope you realize that New York stinks, right now. You're going to be shocked. You've forgotten. It's

Christmas time, you know. You've never seen such crowds. The traffic's at a standstill, choked solid from the Hudson to the East River, and from Fifty-ninth Street to Thirty-fourth. You can get overcome by carbon monoxide just walking down Fifth. Or if the fumes don't get you, a mugger will. They're holding people up in broad daylight. The weather is foul. Oh, the department-store lights are nice, and the tall buildings in the snow—I love the damned place, I can't help it—but nothing's changed up there. Let's understand that."

"I know," Norman said. "I know all about New York. And that's where we're going."

Henny was holding her bracelet in her hand, looking at it wryly. "Norm," she said.

"Yes?"

"Did Iris pick out this bracelet?" She smiled a little at his astonished look, and went on, "I've often wondered. It isn't your style, you know, kid. It's a thing a woman would pick out. Come on. Was it Iris?"

He stared at her and didn't answer. They were standing close to each other, and Henny was looking up at him, straight into his eyes.

"It doesn't matter," she said. "Not any more. It never really did. I love it. But was it Iris? Iris picked it out, didn't she, Norman?"

"Yes, she did," Norman said, "and she knocked Hassim's price down to half. So that's a historic bracelet. Iris and Hassim. A perfect memento of Kinja."

"You liked Iris, didn't you?"

"Yes, Henny. I liked Iris."

"A lot?"

"A lot."

The rest of the information, all there was to know, passed between them in the looks of their eyes, unspoken.

Henny tightened her lips in anger, and her eyes became misty. "Well, you know something? This time I was fooled. Completely fooled. And now she's dead."

He said with difficulty, "I love you, Henny."

"Yes, sure, you miserable bastard. Let go of me! We have to pack."

They sat on the bed all littered with clothing. He kissed her, and buried his head on her bosom; she caressed his gray thick hair. "Poor Norm." She felt his tears on the skin of her throat, and she hugged him close. "Hey! Don't do that, sweetheart. I'm sorry about this. Honest, I am. I'm even sorry for Iris." Tears were starting from her eyes, but she spoke lightly, almost gaily. "You made the place into one hell of a good hotel, Norman. You really did that, you know, honey. And nothing's lost, nothing. Isn't it good that we didn't give up the apartment, baby, after all? We can just go home."